DREAMFORGERS

A SCI-FI THRILLER BY
STEVEN HEUMANN

Printed in the United States of America

First Printing, 2022

ISBN 9798421012535

www.stevenheumann.com

TABLE OF CONTENTS

Special thanks to Becky Heumann.

I would be nothing without you.

CHAPTER ONE

Abbie Kinder rubbed fatigue from her eyes and reread the pseudo-inspirational quote on the side of her Starbucks cup.

'Who's to say that dreams and nightmares aren't as real as the here and now?' – John Lennon.

"That's easy to say when you were one of the most talented musicians of all time," she murmured to herself, taking a seat at the closest empty table. "The rest of us regular people don't find following our dreams quite as easy as you did."

A man in an expensive suit walked past outside the window and yelled into his cellphone. Abbie rolled her eyes. *'There goes another success story living his nightmare,'* she thought.

Laughter pulled Abbie's attention back to the coffee shop. Nana Gayle paid for their lattes and chortled with the handsome guy at the register. Boundless energy seemed to emanate from the 70-year-old grandmother. Abbie wished she could bottle it and drink some each morning instead of her coffee. A yawn forced Abbie's mouth open into a gaping chasm of silver fillings. Uninterrupted sleep didn't seem to equal quality sleep anymore.

Too many late-night Netflix binges. The caffeine would help.

She blinked several times, focusing again on the proudly eco-friendly cup with its green Starbucks logo and kitschy, quasi-meaningful citation. John Lennon may have known music like few others in history, but Abbie found celebrities pontificating about following one's dreams more than tiresome. Dreams and nightmares disappeared in the light of morning never to be remembered, making them about as powerful as a dandelion in a hurricane. Reality didn't care whether you wanted to be an astronaut or a fry-cook; it would beat you down either way.

Latte steam tickled her nose with the fragrance of Colombian beans and cream. She closed her eyes and breathed deeply, hearing the din of patrons around the shop chatting and sipping their brews. A wave of warm relaxation flowed from Abbie's spine and tingled throughout her body. For a moment, her mind seemed to pull away from the world in a flash of colors, voices, and warnings.

Someone cried out for help in the ethereal distance and Abbie bounded forward without thought or worry, as if the entire universe would bow to her power. A purple sword appeared in her hand.

Hot coffee splashed on her wrist, jolting Abbie from the momentary doze. A flash of pain ripped the fatigue from her eyes as she blinked down at brown liquid pooling on top of the table's Starbucks sticker graphics.

"Damn it," she spat, wiggling her left arm and sending droplets of coffee flinging from her oversized sweater sleeve. The light blue cotton turned a depressing shade of auburn next to an existing pink ketchup stain.

Embarrassment burned in Abbie's cheeks, as if her fellow coffee shop patrons would start whispering behind her back like snobby high school cheerleaders. A quick glance revealed the complete disinterest of everyone in the Starbucks, as phones and personal conversations dominated their attention. Still, the temperature seemed to rise by ten degrees as Abbie yanked napkins from a dispenser at the end of the table. She brushed her dark brown hair behind her ear and smelled espresso on her fingers.

"If you didn't like the sweater, you could have told me when I bought it for you," Nana Gayle teased as she walked from the register with her own latte in-hand. "You don't need to spill coffee on it as an excuse to get rid of the thing."

Abbie smiled despite the uncomfortable burning sensation on her skin. She dabbed at the spill, hot liquid soaking into the cheap Starbucks-branded napkins. "Well, you know how passive/aggressive I am about sweaters."

"You're far too direct to be considered passive/aggressive, sweetie," Nana said, winking playfully. A faint lavender scent danced from the older woman and reminded Abbie of childhood summer evenings reading *A Tree Grows in Brooklyn* together on the third-floor balcony of Grandpa's condo. Lean and athletic, with long gray hair pulled back into a ponytail, Nana certainly didn't look like the traditional grandmother. Her penchant for flirting with cute cashiers and using four letter words whenever possible made her seem born from the 90's instead of the 50's.

"Life's too short to beat around the bush," Abbie replied as she tossed the wet paper towels toward the garbage a few feet away.

"So, does that mean I can jump the hedge and ask you about Emma's gallery offer, then? Please? Please, please, please?" Nana asked, looking down at her granddaughter with an apprehensive but excited gleam in her eyes.

Abbie squeezed her cup, almost popping a hole in the cheap paper. "Dad told you, didn't he?"

"Your mom, actually, which surprised me since I thought she was trying to force you into a job with that insurance adjuster she kept setting you up with. She also said you were thinking about turning it down."

"So, this is why you wanted to take me out for coffee," Abbie said as she wiped her wet hands on her jeans. "And here I thought we could spend some quality grandmother/granddaughter time together."

Nana's lips compressed ever so slightly. "Now you're being passive/aggressive. Tell me about the offer so I can convince you to take it."

Abbie grabbed her half-full coffee cup and stood, running her finger along the tabletop, and feeling the cheap vinyl used on the sticker graphics covering the veneer. She would have used a thicker textured plastic as opposed to this thin crap that cracked easily and needed to be replaced every two months. She thought about leaving her card with one of the baristas and giving them a quote for the higher-quality printed material but figured it would be a waste of time.

"I like working at the Sign Hub," she said. "I get to be creative and help businesses with their print needs. It's not like I'm working at a McDonalds flipping burgers or something. I don't need Mom trying to find me a higher paying job, and I sure as hell don't need Emma's charity."

"It's not charity when you've earned the opportunity," Nana assured.

"Did I earn it? Really? Look, you may be my favorite person in the world, but I don't want to talk about this even with you, Nana. You still want to walk through the plaza, or was that a ruse too?"

"Beats standing here listening to co-eds cackle." Nana nodded her head toward a group of women in University of Utah hoodies laughing loudly in the corner. "You have any coffee left in that cup?"

Abbie sloshed the liquid back and forth. "More than enough to keep me alert for the next few hours."

"Let's go then. Oh, and by the way, you're my favorite person too. Don't tell Emma or your grandpa. Or your dad."

"Your secret is safe with me."

Brisk air hit Abbie in the face as she pulled the door open and stepped into morning sunlight. A chill rippled up her back; goosebumps forming along her forearms. While warm enough to avoid needing a coat, the March weather still seemed a bit too frigid for a walk outdoors. Nana never seemed to mind though. She would jog before sun-up on the coldest day in January without a jacket.

Towering office buildings loomed along the pathway, kissing deep blue sky. Retail space dominated the ground level of the adjacent high rises with bright signage and photos of impossibly beautiful women hanging in the windows. Well-dressed professionals scurried by on their way to what Abbie assumed had to be vital corporate meetings, by the self-important scowls on everyone's faces. Printed advertisements for the St. Patrick's Day Festival hung from lamp posts along the promenade in bright greens and gold. Pride swelled in Abbie's chest at the sight. She had designed and printed the posters for the city the month before. A homeless man with a cardboard sign reading, 'Veteran. Anything helps,' wiped his hands on one of the banners; she hoped it wasn't a commentary on the design quality.

"If you don't want to talk about Emma's offer for your art," Nana began as they walked past a bakery on their way to the open plaza, "…we can always go into how I can set you up with that hedge fund manager in my building."

"You've got to stop," Abbie chuckled. "The last blind date you sent me on with that money manager was enough dating all by itself for the next month. His business card was worth more than my car, and he made sure I knew it."

Nana handed a five-dollar bill to the veteran as they walked past and ascended the steps toward the plaza. "Geoff is very nice. And you need to stop judging men by their business cards."

"I only judge them by their business cards if they throw it in my face how much money they make. The more expensive the business cards, the more shallow the guy. It's a turn off."

Nana took a long slow drink of her coffee as they entered the plaza. Generators hummed loudly as city employees dismantled the outdoor ice-skating rink in the center of the square and began constructing temporary stages for the spring concert series. Abbie had already begun work on the poster designs for the city council.

"You look tired," Nana said.

"I'm fine," Abbie replied.

"You looked tired at dinner last Friday too."

"You sound like Mom. I'm fine," Abbie repeated. She took a quick sip of coffee and burned her lip. "I just need a new pillow and fewer late nights watching Netflix."

"You were nodding off when you spilled your coffee, weren't you?" she asked.

"I just wasn't paying attention."

"Is everything okay with work? Have you been exercising, or at least playing soccer with friends like you used to?"

There it was. Most grandmas tried to fatten you up. Nana Gayle wanted to slim you down. Every problem in life could be fixed with a workout. Abbie hadn't been to the gym since before Thanksgiving and noticed she'd put on a few pounds; not much, but enough she knew Nana would eventually comment. It had taken longer than expected for her to bring it up.

"Work is fine," Abbie said, avoiding the exercise portion of the question. "The past couple weeks I just haven't slept well."

"You know…" Nana began, stepping over a hose running from the skating rink to a portable water tank. "Starting your morning with a good workout will actually help you sleep better the next night. Your grandpa and I have a routine that's pretty simple."

Abbie's leg vibrated; a buzzing sound emanating from her pocket. "I know, Nana," she said as she pulled out her cell. "It's been hard to wake up early lately. I have been drawing more, though, so that's good. I've been feeling inspired in the morning, I guess."

"Are you taking Emma up on her offer then?" Nana couldn't contain the excitement in her voice.

"Sorry," Abbie said, unlocking her phone. "Give me a second." A text from her boss, Darren, flashed on the screen. *'Did you have a design consult scheduled this morning?'* it read. *'A doctor guy is here waiting for you.'*

Doctor-guy? Abbie tapped her calendar app to verify her schedule, confirming she had a logo design appointment with the owner of a new soap boutique at 1:00 that afternoon, and nothing else until Thursday.

"Everything okay?" Nana asked.

"Yeah, just work stuff," Abbie said. She typed a quick response of *'Don't know who it is. Won't be in for another 30. Have Dan take care of it.'*

"You said you were drawing more? I know you don't want to talk about Emma, but are you going to submit something?"

"No," Abbie answered quickly. Too quickly. In truth, she hadn't fully decided whether or not she would submit any art to premiere alongside her sister's in New York. Emma had always been the supremely talented one in the family; taking after Dad with her ability to create both abstract and commercial art. A scholarship to Juilliard had been offered her junior year in high school because of Emma's brush strokes and eye for detail. Everything she touched seemed to have been kissed by angels. Abbie on the other hand always preferred cartooning and graphic design. Painting portraits or creating interpretational layouts seemed way beyond her skill level, despite Nana's insistence to the contrary. Emma's offer to show some of Abbie's art alongside her own was a sweet, though from Abbie's perspective also condescending, gesture; one looming like an impenetrable wall before her that could never be scaled by someone of Abbie's pedestrian ability.

"Why not?" Nana asked as she took another sip of steaming coffee.

Abbie opened her mouth intending to spout some rhetoric about not needing to prove herself to uptight Manhattan socialites but found no words forming. In truth, she would love to draw an image worthy of such an opportunity. But despite her best efforts, nothing had materialized.

"I don't know," she admitted finally, looking into Nana's kind eyes as they walked under one of the large cottonwood trees at the north end of the plaza. Sunlight filtered through the bare branches and cast dancing shadows across the older woman's face.

"You're good enough. I've seen you draw some amazing things."

"Not like Emma. I design logos and cartoon heads. I've never created anything that stood out. I mean, I woke up the other day and drew something pretty cool, but it's still nothing like what Emma paints."

Abbie pressed the photo app on her phone and scrolled until she came to the image of detailed pencil lines forming a butterfly with large eyes and playful smile. Half photo-real, half cartoon, the black and white drawing expressed personality and passion that most of Abbie's drawings couldn't match.

"That's really stunning," Nana said, taking the phone and examining the artwork more closely.

"I sent this photo of the drawing to a boutique client to maybe use for their logo design," Abbie said, inwardly beaming that

Nana seemed genuinely impressed by the artwork; not just because it had been created by her granddaughter, but because it was actually good. "Like I mentioned, I've been waking up and drawing more the last few weeks. Most of the art is pretty random. Just stuff; insects or shapes. I guess I've felt particularly creative after a bad night's sleep. I don't even know where I came up with that butterfly, but it turned out pretty great. The client loved it."

Nana handed the phone back and stopped on the sidewalk running along 200 South Street. A delivery truck rumbled by, spitting exhaust into the crisp morning air.

"This is what you should be doing," Nana said over the traffic sounds bouncing off the downtown buildings, "You're wasted at that printing place."

"I like working there," Abbie insisted.

"Then why are you so tired all the time? If you love something, it should *give* you energy, not take it away."

Abbie tried to think of a response that wouldn't lead Nana into a discussion of energy work, chakras, and aura cleansing. Nothing came to mind.

"Your dad would cheer you on if you took the risk and quit your job," Nana said. "I know he wishes he had done something like that. And Emma would be happy for you too. Don't pass up this chance because you're scared or don't think you're good enough. That's not you."

A bus drove by with a massive graphic for a local realtor on the side, big red and orange words reading: 'Best in Utah!' Abbie tried not to get distracted by the vinyl wrap's clashing color design.

"I know they would all be supportive if I tried to sell my art full time," she said, looking back at Nana. "But it would be half-hearted support. Everyone knows I'm not the gifted one. I draw pretty good, but not like Emma. They'd be happy, but cautious, and I don't want cautious support. Either way, Dad and I don't talk about it much, and Emma's offer is just beyond my ability. And no matter what Mom says, she doesn't think I'm good enough. If she did, she wouldn't be trying to get me that job with State Farm."

Nana's lips pressed together as if catching a string of irritated words directed at Abbie's mother. She squeezed Abbie's shoulder softly and smiled with a warmth only a grandmother can conjure. "Connie has always played things safe. There's nothing wrong with that, I guess. Anyway, if you're still not sleeping well, you can always come and use the guest room at the condo. Sometimes it's nice to sleep away from your apartment; and Grandpa will cook breakfast for you as always. You could stay for a couple days if you wanted...maybe try your hand at creating something for Emma's show."

The thought of waking up to the smell of scrambled eggs with potatoes and bell peppers mixed in made Abbie breathe deeply through her nose and catch a lung-full of tailpipe fumes. She coughed and took a cleansing sip of coffee.

"I might take you up on that this weekend, maybe," Abbie said with a smile. "As long as I don't have to wake up early to exercise with you and Grandpa."

Nana tossed her empty cup in a garbage can on the curb with an exaggerated pout on her lips. "I won't make you get up."

"Or push me to draw something for Emma's show," Abbie said with a pointed finger.

"No promises. Have an excellent day at work, even if you are too good for that place."

An electronic buzzer rang as Abbie opened The Sign Hub's front door and smelled the familiar fragrance of ink and plastic. A six-foot-long Epson industrial printer across the room pumped out a banner reading, 'Grand Opening' in bright red letters. A cluttered desk to her left rattled as head designer Dan popped his head up over his computer monitor to see who had entered. Darren sat across from him on his usual perch behind the counter just to the right of the entry on a slightly elevated platform. A pair of glasses hung on a chain around his neck, as if he were an 80-year-old man instead of in his mid-50's. His salt-and-pepper gray hair hadn't changed in length or style since the day she started as a designer four years earlier. In fact, the office itself seemed completely unchanged in that time aside from the thousands of banners and exterior business signs that had moved through the shop over the years.

One difference caught her eye this morning though. The 'Doctor-guy' Darren had texted about earlier sat in a chair next to Abbie's desk. His thick mustache and mocha skin reminded Abbie of one of her math professors at Southern Utah University who had always laughed at silly jokes and spoken in a thick Hindi accent. The visitor wore a pull-over sweater, tie, and tan pants. His fingers tapped nervously on a pale-yellow file folder on his lap.

"Good morning, everyone," Abbie said cheerfully.

"Hey," Dan waved. "I got a call from Rachel with the city offices. You have the concert posters designed yet?"

"I told her I'd email them by Friday," Abbie replied. "They're always so impatient."

"But they pay on-time," Darren smiled without pulling his eyes from his computer screen.

Abbie returned her attention to the man sitting beside her desk and stepped forward with an outstretched hand. "I'm Abbie.

Darren texted me earlier you were here, but I don't recall setting up an appointment."

The man stood, eyes darting to the side quickly. He took Abbie's hand and shook lightly. "I didn't have an appointment," he said, hint of a midwestern accent to the words.

"Dan could have helped you," Abbie said, nodding her head toward her coworker. "You didn't have to wait around for me all this time. You looking to do some new business signage, or need design work?"

"No, um…" the man hesitated. He remained standing as Abbie took her seat at the desk. "This is going to sound strange. I'm Doctor Riann Chabra from the Huntsman Mental Health Institute at the U of U. I'm actually here because of a patient. Have you ever been to the Health Institute by chance?"

"I haven't," Abbie answered.

"Are you familiar with a man by the name of Conrad Rossi?" The doctor pulled the folder from under his arm and took a photograph out. A bald man in his late 50's or early 60's stared back at Abbie, face expressionless, head cocked to the right with his shoulder lifted slightly toward the ear. His eyes seemed vacant and thoughtless somehow, as if the man stared past the photographer toward empty space.

"No, I've never met him," Abbie answered. "At least I don't recognize him."

Dr. Chabra took a deep breath and sat back down in the visitor chair. He leaned forward and rubbed his fingers against the file folder. "You've never met him?"

"No. What's this about?"

"Mr. Rossi is one of our patients…and has been for the past 15 years. He suffers from a condition known as Catatonia, which stems from his schizophrenia. He's completely non-responsive to people and spends most of his time drawing shapes on pieces of paper. He doesn't have any family except for a nephew who used to visit him regularly. Most importantly, he has no real contact with the outside world. He doesn't have the physical or mental capacity to use a computer, and he doesn't recognize or acknowledge people he meets; not even family."

"Okay…" Abbie said, hoping the doctor wasn't about to say she was this guy's long-lost niece or something and she would have to take care of him for the rest of his life.

Opening the folder again, Dr. Chabra pulled out a thick piece of cardstock covered in colored scribbles, as if a group of kindergartners had each taken a crayon and went crazy on the paper. In the middle of the formless mess in a clear spot free of other doodles, read the name, 'Abbie Kinder' in the most beautiful calligraphy Abbie could imagine.

"A few days ago," Chabra began, "Mr. Rossi started writing this name on pieces of paper." He pulled out several more pages; 'Abbie Kinder' written magnificently in the center of each. "I actually had my intern film him writing the name because I'd never seen anything like it."

Abbie took one of the pages and examined it to make sure the name hadn't been printed. Deep pencil marks dented the page, evidencing the hand-drawn nature of the letters.

"It's good work," Abbie admitted. "The lines are very straight, and the serifs look amazing. Why do you think I'm the Abbie Kinder he's writing about though? I mean, what if he knew an Abbie Kinder in high school or something?"

"I thought the same thing," Chabra agreed. "Until two days ago…when he started drawing these."

Out of the folder came another paper, this time with the sophisticated pen strokes of a master. Abbie's face, hair blowing in the breeze with a stern look in her eyes, filled the page like something from a Drew Struzan movie poster. Everything from her tapered nose to the mole on the right side of her jaw appeared in the sketch. Over her shoulder floated a butterfly, eerily similar to the one Abbie had sketched a few mornings before. Perfectly shaded, the drawing made Abbie's artwork look rudimentary by comparison.

"Saturday afternoon, I came into the hospital and saw Mr. Rossi drawing that picture," Chabra said, eyebrows squeezing together below his forehead. "I saw him drawing it with my own eyes. Then yesterday he drew two more."

Dr. Chabra pulled another picture from the folder, followed by a third. One featured Abbie with a broad smile, and what looked like a line of white make-up moving down her forehead, past her left eye, ending with a dot on her cheek. In the other she held a broad translucent sword of some sort over her head while crying out in anger. Each appeared more perfect than the last, with skilled pencil strokes cross-hatching and twirling in perfect symmetry.

"What is this?" Abbie asked, suddenly feeling warm and uncomfortable in her blue sweater.

"He's been writing your name and drawing you," Chabra continued. "A person that, as far as we know, he's never met."

"What is this?" Abbie asked again. She looked over at Dan, who listened to the conversation with interest. "Is this a joke or something? Dan, are you screwing with me? Darren?"

"I'm not," Dan answered.

Darren shrugged and sat forward in his chair as if watching his favorite drama.

"I assure you, this isn't a joke, Miss Kinder," Chabra said, taking back the drawings and slipping them into the file. "This is potentially one of the most incredible instances of lucidity I've ever seen in a patient."

Abbie laughed nervously. "I'm serious. Who put you up to this? If it wasn't you Dan…was it Kelly? Did Damyon pay you to mess with me?"

The chair squeaked as Chabra sat back and placed the folder on his lap. "Again, Miss Kinder, this isn't a joke. I searched your name on social media and there were a handful of Abbie or Abigail Kinders across the country. I looked for any living along the Wasatch Front and found you. It was easy to match the drawings to your pictures on Facebook. That's how I found you. I didn't want to call because I know this is crazy and without some sort of proof no one in their right mind would believe it."

"Okay," Abbie said, sitting forward. "Let's say this is true and you're really a doctor at whatever research place at the U of U. What do you want me to do about any of this? For all I know you're some perv who's drawing pictures of me as a fetish or something."

Chabra nodded. "I understand. This is really odd. Look, what I'd like is for you to come up to our offices at the university and sit down with Mr. Rossi while we film and see if he responds to you. That's all. We'd reimburse you for gas and your time. I can't tell you how unique this is."

"What if this guy just saw a picture of me on the internet or something and now, he's drawing it from memory?" Abbie asked, seeking a logical answer to what seemed on the surface a complete impossibility, if not some prank.

"Mr. Rossi has suffered from varying levels of Catatonia for 20 years," Chabra said. "He's never been on a computer in that time. Honestly, I'm not sure where this has come from. You're both here in Salt Lake, so there's a possibility of contact somewhere at some point, but I have no idea where that could have been. Maybe someone came into the hospital, and he saw a picture of you, or a nurse was on Facebook or something and a photo of you came up. I have no idea. Either way, it's extraordinary for a person with normal capacity to be able to draw pictures like these completely from memory, let alone someone with cognitive impairments. What I do know is that a change of this magnitude is unprecedented in my field of study. With his schizophrenia, the drug regimen that usually works on Catatonia patients hasn't been effective. Like I said, this sort of thing has never happened before."

"This is really weird," Abbie admitted. "Is he an artist…or was an artist before he…you know?"

"According to his files he's been in and out of hospitals since he was a teenager. There have never been any indications of any artistic ability beyond the average. But the brain is an amazing thing. Sometimes after strokes people have been known to be able to speak languages they didn't speak before, completely without an accent. This may be a case like that, but we won't know until we do more tests. If you could help us with that, you could be a part of changing how we think of brain functions and the mind. It's very exciting."

The words poured quickly out of Chabra's mouth, corroborating his exhilaration. Abbie didn't know quite what to think, but the more the doctor spoke, the less she got the impression this was an elaborate hoax.

"Here's my card," Chabra said as he pulled out a thick trifecta business card with gold embossed lettering. Abbie had ordered cards like this many times for high-end clients working in law firms or downtown offices and knew they were $250 per 1,000; one of the most expensive printing options. "If you can come down at some point in the next few days, it would be greatly appreciated. Like I said, we'll pay well for your time."

Turning the card over in her fingers, Abbie grappled with the implications of the conversation. If real, the situation was fantastic beyond reason. She had watched documentaries on PBS about the wonders of the human brain, and always came away with a sense of wonder. What if this guy really did have something unlocked in his cerebellum that allowed him to suddenly draw like one of the great artists of history? Such a thing would revolutionize the sciences and our understanding of our own brains. Goosebumps rippled up Abbie's arms at the thought of this being real.

Of course, it could just as easily be a joke, or a mistake, or some other far likelier scenario. Abbie still had her doubts. All the website and email info on the card seemed legit, but in the 21st century, you never could be sure what angle people were coming from.

"So, he just started drawing her?" Dan asked from his desk across the office. "That's weird."

"It is, and that's why I'm here," Chabra replied. "I wouldn't have come otherwise."

"I might be able to come by on my lunch break tomorrow or Wednesday, maybe," Abbie said finally, rubbing the resurging fatigue from her eyes. "When you say you'll pay me for my time, what does that look like exactly?"

Chabra stood and rubbed his hands together with the file in between, seemingly excited at the possibility of Abbie coming to his offices. "This is important to our facility. If you can come down tomorrow, I'll pay you $200 an hour. I wouldn't think it would take more than a couple hours, but I want you to know, this is important. I'm excited you're considering it."

$400 for two hours of work? Abbie could take a risk for 400 bucks.

"Alright, I have a design consult today at 1:00, but I can come tomorrow over lunch," Abbie said. "Is that cool if I take a long lunch tomorrow, Darren?"

"Yeah," her boss answered. "You don't usually take time to eat most days anyway."

"Awesome." She looked at the card and then back up at

Chabra. “It says here you’re at Research Park. Is that across from the cancer institute just past Fort Douglas Museum?”

“Yes,” Chabra said, practically bouncing on his toes. “Thank you so much. I know this is weird, but your participation could really help our studies. Everything is on the card. If you need to call me directly, the number is there, or you can call the offices at the 800 number as well. Thank you so much, again!” He backed toward the door and ran into the cutting table in the center of the office, knocking over a cup full of X-Acto knives. “Sorry about that…We’ll see you tomorrow at what, 12:30?”

“12:30 is fine,” Abbie agreed.

Chabra exited quickly, gushing ‘thank you’ at least three more times.

“You think this thing is real?” Dan asked, eyebrows raised.

Abbie flipped the card on the desk and shrugged. “For $400 I’m willing to suspend my disbelief. If he wanted me to go to some shady back alley, I’d probably flip him off, but I’ve seen the Research Park buildings from the soccer field stands at the U. They’re nice offices.”

“Just keep your phone close and call if anything seems weird,” Darren added.

Dan nodded in agreement and went back to his design work just as the printer finished a second ‘Grand Opening’ banner before falling silent. Abbie’s fingers clacked against the keyboard as she pulled up Dr. Chabra’s website. A group of smiling physicians stood together in front of a window with the Salt Lake City skyline in the background. Words like ‘rehabilitation’ and ‘pharmaceuticals’ stood out against graphics showing patent improvement rates. Fluffy paragraphs sold families on miracle medical breakthroughs just around the corner.

It all seemed legitimate.

What would she find at the research center besides a schizophrenic guy with a creepy talent?

$400.

Not bad for a day she thought already marred by exhaustion and spilled coffee.

After her one o'clock meeting with Gina from The Bath Bomb Boutique, Abbie spent the remainder of her day trying to finalize their butterfly logo design. At 6 PM on the nose she darted from the building and headed home.

Day-old French fry stink hit her nose as she entered the apartment. Garbage overflowed next to the refrigerator, reminding Abbie she needed to toss the bag in the dumpster before something more disgusting replaced the smell of fried potatoes. Laundry hung from the end of the couch while dishes piled in the sink. Back when she had a roommate, Abbie had been very good about cleaning the apartment and got incredibly annoyed when Rachel left a mess. Now that the chaos belonged to her, Abbie didn't get quite so frustrated, nor was she as quick to pick up after herself. Soon a pot filled with the remains of cheap macaroni and cheese sat atop the dishes like a benevolent ruler. Kitchen clean-up could wait until tomorrow. A few more plates would still fit in the sink.

As Abbie took bites of her mac and cheese, a pile of drawings across the table stared up at her. Most of them had been sketched within minutes of waking up each morning; dancing wolves, strange maze shapes, a cat with octopus tentacles coming out of its nose. Some were definitely weird, but showed promise, while others seemed like a third grader could have done better. Mornings seemed to be her most creative time lately.

'You should draw tonight instead of watching TV,' her inner monologue whispered. *'Maybe you'll come up with something good for Emma's show. No need to procrastinate until tomorrow.'*

"Shut up," she said out loud to no one, while reaching for the remote.

By 11:30 she'd finished her third episode of *Lucifer* and sleep beckoned. She threw on a loose-fitting pair of pink pajama pants and an old *Mumford and Sons* shirt she'd bought at a concert a few years prior. Cool sheets swirled around her as Abbie snuggled in for a restful night, mind filled with thoughts of strange drawings, catatonic artists, and gallery openings where snooty critics made fun of her art. An old lumpy pillow she bought in college twisted her neck slightly, but she endured, pledging to buy a new one over the weekend so she could sleep better.

Despite the uncomfortable padding, Abbie soon breathed deeply, and slipped away from the waking world with the words of John Lennon somehow still in her brain.

"Who's to say that dreams and nightmares aren't as real as the here and now?"

As sleepy fog filled her mind, it seemed Abbie's own voice called out in answer.

"They aren't as real as the here and now," the cry echoed. *"They're more real."*

CHAPTER TWO

Colors sang in Abbie's ears like a gospel choir, as if all the shades in the rainbow suddenly found voice. Her mind awoke on the shores of Consciousness.

For a moment she still felt the sheets wrapped around her physical body and the warmth from the comforter, but those sensations faded quickly as her senses elevated beyond the tangible. Confusion tickled Abbie's brain for a moment as it always did during those first few seconds after entering the dream. Memories flooded her mind; images and feelings from almost a decade of running through fragrant forests made up of concepts like freedom and excitement, while cutting down predators looking to feed on the emotions of innocent dreamers. She remembered relationships with friends and mentors she'd never met while awake and wouldn't remember in the light of day. It was a good existence; much better than the worthless physical one that held her mind captive all day long.

As her perceptions sharpened, Abbie became aware of air currents blowing across her arms. The smell of spring rain and ocean spray mingled in her nose and conveyed a feeling of serenity. Waves crashed somewhere behind her as if she stood on a sea of emotion far from the shore. Slowly, purposefully, she opened her eyes.

A red and orange horizon stretched on forever before her, reflecting in a rippled sea that responded to her every thought. While solid enough to support Abbie's weight, the water shifted slightly beneath her bare feet as small waves bobbed her up and down. Pigments that had no name shimmered on the surface, smelling like sea brine with a hint of tranquility.

Abbie dipped her toe into the warm ocean, distorting the mirror image staring back up at her. Liquid solidified and changed color from bluish orange into green. Thin stalks sprang from the surface until a pastoral meadow covered in tall grass replaced the sea. A breeze blew cool and refreshing, bringing scents of freshly cut lawn and summer barbeque. Several knotted trees grew around her, twisting from sapling to ancient oak in seconds. Birds cried overhead while bees whispered to each other about the sweetness of the flowers.

A pink hummingbird wearing a top hat flew in front of her face and stuck out its tongue. "Watch where you're manifesting," the bird spat in a surprisingly deep voice.

"Keep moving dreamer," she replied, swatting at the bird and sending it whizzing away. Comfortable fabric held tight to her flesh in a purplish gray unitard that covered from her neck to her ankles like a second skin. Her feet remained bare so she could touch the pasture and absorb the feelings shaping the environment around her; the better to ground herself in the conscious realm. Freedom became palpable as she looked out on a world of pure creation.

The real world.

"I need to convince her to go to bed earlier," Abbie said to herself.

Using the term 'her' to describe her physical form asleep in a bed seemed somehow wrong, but at the same time accurate. Were they even the same person? Of course not. That bag of flesh could barely remember the drawings every morning, let alone the extent of her unconscious connection to the world around her. Being the same person would be a disappointment. It was better to think of her separately.

Abbie was now home in a world she understood far better than the tactile one that locked her away each morning. Balmy air filled her lungs with a joy that accompanied entrance into elevated consciousness.

Memories from her day appeared as images in front of her like a sunrise of recollections. Nana Gayle materialized in a three-dimensional impression, ponytail swishing in the wind as they walked in the plaza. Abbie smelled lavender, love, and acceptance. Then she felt contempt for herself as memories of her fear of failure vomited out like putrid smoke, along with the stomach cramps that accompanied eating ice cream 15 minutes before going to bed. Doubt seemed to be Basic-Abbie's defining emotion lately. She wanted more from life but didn't have enough confidence in her abilities to even try to escape her comfort zone. What a waste of a conscious mind.

'That girl doesn't trust herself much,' Abbie thought. *'I completely understand why she wouldn't.'*

Despite her disappointment, a smile spread across her face as she saw Conrad Rossi's picture appear before her eyes.

At last, they had reached the next phase.

The doctors finally figured everything out and contacted her. Perhaps now her conscious brain would be able to start thinking beyond the confines of normal thought and allow her to remember what was really important. Abbie could then fight against Alexander and Catharsis' forces both in the dream and in Basic. She could make a real difference.

"Can't you ever go to bed on time?" an airy voice asked somewhere above her.

"We can't all be as disciplined as you," Abbie said, reaching up and plucking a thought from the air. The idea of safety took shape and churned around her, forming opal armor that glimmered in shades of purple, red, and black. Light and durable, the defensive shell grew harder as she added other thoughts to the mix, like protection, salvation, and a hint of sass.

A woman flitted from above, wearing a white robe that whooshed in misty motions around her slender body. Golden hair, glistening like strings of brass, floated on the breeze and caressed her flawless, statue-like face.

"Moon," the woman nodded.

"Merquery," Abbie replied, taking her index finger and running it down her forehead from her hairline. The action left behind a glowing white line that stretched over her left eye, and ended with a dot on her cheek; the final accent of Moon, her true self. "How far behind am I?"

"Only about an hour," Merquery said. "The others have already gone deeper to search for any signs of Catharsis and his crew. It's up to you and me to cast out the leeches in the forest."

"How many Pursuants are in this section of the dream tonight?" Abbie asked.

"Hanker said he felt at least three dozen coming and going," Merquery answered. "Only a few of any real strength."

Abbie nodded her head and listened for the hum of dreamers. "About the same as the last few days. Good. We can take them."

Fog circled around Merquery as she raised her hands in front of her, palms toward the colorful sky. "I'm pulling us into the woods. Emotional ripples are strong there. Plenty of dreamers congregating and likely to get preyed on. We'll meet up with the conclave again once you and I have cleared the forest. Hanker also told us the plan worked. The doctors contacted you in Basic today?"

"Yes, one of them brought her the pictures he drew and convinced her to come to the hospital tomorrow," Abbie answered, feeling the familiar mixture of emotions swirling as they transitioned away from the tranquil pasture toward a woodland of imagination.

The grass twisted and morphed, transforming into a multicolored forest. Trees of every type, from pine, to walnut, to mangrove and juniper, sprouted and flowered with the accompanying smells of moss and moist earth. Instead of merely green leaves, purple, orange, and pink foliage blew in the wind as boughs waved at the women and blushed. Quiet laughter echoed through the forest along with voices calling out in different languages.

Ghost-like apparitions of men, women, and children of all ages and sizes appeared around Abbie and Merquery. Each dreamer blinked in and out of existence, some smiling, others running, yet others weeping. Their mental projections took shape for a short time, enjoying a brief moment of unencumbered consciousness mixed with their own thoughts, before dropping back into REM sleep. A small girl, no more than six or seven years old, darted past Abbie and shouted in Spanish about hiding in the basement where her brother couldn't find her. Strong emotions of childlike excitement emanated from the girl, filling Abbie with the desire to play outside in the sunlight and blow dandelions into the air. More dreamers appeared in every direction, each experiencing the world differently; not conscious enough to affect their surroundings like Abbie and Merquery.

"How did you react when the doctor told you a man in a mental hospital had drawn pictures of you?" Merquery asked as she reached her hand out and pulled a trail of yellow laughter from a ghostly dreamer flitting past. The misty contrail twisted around her finger and Merquery sniffed at it with a deep inhale. She giggled. "I've always wondered what all of you look like in the Basic realm. I'm sure Hanker looks very much the same as he does here; no self-consciousness to speak of, for certain."

"She reacted about as expected," Abbie said, walking through the trees and smelling ripe grapefruit. "It was all pretty strange for her. We'll have to see what happens. I'm hopeful she starts to figure things out faster now. I'm tired of waiting. Things are getting worse every day. People like Catharsis and Alexander need to be hit both here and in Basic. I need to take control and put my awake-self on the mental back burner."

"It isn't about control," Merquery said. "It's about surrender. Unity."

"You sound just like Hanker."

"I'll take that as a compliment. He's our mentor for a reason. You can't think of yourself as two different beings. You're the same. You're one. Imagine if the dreamers here in the wood believed they were different than their conscious forms. Just because you move from one mental state to another doesn't mean you've changed who you are."

"She and I are different," Abbie replied. "I may live as her while my eyes are open but that doesn't make us the same. I get enough lectures from Hanker. I don't need another one from you."

"I'm just trying to help. Things are getting worse as you said, and the faster we unify our divides the sooner we can become as Alice. We are one person both here in the dream and out there in the world simultaneously, not two distinct individuals."

"And that's how you look in Basic? Flawlessly beautiful and elegant?" Abbie questioned as an ethereal woman passed through her body, leaving behind the scent of young love and unbridled lust. "I'm going to bet you don't have hair made of gold either, 'Query."

"I don't," Merquery admitted as she sniffed the air. "I am…ashamed of some of my physical habits in the Basic Realm, but I am completing the drawings every day and soon I will be unified. Not all of us can be confident enough to look the same in both realms. I'm willing to bet there are things you change about yourself as well, whether you choose to admit it or not."

The duo strolled through the flamboyant forest, soft ground squishing under their bare feet. Dreamers continued to materialize and wander about. Some asked Abbie unintelligible questions while others danced, oblivious of their conscious neighbors. One young man floated into the air as he passed close to an attractive woman, leaving behind a trail of pink frivolity that filled Abbie with a feeling of unfettered independence. Part of her wanted to reach out and pull more of the emotion toward her but knew it would only cloud her thoughts and impede her mission.

As the happiness ebbed, Abbie returned to her own controlled state of mind. "She fell asleep for a second this morning while sitting in a coffee shop, and I was able to enter Consciousness for a moment. I was pleased I could get in so quickly. Training is paying off every day. She spilled coffee on herself, and it pulled me out too soon."

"I took a nap this afternoon," Merquery said as a vine reached down from above and twisted into the shape of a heart in front of her. She continued sniffing. "I find I'm never quite as powerful during naps, but it's always wonderful to interact with and protect dreamers from other parts of the world. I met Ashrylock from Mongolia. I'd heard of him and how he acted as Proctor for an entire city, protecting them from dream predators by himself for over a year. He was very nice. I'm smelling fear coming from the north. What about you, Moon?"

"Yeah, I smell it too," Abbie said. The atmosphere shifted, filling with odors of onion and parsley. Emotions wavered as well, with the forest itself pulling away from a pleasant underpinning to one slightly more apprehensive. Several dreamers looked around with worried expressions. The ground puckered into a series of tiny boils, as if the entire world suddenly broke out in goosebumps.

"They're getting close. Dreamers are confused and trying to wake up."

"I am prepared," Merquery replied. "The fear isn't particularly potent, so I am betting these are weak Pursuants. We should be able to cast them out easily. While we wait for them to arrive, let me ask you this: here in the dream, do you think of yourself as 'Moon' or by your name in the Basic Realm?"

Abbie tripped on a rock and caught herself against one of the trees before standing back up quickly. She grunted in irritation and continued walking.

Merquery giggled playfully. "We have a way of making our stumbling blocks real here, don't we? I'll take that as the answer to my question. You see? You are the same person, whether you want to admit it or not."

Closing her eyes, Abbie held her hands in front of her and imagined rage taking shape. Fingers twitched as a lavender blade, like sharp glass, formed between them, warm to the touch and tingling with the electricity of pure anger.

"Are you using your annoyance with me to help form your sword, Moon?" Merquery asked with a grin.

"A little bit," Abbie said. She swished the purple blade back and forth as the forest darkened further. Trees distorted and bounced as if jumping between two emotional states. Dreamers responded in kind, some changing color from a pale mist of dancing shades to more opaque grays and browns.

Mushrooms grew black and sticky amid the grass; leaves fell and blew on a wind of malice. The trees moved aside as a creature bounded into view. Its hunched shape and long limbs made it appear like a beast from a nightmare; pale, emaciated, and slobbery. A long nose poked from its gaunt, wolf-like face; tongue flicking out and licking its lips.

Abbie knew it was no monster, just a weak man preying on innocents; taking the form of something horrific to elicit his preferred emotional response. An addict getting high on the emotions of unsuspecting dreamers.

Two more parasites emerged from the shadows. One appeared to be a blubbery male in an apron with disgusting fat rolls that smelled of sweat and baked goods. His adjacent colleague manifested as a large man made completely of black obsidian, wearing a fine blue suit and tie. Hawaiian tattoos glowed along his neck like crimson magma. Abbie recognized him immediately.

"It's Koa," she whispered to Merquery as the two women crouched behind a tree to avoid being seen.

"Haven't felt his presence in a while," Merquery said. "Do you think he's still working for Catharsis?"

"He seems to switch it up whenever the wind changes, but I wouldn't be surprised if he's taking orders from the cat. You recognize the other two?"

"I don't. Koa is probably training them, I'd bet.

Dreamers shouted, pulled from pleasant memories, and thrust into bitter nightmares. The werewolf creature pounced on a young girl who cried out for her daddy. Mist cascaded from the child and twisted upward toward the beast's snout. He breathed as if coming up for air after almost drowning and inhaled the terror seeping from the child.

"Better than Christmas morning memories!" he shouted.

Koa smacked the creature upside the head, knocking the beast off the girl and allowing her to dissipate and leave the dream. "Quit screwing around and find Davis. We're not here so you can scare little kids to feel their fear."

"Sorry," the werewolf-man mumbled.

“I can smell him over this way,” the fat hunter pointed toward a clearing in the trees. “We’ll catch him again, don’t worry.” He floated toward an ethereal woman who seemed unsure whether she should linger or run away. He touched her ghostly cheek and moved close, licking his lips. “His fear is pungent, like sweet caramel. This little lady has a bit of it herself, along with some…tasty self-loathing. Can’t we take a minute, Koa?”

Abbie lunged from behind the tree without a word and caught the fat pastry-man off guard.

“Proctors!” the flabby ghoul screamed. He darted out of the way much more quickly than his size would imply just as Abbie’s blade came down to cleave him in two. Before he could mount another cry, Abbie pivoted and sliced through his sagging belly, spilling out smoke and bile that smelled like rotting corn syrup. She thrust up, shoving the blade below his chin and out the top of his head. He shrieked and clawed at her before dissipating like fog in the sun.

“That must have hurt,” Merquery said.

“It’s Moon!” the wolf-creature bellowed. The few dreamers remaining in the area darted in all directions, leaving the Proctors to dispatch their enemies.

Merquery stepped next to Abbie and shrugged. “Why do you always get top billing?”

“Your name is too hard to say,” Abbie smiled before leaping in the air. “And it’s tough to be afraid of someone with golden hair!”

“You won’t banish me so easily!” the pimpled dog-retch cried. He jumped back, taking hold of the fear still drifting with the mist around him. A shield took shape, throbbing like a rapid heartbeat.

The weak emotional barrier did little to slow Abbie’s attack. A single swing of her sword shattered the hastily created armor, followed instantly with a swipe that cut directly down the center of the wolf-thing's head. He blinked for a moment, wafting in two pieces on the breeze as a tear fell from his eye, before billowing like haze into the void.

"Nice," Koa clapped with his rocky hands. "You've set me back like two hours. Thanks Moon." Each word sounded like stones scraping together.

"Glad I could help," Abbie said. She squatted low, sword in front of her. "It's been a while since you've slept in this time zone. I figured you were on the other side of the world or something."

"Maybe I was."

"You should have stayed there," Merquery said. She rose into the air, robes swirling around her.

"What?" Koa asked. "You want to battle? I honestly don't want to fight. What I'm after has nothing to do with either of you. I'm not here hunting dreamers, and I wasn't even allowing Frank and Wally to lick anyone's minds, so why don't you cut me some slack, huh?"

Abbie stepped slowly closer, weapons at the ready. "Then who's this 'Davis' person you were looking for? I'm assuming they ran away from you for a reason."

"We don't need to do this, Moon," Koa said, twisting his neck to the side with a sickening crinkle.

"I think we do."

"Fine."

A shockwave blew from Koa's feet as he leaped toward Merquery. Black blades grew from his fists. He swiped at the floating blonde with a growl. Merquery spun to the left and avoided his attack with ease. Her gold hair coiled around his arms as he moved past, holding the rocky man tight in the air. Sensing her opening, Abbie jumped over and sliced off his craggy legs with a slash of her sword.

Koa bellowed in pain as Merquery dropped him back to the ground unceremoniously. He pushed himself up and tried to reform his severed limbs from the dirt beneath him, but Abbie stepped over and came down with her blade, cutting off his right arm, followed swiftly by his left. Koa balanced on his torso, staring Abbie in the eyes with less anger than she expected.

"Your heart's not in this fight, Koa."

"I told you…I didn't want to brawl," he grimaced.

Lips scrunched together as Abbie tried not to roll her eyes. "In that case, you chose to work for the wrong people." Her sword flared dark purple and disappeared. Abbie brought up her fists instead, smashing Koa's head between her knuckles like a punishing vice. Pebbles crumbled to the forest floor and then disintegrated as Koa's mind was severed from Consciousness. He would be back of course, but at least Abbie had slowed him down, whatever his agenda had been.

"That was strange," Merquery said, picking up one of Koa's rocky sections as it dissolved between her fingers. "I've never battled Koa before myself, but he has a reputation as a powerful Pursuant. Why did he let us win so easily?"

"I don't know," Abbie admitted. "Nothing has been making sense lately when it comes to Catharsis and his crew."

With the Pursuants excised from the area, the forest seemed to breathe a sigh of relief. Color returned along with an overall feeling of calm. Abbie closed her eyes and let the emotion wash over her. Dreamers began popping up again, speaking sentences without nouns and manifesting memories of Halloween and first kisses.

"And here I thought you two would have some difficult fighting ahead of you," a man's voice said from somewhere behind

Abbie. "We came as fast as we could, but Catharsis had plenty of leeches slithering around like always. Ours weren't as easy to dispatch as yours, apparently."

Abbie smiled as the smell of fresh lilac-infused confidence expanded around her, with the hint of freshly baked cookies.

"What the hell happened?" Another voice, this one a bit higher with a British accent, asked. "Did you guys get the easy shift or something?"

Abbie opened her eyes and turned, feeling the familiar rush of emotion that always followed her conclave. Pinely Daymare, tall and lanky, wearing a pointed green hat and a British flag as a cape, leaped from one tree to the next before hitting the ground like a Cirque de Soleil acrobat. The symbol of a compass with a lightning bolt across it covered his chest like a superhero emblem. He pressed his nose close to the singed grass where Koa had just been excised and sniffed, rubbing his pointed chin. Aspira, with her cat-like features and pink fur, purred up next to him and played with Pinely's ears. A coarse red tongue flicked out of her mouth and licked her whiskers. Short and stout Proctor Gaze stomped forward like an angry bearded dwarf in orange armor; Tommy, who manifested as a college student with nothing more than jeans and a different 90's band t-shirt for his armor (tonight was *Collective Soul*); and massively oversized and over-gunned Brainstorm, filled out the group's ranks, each with their colorful physical constructs and array of weapons at the ready.

Finally, Hanker strolled through the trees bringing with him all the warmth and atmosphere of a bakery filled with fresh confections. His bald head nodded toward Abbie as he adjusted his yellow and blue emotional armor across his chest; a white eagle emblem blazed across the front like a beacon in the forest. Wrinkles etched deep in his forehead, but jovial energy flowed from every aspect of his awareness. He looked almost exactly as he did in the photos Dr. Chabra had shown her earlier that day: Conrad Rossi, the poor catatonic mental patient. Even with enough psychological power at his disposal to rewrite the fabric of the world around them, Hanker never needed to make himself look intimidating. While tall and broad, the only time he ever seemed even slightly menacing was when banishing particularly cruel hunters to the waking world. He smiled and walked slowly toward Abbie; arms open wide.

"You came as fast as you could, huh?" Abbie joked as she gave her mentor a hug. He stood twice as tall as her, like a cuddly grizzly bear in armor made from fragments of kindness and empathy.

"Well, you know Pinely," he grinned. "Always needing to take a second to talk during a fight."

"Humor is a powerful weapon, captain," Pinely said with an exaggerated bow. "We can't all be like Moon and have anger raging constantly. Without me you'd be morose all the time like Brainy."

"It's Brainstorm," the giant, muscularly swollen young man informed with indignation, while strapping a comically massive gun to his back. Knives and other smaller pistols seemed to cover every inch of the Proctor's body.

Pinely jumped to an overhanging branch and cocked his head to the right. "That's the stupidest name you've come up with yet. I liked 'Mental-Surge' better than 'Brainstorm.' And you don't need to make yourself look like you just ate ten Dwayne Johnsons either. A little subtlety can go a long way."

"He's not wrong," Tommy agreed with a disinterested wave.

"At least I don't wear old band t-shirts or have a stupid lighting compass as my logo, like some Flash reject," Brainstorm seethed. He reached back for his mammoth cannon, ready to start a fight.

"Leave each other alone," Hanker said as he looked down at

what remained of Koa. "We're a team, remember. Pinely, Brainstorm is young. Give him time to find himself here before you make fun of his name choices. If I remember, you originally wanted to go by Claptrap until you found out that Proctor from India already claimed that title."

"Claptrap's a stupid name," Brainstorm mumbled under his breath with a smile. "Barely worse than Daymare..."

"Yeah, yeah," Pinely said as he jumped down and put his arm around Aspira. Several dreaming women circled Pinely like smitten spirits. One of them whispered in his ear and he chuckled. Aspira hissed at the intruders, and they fluttered away.

Abbie kicked at the pile of rubble and looked at Hanker. "Koa went down surprisingly easily. He was hunting someone specific with a couple of lightweights. He's still working for Catharsis I think."

"Working *with* Catharsis," Hanker corrected. "Koa is one of those Pursuants that's hard to pin down where his allegiances lie. It's becoming far more common these days. Between Catharsis' powerplays and Alexander pulling everyone's strings, it's hard to know who to trust. I miss the 80's. Half of the Pursuants manifested like they'd stepped out of a *Mad Max* movie. So much easier to keep track of who you needed to banish."

"Can we cut the chatter and get back to the good news," Gaze interrupted. "The doctors finally contacted Moon about the pictures you drew."

A broad smile brightened Hanker's face. "Yes, they did. Dr. Chabra wouldn't shut up about it when he got back to the hospital. He sat in front of me and went on and on about it. I think he likes that I can't talk, so there's no chance of him being interrupted." He turned to Abbie and took a deep breath. "How did you react?"

Abbie kicked at the grass. "She didn't know what to think

about any of it. I doubt she would have even agreed to go to the hospital to see you if it wasn't for the money."

"Be patient with yourself," Hanker said, placing his large hand on her shoulder. "We weren't sure how this was going to go, or how you would respond. Our best hope is that you'll open your mind to the possibility of our conscious connection and hopefully unite so you remember the dream. There's no guarantees at this point."

"So now that the doctor made contact, how long until Moon can break through and remember in the waking world?" Aspira asked.

"I don't know," Hanker admitted. "This experience will for sure push her conscious mind toward expansion, as have the daily drawings. Unifying is difficult, and everyone takes their own time when accomplishing it. I've had very few students be able to merge, but the need is greater now than it's ever been."

"Tell them about Rêver and Mechtat," Pinely said, face less colorful now than it had been.

"Who are they?" Brainstorm asked.

Hanker scratched his nose and waved away a small red bird trying to serenade him. "Later. First let's prep for today's drawing before we re-enter the fight. I don't want any of you falling behind in your memory progress."

The grove filled with light as Hanker raised his arms to the sky. A giant image of a wave encased in a glass globe appeared above them, colors dancing in its curl and shedding glowing sparkles of creativity like lightning bugs on a summer's night. Salty sea spray seemed to accompany the design with laughter and the sound of gulls. Abbie breathed in the feeling of childlike warmth that emanated from the vibrant swirl, writing every detail into her subconscious so that upon awakening, her Basic Realm self would feel compelled to draw the image. Each sketch brought her closer to awakening her mind and finally throwing off the shackles of her mundane physical existence.

"Absorb the feeling of the wave as much as the picture itself," Hanker said, eyes closed. "Feel the twist of the water and the power of its crash. Smell the ocean. This is the image that moves from mind to hand today."

"This is the image that moves from mind to hand today," they all repeated in unison.

Light faded along with the image, but the emotions remained.

"That was a good one," Pinely smiled.

"Do your best to add more detail this time," Hanker continued. "The more detail you remember while awake, the closer you'll come to unifying."

"We get it," Gaze interrupted gruffly. "You say that every night. Go back to what Pinely said about guys named Rivers and Matches."

"Rêver and Mechtat," Pinely corrected.

"It doesn't matter. Whoever they are, I'm betting something bad happened to them, just like Crawbridge and Gandlefish."

Shoulders slumped slightly as Hanker bowed his head. "Pinely and I learned earlier tonight that the identities of two more Proctors from Europe were discovered last week; Rêver and Mechtat."

"I've heard of Rêver," Merquery said.

"Before I moved to the states, he was quite the presence in the French dream zone," Pinely replied.

Hanker nodded. "As of three nights ago, neither of them has reentered Consciousness. It's believed that once their identities were discovered, someone, probably Catharsis or Alexander, had them killed in the physical world."

The conclave fell silent.

Flowers withered slightly at Abbie's feet. She rarely thought about the dangers of her calling as a protector in the dream, and how vulnerable she really was out there in Basic. Rêver and Mechtat may have been as oblivious to their connection to Consciousness as she was while awake. They may have been going about their day, and then boom, somebody kills them because of what they did while sleeping. A scary thought: one Abbie pushed from her mind immediately so it wouldn't impact her ability to fight and defend.

Stocky Gaze stepped forward; mouth pulled down to his beard in a familiar scowl. "More dead Proctors. And what are we doing? Waiting while you draw pictures of Moon. It's bullshit!"

"Calm down, Gaze," Pinely said, grabbing his teammate's arm.

"No, Daymare! I want to talk." Gaze pulled away and stared at Hanker. "Why the hell are we wasting time having you draw pictures of Moon in Basic, Hanker? It's pointless! You focus on her like she's the only one of us close to remembering the dream. I'm doing the sketches every day. My physical self is close to bridging the gap and remembering everything. I don't see you drawing pictures of Merquery for doctors to find; or writing my real name in Basic."

Armor clinked lightly as Hanker turned and towered over the much shorter man. "If you lived 20 minutes from the hospital where I sit and scribble all day long while trying not to piss myself, I'd be drawing pictures of you, Gaze. But you don't. And you think it's easy for me to exert control over my catatonic body even for a few minutes? I'm doing this for a reason."

"It's not just about the fact that Moon happens to live close to wherever you are, Hanker," Gaze said, seeming to grow taller. "What aren't you telling us? I'm tired of being in the dark when you're taking risks like drawing attention to yourself out there. What you do affects all of us. If some Pursuant figured out the mental patient drawing pictures of a stranger happens to be the great Hanker, how long you think it would be till they figured out who the rest of us are? We'd be dead; dirty and permanent. So, I ask again, what aren't you telling us?"

The other team members looked around uncomfortably. Several dreamers floating just beyond the group whispered and pointed as if intrigue by their favorite soap opera. Pinely scratched his neck and whistled quietly. Merquery ran her fingers through her hair while concentrating on the grass between her toes.

"I need to talk to Moon alone for a moment," Hanker said after an awkward pause.

Gaze grumbled like an irritated troll. "Fine."

"We'll be back in a minute," Hanker said to the crew. "Reinforce your emotional connections and focus on the image of the wave. We'll head into battle after Moon and I get back."

Abbie followed her teacher farther into the trees away from the conclave. Brightly colored insects buzzed around while singing conflicting melodies. Feelings of resentment lingered on the air despite the distance they put between them and the team.

"What's wrong?" Abbie asked as Hanker looked back over his shoulder.

"You haven't told anyone what happened last month with Alice Ashling, have you?"

"No," Abbie answered. "Of course not. The moment it went down I knew to shut my mouth. It's not every day one of the most powerful dreamers on Earth links with your mind during a battle. It leaves an impression."

"Good." Hanker stopped underneath a towering pine covered in yellow roses and glanced back and forth as if checking for hidden listeners. "Last night I swam in the River of Subconscious to see if I could learn anything new or see what patterns were emerging across Consciousness. I stayed asleep a little longer than usual and sniffed around the dream city of Guāng too."

"I hate that place," Abbie spat. "It always feels like a million frustrated businessmen trying to unsuccessfully close a deal."

Blinking slowly as if to say, 'please pay attention to the important words coming out of my mouth,' Hanker continued. "Be that as it may, I heard whisperings about you and what happened with Alice. There's a lot of chatter linking the two of you. I think that's what Gaze was implying. People, dangerous people, are looking closer at you than they ever have, which means they're looking at the rest of our team as well. I understand Gaze's concern, despite his lack of tact. We're all in danger because of that mental link with Alice."

"It wasn't my fault," Abbie said, suddenly defensive that Hanker would accuse her of putting all of them in jeopardy. "I didn't even care that she was there during the fight. I don't get star-struck like those idiots from that religious conclave. They practically worship her. As far as I'm concerned, she's over-hyped. Alice has helped us in a fight with Catharsis all of one time. One time! I don't see her out here every night cutting hunters down like we are. She may be powerful or whatever, but she's a non-entity. She linked with me. I wasn't trying to…"

"I know," Hanker said calmly. He placed both hands on Abbie's shoulders. A warm feeling tingled from his palms. "I know. Alice is very powerful…and very dangerous. And I'm not worried about what thoughts she might have gleaned from you concerning all of us. I'm worried about what you gleaned from her."

"Again, I didn't have any control over what thoughts were on her mind," Abbie continued. "I didn't want to know where---"

"Shhhh!" Hanker hushed. His eyes darted around the forest as if the trees would pass along anything they said. "We don't need to talk about details. All I wanted you to know is that powerful Pursuants are focused on you. If they think you have information on Alice, they'll come after you, and it won't be to cast you from the dream. Catharsis, Alexander; they all want her out of the way. They'll try to pry whatever they can from your mind as painfully as possible. I don't want you straying far from my side over the next few weeks. Got it?"

"Everybody on the team knows we're keeping something from them. Gaze is the only one pissy enough to complain about it though."

Hanker blew out a breath. "I know. He'll get over it. As long as you haven't told anyone else, there won't be more than rumors flying around. We can deal with rumors. Gaze can deal with rumors. You just need to be careful. And you need to remember the dream in the real world before things get really out of hand up here."

"This *is* the real world," Abbie whispered under her breath.

"Stop it," Hanker said, sounding like a patient tutor. His fondness for her emanated from his fingers, smelling like chocolate chip cookies straight out of the oven. "You still consider yourself two different people. That's the first and last obstacle you need to overcome."

"Merquery already gave me this sermon tonight," Abbie said. "I just need to keep fighting in here and hopefully my physical self will catch up."

Hanker nodded. "The lengths we've gone to aren't for nothing, Moon. But I can't draw any more pictures of you for the doctors. I can barely force my body to scribble basic shapes anymore. I'm spent out there. When you come to the hospital tomorrow you need to push past your pedestrian way of thinking. Your synapses need to expand beyond their physical confines. Pay attention to our connection. I know you'll feel something when we're together. You'll have vague memories of our friendship. I'll do what I can to help, but there's no guarantee. Your link with Alice has accelerated everything. This is our Hail Mary pass to get you to unify and remember Consciousness before the tide turns for the worst. If it doesn't work, we're in real trouble."

"It'll work," Abbie said, looking into her mentor's kind blue eyes. "When I see you tomorrow, I'll remember. I know it."

Unfortunately, Abbie didn't feel as confident as her statement implied.

CHAPTER THREE

Disinfectant filled the air, irritating Abbie's eyes. She sat in an immaculately clean square white room with three different cameras surrounding her on tripods. A window to the left peered out on Red Butte Canyon to the northeast. Dr. Chabra and four other white-coated psychologists stared at Conrad Rossi as he pressed a red crayon to paper with slow but forceful strokes. Blank pages, thick drafting pencils, and a Crayola box littered the table in front of him. A series of wobbly ovals filled Mr. Rossi's paper canvas without rhyme or reason. Veins on his hand stood out against loose skin as he left behind a heavy layer of crimson wax with each twitching turn of the wrist.

Conrad Rossi himself seemed completely detached from the world. He looked at neither the paper, the doctors, nor Abbie, staring instead at somewhere near the meeting between the wall and floor, or the air between, or the nothingness beyond the room where his eyes couldn't even see. Closely cropped gray hair sprouted from over the man's ears, head cocked to the right, shoulder hunched slightly just like the photo Chabra had shown Abbie. The expression on his face seemed neither positive nor negative; just sort of *there*, as if no emotion existed below the surface.

For some reason Abbie felt strangely connected to the man. She didn't understand it; she didn't recognize him or know Conrad Rossi at all, but for some reason his simple coloring made her smile, as if she understood some great effort went on in his brain at that very moment. The comfortable feeling dissipated quickly however as the doctors constantly interrupted, trying to force Rossi to respond in the way their research required.

"Mr. Rossi," a female physician said, leaning forward with a fake kindergarten-teacher-smile. "Do you see Miss Kinder? Would you like to show her how you can draw?"

Rossi made no sign he understood or cared what the woman had to say or that she even existed. More ovals filled the page with the same methodical pace Abbie had observed for the past 20 minutes.

"Zoom in on what he's drawing," Chabra ordered one of the other doctors. A young MD with slicked back blond hair darted to the closest camera and adjusted the settings. Abbie stared at the drawing and noticed no change in the rhythm or quality of the work.

Hospitals in general made Abbie uncomfortable, but especially those dealing with psychiatric disorders and disabilities. As a five-year-old, her family went with a church group to do service at a local children's hospital. Abbie remembered the kids with extreme birth defects giving her nightmares for days afterward. Her young mind didn't know how to process the reality of such tragedies on innocents even younger than her. Now as an adult, she avoided hospitals at all costs. Sitting across from Mr. Rossi didn't expand her understanding of mental health or make her feel less anxious.

And yet she couldn't shake the feeling that Conrad Rossi was important to her somehow. Perhaps the crazy was rubbing off.

Dr. Chabra stepped over to Abbie and lowered his mouth close to her ear. "Perhaps if you spoke with him, that might elicit some sort of response."

A deep breath filled Abbie's lungs as she nodded her head.

"Mr. Rossi," she began slowly. "I'm Abbie Kinder. Dr. Chabra showed me some drawings you did of me, and some nice…names you wrote."

The whole thing seemed silly. If the guy had indeed drawn the pictures and written her name like the doctors said, wouldn't he have shown some sort of reaction at this point? Did they want her to dance for him or hold his hand so they could get the data they wanted? There were limits to what $200 an hour would get them. This wasn't Vegas after all.

The doctors whispered to each other and wrote hurried notes onto digital pads. One of them moved the camera to Abbie's left a little and then stood back with the others. Another ten minutes went by without Rossi so much as pulling his eyes away from the wall.

Without speeding up his movements, Rossi pulled another piece of paper over and began scribbling again. Instead of ovals however, the red shapes appeared to be cursive, lowercase A's. The letters didn't have the form of the calligraphy Chabra had shown Abbie back at the sign shop, but they definitely had more structure and thought than the previous doodles.

"Look," the blond doctor said, pointing at the page. "He switched it up."

"Are those A's?" one of the female physicians asked while typing quickly on her digital pad.

Chabra tapped a short physician with a high ponytail on the shoulder. "Make sure all the cameras are getting this." She ran dutifully to one of the camcorders on Abbie's right and fumbled with the lens.

Just as quickly as he'd begun though, Rossi returned to the shapeless scratches he had produced prior. Burgundy lines twirled across the page and began covering the letters as his hand moved back and forth.

“Get the paper before he writes over what he’s drawn,” Chabra ordered with a pointed finger. The blond zoomed over and yanked the sheet away, leaving a crayon score across the page. Rossi continued making circles on the table for a moment before dropping the crayon and breathing heavily through his nose.

“We should take him back to the group area for his afternoon color therapy,” the ponytailed doctor said.

“Okay,” Chabra replied. Sweat accumulated on his forehead and he wiped it with his sleeve. He chuckled excitedly. “Okay, yeah, have the orderlies take him back. Stop recording and make sure the files get uploaded to the server so I can share them with Doctor Schvaneveldt in Chicago.”

Clinicians scurried around the room like worker ants in search of sugar, paying no attention to Abbie at all. She eventually stood and grabbed her purse off the floor.

“Could we have you come back sometime in the next few days, Abbie?” Chabra asked as several orderlies helped Rossi stand and led him out of the room. “These things can take time. We’ll of course continue to compensate you. In fact, Nurse Brandt brought me your check a couple minutes ago. Here you are.”

Chabra held out a printed money order. Raised ink on the bordered edge rubbed against Abbie’s fingers as she took the $400 payment. The check itself felt expensive, filling Abbie with an air of importance.

“Sure, I can come back another day,” Abbie said. She yawned and stretched her back as if the easy money didn’t excite her. “Anything for science.”

Chabra practically skipped over to the door and opened it for her. “That was amazing, wasn’t it? I know it didn’t seem like much, but in terms of data, that was incredible to see him draw even something simple like those letters while you were here. I definitely think he feels some connection with you."

The temperature dropped slightly as they entered the research center's main lobby. An Amazon delivery guy held the front door open while trying to bring in a dolly laden with boxes of cleaning supplies. A cool wind entered through the opening and hit Abbie with surprise force.

"I still don't get why I'm somehow important to Mr. Rossi," Abbie admitted with a shiver.

"I don't know yet either," Chabra said. "But the more we look at the tapes and maybe do a few brain scans, we'll get closer to the truth. You're important in all of this, whether we understand why or not. When can you come back in?"

"A client scheduled a design appointment tomorrow at 1 pm, which will take most of the afternoon, and I have the same on Thursday, but Friday I can make it work pretty much whenever."

"Let's plan on the same time Friday then. A couple of hours again." Chabra held the door so the Amazon driver could dislodge his dolly, and Abbie slipped out with a wave.

"See you Friday."

As Abbie stepped into the bright afternoon sun, she took a breath of Salt Lake's pre-spring air. The cold breeze blew from the north, dropping the temperature into the mid-40's. The sweater kept her warm enough as she jogged toward her ugly green Nissan Sentra.

"Are you Abbie?" a man's voice called from behind her. "Excuse me, are you Abbie?"

She turned to see a tall man with black hair and a firm jaw running along the pavement. He looked a bit like the star from one of her favorite Netflix shows, *Kim's Convenience*, but with slightly longer hair. He wore an expensive designer maroon jacket she'd seen on several billboards around town, a white V-neck shirt and tight gray jeans. She would have thought he was unusually attractive had he not been a stranger shouting her name in the parking lot next to a psychiatric hospital.

"I'm sorry, are you Abbie?" he asked again, stopping in front of her and catching his breath.

"...Yeah," Abbie answered.

"Oh my gosh," he smiled. "You're real. I mean, you're a real person."

"I am," Abbie agreed, eyebrows raising as if to say, 'duh.'

"I'm sorry," the man chuckled. He held his hand out for her to shake. "I'm Vincent Nguyen. I'm Conrad Rossi's nephew. When the doctors called me about my uncle drawing weird pictures of some woman, I thought it was crazy. I'm in town from Vietnam where I've been working the past couple years, and when I came by the research center, they told me they found you, but I didn't believe them."

"I wouldn't either," Abbie said, taking Vincent's hand and shaking lightly. She relaxed, knowing he had a connection to Rossi and wasn't an escaped mental patient. "The whole thing has made the last two days pretty odd."

"Well, I appreciate you coming down," Vincent said. A gust of wind wafted a soft scent of sandalwood from the dapper gentleman. His warm smile seemed to raise the temperature of the March afternoon.

Abbie pushed her hair over her ear and suddenly wished she had worn a nicer jacket that flattered her body a bit better than the drapey old sweater. "I guess this is a pretty big deal, from what Dr. Chabra told me."

"Bigger than you could ever guess. Uncle hasn't been responsive much since I was a teenager, so it's cool to think he might be able to start talking or communicating, or whatever again."

“Hopefully I can help,” Abbie smiled, patting her purse and the $400 check currently thawing her pocketbook.

“Can I ask you a bizarre question?” Vincent asked.

“The last couple days have been full of weird questions,” Abbie said, tilting her head to the side and letting her dark hair catch the breeze. “So, sure.”

“What image moves from mind to hand today?”

Abbie paused. Was this guy asking her a riddle or something? She looked around and shrugged. “I’m not sure how to answer that question.”

Vincent waited for a moment and nodded. “Sorry. It was something my uncle would say. I thought you might know the answer, but I forgot you never met him when he could still speak, so…” He reached into his pocket and pulled out a business card, easily one of the most expensive looking Abbie had ever seen. It was black with raised emboss, cropped corners, and gold inlay. $550 per 1,000? It had to be. “Here’s my card. I’m only in town for a couple days, but I’d love to talk to you more about all of this. It’s crazy, right?”

“That it is,” Abbie said, taking the card, and feeling its heft. Could it be real gold inlay? Insane! $750 per 1,000 cards for sure. Shiny words read ‘Vincent Nugyen, CEO Nugyen Consulting.’ Below the title was listed Real Estate, Shipping, Executive Training, and International Relations, along with a quote: *‘Making your business dreams a reality.’*

“Anyway, if you’re up for it,” Vincent continued, “I’d love to take you out to lunch, or dinner, or whatever works for you, and just talk about all of it. I’m excited about what the doctors are telling me, and if you have a part in that, it’s really awesome.”

“Yeah, I’ll think about it for sure,” Abbie said with a noncommittal tilt of the shoulders. In truth, she would offer to go out to dinner with him tonight, but she didn't want to seem desperate.

Vincent stepped away and turned back toward the research building. "Call me and we can go wherever you want. My treat. It was nice meeting you, Abbie."

"Nice meeting you, Vincent," she waved.

The drive down the freeway and back to The Sign Hub took longer than expected in the afternoon traffic, but Abbie didn't mind. Less time at the Hub meant less mind-numbing client work with businesses who wanted $20,000 exterior signs on a $5,000 budget. She didn't mind the design work, but sales calls made her anxious, and the constant flip-flopping of customers caused rage headaches that made her want to smash things.

Her mind lingered on Conrad Rossi's sketches and calligraphy as she exited the freeway. She couldn't deny that his drawing had changed from scribbles to letters while she sat in front of him. If he had in fact drawn the portraits, and the doctors said they filmed him doing it, the man possessed a gift. Abbie dreamed of being able to create images with that much detail. The diversity in the designs intrigued her too. If Rossi had somehow seen a photo of her or maybe caught a glimpse somewhere, being able to recreate her in three different poses and still have the amount of detail those pictures featured? That was an artistic feat. None of them seemed to be copies of any photos she was aware of on any of her social media accounts, so either they had been made from scratch or someone was stalking her…which didn't seem likely, given the circumstances.

Again, the feeling of familiarity warmed her chest as she thought of Conrad Rossi. It was as if he had been a beloved high school teacher, or someone that had changed her life for the better.

'Silly,' she thought. *'I don't know this guy at all. He doesn't mean anything to me. It would be like me thinking I was in love with his nephew after one meeting in a parking lot.'*

Vincent's card bounced in the cupholder as Abbie hit a pothole.

Would she call him?

Why not? Normally the hyper-expensive business card would have turned her off, but his smile and warm demeanor made her willing to wade into potentially shallow waters for a free meal. He was good-looking and obviously successful. Plus, if he lived in southeast Asia there would be no chance of things getting weird between them if anything romantic sparked. Seemed like exactly what she wanted in a relationship right now: good food and a quick wave goodbye. Besides, he was obviously out of her league. Embarrassingly out of her league. This was the type of guy Emma would date after one of her gallery openings on 57th Street, not someone who would be interested in a woman who worked at a sign shop making $20 an hour.

While pulling into the office parking lot, her phone buzzed and rattled. The Bluetooth picked up the signal, feeding it through her speakers.

"Call from…Emma Kinder," the automated voice chirped.

Emma. No doubt wanting to know if Abbie planned to submit a piece of art to the gallery show. The submission wouldn't need to be sent for several months, but the commitment needed to be confirmed as soon as possible.

The green 'answer' symbol flashed next to the red 'decline.' Abbie didn't hesitate, sending the call to voicemail.

She sat for a moment in the parking lot looking at the vinyl Sign Hub logo on the glass entrance. The sun shined directly behind the sign, casting a shadow on her car that seemed to hold her in place.

"I should have answered her call," Abbie said to the empty seat next to her.

In that moment she wanted someone to blame for her hesitation. Mom, Emma, anyone but herself.

But it wasn't her mother's cautious and fastidious nature that held Abbie back. It wasn't Emma's talent and wealth of opportunities. Was it the fear of no one liking Abbie's drawings? The worry of not having a regular paycheck? Would she simply never be as good as her older sister? Any one of them seemed reason enough to make her hesitate.

And that hesitation filled her with self-loathing. In some ways she was her own worst enemy, stuck in a battle with herself she could never win.

Still, life had to go on, and she pushed the feeling aside. The shadows grew long, but Abbie eventually pulled herself from her car and into the office.

If only life had something more exciting to offer.

That thought consumed her the rest of the day and echoed in her mind that night as she fitfully fell asleep.

CHAPTER FOUR

"If only life had something more exciting to offer!?!" Abbie screamed as she entered Consciousness beside a waterfall flowing upward toward floating pink hippopotamuses. She kicked the gravity-defying liquid, sending droplets flying into the sapphire sky. "You stupid cow!" she seethed. Skin held tight against her knuckles as fists squeezed with enough force to crush granite to powder. "You think you have nothing exciting? You can't even understand Consciousness. You're a coward who won't go after anything in your life! You're a whiner! Damn it, I hate you!"

Birds flew from nearby trees at the sound of her raging. Even the hippopotamuses who normally wouldn't give her a second glance, stared with judgmental eyes. A pair of dreamers swam out of the waterfall and wagged their fingers at her childish tantrum.

"Go to hell, all of you," Abbie exhaled in frustration. She stepped away from the waterfall toward oversized ferns that grew in rainbow colors next to an outcropping of clear crystals. Her heartbeat came back under control and slowly she established an emotional connection with the dreamscape. Earthy smells wafted from the ground and helped calm her mind. The humidity seemed more uncomfortable than usual, but she could change that once she had her thoughts back under control.

"She still doesn't remember…" Abbie said, a defeated sting to the words. "How could she not open her mind after Hanker drew her those pictures? He started writing right there in front of her! It's all right there. What else does she need? What's wrong with her?"

Stepping into a muddy puddle, Abbie looked down and saw her reflection in the rippled water. Memories replaced her face on the surface like a television screen. Conrad Rossi scribbled on paper. Dr. Chabra babbled on about his excitement. Handsome Vincent introduced himself in the parking lot and asked her about 'the image that moves from mind to hand.'

Vincent. As Hanker's nephew, he had to have been trained by him before Conrad ended up institutionalized. Hanker had never mentioned him, but her mentor had rarely shared even minute details of his life until he told Abbie his plan for uniting her fractured mind. How else could Vincent quote Hanker's training? Had she met him before in the dream? Was he someone she knew or even with whom she worked closely? Vincent obviously remembered both the dream and the physical world. Why couldn't stupid Abbie?

An irate scream echoed from her mouth as she stomped in the puddle and let mud ooze between her angry toes.

"What's all the yelling about?" A British voice asked from above. Pinely skied down the waterfall in his pointed boots and dropped next to Abbie among the jungle foliage. Ragged strings of fabric blew from torn sections of his cape.

"You don't need to worry about it Pinely," she said with a dismissive wave. "Just dealing with my own crap right now. I'm sure Hanker already told you that I haven't unified yet, even after meeting him today. Where's Merquery? She's usually the one to wait around for me if my Basic-self falls asleep late. Nothing wrong, is there?"

Pinely grabbed her arm and pulled her toward the waterfall. "As a matter of fact, there is. Hanker sent me to find you. Merquery has already been cast from Consciousness. She won't reach her theta state and be back in for probably another half hour at least."

Purple armor formed around Abbie's clothing, and she shook her fingers as if casting off frustration. "What's going on?"

"I don't know," Pinely said as he stepped into the water. "The guy came out of nowhere. Seemed to know where we'd be and hit us fast and hard. Brainstorm has been cut off too. Get in the water and I'll pull us over to the plains. That's where we were when he attacked."

Warm liquid poured over Abbie from her feet to her head as she stepped into the reverse waterfall. Each drop vibrated as it fell toward the sky. The serene moment didn't last long though, as Pinely pulled them deeper into the dream. The fern forest disappeared, replaced by flowing grasslands of yellow and gold touching a gray horizon. Abbie smelled fresh grain mixed with burning hair. Shouts replaced the stream's gurgle. She expected to see her conclave battling one of Catharsis' minions but felt only the echoes of battle. No war raged anywhere in sight. The plain sat empty, besides fields of wheat blowing in the wind with the occasional black scar scoured across the face. Dreamers stood scattered across the area, confused and frightened.

"Where are they?" Abbie asked. Her sword formed in her right hand with a purple flash.

Pinely spun around and stumbled. "They were just here, along with a Pursuant I've never met before. He was powerful and strong."

"It wasn't Koa, was it? He didn't put up much of a fight last night. Maybe he came back to flex some muscle."

"I'd have known if it were Koa, or somebody else I'd fought before, no matter what form they took," Pinely said, still looking around. "This was somebody new. He was feeding on people's inadequacy. Nasty prick, he was."

A chuckle echoed menacingly across the prairie with vapors

of pungent, ammonia-rich disdain. A man in a dark suit and tie smiled at Abbie as he grew from the ground like a dead body risen to life. His skin appeared so black no light could escape it. Only a toothy grin stood out against the empty nothingness of his face. Gray mist drifted from the man's shoulders as if he'd just stepped out of a brimstone shower.

"It's just the two of you Proctors," he began, voice trembling against the fabric of Consciousness. "Your team is tough, but nothing I couldn't handle."

Abbie pointed her sword at the hollow man. "There's no way you cast Hanker from the dream. What did you do, lead them away and then come back here hoping there would be no one left to stop you from feeding on little kids and good-natured grandmas?"

"...Something like that," he admitted.

"I'll give you props, for sure," Abbie said, forming a second sword in her left hand. "It isn't every day that Pinely Daymare gets nervous, so you did something right, you skeevy little leech."

"I wouldn't taunt him, if I were you, Moon," Pinely whispered.

Red eyes glared on the dark man's face. "Moon. I've heard of you. There's a lot of chatter about Moon. Catharsis is very interested in where you are in Consciousness."

"Good for him," Abbie said, pacing to the right slowly. "I'll send him to meet you after I've cut your head off and watched you turn into a steaming pile of crap."

The red eyes narrowed. "Do you have any idea how close Catharsis is right now? He'll be here to back me up in a minute. I've been trained by Alexander himself. I'd let me have my fun if I were you." The suited man suddenly doubled in size, standing at least twelve feet tall. The grass around him died, shrieking as if burned alive.

Uncontrollable laughter burst from Abbie's chest. She hunched over as she giggled. Her humor affected the prairie in every direction. Darkness subsided and sections of grass turned bright pink in polka doted patterns.

"You believe this guy?" she asked Pinely.

"Moon, this isn't someone I would---" Pinely began.

"Anybody who has to make themselves look like a giant to intimidate people isn't someone I'm worried about," Abbie chuckled. "Who are you anyway? One of those rich kids paying Alexander to be trained in siphoning off emotions from people in their dreams? Forgive me if I don't shake in my boots. And you claim to know Catharsis too? You must be really important to have both of them in your contact list."

"I am."

"I bet. So, what's it going to be? You slink away, or do I wake you up screaming with a nasty slice from my blade? Your choice."

The man's shadowed face contorted into a wrinkled manifestation of fury. Eyes bulged; drool spattered his lips. Condescension bubbled from him like boiling ammonium hydroxide. While an effective weapon against half-aware dreamers, condescension was too hollow an emotion for a sustained battle with two trained Proctors. Abbie knew he would peter out before he had a chance to do much damage.

Of course, fat cat Catharsis wielded condescension quite effectively, so she knew there were limits to that logic.

Vines suddenly shot from the ground and grabbed Abbie's ankles. Thorns tore into her flesh, reminding her that no matter where the mind went, pain followed even without a physical body. Pinely jumped aside and formed a double-bladed battle axe from his rage. The shadowed man contorted and twisted to the side like a shifting pile of bricks, avoiding Pinely's strike.

Abbie threw one of her swords into the warping beast's bulbous thigh. "You might as well give up now, whatever your name is!"

"I'm Resin!" the man shouted while lunging at Abbie. Forked spikes shot from his limbs as he merged with the fabric of the savannah. Abbie cut the vines holding her legs and altered perspective so that the attacking Resin suddenly appeared behind her instead of in front.

"You need a few more lessons before you can pull one over on us," she said. "There's more to Consciousness than what you see and smell."

"Thanks for the tip," Resin seethed.

Suddenly Abbie found herself upside down and falling to the ground. Resin appeared to be a quick learner.

"Moon!" Pinely cried. An energy blast cascaded from his axe and thundered toward the lumbering brute.

Abbie twisted and landed on her feet just as Pinely and Resin collided in an explosion of hate and overconfidence. Resin grew larger, like a tornado of tar. His torso spun and swirled, sucking in grass and the emotions holding the area together. Eruptions of orange light shattered against him as Pinely threw splinters of revulsion in his direction.

Joining the fray, Abbie sliced at one of Resin's massive arms and severed it from his perceptual construct. He bellowed and shot barbs of sticky black sludge in all directions. The arm turned to ash and blew away.

"I know how to cast people out of dream sleep too!" the disgusting man yelled. He grabbed Pinely by the legs as he tried to form a larger axe. Another hand tore out of Resin's chest and grabbed Pinely's head. He grew larger still, ripping Pinely in two with a hateful tug. The Brit's legs immediately wafted to nothing on the air, while his head and torso pitched to the right like a bag on the wind.

Pinely's voice trailed off as he faded. "Ouch. You better take this guy seriously. See you in twenty minu…"

A roar filled the forest. Resin howled and smashed a bush into tiny black bubbles. He laughed and reached into the grassy dirt, tossing soil into the air between himself and Abbie. The dust and mud transformed into insects that smelled like manure. They flew at Abbie, but she quickly took control of the emotional remnants of the plain, halting the bugs in midair. The insects swarmed together in front of her and reformed into a granite statue of a hand flipping its middle finger at Resin.

He laughed, sending gray mucus flinging from his twisted mouth. "I like your style. We should meet in Basic and have drinks sometime. I'd pay you for a few lessons on manifesting emotional weapons. It would serve me well when I go into the more nightmarish regions of Consciousness; make it easier to suck out people's terror. What do you say? Up for a date in the real world?"

"This *is* the real world," she replied, swinging her blade back and forth.

"Maybe for you."

"Why don't you go tell Catharsis and Alexander something for me," Abbie said between clenched teeth.

"What's that, oh famous Proctor?"

No words left her mouth as Abbie grabbed hold of her enemy's emotions like a rope. She tugged, pulling herself toward his bulbous form and cut to the center of his consciousness with her sword, severing him from the dream state. White light flashed momentarily from his chest before Resin spat charcoal goo and vomited disappointment like gastric acid. Surprisingly, a smile cracked across his desiccating face.

"See you soon..." he hissed.

Resin shrank, unable to speak further, before slinking to nothing into a smoking black stain on the grass.

Abbie slumped back in exhaustion, gagging on the stench of his burned slime. It had been a while since she had been pushed that far in a fight. It had been a while since anyone had banished Pinely from the dream too. Not since their battle with Catharsis over a month before...when Alice Ashling had linked minds with Abbie.

Alice Ashling.

Resin had mentioned Catharsis' interest in Abbie. She figured the reason had something to do with that mind link.

And what Abbie had learned because of it.

A warm breeze blew through Abbie's dark hair. She smelled baked goods and comfort. The air seemed to twist like a whirlpool a few feet to her right, and out stepped Hanker, Aspira, and Gaze.

"Moon, you okay?" Hanker asked. "I'm glad Pinely found you."

"Yeah, me too," she replied, pulling herself shakily back to her feet.

Dark pus squished against Gaze's boot as the bearded dwarf stepped on Resin's viscous remains. "You cast him out by yourself? Where's Pinely?"

"The same place I assume Brainstorm, Tommy, and Merquery are right now," Abbie answered, head throbbing. "Rolling around in their beds trying to figure out why they're having such a hard time falling back asleep. We've all been there."

Hanker helped steady Abbie as she took a step forward. "That Resin was tough," he said. "The punk pulled us all into a vortex and dropped us into the River of Subconscious. Ballsy move.

It's easy to lose your identity there. He even manipulated perception and hit me in the face with thoughts from the river to confuse me. I didn't even know you could do that. Even I have stuff to learn, I guess. You did good Moon, taking him down. But I can tell it took a lot out of you."

"I needed to use a lot of emotions. Just give me a minute."

The sky grew darker. Screams echoed in the distance as more Pursuants entered the area and began feeding on dreamers. The grass turned gray and limp.

"We need to go now if we're going to help anyone," Gaze said, touching Hanker's shoulder pauldron. "The entire emotional underpinning of the prairie is being affected. We're going to have a long night."

"We can't wait for the others to fall back asleep," Aspira added.

Hanker stood tall and nodded. "Let's share the image for today before we head into battle. At least you guys will have it in case we're separated. You need more time, Moon?"

"No, I'm good," Abbie breathed.

"Alright."

Hanker held out his arms and formed a giant lizard in the air before them, colors dancing on its tail in an intricate diamond design like a glowing tattoo. Abbie wrote every detail into her subconscious. Subtlety and sneaky mischief emanated from the reptile.

"Absorb the feeling of the lizard as much as the picture itself," Hanker said, eyes closed. "Feel the design on its back. This is the image that moves from mind to hand today."

"This is the image that moves from mind to hand today," they all repeated in unison.

Suddenly Abbie again remembered the question Vincent Nguyen asked her in the parking lot in Research Park. *'What image moves from mind to hand today?'*

Vincent had to have been trained by his uncle Conrad. If so, she needed to know more.

Just as Abbie opened her mouth to ask about Hanker's nephew, her body shook. A loud boom rippled slowly through her mind like an earthquake. The environment shifted as if agitated by a giant hand, just as it did every time Abbie had been ripped from REM sleep by an interruption from the outside world.

Something was happening in her apartment.

"Moon, you okay?" Aspira asked. "You're blinking in and out."

Abbie looked through her hands as they faded. The group suddenly moved farther and farther away.

"I'm being pulled from the dream!" she cried. A flash of white severed her mind from its theta state, and she cascaded toward ordinary consciousness.

CHAPTER FIVE

A loud bang shocked Abbie awake. She sat up, heart pounding in her chest. For a moment, the image of a beautiful lizard burst in her mind along with the memory of calling out to a group of friends.

Before she had a chance to regain her bearings, a dark shape rushed at her from the open bedroom door. Light from a streetlamp shone through the partially closed blinds and rippled on the man's face and large nose as he lunged across the bed. A scream rushed up Abbie's throat, but before she had a chance to release it, a rough hand covered her mouth and threw her head back down to her pillow. Hot breath touched her cheek. Terror clawed at every muscle in her body.

"Where is she?" a man's voice asked in a thick Australian accent.

Abbie grabbed at the man's wrists and tried to scream again, but his coarse palm muffled the sound. Body odor stench seeped from the man like dirty water from a kitchen sponge. His body weight pressed her against the mattress, not allowing any leverage to move or escape.

"Tell me where she is!" he yelled again.

No thoughts entered Abbie's mind beyond the need to get the smelly man off her. She released his wrists and instead clawed at his face, feeling her fingernails dig into the skin of his cheek.

The man reared back and pulled his hand from her mouth. “Bitch!” he cried.

Muscle memory seemed to take over as Abbie followed up the scratch with a jab to his left eye. Again, the man shifted in response to the pain, taking his weight off her hips and giving her a chance to roll him to the side. Abbie kicked through the blankets at her assailant and moved out from under him.

“Abbie!” a man shouted from down the hall.

Sitting up, Abbie saw another shape running toward her from the hallway. In that instant her tired mind conjured a kidnapping scenario that ended with her body thrown in the Jordan River. As the second man entered the room, he jumped not at Abbie, but toward the man next to her on the bed. With a grunt and surprised yelp, the two men tumbled off the mattress and thumped onto the floor. Abbie screamed and jumped up, seeing them wrestling in the streetlamp glow still filtering through the blinds. She ran to the door and flicked the light switch.

Bright white pierced her eyes for an instant before her pupils recovered. Blurry shapes refocused. Abbie saw Vincent Nguyen, Conrad Rossi’s nephew whom she’d met in the parking lot the day before, punching a man wearing a black leather jacket hard in the face. A second punch followed until the man stopped moving and went limp.

Abbie jumped toward the nightstand next to the bed where her cellphone sat charging. She yanked the cord from the wall as the screen lit up and asked for her thumbprint.

“Abbie, no!” Vincent yelled as he swatted the phone from her hand. “It’s not safe! They found you. We need to go now!”

“Get away from me!” Abbie screamed. She looked for where the phone had fallen, but Vincent grabbed her by the shoulders.

“Listen to me! We need to run right now. If they find

you…they're going to torture you. You have no idea how far they'll go."

Abbie struggled and pushed Vincent away. "Let me go! I'm calling the police right now!"

Movement across the room caught her eye as the man in the leather jacket pulled himself up and kneeled next to the bed. Blood trickled from his nose. Red scratches covered his cheek, while his left eye remained closed from where Abbie had jabbed her finger. He growled like a pit bull and pulled a silver revolver from his belt.

"God damn…shoot you both…" he breathed.

"Run!" Vincent shouted. He pulled Abbie toward the door and down the hall without looking back. As they entered the living room Abbie saw her front door sitting slightly crooked as if it had been kicked in. Splinters of wood pricked her bare feet as Vincent practically yanked her through the breach and down the stairs to the parking lot.

"He has a gun," Abbie said. Her heart pounded in her ears and drowned out all other sound.

What was going on? She'd been asleep less than a minute before, and now she was running for her life with a stranger, while some guy with a gun threatened to kill her.

"Get in the car!" Vincent shouted as they approached a white two-seat Tesla roadster with its lights still on parked crookedly in front of the dumpsters.

Abbie pulled away again and smacked Vincent across the shoulder. "I'm not going anywhere with you! Who was that guy? Who are you?!"

"I'll explain, just---"

A gunshot split the quiet night, echoing through the apartment complex with the resonance of a thunderclap. The back window of a VW Beetle behind them exploded in shards of shattered glass. The sound made Abbie jump toward Vincent involuntarily and she turned to see the Australian man in the leather jacket standing at the top of the stairs next to her apartment front door. Smoke billowed from the barrel of his weapon.

"Get in the car!" Vincent cried again.

This time Abbie didn't hesitate. She charged around to the passenger side but found no handle anywhere in sight. As she opened her mouth to ask how to get in the car, a beep sounded from inside and the door swung open. Practically diving, Abbie entered the Tesla and slammed the door behind her. She ducked low in the seat to avoid getting shot and smelled the chemical fragrance that accompanied new automobiles. The scent always made her nauseous. That, coupled with the confusion and stress throbbing in her skull, threatened to overpower her stomach with an eruption of vomit.

Vincent threw the car into gear and spun them backward. Tires squealed loudly. Abbie felt herself swing toward the door. Her nausea intensified. She bounced roughly as the car flew out of the parking lot and scraped its undercarriage against the pavement, leaving behind a trail of sparks in the night. The man with the gun was nowhere to be seen as Abbie looked through the back window. Her apartment complex moved quickly into the distance as Vincent drove at reckless speed through the neighborhood. He reached a larger avenue and joined a handful of other cars still on the road in the early hours of the morning.

"What image moves from mind to hand today?" Vincent asked without taking his eyes off the oncoming traffic.

"I think I'm going to throw up," Abbie replied weakly. Her head seemed to spin around and around. Her hands shook violently. Streetlamps streaked at hyper speed through the windows, casting their light in flickering waves that made Abbie feel as if she moved in slow motion.

“Answer the question!” Vincent shouted, no hint of sympathy for her roiling stomach. “What image moves from mind to hand today?”

“I don’t know what you’re saying!” Abbie screamed back.

Vincent reached between them into the center console and pulled a pad of paper out, along with a pen. He tossed them to Abbie and pointed. “What image moves from mind to hand today? Draw it.”

“You want me to draw? What do you---?"

“Draw the first thing that comes to your mind. What image moves---”

“I heard you the first ten times!” Abbie yelled.

The car swerved to the right as Vincent sped around a slower vehicle getting on the freeway in front of them. “Draw!” he ordered, again returning his focus to the road.

Abbie gripped the pen, unable to hold her hand still. What did he want her to draw? Without thinking, she pressed pen to paper and let her hand move on its own. The tremors ceased, her nausea abated, and quickly a shape began to form in blue ink. Scales and large eyes stood out against the white page, a wiping tail twirling across the paper. Though she drew quickly, even Abbie had to admit that the level of detail was impressive, particularly the diamond design covering the creature’s scales. She stopped drawing and stared down at a lizard with bulging eyes, playful smirk, and what looked like a stylized tattoo on its back.

“There,” she exhaled before adding, “Asshole.”

Breaks shrieked, throwing Abbie forward in the seat. She dropped the pad of paper and slammed her hands against the glove compartment to keep from smacking her face into the expensive plastic and leather interior. The car stopped on a dime and Vincent pulled them over to the freeway shoulder.

"Perfect," he said, reaching into the center console again and tossing a stack of papers on Abbie's lap. "Leaf through those real quick. You'll see what I'm talking about."

She looked down at different drawings, some of fish, others of complicated maze designs. The third from the top caught her eye, as it looked strikingly similar to the butterfly she had drawn two days before after waking from a vivid dream. She gasped as she pulled out the next drawing, however. A lizard with bulging eyes and an intricate diamond design on its back stared up at her, almost identical to what she had just drawn. Everything from the twist of the tail to the angle of the face and legs mirrored her own.

"What is this?" she asked, fingers squeezing the paper slightly.

"Those are drawings I did when I trained with my uncle. The same training you're going through right now."

"Your uncle?" Abbie asked. "Conrad Rossi?"

"Yes."

"I only met him yesterday, and he doesn't talk. He's schizophrenic, or whatever. How could he have trained me to do anything? You're insane!"

Vincent leaned back and took a deep breath. "Yet we drew the same lizard, didn't we? And I'm betting you've drawn half the other drawing there too over the last few weeks, haven't you? Uncle tends to use the same designs, like the maze and the butterfly. They're simple, but effective."

The pages shifted on her lap. Abbie had to admit that at least three other drawings in the pile looked scarily similar to sketches she had created the last few mornings.

"Let me guess," Vincent continued, throwing the car back into gear and pulling onto the freeway once more. "You've been waking up in the morning after not sleeping well, but you're filled with inspiration to draw something you've never seen and normally wouldn't create. Does that sound accurate?"

Queasiness suddenly bubbled in her stomach again. The man's appraisal of her recent mornings was accurate.

"Who was that man?" she asked, deciding to get some answers of her own before delving into whatever madhouse Vincent wanted to take her into.

"I don't know his name here in the real world," Vincent began as lights from a semi-truck reflected in the mirror and splashed across his face. "But in Consciousness he calls himself Mozzie; sometimes takes the shape of a giant mosquito to scare people."

Abbie closed her eyes and tried to get her stomach back under control again. "What do you mean: you don't know his name in the real world?"

"I have a lot to explain to you, Abbie, and a lot of it is going to sound crazy, but it's true."

"Just…drop me off at the nearest police station and you can tell me everything there with some cops watching," she said between deep breaths.

"He's going to torture you if he has to," Vincent replied, eyes moving quickly from the road, to Abbie, and back.

"I don't even know this guy. Why is he trying to hurt me?"

"Because you know where Alice is."

Abbie slammed her hands against her thighs and sat up straight. "Who the hell is Alice?! Take me to the police right now!"

"You have to trust me."

"No, I don't."

"I did just save your life, you know," Vincent said with a charming half-smile.

Abbie wanted to smack the smirk right off his face. "For all I know this is some freak show where you and that guy are in it together. Drop me off right here, I don't care."

"You think everything with my uncle was random bullshit?" Vincent yelled, sounding every bit as frustrated as Abbie felt. Dark strands of hair fell over his forehead as his hands gripped the steering wheel. "Some schizophrenic guy starts drawing you, and you think that's normal? I draw the same pictures as you, and you think that's normal? A guy just kicked down your door and tried to get you to tell him where Alice is, someone you don't even know. That shit ain't normal!"

"Well, take me to the police and we can figure it out," Abbie said.

Vincent shook his head. "I can't do that, Abbie. I can't. Mozzie will find you. He'll torment you to get the information he wants."

"The police will protect me. That's what they do!"

"Not if he manipulates them in their sleep, they won't. He'll know whatever access codes he'll need to get at you. That's what they do."

"Who's 'they'?!" Abbie screamed, hands shaking in front of her. She had enough of whatever mystery Vincent was trying to sell.

"Alright," Vincent said after a brief pause. "I'm going to pull into the parking lot of the closest police station we can find. I'm going to leave the doors unlocked, and I'll hand you the keys. Let me at least try to explain everything that's going on, and if at the end you're not convinced, you can leave and go right in and tell the police what happened. You can have them arrest me too if you want.

But remember, I came into your apartment tonight and pulled Mozzie off you. That's got to count for some level of trust. I saved you. I did it even though I knew he was dangerous. And my hand hurts like hell from punching him. Think about that, okay?"

Abbie shook her head. "I'm not going anywhere with you. Open the damn door!"

"Hanker would want you to talk to me," Vincent said slowly. "You recognize that name, don't you? Hanker. It's important to you for some reason, isn't it?"

Hanker. What a stupid name…a stupid name Abbie *did* recognize for some reason. Hanker. She felt suddenly warm, as if her dad had sat down next to her and held her hand.

"You do recognize it," Vincent exhaled in apparent relief. "Hanker. He would want you to listen."

"Who is…he?" Abbie asked. Why did she recognize that name? Had she met someone named 'Hanker' before and just couldn't remember? The word brought her calm and almost made her want to smile.

"Give me five minutes," Vincent continued, "and I'll tell you everything you need to know. If you don't trust me, trust Hanker. Trust what your subconscious is telling you right now."

The car swerved to the right and exited the freeway at the next off-ramp. Abbie looked around, seeing the familiar lights of retail stores along Redwood Road. She remembered a police station about five blocks down across the street from a Walmart. If Vincent pulled in and gave her the keys, she would listen for five minutes. After that, she would shove the key into his eye socket if he so much as breathed on her wrong. Somehow, she knew the exact amount of pressure to use too, as if she had done it to someone in the past.

Such a strange thought.

Abbie breathed and nodded her head. A quick glance at

Vincent's right hand showed her the bruises on his knuckles from hitting the attacker in her apartment. "There's a police station on the right up here in a little bit," she began. "I'll take the keys and give you two minutes to talk. After that you can go to hell."

"I'll take it."

"So, you're saying when people go to sleep, they all dream together, and I protect them from people trying to eat their feelings?" Abbie asked, ready to throw the door open and run toward the entrance to the police station. The well-lit parking lot acted as the perfect safe zone. Several police officers had entered the building in the few minutes they'd been parked. At least one of them looked over at the Tesla with a raised eyebrow. Abbie's heart rate had returned to normal, and she felt confident if Vincent tried anything she would be able to make a big enough scene to get the police to come running. If she needed to use the car keys as a weapon, so be it.

Vincent rubbed the bridge of his nose and grimaced. A police car exited the parking lot and flicked on its siren before wailing into the distance.

"When you say it like that it sounds stupid," he said, face alternating between shades of flashing red and blue.

"It sounded pretty stupid when you said it," Abbie retorted.

"Look, this is actually backed up by science."

"Science backs up that I protect people from having their feelings eaten?"

"No," Vincent puffed. "That consciousness is more of a collective than just being a manifestation of our individual thoughts. Scientists and psychologists like Carl Gustav Jung theorized that all human beings are connected mentally; that we link in a dream sphere and share a subconscious mind. They hypothesize that we can even store memories from our ancestors in this mental space. There are coincidences all the time that are too focused to be random. These occurrences completely shatter probability models and hint at a synchronicity of shared consciousness. It's like two different people on opposite sides of the world inventing the same technology at the same time without ever having met each other or been in contact at all. That's actually happened over and over again throughout history with every major scientific advancement. Inspiration ripples through Consciousness and touches other minds."

A blank stare met Vincent's monologue. Abbie heard plenty of words coming from the man's mouth, but none of them made much sense.

Vincent sat back and bit his lip, as if trying to imagine a better way to describe his abstract mania. "Think of, like, the cells in your body. Each of them has an individual purpose but is linked with every other cell through electrical currents in the nervous system. They are individual, but they're connected. Human beings are the same way. We're all bonded by the energy around us, and that manifests in a shared dream space. That's one of the reasons dreams are so weird and random is because you're interacting with different people's emotions and thoughts all at once. You establish links with a handful of people in the dream at any one time, and they establish links with other people, and those people establish more links, and so on, until in some form, everyone is connected all at the same time."

Abbie shook her head. This sounded like pseudoscience from one of those late-night paid programing shows trying to sell you magic healing crystals. "And so, we all dream together?"

"Not exactly," Vincent continued. He unclipped his seat belt and turned to sit more squarely toward Abbie. "Most people enter what we call Consciousness in short fits and bursts as they dream, kind of like ghosts or apparitions. They're in the space for a short time, touching ideas and emotions from other people. Some dreamers though, particularly people who are incredibly creative, can reach a higher level and stay in Consciousness as they sleep. Those people are able to feel others' emotions and sometimes experience their memories. It's a highly addictive place for that reason."

"I don't get it," Abbie admitted.

Vincent stared forward, lips pressing together as if the pressure helped him search for the proper example. "Okay, imagine if you were having an affair with a married man. That would be a potent mixture of powerful emotions, right? Well, imagine that you could experience those feelings…thrill, lust, danger, whatever, without ever needing to actually have an affair. You could steal those emotions from someone else. It's easy to get addicted to that sort of thing. Some people like to feel the happiness of a child's Christmas memories, others will scare dreamers, force them into a nightmare, and then feel their fear."

The thought of being pushed into experiencing a bad dream made Abbie twitch involuntarily. How many men had she known in her life that would have loved to sneak into her dreams and play around? A revolting thought. Skeptical questions came faster than she could process them.

"Why don't we wake up when one of these predators tries to force us into a nightmare?" she asked.

A sad expression tightened Vincent's lips. "Because you can't wake yourself up from a dream. Only something outside yourself can sever you from Consciousness. Like, have you ever screamed in your sleep and woken yourself up?"

Abbie thought for a second and remembered a time when she shouted so loud that she sat up in bed. "Yeah, I'm pretty sure I have."

"That's because you were able to produce the sound in your vocal cords loud enough to startle yourself awake. It's really hard to do. Controlling your body while in the dream is extremely difficult, even for someone trained, like me. My Uncle Conrad, or Hanker, as he's known in the dream, is one of only a few people who can do it, and even then, it wipes him out for months afterward. Other than something like that, where you scream, waking yourself up is almost impossible. You have to be removed from the dream by someone else, and generally it needs to be violent."

"And I'm one of those people who can reach this higher level and cut people out of the dream?" Abbie questioned, trying to understand Vincent's madness.

"Exactly. I am too. You can be trained to do it, but it takes a lot of practice, kind of like lucid dreaming, only you're able to experience the dreams of others. Some people become predators in that space, hunting dreamers to feel their emotions. Others, like you and me, protect the dreamers from those who would hurt them. We create mental and emotional weapons like swords or even guns sometimes. When your mental strength collides with someone else in Consciousness, you can sever their connection to the theta state, or the mental frequency everyone dreams at. It's like killing someone in a nightmare; they don't die, they just leave the shared mental space. Depending on how gruesome their dispatchment, they may not even fully wake up."

For some reason, the color purple kept coming to Abbie's mind as Vincent described dream combat. Shapes like large shards of glass, glowing in violet hues, seemed to cut the fabric of reality, leaving Abbie confused…and her pulse quickened.

Vincent continued, oblivious to the strange impressions his words conjured in Abbie's thoughts. "So yeah, you cut off someone's head in the dream, or rip them in half, and that's usually enough to disrupt their thought processes. It hurts too, so there's that. You're really good at it, from what I hear, but that makes sense. You were trained by Conrad Rossi, for Pete's sake. My Uncle Hanker is incredibly powerful in the dream state because all he has is his mind. His body and brain don't communicate properly with each other in the real world because of his schizophrenia, so in the dream he's learned and expanded until he can do pretty much whatever he wants. He's your mentor there, just like he was for me."

"Why don't I remember it then?" Abbie asked. She squeezed the keys in her hand, cold metal pressing against her skin. "You'd think if I was running around protecting people all night, I'd remember it."

"It isn't as easy as you think. With training it's possible, which is what my uncle has been doing with since you join his conclave. That's why you're waking up wanting to draw the pictures you do; you're trying to link who you are here and who you are there. Uncle Conrad is training you to remember because things have gotten so bad up there."

Leather upholstery squeaked against Abbie's back as she shifted in her seat. Every word out of Vincent's mouth seemed crazy, but she couldn't deny the warmth she felt when he talked about Hanker…or the strange unease when he mentioned things getting 'bad up there.' She somehow not only knew what he implied but felt an urgency to do something about it. Logically none of it could be real, but Abbie's instincts pushed against that conclusion. Conrad Rossi's drawings, coupled with her own, also made her hesitate when wanting to throw everything he said out the window. Determination eclipsed her fear. The longer Vincent talked; the more Abbie's mind filled with images of colorful forests and the sound of someone saying the word 'moon.'

A knock on the window startled Abbie and elicited a small shriek from her throat. She turned to see a police officer with a thick mustache tapping on the glass, a curious look on his face. Vincent pressed the controls on his steering wheel and rolled down the window.

"Everything okay?" the officer asked. "You folks need anything?"

"Oh no," Vincent chuckled good-naturedly with a wave. "We just stopped to talk, and at this time of night we figured this was a safer place than some random parking lot."

The officer nodded and looked at Abbie.

"Yeah," Abbie confirmed with a slight waver to her voice. "Just talking after a long night."

His mustache furrowed as the officer's lips pressed together. He glanced down at Abbie's *Mumford and Sons* shirt and pink pajama pants. "Alright…but if anything changes, feel free to come inside."

"Sure will," Vincent agreed.

"You got it," Abbie added.

The policeman turned and walked back to the station's front entrance. Vincent blew out a breath and rolled the window back up.

"For a second I thought you were going to tell him you were in a car with a crazy person," he admitted. "Thanks for giving me the benefit of the doubt."

Abbie bit her lip. "Some of the things you're saying…they seem…familiar, if that makes sense. When you said, 'bad up there,' what did you mean?"

Vincent nodded, eyebrows raising slightly. "There always seemed to be a balance in place. For every couple people hunting for emotions, there was naturally a Proctor, or protector, to keep them from going too crazy. That's why we have criminals and cops, right? Some people gravitate toward one extreme and some toward the other. Over the last probably twenty years, I guess, that balance has shifted. Now there are more and more people feeding on dreamers, manipulating them into feeling whatever emotion the parasites want to get high on. And the worse it gets, the more it all spills out into our waking lives. Imagine everyone in the world feeling afraid every night as they sleep; everyone nervous they're going to be preyed on. What effect do you think that would have on societies and nations? On our relationships with each other? On top of that, powerful Proctors have been killed in the real world once their identities were uncovered in the dream. We don't share our real names in Consciousness for that reason. We create our own identities, and it's sick that we have to be so afraid to share who we really are with anyone in the dream for fear of getting assassinated. You see? That's the danger we're facing; a world where everyone is oppressed without even knowing it, and anyone willing to step in and protect them is getting killed. It all started with this lady, Alice Ashling, and a guy we only know as Alexander."

"Okay, you said that man in my apartment tonight wanted to know about Alice and that I knew where she was or something?"

"Exactly," Vincent said with a smile. He seemed pleased Abbie was opening up to his strange perspective. "The story goes that twenty or so years ago two grad students ran an experiment in shared consciousness and were able to dream together in that realm without going to sleep. They had full control to do whatever they wanted despite the emotions and thoughts of other people sharing that space. Afterwards they sort of chose sides, with Alice standing with the Proctors and Alexander with the hunters, or Pursuants as we call them. Now, Alexander trains rich people, or uses technology or something, and shows them how to steal people's emotions and sometimes even personal information. Alice fights against them. It's that simple. No one knows where Alice is, and Alexander would send someone to kill her immediately if he ever found out. On the other hand, Alice would kill anyone who learned where she was to protect herself. They're both incredibly dangerous people. And from what I've been able to gather, you're the only person who may know where Alice is."

"How would I know that? I've never met her."

"You have in Consciousness," Victor replied. "You're kind of a legend up there. You and Alice fought together against a powerful dreamer named Catharsis not long ago. The two of you apparently linked for a moment during the battle, so you likely gleaned some personal knowledge from that mental encounter, like where Alice is hiding in the real world. Whether that's the information you actually got from the connection or not doesn't really matter. It seems everyone *thinks* that you did, so that's enough to send someone after you. The emotion of the link rippled through the realm. I felt it hours later when I went to sleep in Vietnam, long after you'd already woken up here in the States. "

"And so now…what? They think I know where she is? They're going to kidnap me or something? I don't know about any of this dream world stuff. I couldn't tell them anything."

Another police car pulled into the parking lot and two officers exited the vehicle laughing to each other. Vincent tapped against the center console with his finger as if trying to coax words from the back of his brain.

"I don't know what to tell you," he said finally just as the two policemen entered the front entrance. "I've had my eye on Mozzie for a while. When I found out he was coming to Salt Lake, I was afraid he found out about my uncle being Hanker. I think someone very powerful probably came across the doctor's messages about a catatonic man in Utah who could suddenly draw like a master. They must have put two-and-two together. It was dangerous for my uncle to do something like that, but he had to have been pretty desperate, which lends some credence to the idea that you know where Alice is. I've been following Mozzie since he arrived, and when he came after you…I realized I had everything wrong. They had to have known about Uncle Conrad, but apparently Hanker was never their target."

Again, logic dictated Abbie disregard the idea of being hunted because she subconsciously knows the location of some woman, but goose bumps rippled up her arm, nonetheless.

"This is crazy," she said. "It's all insane. Even so, I can't explain it, but it's like my brain is agreeing with you, if that makes sense. I don't feel afraid."

Vincent reached over and placed his hand on top of Abbie's. She flinched but didn't pull away. The aroma of sandalwood filled her sinuses, adding to her calm.

"That makes perfect sense," he said. "You have a powerful subconscious. It's not going to lead you astray. If my uncle was going so far as to force his body to draw pictures of you, you're close to remembering in the waking world, or 'Basic' as we call it. You have to know where Alice is if that's the case."

Abbie glanced down at Vincent's hand on hers quickly before looking in his dark eyes once more. "Do we know each other in this conscious realm?"

A wide smile brightened his handsome face. He squeezed Abbie's hand lightly. "We don't. I operate on the other side of the world, so we don't sleep at the same time. Plus, there are tens of thousands of Proctors and even more Pursuants. It's easy to never meet people beyond your core crew in Consciousness. You're pretty famous though. The name you go by in the dream is known all over the world. You're badass. I heard recently you cut one of Catharsis' most powerful operatives arms off and then crushed his head between your fists before taking out the rest of his squad. The last time my uncle and I talked in the dream he spoke highly of all his trainees, but especially you. 'Fearless,' he called you."

An image of Conrad Rossi drawing circles on paper came to Abbie's mind, juxtaposed with the idea of a tall warrior slicing enemies in half. If what Vincent said was true, that would mean the comatose man, as well as herself, lived a whole other life in a different world that she knew nothing about. She didn't even know her own name or identity in this place. Was she the same, or was she different? Was she disappointed with herself and her decisions in the real world? How could she not be if she were this incredible warrior that everyone looked up to? Those thoughts filled her with doubt. '*Who am I?*' she questioned silently. '*I don't even know myself at all.*'

"What is my name in the dream?" she asked. "If I don't use my real name while I'm sleeping, what do I call myself?"

Vincent dropped his head. "I shouldn't tell you. You wouldn't want me to."

"Why not?"

"It's…personal. It's not my place to tell you."

Again, the word 'moon' came to Abbie's mind. Moon. Calm covered her like a warm spring rain. What did the word mean? Why wasn't she afraid anymore? A man had broken into her apartment; attacked her. Now she sat with a stranger in his car as he talked about dream worlds and fighting bad guys, and yet for some reason she felt almost peaceful. Abbie dug deep to find fear or some lingering doubt about Vincent's claims but came up with nothing. Her instincts told her to stick with Vincent for now, while logic dictated she run toward the police station.

Which would she choose, logic or instinct?

Mom would choose to run. Nana Gayle would choose to stay.

Abbie breathed in deeply and came to a decision.

"Okay," she began. "So, they want me to tell them where this Alice-lady is in the real world? I don't know where she is, and I think I need a little more proof before I jump off this bridge with you. So, how do we do that?"

Sitting up straighter, Vincent grinned. "That shouldn't be hard at this point." He turned back toward the steering wheel and put his seatbelt on with a click. "We need to find a safe place to fall asleep. We don't know how desperate Mozzie is, or exactly who sent him, so it needs to be a place that isn't obvious. Once we find that spot we can rest. We'll meet up in the dream world and work together on a drawing exercise, like what my uncle is having you do for your training. Then, when we wake up and draw the same picture, you'll know. From there we'll keep training until you can remember."

Vincent pressed the ignition button and the Tesla hummed quietly to life with a slight vibration. Abbie looked closer at the keys in her hands and realized the car itself activated from a fob on the chain with the logo for Enterprise Car Rental engraved on the side. The other keys were probably for Vincent's home back in Vietnam. He could have driven them away from the police station anytime he wanted; taken Abbie to some back alley and dropped her body in a dumpster like one of the true crime documentaries she liked so much…but he hadn't.

Could she trust him?

She wanted to, at the very least.

"What if I just tell you where this Alice Ashling lady is while we're in the dream?" Abbie asked. "Wouldn't that solve everything? You could find her, and those guys would leave me alone."

A dismissive chuckle blew out of Vincent's nose. "You would never tell me. Ever."

"I wouldn't?"

"Trust me," Vincent said as the car pulled forward and turned toward the parking lot exit. "Sharing memory with someone is very personal. Whatever information you got from Alice…from what I know about you in the dream, I don't see you giving that to anyone. Out here in the real world it's different though. She wants you two to become one, and if this is the way to do it, the memories will come back to you. From that point, you won't have to tell me where Alice is if you don't want to. You can go to her yourself and leave me behind. And there won't be any hard feelings on my part if you do. Like I said, there's a lot of dangerous stuff going on. I'm here now to keep you safe and hopefully help you unify. Outside of that, you have no obligation to me."

They drove north on Redwood in silence. Abbie tried to picture herself in the dream world. Would she appear perfect and beautiful? Regal and powerful? A fighter?

"Where are we going?" she asked as an image of a purple sword swung through her imagination.

"That's an excellent question. I haven't lived in Salt Lake in about ten years, so my friends are scattered to the wind. I'm staying in a hotel downtown, but I think it might be better to put some distance between us and the city. At this point I don't know what we're dealing with exactly. I know who Mozzie is in the real world, but I haven't been able to find out his real name or who he works for. He's like a ghost. My contacts keep tabs on him for me. At this point I'm going to assume he may know more about me than I'm comfortable with. You know anywhere we could go that won't be easy to find us?"

While more comfortable than before, Abbie still didn't fully trust Vincent, and had limited desire to go somewhere completely untraceable with him. She'd seen too many real-life murder investigation documentaries on Netflix to be that naive. Still, she couldn't go back to her apartment, and worried who else might be working with this Mozzie character. And if Vincent could prove what he was saying, her entire life would be flipped on its head. Instead of being just a graphic designer at a sign shop, Abbie would be a great protector of dreamers. What would that mean if she could remember being in a world of power and strength every night? The possibility excited her…if it turned out to be true.

Was she really more than she imagined? If so, she should be able to think of a place that would be both out of the way, and safe for her just in case she was being played.

Quickly the destination became clear, along with several ways to defend herself and escape should the need arise.

Interesting. Perhaps she *was* more than just a graphic designer after all.

"My Nana Gayle has a cabin out past Woodland, a couple hours from here," Abbie said as they drove through an intersection. "We don't use it very often because we have a better one down at Fish Lake. I don't think I've ever posted any photos from there on social media, so no one should know about it. The entire complex of cabins is gated and has lots of neighbors, but I know the code and can get us in."

Vincent nodded and flicked on his blinker to turn right, back toward the freeway. "Woodland is out past Kamas, right?"

"Yep. I'll show you the way."

They sat in silence as the occasional car passed them in the oncoming lane. Abbie looked straight ahead, unsure of what the night, and the coming day, would bring.

CHAPTER SIX

The keypad beeped as Abbie typed in her personal code on the security pad next to the large swinging green fence. Pale pink sunlight framed the mountains as dawn approached. Cold air bit at her fingers and bare feet as she shuffled back and forth to keep warm. The Provo River gurgled somewhere in the fading darkness beyond the trees, accompanied by chirping birds overhead.

The red light on the gate keypad flashed green, followed by a clicking sound. Abbie turned back toward Vincent, who remained sitting in the Tesla, and flashed a thumbs-up sign. Gravel poked at her cold bare feet as she pushed the gate open, and Vincent pulled inside.

Abbie smiled inwardly as she re-locked the gate behind the car. Nana Gayle had given her a personal code based on her birth date to access the cabin whenever she wanted. Abbie had only used it once in the last five years but remembered that each login at the gate was recorded by the host cabin computer. Break-ins over the years had necessitated the cabin owners putting the security measure in place to verify everyone using the communal property at any given time. Now if anything happened to Abbie, at least people would know she had been there.

A macabre thought, but it gave her some comfort. She didn't distrust Vincent to that extent, but she still didn't fully trust him either.

She climbed back in the car, and they drove a quarter mile down the dirt road to the old cabin beside the water. Pine needles covered the tall, pitched roof, weeds growing wild beside the front porch. It had to have been at least a year since anyone in the family had used the neglected cabin.

"This is the place," she said as Vincent looked through the front windshield at the dark cottage.

"Let's get inside before it gets any lighter out here," Vincent replied.

Boards creaked under Abbie's feet as she shifted logs around in the porch wood pile looking for the hidden key. A spider web tickled her fingers before she grasped cold brass. Unlocking the door, Abbie immediately smelled musty carpet and dust in the air.

"Careful," she said, flicking on the light and illuminating the small front room with its assortment of dated 1970-era furniture. "Normally there are mice in here if no one has used the cabin in a while."

"I'll be fine," Vincent said. He rubbed his finger against the armrest of an orange recliner and came back with several years' worth of grime. "We should get to sleep as soon as possible. I don't know about you, but I'm pretty tired at this point. I'm still on Vietnam time."

Abbie pointed to a hallway on their right. "There are beds in the main area through there, along with two separate bedrooms. I'll take one of those, and you can take the other."

Dust flew into the air as Vincent brushed his hand across the closest floral-patterned couch. "I should sleep out here, just to be safe. If anyone followed us, I'll hear them first. Plus, you can lock the door on the room if it helps you feel safer."

The courtesy was appreciated, but Abbie had to admit that she didn't feel frightened. A calm peace enveloped her.

"That sounds good," she replied. "If you need a blanket, there are some in the cupboard over by the kitchen. How long will it take once we fall asleep for us to reach this…Consciousness place?"

"Not long, if you're half as skilled as your reputation implies," Vincent smiled.

Abbie waved 'goodnight' and entered the small side bedroom. She locked the door behind her with a click. An empty mouse trap sat in the corner next to a torn section of green wallpaper with elaborate leaf shapes and vine patterns. Springs squeaked loudly as Abbie sat on the bed. Rustic smells of stuffy, timeworn blankets wafted from the old mattress and reminded Abbie of why she never cared for the cabin much. She'd brought her boyfriend up here senior year of high school along with a couple other friends but couldn't bring herself to sleep alone in one of the rooms. Now, despite the smell and worry of bugs crawling on her while she slept, fatigue once again grabbed hold of her mind and body. She had no idea what time it was but wanted nothing more than to close her eyes.

What would sleep bring? Would everything Vincent told her prove true, or would she have nightmares of a man kicking down her door and pressing his sweaty hand on her face?

As she lay back and stared at the bowed ceiling above, Abbie tried to make sense of her night. Why had the things Vincent said made so much sense to her? Why wasn't she afraid?

"Because I'm taking over," a voice seemed to say as Abbie's eyes closed and she drifted toward freedom.

Waves of warm, salty sea air wafted against Abbie's face as she opened her eyes on Consciousness. The environment felt different than earlier that night, with green grass growing endlessly toward rounded peaks that twisted like marshmallows on a pink ocean. Pale violet skies smiled down on the world, complete with at least four suns of red, orange, purple, and a surprising plaid. Dreamers faded in and out leaving behind pleasure and confusion in their wake, but fewer than expected. The ground rumbled with the fear of nearby predators.

Consciousness itself pulsed with stronger emotions than Abbie was used to. More voices echoed in her mind. The shapes in the clouds seemed foreign. It had been some years since Abbie had slept deeply during this time of day, and she assumed that fact had something to do with her disorientation. People from the other side of the planet collectively created the dream space now. Different cultures understood the world differently, and thus affected the dream differently. Pursuants here would use distinct fears and enticements to elicit unique emotions from their prey, emotions that would be unheard of in other parts of the world. Everything seemed strange to Abbie; less firm and clear.

Of course, she had just been attacked in Basic, and pulled out of her apartment, so that might have something to do with her tenuous attachment to the area as well.

Her memories of the last few hours began to take shape in front of her. The man with the gun, smelling of terror and the unknown, loomed over the bed. So much fear. Too bad Basic-Abbie didn't know how to fight off an assailant. Another reason she needed to go. That girl was too confused and scared to be of any use. If it hadn't been for muscle memory gained through years of fighting in Consciousness, poor weak Abbie wouldn't have even been able to get him off her. And without Vincent, who knows what would have happened.

Vincent.

He was a tangled puzzle to unravel and piece back together. He'd told Abbie the truth about the dream world as they sat in the car. Her physical self was too inept to understand everything, but at least she didn't run away like a coward.

Maybe she was good for something after all.

Abbie wondered where and when Vincent would appear in Consciousness. They had a lot to discuss. Hanker had never mentioned his nephew before, but then again, Hanker had never told her anything about himself until they formulated the plan to have him draw her in the real world. Here in Consciousness, she would get a better feel for the charming man and discover if he really was who he claimed to be.

"Gang way!" a woman with an Australian accent yelled.

Abbie turned to see a stout redhead in light blue armor leap through the air and land beside her. Long strands of curly hair smacked Abbie's cheek, smelling of earth and wiggling like worms. Her armor glowed with neon light, reminding Abbie of a Proctor she had met once named Argot who loved fluorescents and dancing to the sound of the wind. The woman next to Abbie seemed much too thick and menacing to enjoy dancing. She growled and swung a double-bladed axe, cutting a bush in half just a few feet away. The shrub contorted and screamed, twisting into the face of an angry man made of gray pollution and tasting of hot wax. The visage died away on the air with a curse.

"Sorry about that," the red-headed woman said with a bow. "Ferron is a sneaky bastard. He's taken to masking himself and attacking Proctors before they realize he's here."

"Thank you," Abbie said. Her standard armor formed around her body as she drew the white line down over her left eye with the dot on her cheek. Bare toes wiggled against the squishy ground, feeling for any stray emotions that might reveal another hidden Pursuant. She extended her hand for her fellow guardian to shake. “I’m Proctor Moon.”

“I know who you are,” she replied while stepping past Abbie and looking toward the warping horizon. “Hanker held on as long as he could and told me to watch out for you. I’m Fraelig. You’re long out of Consciousness by this time of night. You’re in for some surprises, I’m sure.”

“Fraelig,” Abbie repeated, annoyed the Proctor had snubbed her outstretched hand. “Did Hanker say anything, or pass along a message?”

“Naw, only that he was worried you didn’t come back in, that’s all. He told me and mine to watch out. Things took a turn for them after you left it sounded like. It’s been a rough night for everyone.” The large woman rubbed her hand against her axe and cracked her neck. A symbol of a kangaroo with sabered teeth glowed on Fraelig’s left shoulder like a brand logo.

“We’ve met before, haven’t we?” Abbie asked.

“I’m surprised you remember,” Fraelig said. “You big important Proctors who hang out with Alice do your thing without needing the rest of us. So single-minded.”

Abbie smiled, though it felt like a scowl, and looked down at the woman’s bright purple boots. “Being single-minded is what makes many of us good Proctors. I shouldn’t have to tell you that. And Alice and I are far from close. Again, thanks for the save. I appreciate the professional courtesy. It’s been a while since a Pursuant has gotten the drop on me. Normally they’re closer to the dreamers when I get here.”

“Australia and Asia bring a slightly different vibe, that’s all. You need to travel more when you’re in Basic. You’ll get a better feel for things.”

"Thanks for the tip," Abbie said, blinking slowly. She sniffed the air and smelled a hint of regret. "Have any other Proctors materialized in the last few minutes?"

"Tons," Fraelig answered. "Proctors are always coming in and out like usual. We got a couple billion people going to sleep right now. You looking for someone specific?"

"Yes, someone very powerful. You might know them, actually. This is closer to their sleep time."

Fraelig shrugged and scratched her armpit. "You got a name for them?"

"I…don't." Abbie admitted. Calling him 'Vincent' would be meaningless in Consciousness since that wouldn't be his identity here.

"Well then, there's not much I can---"

The grass blew toward the women as if a hurricane had formed without clouds. Abbie looked in the distance as the landscape heaved and rolled toward them.

"You have a conclave?" Abbie asked.

"Yep," Fraelig said, spitting into the grass like she had a wad of tobacco in her cheek.

"Are they going to join us?"

Fraelig shrugged. "We don't have Super-Proctors like you and Hanker here normally. My entire crew was beaten and banished about twenty minutes ago. It'll be a little while till they come back in."

An entire conclave banished? Normally Abbie might lose one or maybe two in a night, but never all of them. Even against Catharsis they had only lost three. Either Fraelig's team was incompetent, or things were worse in this time zone than Abbie knew.

The horizon continued to approach, spitting rocks and smoke into the air. Rage and self-importance glided on the breeze and stiffened the grass until it froze in place like a collection of bent sculptures.

"Is losing your whole crew a normal occurrence?" Abbie asked. Her purple blade formed in her hand, ready for battle.

"Not until the last few weeks," Fraelig admitted. "Now it feels like we're lucky to have one of us standing after a fight. It's gotten bad."

Abbie stared at the approaching mass and formed a second sword as a precaution. "Well, now you've got me," she said.

The ground formed a frenzied wave and arched as if to crash against the women. Fraelig seemed nervous, but Abbie just smiled. She leaped toward the mass and swung her swords, shattering the cresting swell. Apparitions spat in all directions like toppling statues. At least twelve hunters materialized, each taking a different form. Several morphed into beasts of varying sizes and shapes, some fat, others sickly thin and wasted. The rest of the Pursuants took the shape of humanoid forms not unlike Abbie and Fraelig, wearing armor or fine suits. One stood like a giant above the rest, hairy and bulbous. Psychic swords flashed and glinted under the light of four suns; comically oversized cannons pointed at the Proctors; eyes glowed like demons trying to intimidate scared children.

Abbie was neither a child nor scared. They'd have to do better than that.

Before any of them could get their bearings, Abbie lunged and destroyed two of them with ease. The Pursuants screamed and disintegrated to ash and bile. The others wasted no time in attacking. Three pulled themselves into the ground and shot up like barbs to block Abbie's assault. Two others fired red rockets from their weapons, which Abbie turned to butterflies with a flick of her wrist. Fraelig cleaved at the giant with her axe as the beast tried to stomp on her like a bug.

"She's a fast one," a hunter cried as he scrambled along the ground, taking the form of a misshapen cockroach. Abbie came down with her blade and stabbed him in the head. The creature's legs twitched. He screamed like a little girl before dissolving into a steaming pile of yellow goo.

"Shit! She got David!" one of the suit-wearing men yelled. "First Ferron, and now David? Rip 'em to shreds!"

A tattooed woman with short blonde hair and revolver barrels for arms shot energy tendrils that crackled like lightning. Fingers of electricity curved toward Abbie, twisting and shifting as if to grab her. She threw one of her swords and hit the woman in the face.

"Gaaaaa!" she shrieked, pulling the blade from her dream flesh and leaving behind a trembling mass of tendrils trying to claw back together.

"You're tough," Abbie said as she sliced another of the hunters and banished them from the theta state. "Normally you guys go down after a hit like that."

The woman snarled and pointed her gun arms at Abbie. Her voice sounded like metal scraping metal and echoed in angry fury. "And normally you Proctors can't hold your constructs solid enough to throw them like that."

"What can I say?" Abbie mused. "I'm special I guess."

"Watch out!" Fraelig yelled from the shoulder of the giant above.

Dozens of arms reached from the ground and grabbed Abbie's legs. Two of the Pursuants converged and tried to cut the Proctor down, but Abbie pushed back with powerful waves of disgust. The terrain rippled like a calm pond before lurching and tossing the hunters into the air. Even the giant tripped, giving Fraelig her opening. She brought her axe down on the creature's head and he tumbled to the earth; a collapsing redwood bubbling to nothing in the frozen grass.

Abbie leaped forward in the confusion and chopped a Pursuant wearing a green suit into two pieces before spinning and cutting him in half again. His eyes went wide. He tried to speak but faded before any words formed.

"You're new here," the woman with the cannon arms smiled. She paced around Abbie and eyed the Proctor with admiration. "How come I've never seen you before? You on vacation or something and decided to make a fuss?"

"I'm Moon," Abbie informed while sniffing the steam tumbling from her blade.

"I've heard of you," the woman said. "You're a bit off your sleep cycle, aren't you?"

Abbie matched the woman's pacing, keeping her distance. "It was a weird night."

"I'm Contrail. It's nice to meet you."

Purple energy glowed in her hand as Abbie shot toward Contrail without a word. The woman fired her energy tendrils, but Abbie cut through them and advanced without missing a step. Just as Abbie raised her sword to strike, a force threw her to the side. She slammed into the rocky ground leaving a crater behind on impact.

Fraelig jumped onto a multi-colored boulder above and held her axe over her head. "I've got you Moon! Just---" Long, thin fingers of smoke and dirt reached up from somewhere behind her and wrapped around the red-headed warrior's throat. With a gasp, she twisted backward and disappeared behind the rock.

The remaining Pursuants ran toward Abbie. She counted five as she pulled herself from the crater where one of them had tossed her. None of them seemed powerful enough to throw her like they had, but it didn't matter. Each of them would wake up with the smell of her irritation in their nostrils.

A blast of white energy built on the horizon and rumbled toward the battle. The Pursuants stopped and looked up, only to be hit by an assault of pale orange arrows. The projectiles flew through the air and hit the three closest assailants in the chest. While not powerful enough to cast them from Consciousness, the arrows offered Abbie the distraction she needed. Targeting Contrail first, Abbie severed the cannons from her arms before plunging her blade deep into the woman's chest.

"Damn it!" Contrail spat. Her dream form began to fade as she clung to Consciousness. "I'll rip your eyes out later tonight!"

Abbie casually blew a gust of breath from her lips and dissipated Contrail's form.

Before the other predators had a chance to react, a helmeted man with long arms and legs wearing pale yellow armor leaped from a shaft of light. Arrows shot from a bow in his hands and hit the remaining Pursuants one after the other. He followed up his surprise attack with a psychic dagger and buried it into the necks of two men in rapid succession. Abbie dispatched the remaining two with a single swipe of her sword. All four hunters clawed at Consciousness before fading to nothing like the promise from a politician. The grass unfroze and began wafting once more in a nonexistent wind. Dreamers once again materialized like flashes of rain in a parched land.

"I tried to help Fraelig, but I wasn't fast enough," the man said. He removed his helmet and tossed his long black hair like a Disney prince. The hair seemed to move in slow motion for a second, and Abbie couldn't tell if he was affecting perception or if she was. A firm jaw and high cheekbones glowed slightly with a warmth Abbie recognized as excitement. He smelled faintly of vanilla.

Even in the dream world Vincent looked almost exactly the

same as he did in Basic. Just with longer hair. And an even better scent.

"It took you long enough to get here," Abbie said, dusting remnants of disappointment from her armor.

"I'm not as fast as you are at falling asleep, I guess," he replied.

Abbie looked over her shoulder toward the rocky outcropping Fraelig had disappeared behind. "Did they banish her?"

"Yeah. There were two over there. They took her out, but I was able to sneak up on them before I made my grand entrance." He smiled and looked at Abbie from her bare feet to her dark hair as if admiring a marble statue at a museum. "You look so much like yourself in Basic, besides the slight bluish complexion. I never know what to expect in situations like this, since some people choose to turn themselves into fiery angels or perfectly beautiful super models."

"I find that sort of stuff takes too much mental energy," Abbie said. "You look the same too…except of course for the funky long hair that looks like it's floating underwater or something."

The air shifted and more dreamers materialized in their vicinity. When Abbie had first arrived, there were perhaps a few hundred in this section of Consciousness. With the Pursuants gone, nothing hindered sleeping minds from filling the space and releasing their stress and doubt across the area. Thousands upon thousands of dreamers converged suddenly. Rooms took shape at random around Abbie and Vincent, along with what looked like a bullet train station. Japanese characters appeared on the walls, changing into smiley faces and crude graffiti of women's breasts. More images appeared as dreamers surfaced in waves. Objects altered at an alarming rate along with conflicting sounds and smells that reeked of urban smog and claustrophobia.

For a moment, the visuals and rush of clashing emotions overwhelmed Abbie. She stumbled and took a breath.

"There are a lot of people sleeping right now," Vincent said. "More than you're used to. It will take a little bit to level out being in deep sleep when this part of the world is online in Consciousness. You're feeling pretty much all of Asia, Australia, and half of India. Billions of people versus the five or six hundred million you usually have access to every night."

Abbie held her hands to the sides of her head and pressed lightly, trying to ease the pressure on her mind. "There's just…a lot."

"I know." Vincent put his right hand on her shoulder and waved his left toward the cacophony of feeling. The area directly around them returned to the pastoral green grass that it had been when he arrived. Natural smells of fresh cut lawn and earth returned.

Opening her eyes again, Abbie still saw the madness flickering in and out just beyond her reach, but at least next to her, peace returned.

"Thank you," she said. "That will help a little until I can get more accustomed to the constant din. She's taken naps before, and I've been able to access Consciousness at this time of day, but never this deeply."

"You'll get used to it," Vincent assured. "Wait, who's 'she'?"

"The me from Basic," Abbie shrugged. The voices dimmed in her mind, but the sound continued pounding.

Vincent raised an eyebrow. "The 'you' from Basic? You're 'you' here *and* there."

"I've heard all this before," she said, standing up straighter and looking around at the weaving world. "Your uncle tells me that all the time."

"It's true."

"I don't care either way, so long as I can get her to remember. Then I can take control in both places. After what happened last night, she's going to need me fighting for her. She'll never be able to do it herself. And thank you for not telling her my name. The word 'Moon' kept coming to her mind, but she couldn't figure it out. I don't think she ever will."

"You don't give yourself enough credit," Vincent said as a bird-sized butterfly dragon with a long tail swooped down and ate a kaleidoscope flower. "Either way, we need to find out who is hunting you out there and how to stop them."

"It's Catharsis and Alexander," Abbie said, hands waving in the air as if her statement was obvious. "They want Alice Ashling."

Vincent's hair blew in slow motion on the wind as he nodded. "So, you do know where she is in Basic."

The air tingled with distrust. Abbie stared at Vincent. Several butterfly dragons flew from the grass and into the unstable array of rooms and offices appearing all around them.

"I'm sorry," Vincent admitted. He held his hands out in a gesture of submission. "I'm just trying to figure all this out too. I'm not pushing for you to tell me anything about Alice. We need to get you to remember in the real world. That way you can make the decision yourself."

"But you want that information too, don't you?" Abbie stepped to the right and started circling Vincent like a lioness. "And don't give me that line you fed my Basic-self about wanting to find Alice to keep me safe. You want to know where she is as much as whoever is pulling Mozzie's strings."

Vincent nodded. "I do."

"Why?"

"Because all of this is partially my fault."

Abbie stopped. She raised her sword and pointed it at Vincent. "Explain."

Shoulders slumped, and Vincent's armor visibly weakened. Tiny cracks appeared along the surface. "I wasn't always the…most dedicated Proctor. Once Alexander started exerting his will over dream space, I had the opportunity to shut him down, and I didn't take it. Standing up to him would have hurt my business in the real world, and I was scared. Now, things are pretty ragged up here because of it, and getting worse."

"So, you want to make amends, is that it?"

"I want to join forces with Alice both here and out there," Vincent said. He stepped closer to Abbie, letting her sword touch his chest. "I can't get anywhere near her in Consciousness. She's too powerful. Most of the time you can't even find her in the dream, no matter how hard you look. I don't know how she and Alexander do it, but they're practically untouchable. It's like they've become part of the fabric of Consciousness itself. But if I can talk to her out there in the physical world, with no armor or tricks or switching perception, I have resources to offer that could help change the tide of what's coming. I have contacts close to Catharsis and Alexander. I have information to share. We can end all this struggle."

"I'll pass the message along," Abbie said as she lowered her sword and turned to walk away. "I appreciate what you did for my Basic-self tonight. I do. But in here, I don't need your help."

"Yes, you do," Vincent called.

Abbie looked back at him over her shoulder and raised an eyebrow. "I do, huh?"

"How are the drawings going?" Vincent asked with a cocky smile. "You remembering things yet? It seems to me you aren't even close to merging your dream-self with your physical-self. Even after meeting my uncle and seeing his drawings of you, you still can't bridge the gap in your mind. Admit it."

The sword flared purple as anger surged from Abbie's hand. "I'm close!"

"You're not!" Vincent waved his arms to the side and turned in a circle as if addressing an invisible crowd. Several dreamers lingered to listen. "How long has Uncle Hanker been teaching you? How long have you tried to wake up out there and found yourself watching from the sidelines? You're the all-powerful Moon, right? Well, let's not forget that now I've met you in here and in Basic. Moon is just a construct. You fight against yourself to prove how amazing Moon is at the expense of your real identity. I know how divided you are."

"It's her fault, not mine," Abbie assured. Her own armor began to fracture in tiny fissures of doubt.

Vincent stomped forward and stood nose to nose with Abbie. "You *are* her! That's the problem. It's not her fault. It's yours. She's only now starting to understand we inhabit two worlds. You've known since you were probably 16 years old, like I did, and yet you still can't unify. I'm the only person who can coax you two together since I'm in both places too. Image how powerful it will be when we wake up and draw the same picture! Your mind will open to the possibilities, just like I told you in the car. You need me; in here and out there."

"You just want to know where Alice is, like everybody else!"

"Yes, I do!" Vincent yelled. The ground shook. All smells died, leaving behind a sterile nothingness. "And maybe I want to make things better. Maybe it would be nice to have someone to talk to about all of this when I'm awake. And maybe I want to finally look Alexander in the eye and then kick his ass."

Emotions slowly creeped back into the area as Abbie

breathed deeply. Vincent never dropped his gaze, staring at the powerful Proctor with as much willpower as she ever witnessed.

Abbie rotated her shoulders, but kept her eyes locked on Vincent. Her armor healed itself with a layer of rosemary-smelling courage. "I guess whether I like it or not, we're stuck together for the time being. You're both asleep at that disgusting cabin in the middle of nowhere. She's not going to run away from you at this point. She will go to the police at the first opportunity, though. It's her way."

"Which is why we need to work together in Consciousness so you and I can draw the same picture. It's the first step. Whether you trust me or not, this is the only way you're going to remember the dream."

The smell of vanilla returned. Grass started blowing in the breeze again.

"And that's what we're going to do," Abbie said. "You help me remember. But if I think for a second that you're something other than what you say, I will carve you from the dream and hunt you every night until you're so exhausted during the day that over time you die of a heart attack."

Vincent's forehead creased and he smiled awkwardly. "Can you do that?"

She touched the purple sword to his cheek. Smoke sailed from the surface with angry anticipation. "I'm willing to find out," Abbie said with a dour grin.

A dark cloud began to form overhead. Chills rippled up Abbie's arm. Several women in armor, one as large as an ancient walnut tree, ran through the grass just beyond the shifting train station and formed a citadel of pearl white with intricate lattices and towers. Thunder rumbled.

"We have more Pursuants coming," Vincent confirmed, looking at the sky. "There should be plenty of Proctors to push them off…hopefully. You never know around here anymore. If you want, we can stay and fight, or I can take us to a Thought Bubble where we can practice our shared image."

Abbie's nose crinkled like a credulous nine-year-old. "I hate those places. Thought Bubbles are like opium dens for freaks."

"If we stay out here, we'll get pulled into the fight," Vincent said, pointing toward the white tower as Proctors and Pursuants began tearing into each other in puffs of colored smoke and remorse. "And I'm pretty sure we have more important things to do than cast out leeches looking to terrorize and get high. You said it yourself; we're in this together for the foreseeable future."

"Fine. Take me there," Abbie said.

Vincent stepped back and looked Abbie up and down. "You should probably make yourself look and feel less conspicuous. Your armor stinks of confidence and power. You'll stick out like a sore thumb in one of our Thought Bubbles on this side of the world. Even here they've heard of Moon."

Biting her tongue, Abbie imagined her armor dripping away like melting wax. In its place she formed a dark green leather tunic with a cape and hood. An assortment of simple knives appeared on her belt, similar to what an untrained Proctor might conjure. Shiny leather pants rippled down toward boots with two-pronged blades sticking out from the toes. Her skin warmed to a standard peach shade, and the glowing line down her face faded away, leaving her looking perfectly pedestrian.

"Is that better?" she asked.

"Very flattering," Vincent said, looking her up and down with a nod.

"What about you?" Abbie questioned. Vincent remained in his gaudy pale-yellow armor and annoyingly perfect hair. "You're not going to change?"

He stepped back and adjusted one of the shiny gauntlets on his left forearm. "This is how I look here, and since this is pretty much the normal time I sleep, other Proctors and Pursuants will expect my light armor and rugged good looks."

"Lucky you."

Vincent smiled and closed his eyes. Instantly the environment swirled like a vortex of color and imagination. Dreamers washed away, leaving behind a faint aroma of roasted potatoes and sugar beets. Abbie allowed herself to be pulled along as Vincent shifted his perception and took them away from the open plains of Consciousness to a more oppressive locale. Mists suddenly hung low to the ground, cutting off the brighter pigments that characterized the dream state. Dust floated slowly on the air; in fact, everything seemed to move at a reserved and languid pace. Columns of stone, like pillars in a colosseum, twirled up from the ground.

"Where are we?" Abbie asked. "There's almost no emotion here at all; no thoughts or dreams."

"We're down a little deeper," Vincent said, walking into the fog. "You ever go this deep into Consciousness?"

Abbie followed him, uncomfortable with the sterility of the area. "Normally the only things down here are Proctors and Pursuants who don't want to be found; wastes doing little more than trying to hide from themselves."

The mist wrapped around Vincent and grew thicker. "And that's more or less all we're going to find. Trust me, where we want to be is close; it just takes a bit of searching. This is one of the top spots in the Asian zones. No one will bother us once we're inside Capacious' Pleasure Palace."

"He likes straight forward names, I take it," Abbie replied, shaking her head.

"Capacious' imagination only extends as far as what he steals from other people. But he's good at what he does."

They continued walking. Occasionally Abbie would get a whiff of some errant emotion, like rancid onion hopelessness, or burnt toast depression. Dark pillars took shape at times through the murk, but no sounds materialized beyond their footsteps.

"So, what kind of consultant are you in Basic?" Abbie asked.

"What do you mean?"

"Your business card said you're a consultant in the waking world. You obviously do incredibly well for yourself, what with that Tesla sports car rental and needlessly expensive business card. Is 'consultant' code for 'smuggler,' or something more nefarious?"

A humorless smile pulled at Vincent's lips. "I don't usually talk about my Basic self while in Consciousness. You of all people should understand the danger of that these days."

"Still," Abbie pressed. "You want me to trust you. You want *her* to trust you out there, right? All I'm saying is that you know a lot more about me than I do about you."

Vincent nodded and blew some of the mist out of his face. "That's fair. Alright, trust begets trust. Here we go…and don't judge. Out there I work with businesses in southeast Asia, Australia, and India, normally with real estate holdings and executive training. I have a lot of contacts I've built up over the years. Companies pay me to get them in contact with the right people at other companies, government agencies, the works. I'll admit, when I first became a Proctor here in Consciousness, I was far less ethical than I am now. I played with emotions, manipulated other Proctors, whatever I needed to do to get information that could help me in Basic. I even made deals with Catharsis when I needed to. Many of those early contacts in my career were forged in Thought Bubbles like we're about to visit. It's how I started building my fortune."

"I'm surprised Hanker allowed you to get away with that.

He's a strict one, for sure, and as your trainer he would have kept a close eye on you."

"He didn't know at first," Vincent said. "Uncle Conrad was always so kind to me in both the dream and Basic. I took advantage of it when things started going bad for me."

Abbie smiled at the thought of her mentor. Hanker had always shown her kindness as well, especially when she had first become aware of her capacity in the dream world. Of course, he could rage with the best of them too, especially at those taking advantage of the innocent.

"That's Hanker alright," she said. "But I'm sure he got angry at you too though. He has a way of coming down hard, but still making you feel worthy, if that makes sense."

"It does, and he did, but not too hard since I never attacked dreamers. I took to manipulating Proctors and Pursuants who were tired of fighting each other. Once I moved to Vietnam, I was in a different sleep time than him, too. Things got pretty bad for me though. I was popping amphetamines in Basic and getting addicted in here too. Something had to give. After a couple years I came back around. Hanker helped a great deal. He and I have since reconciled. Now all my contacts are above board. I still have a lot of friends down here, but now I'm protecting instead of self-serving. Even in the dream I try to keep my nose clean, except for when I have to come to places like this. And…I think we're finally here."

Out of the fog, Abbie could see a granite building approaching, whose entrance consisted of a crystalline revolving door and several Greek statues of gods and goddesses. A scowling man with over-sized arms stood next to the spinning glass. A gray business suit covered his misshapen body; face lined and worn like a dried grape left on the vine long past harvest time. The man grumbled and blubbered his lips as Vincent approached.

"Capacious, it's good to see you again," Vincent said with a bounce to the words. “It’s been a little while.”

“Not long enough, Auspice,” the deformed brute grunted. “What do you want?”

“Just a quiet place for my friend and I to chat without interference or emotional manipulation.”

Capacious stood taller and looked down on Abbie with a bulging eye. Mist wafted from his shoulders smelling like birthday cake soaked in pickle brine. “I got that here,” he said. “But it’s going to cost you, just like everybody else.”

“You’re charging me now?” Vincent asked, giving Abbie a side glance as if embarrassed he wasn’t let inside without a fuss. “I thought we all had an understanding.”

“We do,” Capacious growled. “But I ain’t running a charity here. You cause trouble, and that trouble causes more trouble. Go cry to Catharsis, or Alexander, or whoever’s running shit right now. I don’t care who you are; you’re paying to get in.”

Vincent took a step toward the man and squinted. After a moment he seemed to soften and nodded his head. “Fine,” he said. “We’ll pay. What do you want?”

A guttural noise that Abbie assumed had to be a chuckle, rumbled from Capacious’ throat. “Not much. I want a taste of lust. I don’t care from what memory or when, just pure lust. That’s the price of entry.”

Veins bulged in Abbie’s neck. Her purple blade took shape in her hand, fed by hot indignation. She would cut this asshole from the dream and walk past his smoldering turd-shaped heap long before she gave up a lustful thought.

Vincent reached over and touched her wrist. “It’s fine,” he said, eyes locked on Capacious. “I’ll pay for both of us.”

“What are you---” Abbie began.

“It’s fine,” Vincent repeated. He stepped in front of Abbie before she could put this leech in his place and closed his eyes. Mists rose from Vincent’s cheeks. Capacious stepped closer and breathed deeply, inhaling memory. Color ran up his wrinkled face, split by a slow smile. Eyelids fluttered as Capacious swayed slightly like an unsteady drunk man.

“Oh, that’s good…” the disgusting man breathed. He glanced over at Abbie. “Yeah…real good.”

“Are we done?” Vincent asked, stepping back.

Capacious nodded with a sneer and stepped aside. He waved them toward the rotating door. Armored boots clanged against the stone ground as Vincent stomped forward past Capacious. Abbie followed, ready to slice the fat bastard in two if he so much as winked at her.

They passed through the revolving glass and entered a towering golden hall with rooms and alcoves on all sides. Passion, frivolity, and dejection glided on the air like orange blossoms and burned cotton candy. Opulent images of people, shapes, and animals were engraved on columns of polished brass that shot up three stories tall. Silver platters laden with fruit and seared meat floated around the hall as naked women with bird wings, and in some cases cat heads, danced in the air overhead. Hundreds of people, both Proctors and Pursuants, some looking like sexy demons, others taking the shape of comic book superheroes or anthropomorphic animals, filled every surface in a frenzied rush of abandonment with a hint of depression.

Abbie grit her teeth in disgust. She had been to Thought Bubbles before, but not since she was a teenager just grasping her ability to move freely through the dream. These places always offered plenty of emotion sharing and crazy sexual escapades, but underneath all the pomp and feverish carnality lay a layer of self-hate that made Abbie physically nauseous. People couldn’t hide their despair no matter how they tried to drown it out. Abbie always saw through the illusion to the desperate people looking to feel anything but their own inadequacy.

"Here we are," Vincent said, interrupting Abbie's critique.

"Why did you do that?" She asked. "I could have cut that prick down. You didn't need to pay him anything."

"And what would that have solved?" Vincent turned to her with a slight frown on his lips. "If we'd attacked Capacious, we would have destabilized the entire area. Everyone would have fled, leaving the palace to crumble to nothingness, only to be reforged somewhere else. I know a lot of these people. I can't go around overturning tables and making a fuss. It was a couple errant thoughts. A worthwhile payment to get us somewhere we can disappear for a bit."

Vincent led Abbie down a wide set of stairs toward the ground level of the berserk party. Several people shouted to 'Auspice' as the two weaved through the crowd. Vincent nodded and smiled, waving to several women beckoning for him to join them in a dance. No one seemed to notice Abbie or care she was there at all. An alcove with a large table and red curtains burst into laughter as a man in a clown costume tumbled into the air after siphoning pungent red emotion from one of the women sitting next to him. Abbie wondered what they were sharing but decided it best not to think too much about it. No need to encumber her thoughts with images of people wasting their dreams perceiving emotions that weren't even theirs.

At the end of the great hall, Vincent turned left and took them into a smaller area where sensations ebbed to more normal levels. Pillars continued to reach high above, but the colors dimmed, with less detail on the walls and polished floor. Fewer people crowded the space, though those that did seemed waifish and dull; eyes sunken and faces expressionless.

"Let's go in here," Vincent said, pointing to a green curtain hanging over an arched doorway. He held the thick drape aside and led Abbie into a sitting room with several red velvet couches, small tables, and a morphing wall that twisted in shades of turquoise and gold. Incense hung on the air. "We'll be left alone in here."

"You sure, 'Auspice'?" Abbie asked.

A smile spread across Vincent's face, revealing perfect teeth. "I'm sure. No one will bother me while we're here."

Abbie took a seat in the closest chair. A feeling of relaxation and fatigue overcame her. "Yeah, you seemed to have a lot of friends out there. Wow…this chair is comfortable."

"Everything here is meant to heighten the senses and trigger emotional responses," Vincent said, taking a seat across from her. "Capacious and his patrons know what they're doing. They may be hedonistic, but they have skill, that's for sure. I don't come here very often, since I tend to feel the same miserable emotions you were apparently feeling."

"Was it that obvious?"

"If you had less control, you would have puked your disgust all over the place," Vincent said. "I get it though. Under all the distracting emotion in places like this there's always that feeling of…misery. These palaces are hard to process psychologically since people are trying to hide and forget and wallow; throwing up facades to make themselves look and feel better than they actually do. It's like going to a Hollywood party. So much fake emotion. I always feel overwhelming pity, which tends to kill the vibe pretty fast." He tapped his finger against the table and glanced down quickly. "There's a lot of sadness and fear down this deep; tends to create darkness and emptiness. There's nothing scarier than nothing. You ever fight in nightmare realms at all? Go down there to help people out?"

"Not usually," Abbie admitted. "People are typically so lost in nightmares that you can't do anything to help them. You?"

"Once or twice," Vincent said. "It's depressing. Tons of Pursuants to kill though. If you ever want to take out your frustration, head down there. You can't take a step without crushing the head of some ass getting high on fear. It's kind of like coming to Thought Bubbles, only fewer naked people and more self-respect."

"How about we focus on why we came here in the first place?" Abbie said, changing the subject so she wouldn't have to think about the people trying to escape their lives on the other side of the curtain. "We need to figure out who is hunting me, and who they work for."

"First thing's first," Vincent interrupted. "Let's pick an image to draw when we wake up. The sooner you start trusting me, and more importantly yourself, the sooner you'll start to remember. You have any thoughts on what that drawing should be?"

Abbie sat back, letting the feeling of contentment rising from the chair envelope her for a moment. "What if we drew a joy archetype, like a dog, or a rabbit."

"I like the dog idea," Vincent agreed. He held his hands up as light began to fill the room. "But we'll need to make it unique, with details that will stand out so there's no question we've drawn the same picture."

A cheerful puppy appeared in the air before them, smiling broadly with its tongue hanging out. Abbie grinned, raising her own hand, and adding to the image. The dog's eyes grew bigger and more cartoony, while bone-shaped spots appeared across its back.

"Those are great details," Vincent said. "This is the image that moves from mind to hand today."

"This is the image that moves from mind to hand today," Abbie repeated. She closed her eyes and opened her mind just enough to let the image inside. The dog filled her with warmth and joy, searing the likeness in her subconscious. Slowly the puppy morphed in her thoughts, replaced for a moment with a smiling vision of Vincent. She opened her eyes and banished the idea quickly. Vincent still sat in front of her with his eyes closed; the dog rotated above them.

"Alright, I think that will work," Vincent said as his eyes opened. "That was a good choice."

"Thanks." Abbie looked away quickly, feeling a warm rush of excitement that made her uncomfortable. Perhaps her Basic self was influencing her emotions. She couldn't have that. *Control, control, control,* she repeated to herself.

"Now that we have the image out of the way," Vincent continued, "we need to move onto---"

A shudder ran along the floor and through the walls, shaking the palace construct. Cracks ran up the pillars. Shouts vibrated through the space with a hint of anger, fear, and awe.

Abbie stood and moved toward the green curtain leading back into the adjacent hallway. "What's happening? Did someone take out that Capacious guy?"

"I don't think so…"

The two ran out of the room and back toward the sumptuous main hall. A group of drug-addled Proctors and Pursuants staggered into the side area, looking nervous and scared. One minute they had been buried in an avalanche of pleasures, and the next, thrown into confusion and doubt.

'Serves them right,' Abbie thought as she brushed them aside and continued running. More shouts emanated from the ballroom.

An earthquake rumbled and shook, sending ripples along the marble floor and leaving behind chunks of broken stone. People cried out and poured from the main hall like water from a dam.

Emotions throbbed in all directions in waves of pure apprehension. Gold flaked from the edges of pillars; curtains and drapes withered to rags as if years passed in an instant. Steam and smoke billowed behind the fleeing dreamers.

Abbie pushed through the crowd and made it to the ballroom first. There she gazed up at a familiar enemy. A giant, twenty-foot-tall pink cat with purple stripes, a sinister mouth, and drool-flinging tongue, dominated the space. His orange feline eyes with their black vertical slit, glowed with a cruelty Abbie had witnessed firsthand less than a month before. Lightning crashed around him, bursting into sparks of superiority. Dark purple clouds fluttered from the tabby and obscured his lower body as if only part of his form had materialized inside the hall. Over the cat's right shoulder darted what looked like a man-sized mosquito with thick black wings and a long, barbed proboscis. A blonde woman manifesting as a brilliant, winged angel bobbed up and down over his left.

"Catharsis," Abbie spat. It had been a month since she had faced the damned cat with Alice by her side. Swells of confidence and tenacity blew from the misty feline in fragrances of lilac and calamari.

"Shit," Vincent breathed behind her.

"Ah, Moon…" Catharsis said in his deep, sing-song voice. "Or should I say Abigail Elisabeth Kinder? I always like knowing exactly who I'm dealing with both in here and out there. It makes things easier. And Auspice! What are you playing at?"

"Just doing my job," Vincent said, stepping next to Abbie.

Catharsis swatted at a man dressed in a Superman costume as he tried to run from one of the side alcoves. Before the wannabe superhero got halfway across the room, the cat smashed him into a puff of blue and red aerosol. "We'll see," he said, twisting his neck completely sideways and licking his paw where he'd just squashed the Man of Steel. "This guy had delusions of grandeur. Tastes like chicken."

"What do you want, you pathetic cat?" Abbie asked. Armor reformed around her body in shades of purple, red, and black. "It's been a while since I've seen you."

"I travel a lot," Catharsis said, stepping forward and smashing a table beneath his oversized paw. "I can't spend all my time in your little part of the dream. It's good to have a presence around the world when you have an organization like mine. If I stayed in a single sleep cycle like you do, I'd be out of business. And all I want to know is where Alice Ashling is hiding. I know you gleaned her location."

Double blades flashed purple in Abbie's hands. She stepped toward the feline, rage billowing from her shoulders in a radiant cloud. "The last time we saw each other I pretty much neutered you, if I remember correctly."

"And last time you had that bitch Alice with you," Catharsis countered. "This time I don't think she'll be here to help out. Plus, I've got Mozzie with me too. He told me about his little break-in earlier. Don't worry, he's good at finding people. I have a feeling you're not going to get too far before he catches up. But complicated plans make me anxious, so I'd love to just wrap this up right now."

"How about I simplify things for you," Abbie said as she crossed her blades in front of her, ready to attack. "I'll wake you back up, and we can call it a day."

The cat giggled mischievously. Chills ran up Abbie's spine and settled in the back of her neck.

"No one is going to be doing any waking up tonight, I'm afraid," Catharsis chuckled. "You won't be waking me up, and I sure as shit won't be waking you up."

"What do you mean?" Abbie asked, suddenly confused.

Catharsis stepped forward and cracked his fuzzy jaw to the

side loudly. "I need what you know. That means I need you here. It's good you can't wake yourself up, because if you could, I'd really be in trouble. Don't worry, I brought plenty of friends that want to feed on a piece of Moon's consciousness. Let's get started, shall we?"

The ceiling broke open and rained down droplets that smelled like wet paint. The walls split and tumbled apart. Dozens of Pursuants charged forward in a wave of exhilarated tension. Shapes and shadows morphed into beasts or terrifying men and women brandishing whips and psychic cords, not for banishing Proctors from Consciousness, but for holding them captive…and torturing dreamers for information.

Abbie stepped back, unsure what to do.

Catharsis hissed piercingly, wet tentacles snaking from his nose and eyes like an octopus slinking from the black nothing of the Mariana Trench.

"Let's play!" he slavered, blitzing his prey.

CHAPTER SEVEN

Long odds had stared down Abbie before, but not like this. An ocean of Pursuants crashed around her, slobbery, sticky, and smelling of hot molasses. During her last battle with Catharsis and his cabal, Abbie had her entire conclave with her, plus Alice Ashling, and dozens of other Proctors. Now only she and Vincent stood against the breach. These parasites had only one interest: violate their opponent's minds.

Only one option seemed viable.

Abbie turned to Vincent. "Hit me with your sword and wake me up!" she yelled.

He stepped back and blinked, looking from Abbie to the rushing mob. "I don't want to…hurt you," he stammered.

"I can't wake myself up on my own! Hit me with your sword!"

Vincent hesitated before raising his weapon. His eyelids twitched.

"Do it!" Abbie cried as the first wave of Pursuants jumped forward in a surge of writhing arms. The ground beneath Abbie's feet suddenly lurched, pitching Vincent backward as he swung his blade, missing her by a full two feet. Rock and tile spat into the air. Giant hands grew from the floor and yanked Vincent toward a whirlpool of swirling gravel.

"Moon!" he shouted. Yellow energy fluttered between his fingers in the pale shape of a bow and arrow, but the painful grimace on his face told Abbie he would be crushed long before he could conjure a weapon powerful enough to break free.

Just as she planted her feet to lunge toward Vincent, a shadow churned on the air in front of her, taking the shape of a blackened skull. Abbie swerved and split the skeleton in two with her blade, before decapitating a pair of furry beasts running up on her left.

More swarmed in all directions. Tendrils of energy twisted all around, groping toward her like spastic slugs. Abbie launched herself into the air and threw one of her blades, hitting a man with lobster claws in the chest.

"Auspice!" she yelled.

Vincent was nowhere to be seen; swallowed in a sea of misshapen dream hunters scrambling through the crumbled hall like ants on an injured butterfly.

Coarse insect limbs clawed at Abbie and threw her backward. The large mosquito, Mozzie she assumed, flew her through the air and tossed her away roughly. She slammed into the disintegrating wall of Capacious' Pleasure Palace next to three hunters waiting to capture her. One wrapped a glowing lasso around her neck, but Abbie threw her blade and hit the shadowy figure in the head. The rope evaporated along with the wounded predator, and Abbie jumped up ready for a fight. Her sword flew back to her hand, and she gripped the hilt with determination. The other two Pursuants attempted to coil her with twisting snake-like vines, but Abbie lunged at them and impaled both with her psychic swords.

"Bring her to me!" Catharsis bellowed, voice shaking the walls. Octopus arms continued writhing all around him, as if his feline body was made of nothing but limbs and tentacles.

The angel woman who Abbie had seen over Catharsis' shoulder dove from above, flapping wings of alabaster like she descended from heaven. Abbie tossed one of her blades and hit the blonde woman in the upper thigh. With a cry of pain, the angel twisted, lost control of her flight, and smacked face-first into the stone wall.

Catharsis roared as his acolyte stumbled back to her feet and then fell over again. The sky above erupted in fiery shades of orange and red. Shafts of cobalt lightning hit the ground and held in place like plasma behind glass. Fear and anguish roared like currents on an angry ocean. Catharsis and his conclave did everything in their power to affect the environment's emotional underpinnings. No lingering arousal or playfulness remained from the party, only fear, hate, and animosity.

Pursuants thronged in all directions. Abbie pivoted, cutting the hair of a woman using her long strands as a snare before embedding her dream blade in the woman's chest.

Each time she dispatched an enemy it seemed two more appeared. She wouldn't get much further without help.

"Auspice!" Abbie screamed again while scanning the battlefield for Vincent. "Auspice!"

No arrows shot through the air. No aid seemed imminent. If Vincent had been expelled from the dream he could come and wake her up, but Abbie had seen whirlpools like the one that swallowed him before. They tended to pull dreamers into confusing emotional quagmires; hard to get your bearings and hard to escape, even for someone trained like Abbie.

Out of the corner of her eye she saw a pair of armored Proctors who had been dancing in the hall before Catharsis arrived, fighting with a group of Pursuants. They were brave to come to her aid, she gave them that, but they would be no help at all after clouding their minds with emotionalized sex and artificial joy. They had barely entered the fray when they were cut down by a group of hunters manifesting as jagged-clawed werewolves.

The rest of the marauders set their sights on Abbie.

"Lick her mind!" a man blathered, hunched over and twisted like a gaunt contortionist. Two blubbery globs of green slime with arms and legs came up behind the thin wretch and laughed.

Abbie kicked the stooped hunter in the face as she jumped over him. In the same movement she swiped backward with her sword and felt the angry blade sever the man's tie with the dream world. He wept and disappeared. The two green slime monsters soon followed their twisted compatriot out of Consciousness as Abbie split their minds with ease.

Emotions became more and more oppressive as Abbie turned to face the unending avalanche of Pursuants. They clamored past Catharsis to enslave their quarry. Once again, the sheer volume of dreamers began to take its toll on her mind. Shapes warped, smells became sounds, and Abbie's grip on Consciousness slipped.

A chain pulsing with anticipation wrapped itself around Abbie's ankle and yanked her to the ground. She hit hard against what remained of the grand hall's stone floor, leaving a crater behind. A ripple of dread cascaded across the environment.

"Hold her!" Catharsis laughed. "Hold little Moon for me!"

More cords spun around her arms and legs, jerking Abbie back onto her knees.

Already she could feel the pull of emotive parasites trying to nudge her psyche open. Abbie wouldn't betray Alice. She wouldn't be mind-flayed by weaklings and terrorizers. Reaching deep into her mind, Abbie grabbed hold of a powerful memory. The smell of bacon mingled with the melody of *Leader of the Band* by Dan Fogelberg. Grandpa Carl mixed pancakes with a wire whisk while Abbie's older sister Emma drew an impressive picture of Wonder

Woman with brand new crayons. Nana Gayle walked into the kitchen grinning, saying, *'There's my little Abbie, all awake and ready for breakfast!'* Nana picked up the young girl and gave her a hug, filling Abbie with love and acceptance.

Pure emotion exploded from Abbie in a shockwave. The chains holding her crumbled like dry bricks in a nuclear blast. The closest Pursuants blew apart in shredded pieces of perception, while the rest tumbled back as if hit by a cyclone. Even Catharsis stumbled and shrunk slightly from his towering, self-important height. Trees sprouted around Abbie in vibrant greens and blues. The smell of pancakes and syrup circled on eddies of playful laughter. Storm clouds dispersed. Warm sunshine illuminated the area with a feeling of serenity.

Abbie stood and surveyed the beautiful destruction around her. Pursuants bumbled forward with bewildered faces. A man with an elephant head rubbed his crooked trunk and moaned.

Clapping echoed on the breeze as Catharsis, now quite a bit smaller than he had been before, but every bit as menacing, smacked his paws together. "Bravo, Moon. Not many Proctors would be able to pull something like that off. And here I thought it was all Alice the last time we tangoed. I'm impressed, and that doesn't happen very often. Auspice knows what he's talking about, I guess."

"You're not getting Alice's location from me," Abbie said, breathing deeply. What did he mean by 'Auspice knows what he's talking about?' Was Vincent in league with Catharsis? Wouldn't be that big of a surprise if the charming bastard was playing all sides.

If so, Abbie would take great pleasure in severing Vincent's arms from his body.

Before she could ponder further, Mozzie landed in front of her in a gust of wind and dust. He smacked her with one of his heavy wings. Abbie stumbled but didn't fall.

"Oh Moon," Catharsis said in a high-pitched voice. "You can't wake yourself up, and we're not going to do it for you. Eventually you'll break. Grab her, Mozzie."

The mosquito's buggy-eyed face mutated until the man who had attacked her in the apartment smiled like an asylum patient. Mozzie dove toward her on odious wings, long thin limbs clawing like a spider.

Instead of backing away, Abbie charged and took the insect-man by surprise. Ducking below him, Abbie threw her sonic blade, twisting it through the air as she would a boomerang. The glowing sword amputated the arms on Mozzie's right side before burying itself in his thorax. Mozzie howled, face transforming back into a mosquito with a sharp extended proboscis.

But he didn't dissipate like most other Pursuants would after such a powerful hit.

Mozzie was strong, without a doubt.

Too bad for him, he was also slow. Abbie jumped on him, forming a second blade, and shoving it just under his hairy insect chin.

This time the bug choked on black pus and drooled leathery tar onto Abbie's armor. He burst open and flopped into a smear of coarse slime in the dirt.

"Well, shit," Catharsis said, picking between his sharp teeth with a retractable claw. "I guess the rest of you are going to have to do it."

Once again, the mass of Pursuants rushed forward on a wave of frustration. The trees Abbie had manifested shriveled to black and died as quickly as they had grown. Clouds reformed, cracking thunder that rocked Consciousness.

Abbie reconstructed her swords and stood unshaken. There would be no victory for Catharsis today. No matter the odds, Abbie would not let herself entertain the thought of defeat. Self-actualization meant something in the dream. If she had to, Abbie would manifest victory from the minds of her enemies.

A cry pulled Abbie's attention behind her. She turned to see red hair and neon purple armor bounding toward her on footfalls of floating bubbles.

"I got you, Moon," Fraelig shouted as she cut down four hunters with a single swing of her massive ax. "It took me a bit to get back to the dream, but I'm here now! I followed your power."

"Stop her!" Catharsis ordered.

Abbie ran toward the strong and savage Proctor. With a thought, her armor dissolved, leaving Abbie completely vulnerable. "Cut me down!" she screamed. "Banish me from the dream now!"

Fraelig paused, mouth hanging open and eyebrows arched.

"Do it!" Abbie commanded. "Do it now!"

"You want me to---"

"Do it!"

Pursuants lunged forward with grasping tentacles and fingers of electricity. Before they could grab hold of Abbie, Fraelig swung her ax and slammed it against Abbie's head.

A forceful splitting headache tore through Abbie's mind. She welcomed the pain, feeling her connection to Consciousness fray.

"Thank you!" Abbie said as the world flashed in a blinding display before fading to nothing.

Sunlight shined through the window, reflecting off specks of dust as Abbie lunged forward in bed. She sat up, breathing heavily, smelling musty fabrics. A memory of pancake breakfast lingered on her thoughts for a moment before retreating. Sweat ran down the back of her neck, though she felt cold and clammy. Her head hurt.

She gasped for a few seconds trying to remember anything she had been dreaming, but found only fragments of shifting rooms, cats, and more pancakes.

Jumping off the bed, Abbie unlocked the door and ran into the front room. Vincent opened his eyes as she entered and adjusted himself on the couch.

"What happened?" Abbie asked.

Vincent rubbed his eyes and took a deep breath. "A lot," he answered. "Before we say anything though, we need to draw." He stood, leading Abbie to the kitchen table across the room. "Is there any paper here in the cabin? I forgot to ask last night."

"Over here." Abbie darted to a drawer next to the old pale green oven and pulled out a stained pad of lined writing paper. A collection of worn pencils and broken crayons littered the bottom of the bin. She grabbed two semi-sharpened Number 2's and handed one to Vincent before tearing a few pages from the notebook.

"What image moves from mind to hand today?" Vincent asked.

Abbie took her page and moved to the couch so she and Vincent wouldn't be able to see each other's drawings. She blew dust from the coffee table and laid the paper in front of her. "What image moves from mind to hand today?" she whispered to herself.

Closing her eyes, an impression of a playful puppy appeared. Graphite touched stationary as Abbie allowed her hand to move freely. The dog took shape on the page with cartoon eyes, tongue hanging out of its mouth, and a series of bone-shaped spots across its back. Drawing the image filled her with happiness and she smiled as she added the last few details.

"You ready?" Vincent asked without turning around.

Abbie held up the picture of the dog and nodded. "Ready."

Vincent turned. A drawing of a puppy, not quite as detailed as Abbie's, filled his paper. The canine's tongue hung out of its mouth, big playful eyes bulged, and a series of bone-shaped spots covered his back.

A gasp echoed through the room before Abbie realized she had made the sound. Her heart pounded. She took Vincent's drawing and placed it on the table next to hers. The angles were the same, even the number of bone spots.

They had drawn the same picture.

"This isn't possible…" She stood and stepped away from the coffee table, hands shaking. Her breaths became ragged, and Abbie thought for a moment she might hyperventilate. Sure, she had felt emotions when Vincent had spoken about certain aspects of the dream world and the people there, but now being presented with something more concrete terrified her.

Suddenly she didn't want it to be real. She didn't want to live another life as an amazing warrior. She didn't want the responsibility of saving people against impossible odds.

Vincent grabbed her shoulders lightly and tried to get her to look at him. "Abbie, it's okay. It's okay, just take a breath."

"How did you do that?" she asked, voice cracking. "How did you draw that?"

"We talked about this. It's okay. We met in the dream, just like I told you."

"No!" Abbie shouted. A bird outside the window flew away suddenly at the volume of her voice. "I can't…it isn't…" Words and breaths merged until Abbie didn't know where one started and the other ended. It was one thing to entertain the idea that perhaps an entirely separate dream world existed every time people closed their eyes; it was another altogether to have hard evidence in front of you that was created by your own hand.

Air caught in Abbie's throat, and she choked. The room spun. It couldn't be true. She didn't live a completely different life when she slept.

"Abbie. Breathe," Vincent said. "Take a second. This is a lot, I know."

Softly, but with enough force to exert control, Vincent pressed Abbie back to the couch. The cushion compressed beneath her as he sat and filled her lungs. Vincent took the chair across from her and leaned forward.

"That's good," he continued. "Just keep breathing for a minute. I know how you feel. This happened to me too. I knew something was up when I first started figuring things out because I had been drawing weird stuff every day. I felt a bizarre connection to my uncle at that time too. He had been in the hospital for a while back then, but he could still talk. He didn't make sense a lot of the time. The morning I woke up and remembered everything from Consciousness, I had a panic attack. It's a lot…to realize there's a whole other world you're a part of that you didn't even know about."

Tears fell from Abbie's eyes, and she sobbed. "I don't want it to be real."

"Why not?" Vincent asked.

"Because what does that make me? If I'm something important there in that world, but I'm nothing here, what does that make me?" Abbie wiped at her tears and sniffed. "I hate myself half the time as it is because I'm afraid to be bold and take chances. My sister Emma does everything right and I compare myself to her all the time. Now there's a comparison to a whole other version of myself that's apparently super awesome? Screw that."

Vincent smiled and looked at the floor. He gazed back up at Abbie and scratched his chin. "You and she are the same person. It's funny because I told you this in the dream too. You're the same person. Once you're able to remember everything you'll know what I'm talking about. There aren't two Abbies; one here and one in the dream. There is one Abbie."

"Then what's the point of all of it?" she asked, holding Vincent's gaze. "You said we protect dreamers, right? We cast these pursuer-guys out of the dream, so everybody is safe. But then they just come back into the dream when they go back to sleep, right? What's the point? Is it just another treadmill we get to run on?"

The couch squeaked as Vincent moved next to her from the chair. "The dream is beautiful and wonderful, where people experience their emotions and fears in a safe place. You can swim in rivers of subconscious thought and learn things about the past that no one remembers. And for dreamers like us that get to roam freely on a higher level of consciousness, it's a world of infinite possibilities. But until things are balanced again, it's going to grow darker and more oppressive. So, to answer your question, yes, there's a point to all of it. We fight back the darkness, even if it's going to come back again an hour later. We make sure regular people are creating their own nightmares, not being forced into one by some asshole who wants to feel powerful. We don't stop. And since it's all spilled over into your real-world life, we need to focus on helping you remember. Right now, we need to find Alice out here in Basic, and keep you safe. She'll know what to do for you. Trust that. And, if it makes you feel any better, I've never heard of your sister Emma in Consciousness, so at least up there you're the superior one in the family."

Abbie laughed, letting her fear temporarily wash away. Tears stopped flowing down her cheeks, and she sniffed again. “Alright. Well, if this whole crazy shitstorm is real, I guess I have to learn a few things, don’t I?”

“That you do,” Vincent grinned.

“So, what happened in there, anyway?”

“We fought a giant cat, I gave up some lustful thoughts to get us into, basically, an emotional crack house, then we got attacked, I got pulled into a whirlpool of dark emotion that I had a very difficult time escaping from, and you wore tight leather pants, which were easy on the eyes.”

“Nice,” Abbie laughed. She wiped at her cheeks. “I’m sure I didn’t shave off a few pounds here and there in order to make myself look good.”

Vincent sat forward and took Abbie’s hands in his own. “You look exactly the same in there as you do out here. You’re perfect wherever you are.” He coughed and looked away, as if embarrassed by what he’d said. “I mean…you don’t change the way you look, which is good because it means you’re not self-conscious and vain.”

“What do you look like in the dream?” Abbie asked.

Vincent snorted a little and looked up at the ceiling with a sideways smirk. “Oh, I make myself look like the most beautiful thing in the universe: a chocolate donut with cream filling and sprinkles.”

Laughter filled the cabin as Abbie’s head pitched back and her chest shook. Vincent’s hand continued to hold hers.

“Abbie, I need you to think about Alice, and where she is,” he said, voice suddenly growing serious. “Right now, she is the safest person for you to be with. She can help us navigate what’s going on. I have contacts and resources to share with her too that will help undermine Alexander and whoever else he’s working with.

I told you all of this in the dream, so I should share it with you out here as well. There needs to be open honesty between us for this to work. I want to find Alice as much as you do, but it's your choice on what you share with me. Everyone knows who Alice is both in Consciousness and in the real world, but she's stayed safe for decades despite being hunted by the most dangerous men on the planet. She'll know how to protect both of us."

"How do I find her?" Abbie questioned as warmth moved from her clasped hands to her chest. "I still don't remember anything from the dream beyond the dog we drew."

"Just close your eyes and focus on an emotion." Vincent held her hands tighter. "You tend to be…angry quite a bit in Consciousness. Your weapons seem to always be made from your rage. Focus on that emotion. Then think of the name 'Alice Ashling' again and again. I promise you; something will register, and a flash of memory will shake loose. Your mind is opening up to all of this now. It will start to get easier."

Air filled Abbie's lungs as she nodded and closed her eyes. Dark shapes swirled in her visual field. "Okay," she said. "I'll try it. Anger. I can do anger."

"Remember Alice Ashling," Vincent coaxed. "Alice Ashling. Find a way to trigger your anger."

'Alice Ashling. Alice Ashling. Alice Ashling.' Abbie repeated in her mind. *'Anger. Anger. Anger.'*

Nothing came to mind. How would she spark her rage? It's not something she had ever tried before. What made her angry? What made her resentful?

Pictures of her mother telling everyone at Christmas the year before about how amazing Emma's gallery photos looked on Facebook, flickered through Abbie's psyche. Clients requesting new designs and then complaining they weren't as good as the originals.

Traffic on a Friday afternoon. Mom's passive/aggressive attempt to get her to work for an insurance agent. Abbie wasting her life, unable to quit her job or take a risk on her art.

Anger. Rage. Frustration.

'Alice Ashling. Alice Ashling. Alice Ashling.'

An image of sharp mountain peaks came into focus like the back of a spiked dinosaur.

'Alice Ashling. Alice Ashling. Alice Ashling.'

Crystal lakes took shape. A river wound into the distance. Feelings of safety flooded Abbie's brain and rippled down her arms in goosebumps. Alice was here. Alice was safe. An image of a saw blade flashed just before a voice in Abbie's head screamed for her to stop. The voice grew louder, tearing at her mind in a power struggle that shattered perceptions and pushed Abbie out of her own thoughts.

A bead of perspiration dripped from her forehead down her nose. Abbie opened her eyes as a wave of fatigue threw her back into the couch cushions.

"Are you okay?" Vincent asked. He held her hands tight and caressed her thumb.

"That was…weird."

"What did you see?"

Abbie sat up. "Mountains; jagged ones. Rivers and lakes. A saw blade too, which was bizarre. And then it felt like someone else was there. Someone yelled at me to stop and then, like, attacked me or something. That's all I remember."

"It's enough," Vincent said. He sat forward and pulled his cellphone from his pocket. "Damn it. There's no service up here."

"Let me see." Abbie took his iPhone and tapped the Wi-Fi app. Three locked networks appeared. The first server, named

RiverRat042478, Abbie didn't recognize, but the second, guysmileyHost, was exactly what she was looking for. "The host cabin has Wi-Fi. I remember the password. Hopefully, it hasn't changed in the past couple years."

After typing in the code, a 'connected' prompt opened. Internet access was granted. Vincent took back the phone and started searching 'spiked mountains' and 'sawblades.'

"I'm betting the impressions you felt are connected," he said while scrolling through Google images. "Normally our brains try to get ideas across in the simplest way possible."

Photos of table saw blades with mountain art painted on them slid down the screen, followed by video links of a bicycle with saws for tires riding across a frozen lake. Finally pictures of angular peaks showed up in the feed. A panoramic portrait of a couple getting married with a series of sharp mountains behind them caught Abbie's eye.

"That one," she pointed. "Those are the mountains, right there. That's what I saw."

Vincent laughed. "The Sawtooth Mountains in Idaho. I told you everything was connected. That's why your mind showed you the sawblade. It was trying to give you the info you needed."

"So, Alice is somewhere near the Sawtooth Mountains?" Abbie asked. "I doubt that's a small area. It's not much to go on."

The coffee table scratched against the floor as Vincent pushed it out of the way and stood. "It doesn't matter. We head there anyway. We keep dreaming together and drawing more pictures. The closer we get, the more details you'll remember. It's our best bet."

Abbie stood as well, feeling a headrush that threatened to send her back to the couch. She recovered and breathed deeply. "What about the guy who broke into my apartment? What if we go to the police now? We can say we were frightened and ran off. I'm not going to tell them you're crazy at this point. They can help find him."

"I…I don't know, Abbie," Vincent said. He looked to the ceiling and put his phone back in his front jean pocket. "We're dealing with very powerful people here with a lot of resources. I knew a Proctor in Indonesia whose identity was discovered in the real world. Guys like Alexander were able to track him down from a single call to his parents from a random pay phone in Jakarta. We have to be extra careful. They know who you are. They know the people in your life."

"I get that, but if the police arrest this Mozzie guy, maybe they can find out who he works for."

Strands of black hair fell over Vincent's eye as he shook his head. "I have contacts all over Asia and Australia and I couldn't even learn his real name."

"I'm just saying---"

Vincent put his hands up to stop Abbie from continuing. "If you feel that strongly about it, we can go to the police, but if we do, they'll report it, and they'll list where you are in their system. That will give Mozzie a chance to find you. It's better if we head straight to the Sawtooths now without letting anyone know. It's safer."

"I can't just run off to Idaho without telling anyone where I am," Abbie said. "I need to at least call my mom and grandma."

Vincent's tongue poked against the inside of his cheek. He looked down for a moment and nodded his head. "Alright. How about this? Let's drive into Kamas and you can call your mom from one of the stores there and tell her you're alright. Don't say where we're going, just that you'll call her back in a couple days. If you want, you can call the police too and tell them you're afraid for your safety and you'll be hiding out until they catch the guy who broke into your apartment. It doesn't need to be detailed, just believable.

You can call them all if you feel better about it. That sound fair?"

The thought of giving such vague information didn't sit well with Abbie. Mom and Nana Gayle would be freaked out and think she'd been kidnapped or something. On the other hand, Abbie now began to accept the fact that an entirely separate dream world existed where she was being hunted for information, and one of those hunters had broken into her apartment the night before in the real world.

"Okay," she replied. "That sounds alright. This entire thing is crazy, but if all of this dream stuff is real…I guess I've got to trust you on this one."

A calm smile brightened Vincent's face. "Getting Abigail Kinder to trust you is a pretty big deal, either here or in the dream, so I'll take it gladly." He looked around the room and pointed toward the hallway. "The bathroom's down there, right? Let me use the 'little boy's room' real quick and then let's hit the road. It's getting late, and I think we should drive through the night without sleeping. Catharsis will have Pursuants waiting for you in your regular sleep schedule. They're not trying to cast you out of the dream anymore. They are trying to siphon information from you. Catharsis is dangerous. Best to keep him off-balance. Maybe in a couple hours we can find a quiet spot to pull over and sleep for a little bit."

"Who's Catharsis again?"

"Oh yeah, sorry," Vincent said, snapping his finger. "Catharsis is the giant cat we fought. He's a powerful guy both out here and in the dream world. Nobody knows who he is, but he can have people killed with a single order, apparently. Don't worry, you've met him before. Unfortunately, I'm sure you'll meet him again."

Vincent stepped toward the hall, but Abbie grabbed his arm and pulled him back.

“Wait,” she said, eyes blinking quickly. “What’s my name in the dream? Just tell me.”

“I can’t,” Vincent confirmed. “But, if you think about it, I’m pretty sure you already know.”

Turning, Vincent walked down the hall toward the bathroom.

“Moon,” Abbie whispered. The word came to her again and she somehow knew. “Moon,” she repeated with confidence. “My name is Moon.”

Vincent stopped and looked over his shoulder. He smiled and opened the bathroom door, stepping inside without a word.

Images of wide-open spaces and orange skies with four suns shimmered in Abbie’s imagination. Power and peace rushed through her body. Freedom seemed to take the shape of a purple sword.

“My name is Moon.”

CHAPTER EIGHT

"I'm going to be fine, Nana," Abbie said, ear pressed against the antiquated courtesy phone at the Kamas Food Town supermarket on State Route 248. An old woman in glasses sat behind the customer service counter pretending to read *The National Inquirer* while obviously eavesdropping on Abbie's conversation. Twangy country music ballads played from speakers overhead, adding to Abbie's discomfort.

"You need to come home right now," Nana replied, worry evident in her voice. "After the police called your mom this morning, we've been worried sick about you. They said there were gunshots and everything. What is going on?"

Abbie rubbed her ankle with her left big toe nervously, feeling the soft fabric of Vincent's socks against her skin. She couldn't enter the store barefoot, and luckily one of his travel bags remained in the trunk. Expensive black fabric now hugged Abbie's feet and slipped against the linoleum floor, contrasting with her pink pajama bottoms and *Mumford and Sons* shirt. While too big, the socks still fit surprisingly well.

"Like I said, I'm okay," she repeated to her grandmother. "I can't tell you everything right now, but I will, I promise. You'll need to call Mom after we're done. I don't have my phone and I never bothered memorizing her cell number. Just tell her I'll contact you guys in a couple days."

"A couple days?!" Nana Gayle's volume forced Abbie to hold the phone farther from her ear. She glanced around the store to see if anyone beside the old checkout lady could hear the exchange. A young mother with two kids patiently told her little boy why he couldn't buy *Frosted Flakes* and have them for dinner. Other than that, the store seemed empty. The woman behind the counter slowly turned the page on her magazine, ear tilted toward Abbie.

"Yes, in a couple days," Abbie continued, gripping the coiled cord that ran from the phone base to the handset. "Just know I'm okay and safe, and that I'll be able to give you more details later. Don't stress out."

"Don't stress out, she says," Nana mumbled.

Vincent turned the corner next to a rack of fresh baked bread, holding a rotisserie chicken in a plastic container, along with a few bags of chips and orange soda bottles. "I'm going to get some more snacks and check out," he said. "And before you call the…you know who, come get me first. I can help. I'll be on the candy aisle."

Waving her hand as if to say, 'that's fine,' Abbie returned her focus to the phone. "Nana, I've got to go. I still need to make another call. Contact my mom and tell her I'm okay, and I'll call back later."

"Who's with you?" Nana Gayle asked. "I heard someone talking to you. Are you alone? Are you being forced to do anything?"

"Nana, I've got to go. I love you. Bye." Abbie hung up the phone and handed the base back to the woman behind the counter. "Thanks for letting me make the call."

"Everything alright, hon?" the woman asked as she pushed her glasses down her wrinkled nose. The look on her face registered more judgment than concern.

Abbie looked at her name tag. Lucinda. "It's all good,

Lucinda. Thanks. I'll be back in a minute, if that's okay."

"That's fine, hon. I'll be here. You from Salt Lake?"

The little boy started crying next to the cereal aisle, pulling Lucinda's attention away from Abbie. She used the wailing as her opening to scurry away from the prying woman. As she walked past dairy cases full of milk and eggs, Abbie looked around for Vincent. She knew he didn't want her to call the police, but she appreciated the fact that he wasn't pushing her not to. Vincent had a lot to lose if his identity was discovered. Would someone kill him just to make sure he couldn't protect anyone in the dream? It certainly didn't seem out of the realm of possibility after what Abbie had experienced over the last 12 hours.

Signs hung above each aisle designating where to find everything in the store. Peering down to the far end of the supermarket, Abbie saw 'Cookies, Candy, Snacks,' in bold yellow letters. Vincent's socks glided along the plastic tiles as Abbie made her way past different end caps full of plastic flowers, nacho-flavored corn chips, or discounted fabric softener. The smell of cleanser mixed with sauerkraut stink as she walked past a teenage boy with a nametag mopping up a spill on Aisle Five. A handful of shoppers filled their carts along the way. Abbie gave each a friendly smile. One stooped gentleman with a twirled white mustache winked at her as he pulled a box of protein bars from the shelf. Abbie yawned and continued walking.

The clock over the bathrooms ticked 2:15 in the afternoon. Abbie felt as if it were 2:15 in the morning and wanted nothing more than to close her eyes and sleep. She'd gotten at least four hours in the cabin bedroom but didn't feel rested at all. Getting half a night's sleep will do that.

Of course, maybe fighting predators in a dream world didn't lead to a quality slumber either.

She still couldn't quite wrap her brain around it all. Even so,

Abbie couldn't deny what she saw and felt when thinking about Alice Ashling. She hadn't imagined those mountains, or the sound of the voice yelling at her. If everything turned out to be true, it made sense that she had been so fatigued lately. Things in the dream world had gotten bad, and she had to fight harder than before. Hopefully once she remembered everything, Abbie could find a balance that allowed her to rest and protect at the same time.

The candy aisle approached, and she turned the corner expecting to see Vincent. Only rows of Oreos and Snickers bars stared back.

"Where'd you go, Vincent?" she whispered to herself as she slowly walked down the aisle. A country music song about a woman running away from an abusive relationship dripped from the speakers above. Abbie shook her head and imagined something more upbeat playing instead.

The sound of slow footsteps behind her mingled with the depressing music.

Abbie turned. "We should get some beef jerky---"

Mozzie stepped toward her. His eyes squinted; mouth pulled up in an angry smirk. The same large nose she had seen the night before in her apartment flared as it approached.

Abbie pressed herself against the shelves with nowhere to go. Hershey bars tumbled to the floor and broke in their packages. She tensed but stood tall. For the first time Abbie got a good look at her attacker's face. Mozzie's large, crooked nose dominated his features. Lines on his cheeks and forehead dated him in his forties, by Abbie's guess. A large bruise swelled under his right eye, with several half-scabbed scratches on his cheek. Instead of the sweaty smell Abbie remembered from the night before, pungent wintergreen medical cream reek, like what Grandpa used on his sore muscles, permeated the area around Mozzie. A black leather jacket, simple white t-shirt, and jeans made up his ensemble.

"I don't like beef jerky," Mozzie said in his Australian accent.

Abbie swallowed, lip quivering slightly. More candy bars hit the linoleum.

"It's been a while since anyone cast me out of the dream," the Aussie continued. He reached slowly around Abbie and pulled a package of Reese's Peanut Butter Cups from the shelf. "You're a skilled one, you are." Chocolate and peanut aroma tickled Abbie's nose as he opened the package and tossed one of the candies in his mouth.

"What do you want?" Abbie asked. She tried to shift to the right, but Mozzie put his arm against the shelf to block her move.

"I'm sure your little friend told you everything," Mozzie said, eating the second Reese's and chewing slowly. "Where's Alice? You tell me and I leave you alone. It's that simple."

"Right…You'll just leave me alone." Heart throbbing in her chest, Abbie wondered if the man still had his gun on him. "How did you know we were here?"

Mozzie smiled and pulled another candy bar from the shelf. "It's pretty easy to track a brand-new Tesla roadster. You just need to know where to look. Rental companies get a little twitchy about big investments like that. GPS trackers are common."

Abbie glanced up and down the aisle, hoping someone, anyone, would turn the corner. "I don't know where Alice is. But if you don't back away from me, I'll scream."

The Reece's package crinkled as Mozzie opened his second treat. He moved a bit closer, eyes on the chocolate in his hand. "You're not so scary here in Basic. I worried you might have a bit more of Moon in you. That'd cause problems. But you're not Moon, are you? Don't remember both worlds yet. Lucky you. You can scream if you'd like. It won't bother me, sheila."

A blur of movement to their left caught Abbie's attention. Before she could tell who it was, a silver Ruger GP100 revolver like her Uncle Eric owned pressed against Mozzie's right temple.

"You've got enough problems as it is, Mozzie," Vincent said. He held a plastic bag full of snacks and drinks in his left hand, the gun in his right as if he'd just robbed the supermarket. "I'd hate to have to make things worse for you. But I'd just as soon not draw any more attention to us if we can avoid it. You okay, Abbie?"

"I guess," she breathed.

Air sucked through Mozzie's clenched teeth as he stepped toward the middle of the aisle and raised his hands. The Reese's candy thudded against the floor and rolled toward Abbie's foot.

Vincent flicked the gun to the right twice as if motioning at the store's exit. "How about we go outside and have a little conversation. No need to make a fuss here in the---"

"Hey!" a young man's voice shouted from their right. Abbie looked down the aisle and saw the teenage stock-boy who had been cleaning spilled sauerkraut a few minutes before. He stood at the end of the walkway, mop in-hand, pointing at Vincent. "You can't pull your gun in the store man! I'm calling the sheriff!"

"Give me the gun, Auspice," Mozzie said.

"No!"

Mozzie squinted and yanked the revolver from Vincent's hand before slamming himself against the shorter man. Vincent fell into the shelves and knocked more chocolate bars to the ground.

"Lucinda!" The teenager shouted as he ran away. "Call the sheriff! We got a fight going down!"

Mozzie and Vincent fell over and rolled on the floor, each trying to pry the pistol from the other's hands. Abbie stepped back and looked around. Next to a selection of discounted Valentine's

Day chocolate boxes marked with yellow clearance tags, sat a wine bottle filled with M&Ms. The pink label read, *'For My Sweet Valentine.'* Abbie grabbed the glass container and swung it as hard as she could at the back of Mozzie's head.

A resounding *thunk* sound was followed by Mozzie cursing loudly. Abbie had expected the bottle to break, but it stood up to her assault with no apparent damage. She brought it down again. This time Mozzie rolled to the side and cradled the back of his head in his hands.

"Shit! God damn it!" The Australian bellowed.

Vincent bounded to his feet and grabbed Abbie's arm. "Run!"

The two bolted down the aisle just as the old man with the twirled mustache poked his head around the corner to see what all the yelling was about. They plowed past him toward the doors. Abbie's socks slipped on the smooth tile, but Vincent held her close, so she didn't fall over.

"Hey!" Lucinda yelled from the customer service desk, arms waving. Her glasses almost fell from her nose as she shook. "You stay right there! Don't you leave the store!"

The automatic doors opened. Abbie and Vincent charged into the bright afternoon sunlight without looking back, almost knocking over a woman talking on her cell phone just outside the supermarket. Pebbles gouged into Abbie's feet as she ran. The socks did little to protect her soles from the uneven asphalt. The white Tesla sat exactly where they parked it twenty minutes before.

"Go, go, go!" Vincent shouted as he rounded the car and the doors opened for them.

Abbie hurled herself into the passenger seat almost exactly the same way she had the night before, wine bottle full of M&Ms still in her right hand. She sat up and looked out the windshield toward the front entrance expecting to see Mozzie chasing them, guns-blazing. No one else exited the store, except for the teenage employee who stumbled out and looked around frantically.

"Hold on!" Vincent yelled. He tossed his bag of groceries to the floor and threw the car into gear. They tore backwards into the parking lot before spinning toward the highway. A black pick-up truck honked and swerved as they maneuvered recklessly between cars.

"I don't see him," Abbie said as they bounced over the sidewalk onto the street.

"He won't be far behind," Vincent replied. "How the hell did he find us? We're in the middle of nowhere!"

"He tracked the car," Abbie answered as they passed another truck and turned north onto Kamas Main Street.

"How did he track the car?"

Abbie watched the road as they blew past buildings and homes at way past the speed limit. "He mentioned something about rental companies putting trackers on their cars."

"Shit!" Vincent yelled, slamming his hand against the steering wheel several times.

"Does that mean he knows who you are now?" Abbie asked. "If he found the tracking number, he would have found your I.D. info too. He called you 'Auspice.' Is that your name in Consciousness?"

Vincent nodded. "It is. Mozzie and I have known our dream identities for a few years now, after an unfortunate run-in with a particularly seductive Pursuant contact I worked with. I've never been able to discover his real name, and as far as I've known, he hasn't known mine. That may have just changed, unfortunately."

"What do we do?"

"It doesn't matter," he answered. "I'm more worried about the police at this point. I was hoping we could get out of there without…It doesn't matter now. At least we know how he did it. We're going to need to ditch the Tesla and find something more innocuous." He glanced at the rearview mirror, eyes twitching fast. Sweat dripped down his temple and ran through light stubble on his cheek. For the first time since they'd met, Vincent appeared truly anxious, and it didn't help Abbie's already frayed nerves. "That did not go the way I wanted it to."

They drove in silence for a few minutes as the town grew sparser and farmland began to dominate the view. Fallow fields ran all the way to the foothills of mountains, smelling of freshly plowed soil waiting for the year's first round of planting.

Watching the world blow by, Abbie's thoughts seemed suddenly clear, as if puzzle pieces in her mind started falling into place. She closed her eyes and took deep breaths. Everything seemed to be in extreme focus. The M&M bottle turned over and over in her hands. Sunlight reflected off the glass surface in twisting shapes of white and yellow. Colorful candies shined in red and pink. A spot of blood clung to the label and obscured the barcode where she'd slammed it into Mozzie's skull.

She had acted and attacked her assailant.

But not soon enough.

Disappointment flowered in her chest. Thoughts of a dozen different ways she could have handled Mozzie without Vincent's help suddenly appeared in her head.

'Moon would have taken him down with no problem,' her inner critic chattered. *'Moon would have beaten him all by herself. Moon wouldn't have been afraid.'*

Moon. Abbie already disliked this better version of herself. Mozzie seemed to have respect for her dream persona, but none for her.

'Well,' Abbie thought to herself, *'I don't care how amazing this Moon is. Life isn't so hard when somebody else has to worry about everything and all you have to do is show up and fight people. In a dream you don't have to pay rent, do you? You don't have to eat. You can't die, right? Moon isn't so special. Moon has it easy.'*

"Are you doing alright?" Vincent asked. "I'm sorry I've been so quiet. I just don't usually play defense, is all."

"I'm okay," Abbie said. "I just feel…different. Like I'm seeing more things, but I'm also being critiqued from the inside out, like a voice in my head is judging everything I do. This whole situation is so messed up."

"You're doing amazingly well," Vincent continued. "This time yesterday you were meeting my uncle at a hospital, and today you're hitting guys over the head with wine bottles. I'd say that's a pretty big leap. Are those M&Ms?"

"Yeah," Abbie chuckled. She held it out for Vincent to take. "You want some?"

"No, thanks," he grinned. "Those are stolen goods now."

"Where are we going to get another car?" Abbie asked, ignoring Vincent's attempt at humor. "Mozzie is probably tracking us right now."

Vincent nodded his head and turned the air conditioning on. He continued sweating. "I don't know. I have a couple thousand dollars in cash on me, so we could find somebody selling an old clunker and buy it outright."

"You carry a couple thousand dollars on you at any given time?" Abbie questioned.

"Do you have any idea how expensive those socks you're wearing are?" Vincent asked, pointing to Abbie's feet.

"No."

"If you did, it wouldn't be a surprise that I carry that kind of cash with me."

"Where did you get the gun?" she asked. As far as she knew he didn't have one before they entered the supermarket.

"I saw Mozzie come into the store right when I was checking out," Vincent said. "I ran back to the customer service desk to find you, but you weren't there. As I was running, I saw the old guy with the curled mustache."

"Yeah, he winked at me when I walked by him."

"He was open-carrying and had a revolver in a holster on his belt," Vincent continued. "I pretended to trip into him and lifted it without him knowing. He was a really nice guy though. Helped me stand up after and apologized like it was his fault."

"Why were you checking out?" Abbie questioned. "I thought you said to meet at the candy aisle."

Vincent looked down at the bag with the Kamas Food Town logo sitting on the floor between his feet. "I did, but I figured we'd have too much to carry, so---" His eyes shot up to the rearview mirror. "Shit."

Flashing red and blue lights reflected in the back window. Abbie's heart started beating faster again as she made out the shape of a sheriff's cruiser less than a mile behind them. A siren wailed in the distance just loud enough to be heard over the Tesla's engine purr.

"There's a sheriff behind us," Abbie said, sitting up straighter.

Staring forward, Vincent pushed his foot against the accelerator and sent them screaming even faster down the highway. Trees and farms became a blur. Abbie held tight to the armrest, fingers gauging into the upholstery.

The road arched to the left along a hillside and the police car disappeared from view. Several houses on the west side of the road sped past. Two more homes rushed toward them, followed by another bend in the highway going back toward the east. Vincent pressed the brakes and slowed them quickly without squealing the tires. The first house on their left had a garage on the south end of the residence. The door sat open with no car parked inside.

"What are we doing?" Abbie asked. "Are we going to randomly hide in somebody's garage?"

"You got any better ideas?" Vincent pulled the car into the vacant garage and threw open the car door, hitting a lawn mower. He ran over to where the garage door controls hung against the wall next to a freezer and smacked his hand against it. Gears rumbled and chains squeaked as the door lowered from the ceiling and cut them off from the sunlight outside.

Abbie sat, pulse thumping in her neck. The scream of a police siren built, and then changed frequency as it passed. With each second the sound grew fainter. Abbie's heartbeat slowed. Even so, she knew they had traded one danger for another. They may have escaped the Sheriff, but Mozzie could find them easily now.

Pacing back and forth, Vincent seemed to share her concern. "We can't stay here," he breathed.

The garage offered Abbie no ideas as she looked around for anything that could help them. Bicycles hung from racks on the front wall. They couldn't exactly ride to Idaho. Shelves full of tents and sleeping bags sat off to the right. Hiking wouldn't be an option. She remained seated in the car, racking her brain for anything that could get them out of this situation.

One possibility took shape. She opened the door and stepped from the car, holding her hand out toward Vincent.

"Give me your phone," she ordered.

"Why?"

"Just do it!"

Vincent hesitated. After a moment, he shrugged and threw his cell to Abbie. She tapped his internet app and found that even in this rural area they were still close enough to Kamas to have some signal. Typing *'cars for sale Kamas Utah'* into the search engine, Abbie soon saw three listings within five miles of their current location.

"Okay, we have three cars for sale by owner in the area," she said, eyes focused on the phone screen. "None of them are selling for more than 15 hundred dollars. This one looks good. It's a white, 1995 Cutlass Ciera Oldsmobile. 185 thousand miles. Says it runs well. They want $999 for it."

A second police siren echoed in the garage before moving down the road and growing quiet again. Abbie breathed in relief.

"Where is the person selling the car?" Vincent asked as he took the phone back and scrolled the screen with his index finger.

"There's an address, but I don't know these little towns at all," Abbie informed. "Best we can do is give the guy a call and go pick it up."

Vincent rubbed his eyes and leaned against the wall next to the freezer. "It's a good plan. Let's make the call. We need to get out of this garage before someone comes home and calls the police on us. Plus, the sheriff might turn around and loop back if they can't find us. We need to move now, or we'll be more screwed than we already are."

"She hasn't been driven much in the past couple years, but I started her up last week and she ran pretty good."

Wind blew from the south, kicking up dust next to the weathered barn and sagging Oldsmobile. The farmer, Danny Ray, fidgeted with his green John Deere ballcap as if excited at the prospect of selling the piece of crap vehicle. He scratched his chin and pulled a rag from his coverall pocket.

"We can check the oil if you want," Danny continued. "I promise you, she's in good shape for being this old."

Abbie dragged her finger along the dirty white hood of the Oldsmobile, coming away with more grime than she expected. Dust covered the entire vehicle, save for a few recent handprints here and there. Afternoon shadows lay across the fields. Dark storm clouds gathered over the hills to the west.

"You want $999 for it?" Vincent asked.

"She's worth $1,500, for sure," Danny assured.

"Let's call it $1,500, then," Vincent said.

Danny scrunched up his nose, leaving lines of dirt in the creases on his face. "You want to pay more than I'm asking?"

"Yeah," Vincent said, looking back at Abbie. "But I want you to do a favor for me."

"What favor?"

"You see that Tesla right there?" Vincent asked, pointing to the white roadster parked next to a rusted tractor.

"Yeah."

"I'll pay an extra $500 if you drive that car to Evanston on the country roads out here. I'll throw in another $500 if you park it in the McDonald's parking lot right there at the first exit and leave it for pick up. That'll be two grand all together. You willing to do that for me?"

Wind blew stiff, almost knocking Danny's hat from his head. "$2,000?" he asked. "Just for driving that car to Evanston and then parking it at a McDonalds?"

Vincent smiled. "Can you do that? She's a hell of a fun drive."

"There's no drugs or anything hidden in it, are there?" Danny asked, eyebrows dropping in suspicion.

"I assure you, definitely not," Vincent laughed.

"Why you want me to drive it to Evanston then? That sounds a little weird. We'll have to take two cars to get back home. My wife doesn't like to drive much."

Abbie stepped forward and took Vincent's arm, rubbing it affectionately. "It's ridiculous, but I don't like driving in the Tesla. It's tight and uncomfortable. I like to lounge around a bit. We're taking the sportscar to Evanston for my brother, and I've been complaining all the way. I know, that makes me sound like a spoiled rich girl, but I like something more roomy, and when I saw the ad for your Oldsmobile, I just had to have it. I told my boyfriend I would make it worth his while in the back seat, or even while he drove, if you get me." Abbie winked and continued. "Sometimes rich people can get away with that sort of stuff, Right honey?"

"You got that right, sweetie," Vincent beamed like a doting boyfriend. "Anything for my baby."

He put his arm around her and drew Abbie close. His skin smelled faintly of sandalwood; surprisingly good for a guy who hadn't showered in more than a day. The warmth from his body tickled her arm as she wrapped it around his waist and slipped her thumb into one of the belt loops on his pants.

It felt natural being this close to him. It felt right.

Before her mind wandered any further into romantic fantasy, Abbie coughed quietly and returned her attention to Danny Ray.

"We figured we'd do something silly and let someone else have fun with the sports car for a little while," she continued. "We're going to take an extra day or two driving and…experiencing the roads out here." Abbie giggled and batted her eyes like an innocent doe. Vincent pulled her even closer and chuckled in response to her thinly veiled metaphor. Again, she smelled sandalwood and pictured her and Vincent standing on the beach somewhere before shaking the image off and continuing. "My brother will pick up the car, so you can just leave the key fob with the manager at the McDonalds and tell her Drew will be by to pick it up. She'll know who you're talking about."

Rubbing his stubby chin, Danny nodded his head. "I don't know…"

"Hey, you like M&Ms?" Abbie asked.

Danny chuckled, as if amused by two horny rich people slumming it in the country. "I sure do, little lady."

Opening the car door, Abbie grabbed the wine bottle full of chocolates and handed them to the farmer. "Here you go," she said with a broad smile. "Enjoy!"

"Well, thank you. I suppose I can drive out there for an extra $1,000 over the price of the car. Just make sure I have your number in case there's any problems." Danny rubbed his finger along the bottle, stopping at the smudge of blood on the label.

"I spilled some red wine on it earlier," Abbie said quickly. "I got a little tipsy!" She laughed as if the thought of getting drunk on red wine was the funniest thing in the world.

"My wife will sure enjoy these, for certain," Danny said. "It might make her more eager to drive the truck into Evanston. And the money will go a long way too. Again, just make sure I have your phone number before you go. Is it the same one you used when you called me?"

"It is," Vincent smiled. "There's enough charge in the Tesla battery for probably three hours. If you do want to drive it a little more than that, I'm fine with it, just make sure you find a charging station if you do. I wouldn't want you getting stranded somewhere. Park it at the McDonalds and her brother..."

"Drew," Abbie said with a smile.

"Yeah, it was Drew who was going to pick it up. He'll grab the fob."

Vincent and Danny switched keys and the farmer beamed when Vincent piled 20 one-hundred-dollar bills in his calloused hand. They threw the excess baggage into the back seat, and the Oldsmobile started right up with a lethargic rumble. It sounded almost unbearably loud in Abbie's ears after the quiet of the electric Tesla. They pulled back onto the state route from the dirt road and left the little farm in the rearview.

"I told you he would need a better reason to take the car to Evanston," Abbie said as they turned toward the main highway.

"You were right," Vincent agreed. "I assumed any farmer would just take the money and the car and enjoy the ride. No one would have asked any questions in a rural town in Vietnam or Cambodia."

"Good for them. Here in the States, even Kamas-farmers are too wary for that kind of crap."

"At least it will throw Mozzie off our trail for a while," Vincent said. "And the police. Long enough so we can put a little distance between all of us and get some sleep." He rubbed his fingers along the steering wheel. "And may I say, you are an impressive liar. The trick with the M&Ms was brilliant. You skipped over his doubts and made him feel warm and fuzzy with a gift. Textbook stuff. Really nice."

"You're not so bad yourself," Abbie said. "Maybe it's something about us being dream-buddies."

Abbie cringed at the 'dream-buddy' remark. *'That was a stupid thing to say,'* a voice whispered.

"Maybe there's something to that 'dream-buddy' thing," Vincent said, not seeming to notice her embarrassment. "I don't have many people I get close to in the dream." He cleared his throat and glanced back and forth quickly. "And I mean…you know, by 'close,' I mean friends. I don't have a lot of friends in Consciousness. I'm not getting close, like *close* to people…women…you know what I mean. Everything is business. All my relationships feel transactional."

"Transactional?" Abbie smiled. "How *transactional* are we talking about? $100 an hour?"

Vincent's eyes went wide. He jerked the steering wheel slightly and swerved the car enough to rock them back and forth. "No! That's not what I meant by that. I didn't mean 'transactional' like… *'transactional.'* I would never…you know, I respect---"

"I was joking," Abbie said, broad grin pinching her cheeks. "I can't see you needing to pay for someone to want to spend time with you."

"You'd be surprised," Vincent replied, fingers loosening their tight grip on the wheel. "You've never heard me snore before."

"That bad, huh?"

"Oh, I'll keep you awake all night." Vincent dropped his head as his cheeks flushed. He closed his eyes slowly. A thin smile pressed his embarrassed lips tight together. "You know what I mean by that. I'd keep you awake with the snoring."

Abbie reached over and patted his shoulder. "Of course. Of course."

Taking a deep breath, Vincent glanced down to Abbie's feet, where the Kamas Food Town bag fluttered against the lower air vent. "On that awkward note: is there any chicken left, or did you eat all of it?"

Abbie reached into the shopping bag and pulled out the plastic container with what remained of the rotisserie chicken. "There's a wing left…some of the breast meat along the sides. Sorry, I was hungry. At least you got both of the legs before I picked it clean."

The pair drove for another half hour, reaching the wide concrete and asphalt expanse of Interstate 80. Turning west, Vincent drove the rattly old car toward I-84 and eventually I-15.

"What time is it?" Abbie asked with a yawn.

"After four," he replied. "We should drive to the next little town and find a spot to pull off somewhere out of the way and sleep for a bit. We're both tired and thrashed at this point. And while we kind of know where Alice is, we don't know near enough. Another shared sleep will help, along with a shared drawing. I don't think we should stop and rest during the night. Catharsis will come after you. Let's keep him guessing. Sound good?"

"Not as good as a comfortable bed," Abbie admitted. She stared out the window, feeling suddenly sad.

"How are you doing?" Vincent asked, as if aware of her abrupt emotional shift. "I mean, how are you really doing?"

Tears filled her eyes, but Abbie held them in despite her desire to burst out crying. "I just know my…Nana Gayle is so worried about me, and I couldn't tell her what was going on. I'm always honest with her."

"It's alright to cry, if you want to cry," Vincent soothed. "I'm not going to judge."

Even with his permission, Abbie still didn't want to get too emotional in front of him. He'd already seen her at her worst, but her feelings now seemed more intimate…more private. She didn't want to share.

"It's okay," she said, regaining some emotional control. "A lot has happened, and I just need some time to process. If this were the day I had planned originally, right now I'd be finishing up a design meeting with a client from a local burger place and looking forward to wrapping up the workday. Now I'm driving across the state with practically a stranger, and if I were to explain any of it to my family or friends, they would have me committed. I just want to talk to my Nana, that's all. I want to call my boss, so he doesn't think I flaked out."

"You like your job?" Vincent asked.

"Yeah, it's fine."

"But you want to do more?"

Thoughts of Emma's gallery offer seemed to suddenly drop in Abbie's stomach like a cinder block. She had worried so much about not being good enough that she didn't even allow herself to think about the possibility of creating something worthy to show alongside her sister's art. The last time Emma had called her, Abbie even declined to answer. Now the opportunity had likely been taken from her permanently. She sat in a car heading into the unknown, looking back on her hesitancy with disdain. What had she been so afraid of?

'I should have answered Emma's call,' she thought.

"Doesn't everybody want more?" Abbie said finally. She looked away, concentrating on the grass flying by on the side of the highway as vibrations nudged her from side to side.

They sat silently. Abbie didn't want to talk anymore.

After another 40 minutes of driving, Vincent pulled off in the small town of Morgan. A closed-down rock quarry caught their eye just outside of town, and they parked behind an abandoned portable office trailer with broken windows. Shadows fell on the area, cooling the car and giving the illusion of evening.

"This will be a good spot, I think," Vincent said as he turned off the Oldsmobile. "I know this isn't going to be the most comfortable sleep, but hopefully we're tired enough it won't matter."

Abbie pressed the button on the side of her chair and lowered it back so she could get more comfortable. "Yeah, I have no doubt I'll be able to fall asleep," she yawned. "How long until we should wake up?"

"I'm thinking two hours," Vincent said, lowering his seat back as well. "I'll set an alarm. It won't be particularly restful, but hopefully it will be enough of a break to get us through the night without needing to stop. Remember, Catharsis and his crew aren't trying to wake you up. They're trying to capture you so they can experience your thoughts. It's dangerous. When we get into the dream, I suggest we don't engage any Pursuants or draw attention to ourselves in any way."

"Will Moon be…okay with that?" Abbie asked. "You know her better than I do."

Vincent sat closer and moved his left hand to Abbie's scalp. His fingertips rubbed through her hair, sending relaxing chills through her entire body.

“You know yourself better than you think,” he said, fingers circling in soft caresses. “Don’t doubt your abilities out here or in the dream. You are in control, not some other person. Remember that.”

A warm feeling filled Abbie’s chest as she closed her eyes. Vincent’s hand continued rubbing gently until Abbie lost all sense of time, self, or space as her mind receded from the waking world.

CHAPTER NINE

Warm water surrounded Abbie as she floated toward Consciousness. Familiar sounds, emotions and smells of brine swirled around her. She broke the surface of a tranquil sea and planted her feet. The water shifted under her, but Abbie stood firm, like an angel controlling the elements.

"I am Moon," she whispered, as if needing to convince herself of her own superiority.

In the distance, a city of bright light shined. Buildings extended from both the ground and the sky. Clouds moved as if in fast-forward, a mad shuffling of thought and memory.

She had glimpsed this scene before a handful of times, normally when her Basic-self was sick and fell asleep particularly early. Europeans and Africans loved their city of illumination. The jungles surrounding the construct were particularly dangerous, but the metropolis itself was a dreamer's utopia of strange experiences and emotions. Abbie preferred the open spaces and forests of her mind, but fantasy cities were sometimes enjoyable as well.

Focusing back on herself, Abbie's recollections of the day took form in the water at her feet. Shapes twisted in vibrant colors that accented the smell of salt water. Mozzie's crooked nose pressed close to her. Vincent held a silver revolver. The sound of a wine bottle full of M&Ms smashing against bone. Vincent rubbing her scalp. Vincent smiling. Vincent holding her hand as they ran.

Vincent.

Abbie grimaced and disrupted the ocean with a frustrated wave of energy. The blast cratered the water in a massive ripple, like a boulder smacking the surface of a lake. Salty spray hit her lips, thoughts of Vincent on a breeze.

“Stupid,” she spat. With a wave of her hand the sea turned to dry ground around her. Pink trees with lavender leaves grew from nothing, filling the space with a forest more to Abbie’s liking. A sandy beach ringed the grove. Orange and white fish flew from the water and swam on air currents. They circled Abbie, humming in unison like a choir. One of the flounders stopped, blinked its large round eyes, and smiled with pearly bucked teeth.

“She hasn’t fallen for someone this fast since that guitar player Nick, sophomore year of college,” she said to the fish, who twisted upside down with a gasp. “That didn’t turn out well, unless getting blackout drunk a few times and eventually finding him naked with your roommate is considered a positive relationship. You can’t know anything about a person after less than a day, little fish. Don’t be that stupid. It’s dangerous.”

The fish giggled and swam off after its gliding school. Dreamers began appearing around Abbie’s small island as if beckoned by the pleasant atmosphere. She drew the white line down her face as always but hesitated to form protective armor. Vincent had been right to suggest lying low and not drawing attention to themselves. Catharsis’ attempt to capture her had gotten too close to succeeding. Now the need to link her waking and dream personalities became more critical than ever.

Instead of armor, Abbie created a shiny purple bodysuit with a long yellow cape that could wrap over her arms. She normally avoided needless frills like the cloak but felt it would make her less noticeable as Moon the Proctor.

She had to admit, Vincent understood the subtlety of

Consciousness better than Abbie did. The clothing made her feel different, and thus put out a different vibe than what she would create as Moon. When in the dream, she was a blunt instrument, straight forward and bold. Vincent seemed to recognize the nuances, emotions, and people more fully. She could learn a thing or two that might help to unite her mind.

Should she just tell Vincent where Alice was and speed things up?

No. She still didn't trust him enough for that. Basic-Abbie had been smart to pick up Mozzie calling Vincent 'Auspice' before they struggled for the gun. Vincent should have told her that Mozzie knew his identity in the dream the first time they had met. If he hadn't told her that, what else had he not told her? Charming or not, skilled in the dream or not, Vincent still held his cards too close to the chest for Abbie's liking.

No, not Abbie.

"I'm not Abbie," she whispered. "I'm Moon. Abbie is weak. Moon is strong."

The thought of her name brought a smile. Things weren't a total loss. Basic-Abbie had remembered her real name while awake, so maybe she was getting closer to relinquishing control of her conscious mind. It was the only way any of them would be safe.

A cold wind blew through the forest, freezing several of the trees in a thick layer of ice. Snowdrop flowers bloomed and drooped; their sweet fragrance mixing with snow on the wind.

"It's been a little while, Moon," a sweet voice said, like a kind aunt happy you've come to visit. Abbie hadn't heard that voice in over a year.

"It has, Malva," she responded as snowflakes swirled and crystallized in front of her. A pale queen wearing a pointed crown coalesced from the frost. Short hair stuck out from their scalp like ice sickles. Their white dress cut off just below the knees and billowed up and down on the air. Blades protruded from the bottoms of Malva's bare feet as if ice skates grew from their very flesh.

"I see Merquery almost every night before I drop out of Consciousness," the regal being said as they stepped lightly toward Abbie. "Hanker sometimes too, but anymore, you seem to go to sleep later and later."

Abbie hugged Malva and stepped back to look at their crystalline form. "What can I say? No discipline in my Basic-self. No perspective. Just today she thought about how much easier my life is than hers. Can you believe that?"

"It's too bad you haven't taken control yet," Malva said.

"Hanker says we're the same person and that I shouldn't think that way," Abbie replied. "He says it's not about control, but unification. I have a hard time seeing it that way."

Malva opened their mouth and caught a snowflake on their tongue. "Hanker doesn't know everything."

"Have you done it yet? Taken control?"

Malva shook their head. "I'm old. I decided it wasn't worth the effort anymore. You have more powerful dreamers now, people like Catharsis and that El Ascendente guy in Bolivia controlling people and oppressing thousands at a time. I can't compete with them anymore. Since I made that decision, I enjoy myself much more here than I ever did before. I don't participate in the fighting at all these days. I even started an affair with a woman from Iran who sometimes manifests as a lovely spider. We have a few hours together a night, It's wonderful. You should try it."

Wonderful? Abbie couldn't use that word to describe her experience in the dream over the last few months. Too many battles; too much anger; too many Proctors disappearing and never coming back into Consciousness. Proctors like Rêver and Mechtat, who

Hanker implied had been killed in Basic.

"What about Rêver and Mechtat?" Abbie asked. "You've had to have worked with them over the years; they're from Europe after all. Hanker told me they haven't entered Consciousness in days. They may be dead. That doesn't sound 'wonderful' to me."

Giant snowflakes formed on the air and floated around Malva as they started gliding along the sand toward the water's edge like an Olympic ice skater. "I fought for a long time, Moon. It never stops unless you choose to stop it. Years ago, things were simpler. Now it's one unending skirmish leading to an inevitable war. I don't want to have anything to do with it anymore. Who knows how many years I have left? I'm going to enjoy them, and you can judge all you want."

And Abbie did judge. How could a Proctor turn their back on the innocent? It made sense for the wastes who languished in Thought Bubbles, but for someone who had dedicated themselves to the cause just stepping back one day? Malva choosing to walk away? A disgrace.

"You smell disappointed," Malva stated.

"We are," Vincent's voice echoed.

Abbie looked around as a light throbbed behind the cluster of trees. Bright yellow robes of billowing silk covered Vincent from shoulder to ankle as he strode barefoot, proudly onto the beach. His hair moved in slow motion as always. Without his armor, the Proctor looked particularly majestic.

The snow whipped into a frenzy and formed giant jagged hands of solid ice; sharp fingers pointing at Vincent.

"What do you want, Auspice?" Malva spat.

A mixture of sand and snow crunched under Abbie's feet as she stepped aside and looked at the two dreamers. "You guys have met, I presume."

"That was a long time ago, Malva," Vincent said as an icy index finger grew closer to his eye. He backed away and held his hands up in surrender.

"It wasn't as long as you'd like to remember," Malva said. Their white face cracked along their forehead in angry lines.

"What happened?" Abbie asked. Finally, a chance to get an outside perspective on the handsome Proctor. So much about Vincent seemed needlessly mysterious, and Abbie wanted nothing more than to peel away the layers of pomp and pageantry to see the scared little boy underneath.

"It wasn't a big deal," Vincent assured.

More ice formed around him in shards of razor sickles. "Not a big deal?" Malva yelled. "You came to me specifically to get information. You manipulated me so Catharsis could move in on my dreamers. Not a big deal…" Malva kicked sand, eyes growing pale white.

Vincent looked to Abbie and nodded his head. "Yes, that's all true. But I also told him you were weaker than you actually were, which allowed you to hold him back. I was never loyal to Catharsis; I just didn't have the courage to stand up to him or Alexander. That's not the case anymore. Plus, since then I've been undermining Catharsis at every turn. Just a few hours ago his leeches yanked me into an emotional pit quite painfully before casting me from the dream because I was protecting Moon. She can back that up."

Icy blades slowed a few inches from Vincent's face. Malva looked to Abbie for confirmation.

"I didn't actually see it, but as far as I know he's telling the truth about the last part," Abbie said. She broke off one of the ice sickles. The clear crystalized water turned bright pink and smelled of Raspberry. Abbie began licking it casually like a popsicle. "As for the rest, I can't confirm."

"Moon, come on…" Vincent said as the frozen fingers again began to grow, twisting like a thornbush around his entire body. "I pulled a gun on a guy for you today!"

Abbie smiled like a teasing sister and rubbed her eyebrow. "Yeah, he did. You can let him go, Malva. I'll take responsibility from here on out."

The ice receded, leaving Vincent standing on the beach awkwardly, legs somewhat crooked and arms pulled close to his body.

"Thank you," Vincent said. He dusted frost from his robes and stood up straight.

"I trust Moon, not you," Malva said, drawing dangerously close to Vincent's face. "You say you're different, but people don't change in the dream. They just become a purer version of themselves; more completely who they were to begin with."

"And what does that make you?" Vincent asked, staring back at Malva's white eyes. "Someone who abandons their duty to protect innocent people so they can party with their girlfriend?"

The beach exploded in a rush of sand and snow. Abbie stepped back, blocking her eyes from the shards of what had originally been a very pleasant locale. A towering mass of fine granules swirled into the air, a tornado of contempt, before dropping down in an ear-splitting boom. Vincent flew back and slammed into a tree. The sand settled once more, but no snow or ice remained anywhere on the island.

Malva had vanished.

"You certainly know how to piss people off," Abbie said as she strummed sand out of her hair and buffeted gravel from her cape.

"Yeah, well, it must be my superpower." Vincent staggered back up next to the tree and stretched his neck. "Damn, that hurt. I'm probably going to have some tight muscles when we wake up. I like the cape, by the way."

Abbie reached down and plucked her raspberry popsicle from the beach. Sand covered the treat, and she threw the construct over her shoulder. "So, you have any other Proctors that want to kill you?"

"A few," Vincent admitted. He shook sand from his robes and twisted his pinky finger in his ear. "I told you I had contacts all over up here. I got some of them by doing things that would make certain people mad. But it's those same contacts that are going to help us, and Alice, take down Alexander. In my opinion that makes all the pissy Proctors and whiny Pursuants worth it. Besides, you have more than a few enemies in Consciousness, so you have no place to judge."

"At least my friends trust me," she said, fake smile creasing her cheeks.

"Just wait a little while," Vincent mumbled.

The sword materialized before Abbie even formed the thought in her mind. She ran over and pressed the blade to Vincent's throat. "I trust my friends and they trust me. End of discussion." Abbie stepped back and the sword dissolved. "Oh, and next time I tell you to cut me down and sever me from the dream, you better not hesitate."

Vincent rubbed his neck. "Yes ma'am. And I'm sorry about that. I've never used one of my weapons on someone unarmed before…let alone someone I…work with."

"You were weak."

"Yes, I was," Vincent agreed. He took a deep breath and watched as the orange and white fish swam down from the sky and splashed back into the water. "It won't happen again."

"It won't?" Abbie asked.

"No, it won't."

"Alright," Abbie said, kicking at the sand. "Then tell me, why didn't you say Mozzie knew who you were in the dream? My Basic-self was smart enough to catch on when Mozzie called you Auspice when you had the gun pointed at him. I know you're not telling me everything. You want trust? Everything about you is untrustworthy. One minute you work for Catharsis---"

"Worked *with* Catharsis," Vincent interrupted.

"And the next you're my convenient savior showing up to help. If you hadn't been sweating so badly after the fight at the grocery store, I would have thought you knew exactly what was going to happen next."

Vincent sat down on the sand and kicked his feet in front of him. "Well, I don't know what's going to happen next. I have no idea how all of this is going to end. I've screwed people over, yeah, but that's never been who I am. Hanker taught me well, but I got wrapped up in the emotion of this place. My pill addiction in the physical world didn't help either. I know you're the perfect protector Moon, but the rest of us don't have that luxury."

"You didn't answer my question."

"Yes, Mozzie knows who I am because I was stupid!" Vincent yelled. He smacked his palm against the sand as he said the word 'stupid.' "The only reason he hasn't killed me is because I have intimate details on people close to him that will be released if anything happens to me. Happy? Even now I have to play dirty just to stay alive. Again, I bow to your superiority at never having to stick your hands in shit to pay for your past sins."

Abbie stood silently for a moment. She didn't trust many people. Deep relationships were important to her, but building those relationships took time and effort. In the dream…hell, in the real world, she rarely took the time to foster those connections.

Did she want to start with Vincent?

Not particularly.

Still, he'd proven himself in the dream and in Basic enough for her to give him the benefit of the doubt.

"Alright," she began. "We need to have a level of trust if this is going to work. So far you haven't screwed me over, but that doesn't mean you won't."

"A ringing endorsement of your ability to trust," Vincent muttered with an eye roll.

"But…" Abbie paused and held up her index finger. "What we've done so far has worked. My Basic-self remembered my name. Our thoughts mingled and I came to the forefront a bit during the drive."

"When you were feeling self-conscious?" Vincent asked. "I figured that was you berating yourself for not living up to the greatness of Moon."

"You want to keep working together or not?" Abbie spat. The purple blade reformed in her right hand.

Vincent stood and nodded. "Yes, but one of us is going to need to open up for this to work, and if it has to be me then so be it."

"What are you talking about?"

"Let's work on the shared picture for a second first. Then I'll let you into my thoughts and you can see for yourself who I am underneath all of this dream flesh. You can stay as closed off as you want, but I don't need to keep defending myself and apologizing for my bad decisions anymore. Give me a minute to center myself. I suggest you do the same."

"I'm fine," Abbie assured.

"No, you're not." Vincent walked over to her and planted his feet in the sand. "Right now, you're a jumble of disapproval.

Everything about your stance and facial expression screams judgement. You're annoyed at Malva, you're annoyed at me, but that annoyance quickly jumps to rage. Take a breath and choose to feel something else. You're naturally more on the aggressive side of the emotional spectrum. But aggressiveness and optimism are closer than we think. Switch over to that and see if you can feel some serenity."

He sounded like Hanker, and for good reason.

Again, Abbie admitted to herself that Vincent's patient understanding of mental and emotional interaction exceeded hers. He seemed to feel no judgement for anyone, allowing him to work through psychological impediments and focus on the problem at hand.

No judgement. Abbie could give it a try. She focused on the world around her, seeing what was, not what she wanted it to be.

The breeze blew warm and fragrant. Lights in the city of illumination on the horizon dimmed and went out as dreamers in Europe and Africa slowly began to wake up in the sunlight of a new day. The handful of apparitions dancing around the island faded one by one until only a few remained to enjoy their fantasies. Quiet descended. The peace of the Atlantic Ocean and a relative dearth of dreamers filled Consciousness.

Abbie closed her eyes and smelled vanilla radiating from Vincent's robes. "I wonder what it would be like to live in the middle of the Atlantic or Pacific Oceans when for hours on end there are so few dreamers to clutter up everything."

"It would be peaceful," Vincent replied. "And boring. And lonely."

The water retreated, turning Abbie's forested island into a continent of blue Mountains, orange skies, and insects the size of dogs.

"What image do you want to use today?" she asked. Vincent wasn't perfect, but neither was she. They needed each other. Abbie would continue to be wary, but at least accept Vincent as her ally for the moment.

Sand transformed into grass beneath their feet, and Vincent looked around with a smile. "I've always loved trees," he said. "How about you?"

"Yeah, I obviously have a thing for forests."

Pearly teeth shined between Vincent's lips. He waved his hands over his head and a massive Banyan tree with extended roots formed in the space between them. A symbol of a moon with six stars around it lit up on the trunk. White flowers bloomed in the branches and rained down cinnamon pollen like glitter.

Opening her mind, Abbie accepted the image and felt the kindness in its limbs and leaves. Safety glowed from the plant in a blaze of goodness and compassion. Vincent's eagerness mingled in the tree's fibers, eliciting a chuckle from Abbie.

"This is the image that moves from mind to hand today," Vincent chanted.

"This is the image that moves from mind to hand today," Abbie repeated.

Bark and boughs disintegrated on the wind, leaving Abbie and Vincent to feel the remnants of the construct. Dreamers wandered into the space and floated about. A little girl's voice whispered, *'There was a tree, but now it's gone in Tyler's ear. Tyler's ear is gone.'*

Abbie opened her eyes. The wispy child laughed and wafted into the canopy above.

"That felt good," Vincent said. "Really good. That was a strong, powerful image, I think for both of us."

"It's nice, not fighting anyone for a little bit," Abbie said as an old man dreamed of flying and took off into the air with an exhilarated yell.

Several ghostly women circled Vincent and called out for him to join them at the bar for some roast beef and tennis. He blew them a kiss and walked over to Abbie. "How long has it been since you've simply enjoyed yourself for a night?" he asked.

"A while," Abbie acknowledged. "I tend to be pretty focused. Not sure if you've noticed."

"Ah, I only ever see you relaxing," he waved, playfully.

Despite her attempt to remain stoic, Abbie smiled broadly enough to show teeth. "It feels like the last couple years it's been all about running from one battle to the next. The last few months have been even worse. Proctors dying, the whole thing. I can't turn my back on the victims of all of this."

More dreamers blinked in and out of Consciousness, leaving behind humor, uncertainty, and sometimes sadness. No predators encroached to harass anyone. Musical notes vibrated from the trees in pleasant harmonies.

"This is how it should be," Abbie continued. "It would be nice to experience this more."

"You still can," Vincent said. He took her hand and looked Abbie in the eyes. "I'm not saying every night, but we all need a break now and then. Pursuants aren't everywhere at once."

Abbie pulled her hand away. "Not yet, they're not."

Vincent nodded in concession. "Well, I don't want things to get to that point. And I'm going to prove it to you."

Stepping back, Vincent took a deep breath and opened his mind to Abbie. Conflicting images of a boy playing in the dirt slammed against feelings of worry as someone fell into water and gasped for air. The environment changed around them. Trees softened like marshmallows, leaves drying toward lively shades of pink. Clouds rounded like cartoons with a smiling sun peaking over the edges. The world seemed to relax, lifting Abbie into a zone of comfort and appreciation.

"What are you doing?" she asked.

"Letting you in," Vincent answered. He closed his eyes as a stiff breeze took his hair and blew it backwards over his shoulders.

More memories flooded Abbie's mind. Bacon fried and filled a wall-papered kitchen with its salty savor. A young woman leaned in for a kiss, spilling excitement and apprehension into the world. Conrad Rossi, a decade younger at least and lucid enough to interact, sat across a table with a pencil between his fingers.

'What image moves from mind to hand today?' he echoed.

'I drew some kind of grasshopper, or something,' a teenage boy's voice replied as if spoken through water.

Conrad held up his drawing: a green insect with long legs and wings. *'So did I. Soon you'll remember Consciousness, and you'll know I'm not crazy. You're doing great, Vinnie.'*

'I want to be called Auspice in the dream, and wear cool armor, and be a protector like you,' the boy said excitedly.

'You can be anything you want.'

Time shifted and blurred. Catharsis danced in a dark forest, bright pink and self-important. Fear surrounded Vincent in pungent waves of sickly caramel.

'You talk a big talk, Auspice, but Alexander knows his business here in the dream better than you do.'

'I can get what you need,' Vincent resounded.

Catharsis spun around in a rosy fog and smiled his Cheshire Cat grin. *'Oh, you'd better. Your reputation is impressive, but unless you're twice as good as people say, you have no chance.'*

'I always have a chance.'

Emotions flooded Abbie's mind again. Her own barriers stood firm, but Vincent seemed to make no attempt to gain access to her thoughts. He only shared with her, not seeking reciprocity or any type of exchange. He was open and vulnerable, letting her wander where she would. Memories surfaced all around with laughter, tears, and occasionally shouts of anger.

A young Vincent ran in the rain and played on the floor with Transformer toys. A man towered overhead, smelling of Pabst and sweat, yelling about Vincent being a disappointment. A hairy hand slapped his face. He cried in a corner and pleaded for mercy. A woman rushed over and held him close, whispering that it would be alright. Then the man pulled her away and punched her in the stomach. Vincent stood and ran over, hitting the man as hard as he could, but doing no damage. Fear turned to determination.

The scene morphed and she felt his happiness as Hanker trained him in a red desert with trees that looked like snakes.

Happiness turned to shame as Hanker's face seemed disappointed and betrayed.

'I'm sorry, Uncle,' Vincent said, tears in his eyes. *'I'm trying, but you don't know what it's like to need something like I do. It's just need all the time whether I'm awake or asleep.'*

Hanker pulled his nephew close and hugged him. *'What you need is to let that need go.'*

A dark room materialized. Abbie recognized it as her own apartment. As if looking through Vincent's eyes, Abbie saw herself being pulled down a hallway. Bewilderment screamed from her face as she ran. Suddenly she sat in the Tesla yelling about being dropped off at a police station.

What a lost girl she seemed. Pity filled her chest, but it

wasn't Abbie's pity.

It was Vincent's.

Pity died away and was replaced with admiration. Moon stood her ground, slicing off Contrail's cannon-shaped arms before she shoved her purpled blade into the Pursuant's chest. Admiration shifted to joy. Abbie showed her drawing of the puppy in the cabin. Joy turned to worry as Vincent pointed a gun at Mozzie's head and they rolled around on the floor. Worry morphed into relief as the farmer Danny Ray laughed and thanked Abbie for the M&Ms. Relief grew into affection as he rubbed Abbie's hair in the Oldsmobile. She smiled at him.

'Will Moon be…okay with that?' Abbie's voice fluttered. *'You know her better than I do.'*

'You know yourself better than you think.'

Affection transformed into devotion as Abbie's eyes closed and she fell asleep.

Devotion. Affection. Adoration. Fondness. Love.

Abbie's own emotions suddenly threatened to burst from her mind. The feeling of Vincent holding his arm around her as they bargained with Danny Ray sent ripples along her skin. Memories from Basic seemed to demand her attention in that moment. His stammering as he talked about transactional relationships and tried to reassure her he wasn't being a creeper. Vincent's smile and the way his voice cracked when he got embarrassed.

'Stupid thoughts,' she told herself. *'Stupid girl with a stupid crush. She's so desperate. I'm not desperate. I'm Moon.'*

Even as she thought the words, an image of Vincent calling out her name while being dragged by giant hands into a whirlpool of torment paraded through her mind. The feeling of Vincent's hand on hers as they manifested the image of a puppy to draw. His insecurities laid bare before her now in the ultimate act of emotional intimacy.

She didn't trust him. She didn't love him. She couldn't. Moon was stronger than emotions like love.

Wasn't she?

Abbie stepped back and threw up her walls, figuratively and literally. Towers of brick shot from the ground and encircled her like a barrier. The air grew thick and oppressive. Dreamers fluttered away. Birds cried out and transformed into turtles. Trees blushed, growing deeper into the soil.

Sweat covered Abbie's face. Her hands shook. Never had she experienced someone's thoughts and emotions that purely before. Everyone hid parts of themselves. Everyone held back. Not Vincent. He'd opened his psyche and flooded her with recollection and memory, feelings and worries, inner thoughts and desires. While only a brief glimpse, Abbie felt as if she could have picked through any corner of his brain and dug until every secret had been revealed.

His feelings for her ran deeper than she knew. Deeper than he knew.

"Are you okay?" Vincent's voice shouted from the other side of the stone wall. "I'm sorry about that. Things just kind of come out when you're open."

"Yeah, you were open," Abbie replied. "Give me a second."

Fingers slowly stopped trembling. Breaths normalized until Abbie once again had control over her mental state. A wind encircled her and caught hold of her yellow cape. The walls crumbled, regrowing into the earth like an ancient mound weathered to nothing over hundreds of years. Grass grew between the cracks.

Vincent stepped around the ruined barricade, a worried look on his face. "You can build walls pretty fast."

"It's a talent. I was caught off guard there." She looked at

Vincent and couldn't help but feel admiration. "That was a brave thing, to let me in like that, especially knowing I wouldn't do the same."

"I didn't do it as a down payment for you to open up to me," he shrugged. "I did it because I want you to know me. Not many people do. I hide like everybody else. I don't...want that with you."

He took her hand. This time Abbie didn't pull away. She remembered his sandalwood scent in Basic and wondered whether she liked that better than the vanilla here in Consciousness.

Thunder rumbled and shook the ground. Abbie stepped back as a pounding gale blew through the forest and began uprooting trees left and right. Dreamers disappeared in shouts and screams.

"Pursuants!" Vincent cried. "There's no way they could have gotten the drop on us like this! It must be a group working together."

"No," Abbie breathed. "Something more powerful."

"...More dangerous," Vincent agreed. "Reform your armor before---"

Large stone spikes, six feet long, shot from the ground behind Vincent and rammed through his chest. He screamed, lifted off the ground by the enormous spears. His arms dropped back, feet kicking the air in a last burst of movement.

"Moon..." he gasped, pale mist pouring from his mouth like blood.

"Auspice!" she cried.

Blades formed in her hands, but before she could act, the spikes pulled apart and savagely tore Vincent to shreds. Pieces of his dream form clawed at Consciousness to no avail. His eyes went wide and then twirled to nothing like water down a drain.

"Son of a bitch!" Abbie shrieked. "Show yourself! Catharsis! Alexander! I don't give a crap who you are! Face me!"

Again, the ground roared and roiled. A mass of stone piled up and twisted in on itself. Debris spat into the sky and belched lava onto the grass. Fire erupted before quickly hissing away to harmless smoke. The rocks fell to the side. A large bald man stepped out in blue and yellow armor with a white eagle blazing across the chest, smelling of warm cookies and donuts.

"Hanker?" Abbie asked.

Anger contorted her mentor's normally kind face. The world continued shaking as if the sky itself would come crashing down. Trees burst into flames. Waves of rancid onion throbbed from Hanker and rippled the ground in a tsunami of hopelessness.

"Hanker, stop!" Abbie yelled.

Slowly, Consciousness stilled. Hanker breathed deep. His face softened.

"I'm sorry Moon," he gasped finally, slumping forward with his hands on his knees. "It took everything I had to get here this early. I'm so drugged up right now in Basic, I don't have a lot of control. They're trying to get me to draw more, and I just can't. But I had to find you. We have to hurry."

"Why?" Abbie asked. "What's going on? Did you cast Auspice out by accident?"

"No!" Hanker yelled. The single word wilted the entire area and cast emotion away. "That was the reason I had to get here."

"What are you talking about?"

"Auspice…Vincent…He's manipulating you. He's working for Catharsis."

"No," Abbie said, shaking her head. "He just opened up to me. His mind was accessible. There was no hint of anything like that---"

"It's the truth," Hanker interrupted. He grabbed her arm and pulled her away from the burned trees. “I was worried when you didn’t come back into Consciousness last night. I sent out feelers and swam in the River of Subconscious again before contacting other Proctors to keep an eye out for you. When I came in tonight and felt Vincent’s presence, everything made sense.”

“No, you misunderstand,” Abbie said. “I was distrustful at first too, but just now he---”

Hanker continued walking, yanking her along with him. “We need to move fast. He’ll wake you at any second, I’m sure. The moment I felt his presence I knew what he was doing. He’s keeping you from sleeping at your regular time so that I can’t warn you. This is what he does. He excels at masking emotion and manipulating Proctors and Pursuants alike into giving him what he wants. Alexander and Catharsis need Alice out of the way. Vincent wants to know how they have become so powerful in the dream so he can do it himself.”

Abbie pulled away. “No one is that skilled. I would have seen something in the moment we were linked. Even Alice couldn’t hide herself from me when we connected during the fight with Catharsis.”

A pained look spread across Hanker’s face. “You need to remember everything in the waking world, Moon…Abbie. You need to remember. I don’t have much time. Vincent is so devious. You need to remember.”

“I know! That’s what we’ve been trying to do. I’m closer now with Vincent’s help than I’ve ever been before.”

“He’s selfish and evil!” Hanker bellowed. He grabbed Abbie’s shoulders and squeezed tightly. “I’ve known for a while now that my time was up. Vincent knows who I am. I wasn’t a threat to him before, but once it became known you found out where Alice was, that all changed. That’s why I started pushing so hard for you to remember. For a while I thought Vincent may have turned a corner and returned to his status as a Proctor like I trained him, but now it's clear he has bigger plans. It's only a matter of time before Alexander kills me out in the real world. I knew my days were numbered before, but now it's going to be even sooner because you and I are linked in all of this. You need to remember and take my place in training the others if anything happens to me! You need to stop Vincent! He can't find Alice, do you understand?"

"But everything with the gun, and punching Mozzie, and…"

"Look closer!"

"But I saw Vincent's thoughts! I didn't trust him before, but after that---"

"Look closer," Hanker reiterated. "Read your memories."

Abbie nodded, letting her mind trail off for a moment. Images appeared in front of her from the last 24 hours like three-dimensional slides of a recent vacation.

"Look more closely at the memory," Hanker said. "You'll see I'm telling the truth."

Abbie focused. She felt her fear as they drove away from the supermarket. Calm as Vincent rubbed her head before she fell asleep. Anger at the prospect of living another life she knew nothing about; another version of herself that seemed better in every way. The cabin formed around her with the stench of mold and dust. Vincent smiled his beguiling playful smile.

'Let me use the 'little boy's room' real quick and then let's hit the road,' Vincent said as he stepped toward the hall.

It hadn't seemed out of the ordinary at the time, but now she wasn't so sure. Vincent had hesitated when she asked to see his phone to check the internet. Was he afraid she might see something? Mozzie knew where to find them…which parking lot, which store. Was he tracking the car, or simply checking his texts? Had Vincent gone to the bathroom to send a message?

'Where did you get the gun?' her voice echoed.

'As I was running, I saw the old guy with the curled mustache.'

Suddenly the man from the store materialized. His white facial hair turned up in swirls. He winked at her as she walked by.

'He was open-carrying and had a revolver in a holster on his belt,' Vincent said.

Abbie slowed the image of the winking old man. She looked down at his belt and saw no holster or revolver. Her memory didn't lie. It was too fresh to have mixed with other thoughts and become tainted.

She pictured Mozzie standing on the steps of her apartment holding a silver pistol. The image twisted and morphed, but the gun held in place until Vincent held it against Mozzie's temple.

The same revolver.

'Hey!' the store clerk yelled. *'You can't pull your gun in the store man!'*

Vincent's eyes closed slowly as if a monkey wrench had just been thrown.

'Give me the gun, Auspice,' the Australian had said. The two men rolled around on the floor, both of them afraid; neither of them knowing what to do next.

Sweat dripped down Vincent's forehead in the car as they sped down the highway. Things hadn't gone according to plan. He had to improvise. Dominoes seemed to fall and reform as puzzle pieces. The picture they formed filled Abbie with acidic panic.

Lies. So many lies. Each half-truth became clearer. Tiny moments of deception or a glance that seemed a bit too fast twisted into obvious patterns now that she looked more closely. How did he hide himself so well? No one could be that deceitful. Had he planted emotions as they interacted in the dream so she would feel more affection for him? Was that why Basic-Abbie had become so enamored so quickly?

Memories billowed like cloud, reforming into a giant pink cat with tentacles squirming from its eye sockets. Catharsis lurched toward Abbie in the Thought Bubble. *'Auspice knows what he's talking about,'* the cat said. He knew what Auspice was doing but wanted to speed things along if possible. He was impatient. Vincent's plan required patience. But if Catharsis could extract the information himself, he wouldn't need Vincent's plan anymore.

Catharsis. Vincent. Mozzie. Alexander. Pieces on a chess board that finally came into focus.

Vincent was the knight. Mozzie the Rook. Catharsis the Bishop. Alexander the King.

Abbie was the pawn.

"Shit," she panted. Perspiration covered her body as if the Conscious realm had become an oven of magma and flame.

"You see it," Hanker said.

"Shit!" Abbie repeated more forcefully.

The air suddenly exploded in flashes of white. Abbie stumbled back, aware of the tug that pulled her from the dream.

"What's wrong?" Hanker asked.

"He's waking me up!" Abbie grabbed Hanker's large arm but felt herself being pulled away. "The drawing is already in my subconscious! She'll draw it! She'll trust him!"

"Fight it!" Hanker yelled. He grabbed ahold of her hand to keep her in the dream, but her feet pulled back into the air as if being sucked into a giant vacuum.

"She'll draw the picture of the tree!" Abbie screamed. "She'll remember more about where Alice is! Hanker, help me, please!

They'll kill Alice!"

Her hands slid from her mentor's, and she flew backward. The dream crumbled.

"Draw a skull and crossbones!" Hanker's voice reverberated. "Draw a skull and crossbones!"

The words died off, floating momentarily in her mind before everything went dark. She smelled burnt toast as depression scratched at her brave heart.

CHAPTER TEN

"Abbie, wake up!" Vincent said as he shook her.

"What…What happened?" Abbie's eyes blinked open. Pale light still kissed the sky, but the sun had set behind the mountains. Her tongue scrapped across the roof of her dry mouth, head throbbing. A man's voice called to her from somewhere far away. There was danger.

"We were attacked," Vincent replied. A frustrated breath blew past his lips, and he leaned back in the seat. "They were powerful, whoever they were. Literally ripped me to shreds." He rubbed his neck and twisted it to the side. "I tried to get back in but couldn't do it. I had to wake you up to make sure they didn't do anything to you."

Abbie rubbed her eyes. Fatigue held firmly to her brain, and she wanted nothing more than to go back to sleep. "Something's…wrong. I feel like something's wrong. I…I need air."

The car door swung open, and Abbie stumbled into the cold March evening. Rocks and stones poked at her sock-covered feet and sent her shuffling in discomfort. In the distance she heard the roar of the highway. The sound rolled over the hills, refracting against the cut stone of the old quarry. Deep shadows pressed down from all directions, adding to her anxiety. She leaned against the hood of the Oldsmobile, feeling the cold of the metal. Inner ear spinning her world over and over, Abbie held fast to the car to keep her balance.

Gravel crunched under Vincent's shoes as he stepped around the front of the car and placed his hand on her back. Warmth spread from his palm and helped calm her mind.

"Take a second and breathe," he soothed. "I'm sorry I pulled you out like that. It can be really jarring."

Oxygen filled Abbie's lungs and pushed a wave of queasiness aside. "I'm alright. Just…fuzzy, that's all."

"Let's get into the details of what happened after we draw our picture, okay?" he said. "I really am sorry. If you're deep in the dream and woken up violently, it can leave you fuzzy and even woozy here in the real world."

"I'm okay," Abbie breathed. "Let's draw."

Vincent walked back to his open door and pulled out the same pad of paper they had used at the cabin. He tore off a sheet for Abbie and handed her a pencil before turning his back and walking farther away toward the decrepit portable office trailer.

"What image moves from mind to hand today?" he said in his familiar cadence.

Closing her eyes, Abbie drew without thought or control. Roots took shape on the paper, along with a thick tree trunk, stretching branches, and flowers. For some reason, the smell of cinnamon and vanilla seemed to hang on the air as the graphite laid down dark gray layers across the page. Lastly, in the center of the trunk, Abbie drew a moon with six stars surrounding it.

"I think I'm done," she said. The car's suspension squeaked quietly under her weight as she sat against the hood and ran her hands through her dark hair.

"Me too," Vincent said. He walked back to the car and held out his drawing. As before, the tree looked shockingly similar to Abbie's, right down to the symbol in the bark and the number of flowers among the limbs. "What do you feel when you look at the picture?"

"Kindness," Abbie answered.

"Safety and compassion," Vincent added.

"Yes!" Abbie smiled. "And vanilla."

"I was going to go with cinnamon."

"That too!"

Vincent sat beside her on the Oldsmobile hood. The car rocked backward a few inches before resting under their shared weight. "How are you feeling?" he questioned.

"Cold." Abbie shivered in the night air and rubbed her arms to increase blood flow.

"I got you taken care of." Vincent ran back to the car and came back with his maroon jacket that he had been wearing the night before. He threw it around her shoulders and patted her back. "This should help a bit."

Vanilla overflowed from Abbie's senses. She breathed deep. Vincent certainly smelled good…or his jacket did, at least. Its soft interior captured her heat and held it close for safe keeping. The cold lost its sting and Abbie sat there next to her handsome dream instructor. The thought of danger returned though, and she wasn't sure what to make of it.

"I still feel like something's off," she confessed. "What happened in the dream? You said we were attacked?"

The tale Vincent recounted filled Abbie with wonder. Islands on an ocean of imagination. Ice queens throwing him against a tree. The sharing of thought and memory. Finally, spikes thrusting from the ground and tearing him to pieces.

"I wish you remembered so I could know who attacked us," Vincent said. "But maybe they kept themselves hidden from you too. Who knows? They were powerful, and definitely knew how to destroy someone."

"Did it hurt?" Abbie asked.

"Oh yeah," Vincent admitted. "You feel stuff in the dream just like you do out here. Pain is pain. Your brain responds in the same way."

She placed her hand on his leg. "I'm sorry that happened. I don't remember anything except flashes. Were there flying fish with big eyes?"

"There were!" Vincent laughed. "You see? You're getting closer. Speaking of which: we need more info if we're going to find Alice. Do you think you're recovered enough to give it a try?"

"I think so," Abbie confirmed. Sitting up straight, she closed her eyes and replayed the same angry thoughts she had used earlier that day to help trigger her memory. Traffic. Stupid clients. Mom. Emma. Failure.

'Alice Ashling,' she repeated. *'Alice Ashling.'*

But nothing happened. No images appeared. She pushed against the blackness in her field of vision and tried to force her mind to reveal something, anything, but all she found was a voice yelling about bones or something and telling her of danger.

"I'm not getting anything," Abbie said. "It's not working."

Vincent sat closer to her and put his arm around Abbie's shoulders. "Why don't you try a different emotion. In the dream we chose the tree, which represented safety and kindness. Why not try that instead of anger?"

"Alright." Again, Abbie closed her eyes. Instead of thoughts that pissed her off, she focused on goodness and compassion. Nana Gayle picking her up as a child and telling her breakfast was ready. Her high school art teacher, Mrs. Payne, helping her with an assignment and saying how proud she was. Vincent rubbing her head as she fell asleep. Vincent giving her his jacket. Vincent with his arm around her.

Vincent.

'Alice Ashling, Alice Ashling, Alice Ashling.'

The Sawtooth Mountains loomed on the horizon. A highway weaved alongside a furious river. Sunlight filtered through the trees in a small town. The name 'Stanley' echoed in her thoughts. A small plane took off from a grassy airstrip and flew over a lake so blue it seemed unreal. A plane with a white body and red wings sat parked below in the grass.

The plane. The plane was going somewhere. The plane was taking Alice away.

Just as a dirt landing strip appeared in the distance, Abbie felt immaterial hands wrap around her throat. She gasped but couldn't suck in a breath. She smelled perfume; a soft feminine fragrance that reminded her of a spring meadow in full bloom.

She tried to breathe again, but the pressure grew.

"Abbie," Vincent said, voice panicked. "What's happening? Are you okay?"

Fingers squeezed tighter. Abbie reached up to her neck but felt nothing there.

"Abbie, let go of the thought!" Vincent shouted. "Let go!"

The image of the airstrip crumbled into the blackness of the void. The constricting at her throat lessened and Abbie threw open her eyes. She pitched forward, falling off the car hood and landing on her hands and knees in the gravel. Vincent's jacket fell beside her, no longer keeping the cold at bay. Coughs rumbled from her chest and burned her esophagus.

Vincent shot to her side, kicking pebbles around in the growing darkness. "What happened? Are you okay? What did you see? Why couldn't you breathe?"

"It…was like…" she gasped and swallowed. "Someone was…choking me. Someone from…far away. It was a woman. Somehow…I knew it was a woman."

"Alice," Vincent said. "Do you think it could have been Alice?"

"I don't know. Why would she do that?"

"Alice wants to protect herself; I would bet. She probably thinks you're a danger to her in the real world. Once we find her though, she'll see that isn't the case."

Legs shaking, Abbie stood back up with Vincent's help. He hugged her and patted her back. Shivers tortured her body; not just from the cold, but the feeling of someone trying everything in their power to cause fear and pain.

"Why couldn't I breathe?" she asked finally.

Vincent stepped back and looked at her face. He brushed a stand of hair away from her forehead. "You were touching Consciousness. Someone must have been aware of you looking for the memories. It had to be someone powerful, like Alice. I told you she was dangerous. Anyway, whoever it was, made you think you were being choked, and so your mind made it real. You thought you couldn't breathe, and so you couldn't breathe."

"Is this how those hunters do it in the dream world?"

"Pretty much, yeah," Vincent said.

Brutal chill bit into Abbie's fingers. She sat back on the hood as Vincent reached down and retrieved his jacket from the pebbled ground. Dusting it off, he placed it back around her shoulders.

"I saw more," Abbie continued. "She tried to stop me, but I still saw more. There's a grass airfield just south of a town called Stanley. Wherever she is, you have to fly out of there and land on a backcountry runway somewhere in the middle of nowhere."

"So, we head to Stanley, Idaho," Vincent said, jumping off the hood. "We should drive for a bit and then stop for coffee so we can keep ourselves awake. We'll go back to sleep first thing in the morning."

As Vincent stepped toward the driver's side door, Abbie grabbed his wrist. "Do you think the danger I felt when I woke up had something to do with Alice?"

Lips pressed together quickly and then Vincent opened his mouth to answer. He blinked twice and nodded. "I'm sure of it."

Wind blew from the north and threw the drawings of the Banyan trees across the car hood. Abbie grabbed hers before it could fly away, but Vincent's disappeared into the night.

"We should go," he said.

Abbie stood and grabbed the pencil from where it had rolled into a groove on the hood. The car door slammed, and she could see Vincent's pale outline inside the vehicle as he pulled the keys from his pocket. She paused for a moment, overcome with the need to draw. The car rumbled to life, engine sputtering slightly in the cold. Quickly, Abbie bent over and placed the paper against the vibrating hood. The pencil moved in a circular motion, as if her hand knew what to draw before her conscious mind did. A small skull and crossbones symbol took shape in shaky lines next to her Banyan tree. She stood back up straight and stared at the image, with its dark dead eyes and femur bones set in an 'X' shape behind the skeleton face.

What did it mean? Was it Alice, or something else?

Air blew frigid as wind cried down from the cavernous quarry above. Taking one last look at the ominous skull and bones, Abbie let go of the paper and watched as it toppled away, consumed by the darkness.

"What happened?" Vincent asked as Abbie took her seat in

the car and closed the door. "Is everything okay?"

The skull and bones flashed in her memory.

"No, I'm good," she said. "I'm good. Let's drive."

A steady supply of caffeine kept the pair awake as they crossed from Utah to Idaho. Formless black surrounded them at all times, save for the occasional burst of headlights, or the glow from small towns in the distance. Abbie remained quiet for the most part, contemplating her place in the car, world, and Consciousness. When Vincent had first told her about the dream world and all the craziness that came with it, she had felt deep peace, as if her subconscious confirmed everything he said. Immediately after their first shared dream in the cabin, the emotion toward Vincent had changed to annoyance with a hint of trust. Abbie took that as a sign that even though she couldn't remember what had happened, things had gone somewhat well in Consciousness. Over the course of the day, she had grown to feel rather close to Vincent: half physical attraction, half emotional connection. Everything had moved so fast, there had barely been time to take a breath, let alone delve deeper into one's feelings.

Now when she looked at him though, anxiety coiled like thorned vines in the middle of a well-tended garden.

They talked at times during the drive, but Abbie found herself less and less inclined to continue the conversation. She wanted to believe her worry stemmed from what had happened with the mental apparition trying to strangle her, but for some reason she knew that wasn't it.

By the time morning broke, they had made their way north on Idaho State Highway 75 toward Stanley. Abbie yawned, barely able to keep her lids open anymore. Vincent's eyes looked like a storm of red lightning strikes all the way to his irises.

"We need to sleep," Abbie said, yawning again. Her eyes watered and she wiped at them weakly.

"I know," Vincent agreed. "When I looked at the area on my phone, I saw that there's a lodge across the highway from the airfield. It's the only landing strip in the area, so I'm fairly sure it's the one you saw in your mind, but we'll know when you see it in real life. The pictures showed it's made of grass, just like you said it would be. Anyway, I'm going to book us a room for the day at that lodge. We need to have a little bit more of a rest than I think the front seat of a car will allow. We'll be there in about twenty minutes. Let's get some food and then a room where we can crash. I can barely keep my eyes open."

When they pulled into the parking lot of the Smiley Creek Lodge, Abbie stood in the morning sun to see if anything familiar triggered a memory. Other than the hotel, a restaurant, and a gas station, nothing but pale green grass and rolling meadows stood out against the distant mountains. Snow clung to the benches and sent bitter winds down into the valleys below. Across the road from the lodge stood a rounded, corrugated steel building with an orange windsock blowing toward the south. Three small Cessna airplanes lined up next to the hangar. One had a white body with red wings; a logo of a compass with a lightning strike running down the middle adorning the side. She had seen a similar plane below her in the vision as she left the airstrip.

This had to be the place.

After getting a room for the day, Vincent and Abbie ordered breakfast at the restaurant next door. While waiting for their food, Abbie went to the ladies' room and washed her face. The cold water did little to push back her fatigue. A tired reflection stared back at her from the mirror. Dark bags sagged under bloodshot eyes. Greasy hair fell over her face and reminded her of a drug addict she had known in college.

Where the hell was she? What the hell was going on? While trying to figure out the truth about some mystical dream world, her life had become a waking nightmare.

"Hey," Vincent called as Abbie stepped out of the bathroom into a spacious gift shop full of stuffed teddy bears, shot glasses, and discount t-shirts with 'Stanley, Idaho' blazed across the backs. He walked over from the cash register holding a pair of jeans and a bright yellow long-sleeve shirt with a Native American dream catcher embroidered on the front. "I figured you might want a change of clothes," he said. "I guessed at the sizes. The shirt might be a little too tight, now that I have you in front of me. And there are some hiking shoes over there in the corner that I just saw. I'll get you a pair. What size are you?"

"Eight and a half."

"Awesome." Vincent handed her the jeans and shirt.

"Thanks," Abbie said. She appreciated the gesture but didn't know how to react in her current conflicted emotional state. But a change of clothes would be wonderful, as would having shoes on her feet. Light from the windows seemed to illuminate the shirt as she held it in front of her. "A dream catcher, huh?"

"I thought it was appropriate," Vincent replied, eyes glancing from Abbie's face to the floor and back.

As her attractive benefactor walked over to a rack of hiking shoes, Abbie noticed athletic sports bras hanging along the wall next to backpacks and water bottles. "Grab me a sports bra too," she said, pointing. "Some support will be nice. I want the purple one."

Vincent nodded with a smile and grabbed the purple bra.

"Your wish is my command! And after spending time with you in the dream, it's no surprise what your favorite color is."

Warmth from his tired countenance pushed against Abbie's strange reluctance. What was happening? Part of her wanted to kiss him, while another portion sought to carve his face.

'I'm just tired,' she told herself.

After a fantastic cheeseburger and fries breakfast, followed by a hot shower, Abbie felt like herself again. The shirt proved indeed to be one size too small. Even so, the fresh clothing did wonders for her spirits. She lay down on one of the two double beds in their room and stretched her arms and legs.

"I'm going to give us at least six hours to sleep," Vincent said as he stepped out of the bathroom after his own shower. Steam followed in his wake as if reluctant to leave his side. A towel draped over his bare shoulder and chest, loose black pants covering from his toned abs downward.

"That sounds good," Abbie said, turning away quickly, cheeks flushed with warmth.

Vincent sat down next to her on the bed and touched her knee. "We're so close, Abbie. We're so close it's crazy. You're going to remember everything soon, we'll find Alice, and you'll be safe."

"Then why do I feel like I'm in danger?" she asked, unable to look him in the eyes.

"Abbie," he said, placing his right palm against her cheek and gently pulling her face toward his. Vincent's dark irises seemed to gaze into her soul, kind and vulnerable, yet strong and unwavering. "Do you trust me?"

"…Yes," she answered. Goosebumps tickled her arms.

"If you want, I'll take you back home today after we sleep.

You can go to the police if you feel that's the right thing to do and tell them everything. I don't want you to feel like you're in danger with me. I've asked so much of you. Too much." He looked down. His warm hand caressed her cheek. "I'm only now realizing what these last couple days have done to your mental health. I don't want you hurt in any way. I couldn't handle if anything…We can go home. If that's what you want, I'll do it. I'll do anything you want."

Emotion pulled at the edges of Abbie's lips and threatened to spill out in uncontrolled tears. Vincent wanted nothing more than her safety. He wanted her happiness. How could she doubt that? Here was this handsome, rich, successful man who had been nothing but honest with her. His protection and quick thinking had saved her from unknown dangers, at the risk of his own safety. She had no doubt he cared deeply for her.

And she cared for him too. That could not be denied.

Silence reigned for a moment. Abbie smelled the soap from his damp skin, catching a glimpse of a small mole on his bare left shoulder. He seemed so close; closer than he had ever been before.

Leaning forward, Abbie slowly pressed her lips against his. Vincent's left hand came up to mirror his right, cupping her face and returning her kiss with affection of his own. Their mouths pressed together, lips joining again and again as Abbie's heartbeat rose. She forgot about her need for sleep or to find some mysterious woman named Alice. All she wanted was to feel safe with Vincent and forget everything else in the universe, whether physical or mental.

Vincent pulled away; breath heavy. "I'm sorry, I shouldn't have kissed---"

"I kissed you," Abbie said, leaning forward.

"I don't want…" he began, pulling away. "I mean, I *do* want, it's just, I don't want things to happen because of how tired we are, or because of stress or whatever. If something is going to happen between us, I want it to be for real. Does that make sense? Because we chose it."

Deep appreciation surged in Abbie's heart. Here was a man who wanted something real with her, not just a moment's pleasure. Part of her wanted to kiss him again just because of that, but she refrained.

"When this is all over, and we've found Alice, you and I should probably go on that dinner date you invited me on," she said.

A broad smile revealed Vincent's perfect white teeth. He stood and leaned back on his own bed. "It's a date. I'll take you wherever you want. I'll even wear a tux if you want."

"I'm not high-maintenance." Abbie pulled the covers back and slipped between the sheets. A calmness rushed through her body, as potent as the passion from their kiss. "I just want to sleep and think about all of that later," she said, pulling the comforter up close to her chin. Her eyes closed and the room seemed to fade into the distance.

"Don't worry Abbie," Vincent said from far away. "I'm here to keep you safe. If you can't trust me, you can't trust anybody."

CHAPTER ELEVEN

A flash of lightning struck Consciousness and sent a flow of silver droplets into the air. The orbs hung for a second before slamming into the ground like bullets. Dreamers spirited away, while a group of Proctors and Pursuants stopped their skirmish and walked toward the commotion.

Abbie ascended from a pool of chrome liquid, covered in a sheen of metal that dripped from her in mirrored globes of thought. They floated around her body and coalesced into larger and larger spheres. The emotions of the entire area throbbed in her angry mind, flowing to her in waves of understanding. Without using her eyes, she surveyed the scene before her by pure thought, including how many conscious individuals currently roamed this section of dream space. Five Pursuants, two Proctors. At least three dozen ghostly dreamers dancing here and there, blinking in and out. A gray desert landscape stretched in every direction, sloping upward as if in a giant bowl under a yellow sky. Humpback whales flew like birds overhead, followed by a group of dreamers chattering in some language Abbie didn't recognize.

"'If you can't trust me, who can you trust?'" Abbie quoted under her breath. The last words Vincent spoke before she fell asleep seared into her memory. His betrayal ran deep. He had manipulated her in both the dream and in Basic. If Hanker hadn't arrived when he had and told her of his deception, who knows what information

Vincent may have gleaned from her. Even now they drew closer to Alice, despite her efforts to close her mind. Abbie didn't truly hate anyone, but in that moment, her hatred for Vincent boiled over like maggot infested cheese in a pot full of vinegar.

And she had kissed him. Stupid Basic-Abbie. Stupid lovesick girl!

"Zhè shi shén me?" a woman sitting in a large pink mech suit covered with Hello Kitty stickers asked in Mandarin Chinese. Her comrades stepped slowly next to her, as if intimidated by Abbie's chrome features. Several manifested as creatures from nightmares, while others wore colorful armor like most Proctors chose to create. One of them looked like she had been dipped in honey and smelled of desire.

Which were Pursuants and which where Proctors? Who protected and who hunted? It didn't matter. Abbie smelled lemon. That was enough for her.

With a simple mental command, two of the silver orbs floating next to Abbie shot like missiles, hitting the woman sitting in the mech suit in her head and chest. Violet smoke exploded like viscera from the psychic wounds. She screamed and tumbled from the dream realm in fumes and ash.

The other Proctors and Pursuants bolted like rabbits. Abbie leaped into the air, still covered in her silver liquid body paint. Purple blades manifested, far larger and more serrated than normal. A dark half-moth, half-man creature cowered, before Abbie cut him down with a single blow. She quickly dispatched the others until only one remained; a thin young man dressed in rainbow armor with a sequined cape that touched the ground. He stumbled over a lime cactus and extended his hand toward Abbie.

"I'm a Proctor!" he said in a thick Indian accent.

Thunderclouds formed in the sky and dropped buckets of rain

in a punishing burst. Parched earth soaked up the moisture like a sponge. Chrome cascaded from Abbie's body with the downpour and left a reflective pool at her feet. After a moment of feeling clean, Abbie formed her shiny purple, red, and black armor. The white line appeared down her face without Abbie painting it on like usual.

The rain stopped. Insects flew in the humid air as a bright red eagle landed on a prickly pear and picked at the fruit. A group of dreamers floated over, speaking unintelligible phrases, pointing at Abbie as if seeing a celebrity.

"I'm a Proctor, please!" the young man yelled again. "My name is Sapana!"

"I felt your emotions when I arrived, Sapana," Abbie said, eyeing the scared man in his colorful gear. "Smelled lemon. Admiration. You weren't fighting those Pursuants. You were learning from them; excited by what they were teaching you."

The man stammered; hand still extended. "They were showing us some moves…none of us are very good at combat yet."

"They were training you how to manipulate the emotion of dreamers to help you in a fight," Abbie stated, no feeling to her words. "And I bet you told yourself, 'It's no big deal. I'll feel these emotions and use them to help people.' That's always how it starts." She stepped toward the young man. He scooted backward on his hands and rear, like a crab. "It never stops there, does it?" she continued. "Soon you're manipulating everyone around you."

"No, I just need help fighting…They wanted to have more of a challenge against us so they wouldn't be bored…"

Abbie raised her sword over her head. "You won't manipulate anyone else tonight."

The blade dropped, but with less force than Abbie would usually use. Instead of slicing through the man and cleaving him from the dream instantly, she let it dig into his skull and stop between his eyebrows so he would feel the pain. Tears leaked from his eyes before he faded away in a cloudy burp. The few dreamers still watching the scene shot away like frightened fish, leaving behind trails of steam and apprehension.

The storm lifted higher into the sky but didn't break apart for even a single shaft of sunlight to reach the ground. Darkness continued to cover the area. No trees sprouted from the soggy desert.

"Now you're taking your frustration out on poor little Proctors who don't even know what they're doing?" Vincent's voice called from somewhere behind her. Water splashed in puddles as he approached.

Turning, Abbie stared at the man in his yellow armor, bright as the full moon in a crisp sky. He smiled and stepped lightly, wiggling his bare toes in the water.

"Damn it, Abbie," Vincent said while kicking playfully at the puddle. "I can feel your anger. Hell, everyone within this section of dream space can feel it. You're so pissed at me that you could make me burst into flames. I know what that means."

Abbie glared, blades glowing ever brighter as breaths began coming faster and faster.

"It was Hanker who cast me from the dream yesterday, wasn't it?" Vincent said. "I thought I smelled him but couldn't be certain. He told you not to trust me. I wasn't sure what had happened, but you were quieter during the drive to Idaho, so I was suspicious you may have some conflicting emotions you couldn't quite understand while awake. Hanker. That schizoid son of a bitch just couldn't keep himself in his own time zone, could he?"

A thousand words came to Abbie's mind; words she wanted to shout and scream and use as weapons. But she remained quiet, firm as a Banyan tree. He had already exploited her enough. She wouldn't give him any more ammunition.

"Nothing to say?" he asked, bowing toward her slightly. "I'll get you to talk. Until then, I have enough words for both of us." He turned quickly and held his finger and thumb close together as if illustrating a tiny distance. "I was this close to having you fall in love with me! Shit, I was so close! Damn it, Abbie! I wanted it too; I'm not going to lie. You're amazing."

His words enraged her. *'You're amazing.'* Even now, with everything laid bare, he couldn't stop manipulating.

"And I came at you from so many angles," Vincent continued. "So much work down the damn drain now. Did you know that I used sandalwood oil in the car to help calm you that first night when I was telling you about Consciousness? It's the subtle things that make the biggest difference, you know. I had everything planned. Catharsis almost screwed it up yesterday with his stupid impatience, but I adapted. I really was going to cast you from the dream like you asked, even though I didn't want to; even though letting Catharsis peel your mind may have worked and gotten us the information we wanted. I didn't want to see you hurt. Whether you believe me or not, I don't care. It's true. We could have been something, you and me. I was going to share more of my thoughts with you in the dream this time. And I know, you'll tell me you wouldn't have opened up, but we both know you would have. I wouldn't have gone after any information though, once you let me in. Oh no, that's amateur shit. I would have planted a few strong emotions. We would have drawn a swan, which as you know is a love and pleasure archetype. Then after waking up, I would have kissed you again and our bond would have solidified. Maybe we would have gone further. Who knows? I really wish it had worked. I really do. But Hanker had to show up and screw the whole damn thing!"

"Hanker told me the truth!" Abbie yelled.

Vincent laughed and snapped his finger. "See? I got you to

talk."

Abbie lunged at him, swords flaring in each hand. Just as she brought them down, the world spun and suddenly Abbie appeared behind Vincent. Her sword cut a cactus to pieces, but not her intended target.

"You're good at twisting perception, but not the best." Vincent strolled around as he spoke, kicking at puddles and leaving footprints behind in the mud. "When I appeared as Resin to learn more about you, I was surprised you were so good at it."

"You weren't Resin," Abbie said, twisting around and planting her feet. The memory of a man in a fine suit turning into a tornado made of tar came to her mind. "I can tell the difference between unique constructs when Pursuants change shape. People can't hide who they are."

"And yet, I let you into my mind and you saw only what I wanted you to see; felt what I wanted you to feel. So why couldn't I have done the same two nights ago when I ripped Merquery in half?" Vincent's face contorted, skin darkening from his natural olive to a black so deep it seemed to absorb the light around it. Armor dissolved, replaced with a three-piece suit. The emotions surrounding him altered as well. Pleasant vanilla decayed into ammonia. Resin, the Pursuant Abbie and Merquery had fought two nights ago, manifested in sheets of despair and ooze. No hint of Vincent remained.

"No one can mask themselves that well," Abbie said, spinning in place as tar erupted from the ground and looped around her and Vincent in a loud roar. "It's a trick!"

"It's all a trick!" Vincent shouted as Resin, voice deep and rumbling. "Everything in Consciousness is a trick! You spend enough time swimming in the subconscious and less time fighting pointless battles and judging everybody, you'd be able to figure it out too."

A shockwave blew from Abbie's enraged psyche. She jumped toward Vincent/Resin and crossed her swords in front of her, ready for a killing strike. "I cast you out before. I'll do it again!"

Smoke and rock belched from Vincent's chest and grabbed Abbie in midair like a globular hand. He squeezed mercilessly, pushing her head back with an oversized thumb.

"That's because I let you!" Vincent bellowed.

He tossed Abbie to the ground, but she altered perception and reappeared over her enemy, kicking him in the face. In a single motion she flipped in the air and swiped at his chest, removing the offending arm just as she had during their first meeting.

"You didn't *let me* do anything," Abbie said, standing back up.

"Oh, I didn't?" Vincent asked. His bulbous, shadowy shape shrunk and pulled into itself until once again a warrior of light stood before her. Vanilla replaced ammonia. The cacti in the area seemed to sing in pleasure as he approached. "Resin was a means to an end. I needed to know who I was dealing with after we met at the hospital."

"So, you pretended to be someone else?"

"It's not pretending if you actually believe you're a different person," Vincent said. "That's how it works. I choose to be someone else. Resin has different motivations, etc. It's not that hard for me to make the switch."

Abbie stomped, shard-like blades growing brighter. His talent for deception stretched even to himself. "You can hide who you really are? That's not…I don't…"

"Ah," Vincent grinned, eyebrows pressing down over his dark eyes. "Did I break Moon? Come on, Abbie! You think you understand Consciousness, but you don't."

"I understand you're working for Alexander and Catharsis! I

understand you want to kill Alice so no one can stop Alexander from doing whatever it is he has planned."

Pulling off one of his yellow gloves, Vincent picked at his teeth with a fingernail. "Well, that right there shows how little you know. Everything is political, even here in the dream. You don't even know who's fighting who, or who's working for who. You spend too much time focusing on the little picture, like my uncle Conrad, and not enough time on the big picture. Alliances are forged and broken overnight. Catharsis and Alexander, ptthh," he spat. "You work with who you've got to work with and then you move on. Alexander has his dictators he likes to play with; Catharsis would betray me at the drop of a hat. He even tried to screw my plan by simply capturing you and prying the thoughts from your mind like a moron. Until I don't need either one of them, I play the game."

A purple blade swung at Vincent's head, but he dodged easily and jumped onto a passing cloud a few feet in the air.

"This is all a game to you?" Abbie seethed, preparing for another strike. "This is people's lives. This is the world."

Vincent shook his head and jumped back down to the desert sand. Craters exploded around his feet as if he'd dropped from a hundred miles above. "You have no idea what's really going on, sweet Abbie-poo. No idea. I'd tell you, but I don't think you'd stop trying to cut me in half long enough to listen. It's too bad, because if you and I were to team up, Alexander and Catharsis wouldn't stand a chance. They're afraid of you. Honestly. Come with me and I'll show you so much about Consciousness that has been forgotten. I've delved deep enough to access memories from ancestors a hundred years ago. Just brief flashes, but still. With you by my side, we'll go even deeper. I'll swim the river and find secrets that will rock this plain of existence."

"I'll stop you!" Abbie yelled. The few remaining dreamers in the vicinity flickered like broken lamps and dispersed at the power of her ire. All life seemed to flee from the two powerful forces locking eyes. "You're a manipulative bastard! I'd sooner cut off my own head than spend a second with you."

"Abbie, Abbie, Abbie," Vincent chirped liked a kind kindergarten teacher. "You're amazing, truly, but let's face it: Abbie Kinder doesn't stand a chance against the likes of me, whether I'm with Catharsis, Alexander, or whoever else wants to play puppet master."

"My name is Moon!"

Vincent clapped his hands and snickered. "Right. Moon. Like 'Moon' is a real person and not an ego construct to keep you from accepting your faults. You watch your own life like a television show. It's sad. I'm willing to bet you don't even think of yourself as Moon when you're here. I bet you're Abbie all the time no matter where you are, and you just can't admit it."

"I'm Moon!"

She ran at him and jabbed with her right blade. Vincent blocked with his protected forearm and countered, striking Abbie across the cheek. Spinning, Abbie swiped with her left, but Vincent shifted position and now stood ten feet farther away. He put his glove back on and twiddled his fingers as if doing exercises before a piano recital.

"Whatever you say," he laughed. "Just keep telling yourself you're Moon and not Abbie so that you stay separate. You're so divided you could never beat me here."

"Then, Hanker will stop you!"

"Oh please! If it hadn't been for Uncle Conrad, I wouldn't even know who you are. All I knew was that Moon had learned Alice's location. Since I knew Moon was being trained by my poor, catatonic Uncle, I also knew where to go. Once the doctors called and told me about my uncle's surprise drawings, I knew you must be close to him somewhere. I hopped on a plane and here we are. Easy-peasy.

"I'm all about connections," Vincent continued, "and let me tell you, Uncle Conrad is my best one. He gets to know so many Proctors. Just by meeting with him and crying a little bit about pill addictions and whatever shit I can make up; I always get such good info. He sees through it lately, but for a while I had him turning wherever I wanted. Love is a dangerous emotion that way. I don't go in for that. Keeping things transactional is the only way to go. Certain people needed to know Alice's location. You know where Alice is. I found out who you were thanks to Uncle Conrad's desperate attempt to get you to remember the dream, and then tracked you down as Resin so I could see you work before I sent Mozzie into your apartment to wake you up. Simple. Transactional."

Abbie screamed and brought both her swords down on Vincent. They never hit their target though, as Vincent manifested his own blades and blocked her attack. A smug odor, like thick cologne, pulsed from his orange rapiers. He pushed back against Abbie with force rivaling hers.

"We're going to have fun when we wake up," Vincent said, avoiding a swipe from her blade. "You're going to take me to Alice whether you want to or not. You don't have a choice when you're awake, do you Moon? I've got you wrapped around my finger!"

"She'll feel nervous," Abbie assured, kicking at her enemy. "She'll feel angry and nervous. I'll make sure of it."

"And I'll talk my way around you like I have for the past two days."

Blades swung with powerful force, as Abbie's rage funneled directly into her weapons. Vincent leaped back and avoided being cloven in two.

"You're so predictable," Vincent blathered, apparently

enjoying the sound of his own voice more than a symphony of the most prolific music. "Always with the anger."

"You gotta use what works," Abbie replied. She pivoted backward and ducked low. Coming up fast, she punched Vincent in the face with the butt of her sword. He stumbled. Abbie used the opening to ram both sword points into his chest. They skewered him, poking out his back like prongs of purple fury. He gasped, his own weapons dissipating from his hands.

Vincent looked down at the blades poking out of his sternum. "That hurts," he coughed. "But…remember when I told you in the car…about how when your mental strength…collides with someone else's you can cast them from the dream?" Vincent reached up and slowly pulled Abbie's shard-like swords from his chest. He held them to his sides as if they were now his. Their purple shade fluttered, overcome by Vincent's own mind, and transformed into orange blades of conceit. "I think you'll find my mental strength more than equal to yours."

He thrust with his right hand, just missing Abbie's head as she pivoted. Reforming fresh weapons, Abbie countered by swiping at Vincent's legs. He jumped and twirled, trying to kick at her in response.

They parried and lunged, partners in a violent dance that cut across the desert. Several hunters, manifesting as giant cockroaches, jumped aside as the combatants carved their path like an emotional chasm. Dreamers materialized and cheered as if watching a boxing match or some Olympic event where a gold medal would be awarded to the winner.

Each effective block from Vincent frustrated Abbie. Her attack was perfect, but he kept pace and matched her stroke for stroke. They scrambled up an embankment and Abbie formed giant hands out of the rock to grab her enemy. Vincent destroyed them with a swipe of his sword and fired a blast of dark blue grief. The emotion hit Abbie in the stomach and toppled her backward. A rock scraped against her armor and banged her leg, but the impact of the grief took a greater toll. Her blades sputtered as sorrow clouded her thoughts. A memory of answering the phone and hearing her friend Heidi sobbing about her brother Casey's suicide tore at her heart. Abbie had loved Casey and thought he was hilarious. Why would he kill himself?

Pain, anguish, grief.

Her sadness intensified. The dreamers in the periphery who a moment before had been thrilled by the display of fighting skill, began to wail, and cry. The grief had affected their emotional state every bit as Abbie's. Many wafted away, while others held their heads in their hands and wept.

A hand grabbed Abbie by the hair. "When we wake up, we still need to draw a picture together, don't we Moon?" Vincent growled in her ear. She struggled, but the grief held her firm. "I can't cut you loose until we decide on what we're going to draw. It will need to elicit a powerful emotion. How about something like a bird sitting in a crocodile's mouth? Something to make you sad? You know, I still might be able to get your real-world self to fall in love with me."

Abbie opened her eyes and thought about how mad she was at Casey for committing suicide; how that rage had devolved into emptiness and indifference. That apathy focused into a gray pinpoint and fired from her pupils in a solemn cold so powerful it burned. Energy hit Vincent on the right side of his face and sizzled like liver in a frying pan. He screamed and fell back, hands cradling his smoking skin.

Purple blades swung through the air as Abbie took advantage of the opening. She wanted to cut his arms off; really make him feel it.

Another surge of emotion flashed from Vincent in bluish-gray ripples. Depression snarled like an unseen beast and grabbed hold of Abbie's courage. Thoughts of doubt overwhelmed her. The desire to lie down and do nothing seemed suddenly so rational. Her blades disappeared. Abbie stumbled back, exerting all her mental strength to remain standing. Memories of waking up every Monday morning, staring down another week at a job she couldn't stand, with no desire to move or think or feel. Her fear of inevitable failure if she tried something even remotely courageous in her life. Nothing she did mattered. Little stupid, worthless Abbie. Never enough. Never as good as Emma. Never going to amount to anything. No one cares. Everyone is better off when you're not around.

Vincent trotted over to her, face slowly healing the ashen scars from her assault. "Most of the time you're so in control it's hard to use emotional attacks against you. Guess I got your number, huh? Makes sense. I mean, I do know just where to poke…"

Gray swells intensified, draining the color from the sand and cacti around Abbie. Her armor melted like butter in an oven and dripped in colorless lumps at her feet. Joy died somewhere close by. A crow cawed in mourning.

"You're an easy book to read, Abbie," Vincent continued with a happy bounce to his voice. Abbie stepped back, but he advanced. "Your entire life is like fourth-grade level study. Twenty minutes on your social media pages told me everything I needed to know about you. Five minutes in the car filled in the rest of the gaps. The job you want to escape but never will. The sister you'll never live up to. The mother you can't please. The grandmother you want to emulate but will never match. Even your father is disappointed in you. You're alone."

A weak blast of purple energy petered from Abbie's fingers and popped like a tiny firework against Vincent's chest. He laughed; butterflies materialized on the sound with a sugary scent.

"Don't you know that you're going to work at that sign shop

the rest of your life?" Vincent said, casting a shadow on her hunched form. "You don't have the talent for anything more than that. You don't have the courage to go after what you want. Nana Gayle knows it. Everyone knows it."

Depression intensified. All of Abbie's self-doubt piled on. If she opened her eyes, all she would see would be her failures and missed opportunities.

Vincent was right, wasn't he?

No! He's a liar!

He's right. You're nothing.

No!

Nothing…

He grabbed her shoulders and pulled Abbie's face close to his. "Now, let's figure out what we're going to draw…What are you seeing right now? Show me…" he whispered.

A stone hand made of pure marble broke from the ground next to them. Abbie looked over, trying to keep the image from materializing, but unable to clear her mind. The hand reached, straining its fingers as if in pain at the thought of never attaining its goal. A snake coiled around it, reaching its head back as if about to strike at the wrist.

"Oh, wow," Vincent breathed. He released Abbie and she stumbled. "This is the image that moves from mind to hand today."

"No…" Abbie said, voice weak.

"This is the image that moves from mind to hand today!" he screamed. The world shook, clouds burning off in the light of a piercing blue sun. "Feel the emotion of it! You can't escape it! Burn it into your subconscious!"

Rocks suddenly flew into the air, and Vincent jumped back. The marble hand cracked, breaking in two, falling over and crushing the snake. Abbie's mind cleared. The commotion had not been created by Vincent.

"Shut ya gob, you two pot screamer!" Fraelig shouted as she burst from the hillside in a dramatic explosion of fire. She stood there for a second as if posing: a large, muscular woman in pale blue armor, curly red hair billowing in a stiff wind. Before Abbie or Vincent could get their bearings, Fraelig slammed her fist against the ground. The shockwave tossed Vincent backwards onto a cactus.

"Fraelig!" Abbie yelled. All depression seemed to wash away, replaced with relief.

An oversized canon appeared over Fraelig's shoulder with at least three separate barrels. She fired a volley of orange energy at Vincent in a punishing assault that spit dust and sand into the air all around.

"Get behind me, Moon," Fraelig ordered. "This is the bastard who cut me out of the dream last night. Caught me by surprise, he did, and ran me through. Looks like he had you on the ropes too."

Once again in charge of her emotions, Abbie reformed her blades, ready to strike. "I'm with you! Let's wake this…"

She paused. If they woke Vincent up, he would just wake her up back in the hotel room. They would draw the picture of the stupid hand and snake, and the whole thing would start all over again. She would remember more about Alice, and she would take him there, not knowing her danger. Something had to change.

"We need to run!" Abbie said, grabbing Fraelig's shoulder.

Fraelig looked back at her, still firing the comically massive cannon. "What do you mean?"

"Run!"

Abbie pulled Fraelig toward the top of the hill. The larger

woman tossed the weapon aside and charged through the sand.

"Where are we going?" Fraelig asked.

"Anywhere but here." Abbie looked back as they reached the top of the knoll. Smoke covered the area below, obscuring Vincent from view. Ahead of them, a cliff face loomed, staring down on a river of pure unconscious thought. "Grab onto me and jump!"

"Jump where?"

A shape moved in the smoke below, glowing in a yellow hue. Abbie looked down at the river of thought below.

"Just hold on!"

Strong arms reached around Abbie and pulled her close. Fraelig smelled clean, like odorless soap. She stood so tall her chin touched the top of Abbie's head.

"Alright, I'm holding you. What we doin'?" Fraelig asked.

No words left Abbie's lips as she pulled the two of them into the air before dropping toward the river. They fell; yellow rocks speeding past in a blur. Wind blew through Abbie's hair like a peaceful whisper. The river rushed up to meet them.

"I don't like water!" Fraelig shrieked. She began to squirm, loosening her grip on Abbie.

"It's not real water," Abbie said. "It'll be fine!"

They hit the surface with a slapping splash, plunging into the swift depths. Water surrounded them in cool currents that tickled the skin and the mind. Blue light twinkled on the surface above as they sank deeper. Fear immediately billowed from Fraelig in yellow torrents that spun with the water in twisting undercurrents. Her armor cracked and faded. She panicked, trying desperately to swim toward the surface.

"Fraelig," Abbie said, voice singing on the liquid's flow. "Breathe! You're not really underwater."

Bubbles roared from Fraelig's mouth as she screamed in terror.

"Fraelig! You're not drowning! You can breathe down here just fine. These are just unconscious thoughts. There's nothing to be afraid of!"

No words seemed sufficient. Fraelig contorted and reached, kicked and grasped for air, but nothing helped. Her eyes went wide as a final bubble emerged from her nose. Red hair floated motionless as the Australian's fear got the better of her. Weak spasms shook her thick arms and legs, before Fraelig's dream form dissolved like sugar in a whirlpool.

"Damn it!" Abbie spat. Without Fraelig's help, she wouldn't have escaped Vincent's emotional snare. If she had known the woman was afraid of water…No, this was the best route of escape either way. Fraelig will rouse and be able to return to the dream. But by the time she reached the theta state again, Abbie would be in another part of Consciousness, doing her best to stay hidden.

And to find Alice.

Nothing could be done for Fraelig at this point. Her fear had gotten the best of her. Drowning in a river of thought didn't scare Abbie. Of course, these waterways offered other dangers. It was easy to lose oneself when immersed in the unconscious feelings of others. Errant thoughts would creep in, and you could never be sure whether the idea was yours or someone else's. Occasionally in the past, Abbie would swim, seeing memories reaching back in time. Once she swore she saw a dead body wrapped in a Confederate flag on a battlefield littered with soldiers in blue and gray uniforms. Maybe it had been a memory from a reenactment. Maybe it had been something more.

Vincent claimed he experienced ancient memories that still lingered in the shared mental space. He mentioned something about swimming in the subconscious. He had to have meant the rivers of thought. Abbie didn't want to delve deep enough to discover the truth or lie behind such an assertion. But rivers like this one would likely be the best place for such possibilities; collections of abandoned memory given current.

The flow moved her along quickly. She floated below the surface, feeling the water's cool caress. No experience quite matched swimming under water while breathing at the same time. For Abbie, it was better than flying. The landscape above changed rapidly as dreamers added their thoughts and emotions to the mix. The sun changed colors, clouds came and went, while the sky rippled with sensation. Shapes above twisted along the water's undulating surface, giving the entire world the feel of a colorful kaleidoscope. Slowly, peace descended on Abbie's recently tortured mind. All thought of depression or grief faded like a nightmare in morning's light. Vincent had indeed known which buttons to push, which soft spots to poke. His manipulation knew no bounds. She wanted to be angry, but the water seemed to siphon the vitriol from her mind and body, leaving her rested and restored.

After incalculable time that could have been measured in minutes or hours, Abbie swam toward the surface. Warm sunlight poured from the sky in yellow droplets and rippled like rain on the water's surface. Ethereal dreamers waded in slowly, faces serene as praying monks. They spoke no words, unlike most dreamers who spouted gibberish. These dreamers seemed peaceful and completely satisfied. No conflicting emotions stirred, no repressed desires.

Mud squashed under Abbie's feet as she plodded out of the river. Rolling hills covered in waving sheets of pink fabric stretched to a horizon of green mountains. The extended cloth flags, some of them one hundred feet long, reached toward the blue sky as if being blown by a giant fan. They waved and contorted in peaceful flutters; quiet ruffle sounds competing with the rush of the river. A smell like warm laundry brought an unfamiliar peace to her thoughts. To

Abbie's right, a small, thin man, bronzed skin with glowing lines of gold painted along his arms and legs, cut carrots from a drooping orange willow tree. Age lines covered his face like worn leather. Tiger stripes made from the same shimmering gold paint smeared across his cheeks. Curly black hair fell to his shoulders. He wore nothing but an ornate white smock with geometrical designs of shiny sapphire wrapped around his waist and thighs.

The man bowed his head toward the river. “You shouldn’t swim too long or too deep,” he said with a strange accent. “Easy to get lost.”

“I’ve swam before,” Abbie replied, squeezing water from her hair. “I know how to keep myself safe.”

“Some do,” the man nodded.

“Where are we?” Abbie asked.

The man’s eyebrows moved up slightly. “Everywhere and nowhere. That question has no meaning here.”

Armor reformed around Abbie. Her hair dried instantly. “I know that,” she said with impatient bite. “I meant on the emotional spectrum. There are only a few dreamers here. I can feel it. I’m not overwhelmed with the numbers like I was yesterday. What is the emotional underpinning of this place?”

“Can’t you smell it?” the man asked. He sniffed the air and smiled almost imperceptibly. “Sage and desert hibiscus. Contentment.”

“I smell towels right after they come out of the laundry,” Abbie said.

“To each his own,” the man replied, returning attention to his hanging carrots. “Different cultures, different families, different fragrance. It’s contentment all the same. Naturally, few dreamers come here. It’s hard to reach and even harder to maintain. Stronger emotions like lust and power are always more alluring. Dreamers tend to mix in places where many emotions flow together in confusion and chaos. Still, the river leads some here. It's hard to let yourself flow with the stream without reaching some level of serenity. Especially if you love water. I've never seen you here before."

Abbie looked around. Everything about the area elicited a calmness she couldn't deny…and in truth, didn't want to leave. Even so, she couldn't stay. "My job isn't about contentment."

"You're a fighter."

"Exactly," Abbie agreed.

"No one to fight here." The man slowly waved his arms wide as if gathering in the world. "No one fights here. Nothing to fight."

The words hit Abbie harder than the man could have ever intended. A truth resonated. Some areas of Consciousness were easier to reach than others. On some level she knew this fact already, but it never seemed pertinent before. Why go to a place where no Pursuants would be active? Someone like Catharsis would have an incredibly difficult time reaching contentment and being able to enjoy the respite of peace, especially if he were hunting someone. You can't be content if you're dissatisfied with your existence. People hungry for power could never bring themselves here. Alice had to know all of this as well. Perhaps she traveled these less trodden paths to keep herself out of the fray that tore things apart on more common emotional levels.

"You've heard of Alice Ashling, right?" Abbie asked.

A weariness seemed to slump the man's shoulders. "Yes."

"Does she come here ever?"

"The river brings many things," he said, turning his back on Abbie. "I take heed of none. Not of the powerful nor the weak. Here all are the same. Those like you never remain for long. You can't. None can who seek more than this."

Willow branches lifted off the ground, and the man walked under them into the darkness of the tree as if saying, 'This conversation is over.' He disappeared behind leaves, carrots, and thin boughs. Waving fabric and swirling water filled the sound of his silence.

The ground tilted to the left a few degrees. Abbie looked down at her feet. Concrete stared back up at her where seconds before she had felt grass. Looking back up, the flowing flags and willow trees had been replaced with a shuffling cityscape of morphing buildings and asphalt roads that mirrored back on themselves seemingly to infinity. A dark sky stared down, neither day nor night, just formless gray. Gurgling water still reached her ears from the river behind her, but everything else, from the chemical smell to the feeling of loneliness, stood in contrast to where she had just been. A rush of emotion and thought rattled Abbie's brain. Millions of dreaming people now swelled in her emotional neighborhood. Contentment felt incredibly far away.

"You weren't kidding about not being able to stay," she mumbled as if the man still stood next to her. "Maybe next time you could say something meaningful before hiding in a tree."

Two ghostly young lovers holding hands rushed past her, leaving behind crisp adoration. They leaped into the air and floated over the river before twirling upward.

"Now what do I do?" Abbie asked the empty air around her. Vincent would be searching for her at that moment. Since she had fought against him, he would likely want to reenforce the hand and snake image again to make sure she would draw it in Basic. Abbie needed help, and no one from her conclave would be asleep at this time of day. It felt like forever since she had laughed with Pinely, or taught young Brainstorm how to conjure a sword. Alice was her only hope now, and Abbie didn't even know when Alice would be in Consciousness at any given moment…or whether she would even help her. "Alice, where the hell are you? How do I find you in here before we find you out there?"

Abbie focused on the river. Deep consciousness flowed there. The Content Man had said the river brought many things to his shores. The river flowed throughout Consciousness in different places; a collection of unorganized thought that coalesced in the shared space. Swimming it's waters could be a thrill, as Abbie had experienced many times, but losing yourself, your own identity, was a real possibility for untrained Proctors who had less emotional control. She had seen young men in the past come out of the water confused, experiencing memories of past lives that weren't theirs. Ever after they seemed affected, and Abbie wondered if the subconscious residue from the swims spilled into their waking lives. It had to. If Vincent had swam deep enough, he could have learned forgotten things left over from the past; a dangerous gamble, but one that could have paid off in so many ways.

Could Abbie find Alice by swimming deep into the subconscious?

No. Vincent, or Catharsis, or Alexander would have tried it already. That's probably the reason Vincent explored the river in the first place.

But none of them had a connection to Alice in the dream world. Abbie did. And that connection apparently still existed. The memory of invisible fingers wrapping around her neck as she tried to picture Alice's whereabouts brought a chill to Abbie's body. Somehow Alice had felt the intrusion and fought back.

Abbie could do the same. Only Alice could help her. One way or another Vincent would find the mythic woman now that he had narrowed his search. Abbie might still unknowingly help him do it in Basic. Time wasn't on her side.

Commotion on the street behind her pulled Abbie's thoughts back to the present. A group of dreamers yelled and ran down the sidewalk, followed by a Pursuant dressed like a military police officer with no face. Feelings of powerlessness, smelling of mold in a wet bathroom, poured from the faces of the fearful people.

"Đừng chạy trốn!" the officer called in a deep, thunderous voice.

Before the Pursuant noticed the Proctor next to the river, Abbie formed her blades and stabbed him in the chest. He pulled back, turning into black mist in an attempt to escape. She cut upward and finished the job, leaving his consciousness fractured and unable to remain in the dream. He barked loudly and smelled of fish before collapsing like a shower curtain cut from its rods.

The dreamers stopped and approached Abbie cautiously. Her blades evaporated, and she tried to manifest a calm emotion, like acceptance, to help them recenter in their previous psychological state. Her attempt proved successful. Several of the sleeping people changed color from a pale yellow to a soft white mixed with the brighter shades of their imagined selves.

"You're good to go," she said. They looked at her as if her words made no sense. "Sorry, I don't have time to try and connect with you so we can communicate. Just, move along, or whatever. I have bigger things to deal with."

Turning from the dreamers, Abbie dove into the river. Cold water bit at her skin with far more sting than before, as if the liquid knew of her goal and disapproved. She reminded herself to breathe, since the sensation of water made her instinctively hold her breath. Mind and body pushed together, forcing her consciousness deeper into the stream. The farther down she swam, the murkier things became. At first, light filtered around her in pale shafts, but soon only faint sparkles remained, like specks of glitter on an updraft. The water grew colder as well. Emotions mixed and swirled, nothing distinct taking shape. A wayward thought touched Abbie's mind; annoyance at a person she had never met named Ishaan. An image illuminated her memory: hiking a snowy trail behind a donkey laden with leather bags. Snow hit her face; the longing for a warm meal clawing her belly. A dog barked in a field of wheat as a tractor rumbled by. She smelled pastries and felt lips press against hers.

None of these recollections belonged to Abbie. The deeper she swam, the more thoughts appeared. She closed off her perceptions as best she could but found the constant pounding of ideas and opinions overwhelming. A thought warned her to turn back and swim toward the surface. She knew it came from her own mind. Even so, she refused to listen. Abbie had to find Alice. She couldn't let Vincent win. Alice would help her. Alice would know what to do. Together, she and Alice could stop the darkness from growing. Abbie focused on her own emotions. Using the technique Vincent had taught her in the cabin, she tried to establish a link with her quarry.

'Alice Ashling, Alice Ashling, Alice Ashling.'

Whispers of names and places scratched her ears. A silver statue of a woman fought a pink cat. The image of a dirt landing strip in a forest. Other memories invaded however, and Abbie began seeing buildings on fire, feeling the pain of a broken bone, and the fear at the moment someone slips and begins falling down a set of stairs.

The water spun around Abbie and suddenly she could no longer tell which way was up and which down…if such designations even applied in the subconscious river. A remembrance of hitting someone she loved filled her with shame and anger. Feelings of loss turned her side to side. Someone whispered they loved her, before dying in a car accident.

"Stop it!" she screamed, hands flying to the sides of her head. "These aren't my thoughts! These aren't my memories!"

She tried desperately to swim back up, no longer aware of direction. More and more images, memories, and dark intentions paraded through her frontal lobe. Her name was Abbie…or was it Chenghiz? She had grown up in Salt Lake City Utah…or was it Las Vegas? She was 24 and worked in a sign shop…or was she 76 living in a hut by the beach in Madagascar?

"Alice!" she called, losing sight of who Alice even was. Why was she yelling her name? Was *she* Alice?

Just as Abbie began to black out, something seemed to lift her from the river. Water sloshed around her body with the force of a firehose. Warm air touched her face again. The jumble of images and feelings receded. Her lungs expanded and contracted. She was Abbie again. She was Moon. She had to be Moon.

Abbie washed up on the banks of the river, surrounded by sand dunes that heaved and dropped like tiny mountains until they vanished in the distance. A cough burned her throat, and she spun onto her stomach as if expelling real water from her lungs. Black liquid belched from her lips, like demons being exercised by a priest.

"You went pretty deep," a woman's voice echoed all around. The air itself seemed to tingle as the sound moved across space. "I'm surprised you went that far. Impressed, really."

The warm sand soothed Abbie's mind. She tried to focus on the voice, but found it came from no distinct direction, rather everywhere at once. Sitting up, Abbie looked out over the wide river and dead dunes beyond. A wind blew, carrying dandelion fluff and blossoms.

"Show yourself, Alice," she commanded.

Sand vibrated and shuddered, as if someone had angrily shaken a snow globe. "I don't take orders from you, Proctor Abigail-Moon-Kinder!" the voice bellowed.

"Please!" Abbie implored. "You have no idea how much danger you're in!"

Time slowed. The water on the river's surface held still,

thickening, and changing from a clear blue to opaque silver. Chrome covered the waterway like a shiny pollutant. Then, in the center, a bulge formed as if something rose from the stream. A shapely form emerged of a long-haired woman, shiny as molten metal, eyes glowing like an angel…or a devil. Long robes, as silver and gleaming as the rest of her, flowed on the breeze as if they weighed nothing.

"The only danger I'm in is because of you," Alice said. She walked across the water, reflecting sunlight in a thousand directions with each step. "You're the only threat I see."

"It's not my fault," Abbie said, standing up.

"I know," Alice admitted. The sand sizzled under her chrome toes as she stepped on solid ground. "But it doesn't matter."

"Why not?"

Alice's eyes flared like tongues of fire escaping from captivity. "Because either way…I'm going to have to kill you."

CHAPTER TWELVE

Instinctively, Abbie leaped away from the shining woman. Sand pushed against her feet and up between her toes. Blades manifested in purple flashes of anger. "What do you mean, you're 'going to have to kill me?' I haven't done anything to you!"

"Haven't you?" Alice asked, voice pure and melodic. "You know things you shouldn't."

"You're the one who merged with me during our fight with Catharsis, remember? I only accepted the bond because we were fighting together, and unlike you, I didn't have anything to hide from the great and powerful Alice. We were on the ropes until you showed up, and with your help I defeated Catharsis."

Sand shifted behind Abbie, forming into a giant, disturbing cat shape with tentacles flowing from its mouth and eyes. Other figures materialized all around them; life-sized statues of Proctors and Pursuants from the battle Abbie had participated in the month before. A sculpture of Moon formed next to her, a look of rage on her face.

"What are you doing?" Abbie asked.

"Painting a picture in thought," Alice said. "So you can understand what is actually going on in Consciousness."

Abbie walked around the large sand figures. Shadows stretched across the dune from shapes of oversized insects and multilimbed monsters she remembered from the fight. Hanker and Pinely appeared frozen in a run toward a mass of roaring creatures; all still, all silent.

"I already know about Consciousness," Abbie said, looking back at the glimmering Alice. "And I was at this battle, so I don't need a recap. When Catharsis attacked, I was surprised, but ready. You didn't even show up until later. Before I saw and felt you there, I half thought you were nothing more than a made-up inspirational message Hanker shared to inspire Proctors. The Great Alice was too good to be true, seeming to only show up when she wanted to, and then vanishing like a whisper. All-powerful Alice, protecting Consciousness, but never showing up to really do anything to help anyone."

"I have no need to make my presence known needlessly," Alice replied, voice sterile as surgeon's scalpel. "Your perceptions prove how little you understand of Consciousness. Take this 'skirmish' for example," she said, motioning toward the frozen statues around them. "You see it as you would a battle in the real world. While your senses are more attuned than most Proctors, you experience things here primarily through visual stimuli, just like everyone else. You know only what you see, and sometimes feel, not the intentions behind the actions.

"Let me see if I can help you understand. Catharsis decided to try and overwhelm the Proctors throughout the United States in one push. From a terrestrial understanding it makes sense but falls apart under even the simplest of examinations. He reeked of manipulation. He constantly swirled with emotions of trust and fealty despite his blatant attack. His real goal was simply to show his power so that new Proctors gaining their footing in the dream world would follow him instead of Hanker. He wanted them to grow to trust him and no one else; make them afraid of being on the losing team. In the grand scheme of things, not a bad plan, but also not one likely to change many minds. People are who they are, and the actions of others rarely sway them one way or the other for very long. I wouldn't have shown up at all for such a pointless clash if Alexander hadn't decided to spectate."

"Alexander was there?"

Alice nodded her head. The sand shifted under them, and the entire scene twisted, moving to the right like someone turning a board game on a table. Tracks in the sand left behind by Abbie's planted feet evidenced the fact that she hadn't moved, but the world had. Beyond the other figures, on the periphery of the fight, stood a shadowed man with his hands clasped behind his back. A fine business suit clung to his broad shoulders. He wore no tie or shoes. While his facial features were hard to make out in the sandy construct, a feeling of power, intoxicating and rich as chocolate sauce, poured from the figure. Abbie breathed in the energy and felt lightheaded.

"Who is Alexander?" Abbie asked.

"A threat," Alice answered.

The blades in Abbie's hands wafted to smoke, but her anger remained. "I'm tired of only having half answers. You say you're going to kill me no matter what I do---"

"Yes," Alice interrupted.

"…Then you might as well tell me what all of this is about, so I at least know what I'm dying for. Who are you? Who is Alexander? Why are you going to kill me?"

"Last question first." Alice waved her hand and the sandy statues collapsed back down to the dunes. Dust rose all around, and Abbie coughed on the particles. "I'm going to have to kill you," Alice continued, "because right now you're leading Alexander's agents to my doorstep to kill me and my crew."

"I'm trying to stop them!" Abbie countered.

“Then why are you currently sleeping in a hotel next to the airstrip where I normally fly in for supplies?”

“That’s not…” Abbie stuttered. “That wasn’t my…”

“You don’t remember the dream in the real world.” Alice’s words carried no judgement. “It’s incredibly common. Very few Proctors and Pursuants ever do. Your chauffeur Auspice on the other hand doesn’t have that problem.”

Abbie stepped forward, kicking up sand in her haste. “You can help me. You can make it so that I can remember in Basic.”

“I can’t,” Alice said, silver head shaking.

“Why not!?” Abbie screamed.

Alice’s glance dropped slightly. A frown creased her chrome cheeks. “I’m not a god, Abigail.”

“It’s Moon.”

“In either case, I can’t control Consciousness. Not mine and not yours. No one can.”

A defeated breath blew from Abbie’s chest. She sat on the sand and leaned back on her elbows. “Then what are we doing here? Why are we fighting?”

Sand separated under Abbie’s hands and pulled away from her. The entire desert twirled suddenly like a giant whirlpool. A roar of sound grew with the wind as billions of tiny granules scraped against each other and cascaded into nothing. Like a ravenous mouth, the hole opened wide to swallow the desert.

“Stop this!” Abbie yelled. Sand surged against her feet. She stepped back, trying to escape the inverted tornado guzzling the dunes. She tried to fly away but found gravity holding her as firmly as it would in the real world.

Alice stepped forward and leaped into the void. “Don’t be afraid.”

The silver woman dropped against the blackness until the shadows absorbed her. The chasm grew wider. Abbie scrambled to get away from the expanding hole but couldn't find anything to grab hold of besides more sand. Particles churned in the air, choking and blinding her. She began sliding down the collapsing dune until space captured her and she fell toward oblivion. Silence slurped all the sound away. The sand around her fluttered and sparkled before becoming one with the darkness itself. No light survived. Abbie found herself in a realm of nothing. No emotions, no noise, no color, not even the sound of her own breathing. Her armor had fallen away at some point during her descent, and she felt exposed and vulnerable.

Was this death? Had Alice killed her, and this is what that experience felt like?

A single point of light cast away the darkness. Alice floated beside it, a goddess amongst nothingness.

"You want to know why we fight?" Alice asked.

"Yes. What's the purpose of all of this? Why am I going to die for it?"

"Twenty-three years ago," Alice began. "Alexander Durham and I were in love. Or at least, I was in love with him."

The emptiness exploded in color and memory. Voices echoed, mingled with laughter. A young woman in glasses, about Abbie's age, looked in a mirror and rubbed at a patch of dry skin under her nose. Freckles covered her cheeks; brown hair hung past her shoulders. She was pretty, though seemed unconcerned with such labels. Abbie felt her confidence and smelled sage. A white t-shirt draped over her chest and torso with a large flaming eye on the front and the words: *Middle Earth's Annual Mordor 5-K, One Does Not Simply Walk,* written across the front. A slender man appeared next to her in the mirror and nuzzled his chin against her neck. Greasy blond hair touched his shoulders; whitehead pimples poking out along his jawline. Neither of them could have been older than 22 or 23 by Abbie's guess.

'You coming into the lab this afternoon?' the boy asked. He kissed her cheek and rubbed his hands along her arms.

'Yeah,' the woman answered with a smirk. *'Professor Khatri's not around anymore, so he won't be staring at my chest the whole time like he used to.'*

"That's you," Abbie said. Even with metal skin, the memory matched the features of the silver Alice perfectly.

"It was," Alice confirmed.

"And the guy who needs a shower is Alexander, I take it?"

"Yes."

Abbie's lip curled. This dorky kid certainly didn't have the same presence she felt when Alice showed her the sand statue of Alexander.

Images blurred while others came into focus. Feelings of comfort and excitement tickled Abbie's spine. A university lab formed around them. Two visored helmets on a metal table drew all attention toward them. Cables ran from the head gear to computers and monitors.

'Shared consciousness isn't a thing,' Alice said, while holding one of the helmets. Alice's thoughts in that moment invaded Abbie's mind with judgments about how the helmets looked like something from an anime cartoon she hated, where the camera constantly lingered on the heroine's butt for its 14-year-old male audience.

'Look, you don't have to help if you don't want to,' Alexander said, typing at a keyboard with a yellow pencil between his teeth.

The moment evolved again, and Abbie felt the two lovers

shift into Consciousness. Trees formed around Alice as she wandered. Flowers spoke to her. Catharsis was there too, playful and menacing. The environment took on the appearance of something from the old *Alice in Wonderland* cartoon Abbie remembered from her childhood.

'Why are things changing to look like Alice in Wonderland?' Alice asked as her clothing transformed into a blue and white dress. *'I don't like Alice in Wonderland. Kids at school always told me to dress like Alice every Halloween and thought I'd never heard that suggestion before.'*

Catharsis twisted his head completely around and grinned. *'Again, you need to ask yourself 'Who's doing the thinking?' After all, if this is your mind then it would be you, but if you're sharing this space with someone, it may be them. Of course, if this is a communal space, then you could be sharing it with all kinds of people; all kinds of minds.'*

Excited malice oozed from the feline. Abbie tried to push the feeling away, but it clawed into her flesh and wouldn't let go.

She turned to Alice and pushed the memories aside. "Why are you showing me this?"

"Because you asked why we're here, and why we fight," Alice said. "Twenty-three years ago, I joined Alex for an experiment he had been working on with a professor who had recently been fired for sleeping with his students. I thought he needed the help, so I volunteered. We entered Consciousness together, but without ever going to sleep. Our full minds could commune with the shared space, giving us control no other dreamers possessed. Catharsis latched on immediately. He was already a strong Pursuant. He tasted our power and our insecurities…or rather, Alex's power and my insecurity."

Memories swirled around them again in a deafening blast of sound and feeling, threatening to overpower Abbie's senses. It was as if she stood in front of a giant subwoofer at a heavy metal concert, but instead of music, the speaker pulsed with emotion.

A beautiful blond man stood in front of a castle, hugging Alice. She stepped away and stared at the man's perfect cheeks and chiseled jawline.

'Why do you look like that?' Alice asked the man.

'Like what?' Alexander answered, voice squeaky and unsure, just as it had been in the real world.

'Like a GQ model.'

'What do you mean?'

Alice stomped her foot, frustration magnified by the memory to the point Abbie wanted to crush something beneath her heel too. *'Two seconds before we came in here, you talked about shared consciousness allowing us to worry less about appearances and more about helping each other.'*

'I said that, yes.'

'And now you made yourself look like a movie star? You don't see that as a problem? Nothing hypocritical about that?'

"This is where things began to fall apart," the silver Alice said as she floated away from the vision. "Catharsis tried to push things as he always does, but I pulled myself out. Alex woke up a minute later. I destroyed the helmets and Khatri's computers, but the damage had been done. A wedge formed between Alex and me. Within a few weeks he'd dropped out of school and told me we needed to take a break. He said it had nothing to do with the dream world, but I knew that wasn't true. We both were having the same experience every night. After our little experiment I could enter Consciousness and remember everything the next morning. I didn't have the same power and control as I did while hooked up to the helmet and computers, but I was still strong. Hanker helped me get my bearings and taught me to navigate. It was amazing."

"Hanker never mentioned that to me," Abbie said, feeling somewhat hurt her mentor never told her about his connection to Alice.

"That's not his way. Hanker is very private. It seems the person he's been the most open with is you, and even then, he holds things close to the chest. I would guess you know more about him than any other living person.

"Anyway, over the next few years things in the dream world began to change. Pursuants multiplied, and Alexander became more and more of a presence than before. Things turned dangerous, and a darkness spread that started to affect dreamers all over the world. Anger festered more readily. Places in the dream that had been peaceful and imaginative transformed into threatening locales that stank. Everyone knew Alexander was training people to hunt in the dream, but no one could stop him. No one knew who he was in the real world. Except me. He seemed to grow more influential with each passing year. I needed to know what was going on, so I looked him up in the physical world and called him. He had penthouses in both Tokyo and New York at that point."

An upscale Italian restaurant coalesced around Abbie and Alice. Warm bread and marinara sauce lingered on the air. Alexander, now in his late twenties, sat across from Alice, smiling in a dark suit. His hair, short and perfectly slicked back, no longer needed to be washed. Charisma radiated from his handsome face. Alice sat across from him at the table. A tight red dress hugged her body, making her look like a display piece that contrasted with the girl in the mirror wearing the *Lord of the Rings* shirt. She matched Alexander's million-dollar style with beautifully curled hair and make-up. Alice laughed attentively as Alexander spoke, but Abbie felt her apprehension and a hint of dread.

'I'm so glad you let me pick out that dress,' Alexander said between bites of ravioli. *'You look amazing.'*

Alice took a sip of red wine. *'Thank you. I'm excited to see your apartment so I can look out on Central Park. I can't believe you're the same guy who used to think Hot Pockets were the pinnacle of fine dining.'*

'You'll find some things have changed about me,' Alexander said. *'For the better.'*

Self-loathing washed over Abbie suddenly, and she twisted as if blown by a stiff wind. "What was that? I feel nauseous all of a sudden."

"It's my disgust," Alice answered, waving her hand in front of her face as if shooing away the emotion. Her shiny silver skin seemed to dull, as if tarnished by the fingerprints of a thousand touches. "I went back to his apartment and slept with him so I could find his research. I had hoped that night I would get what I needed, but he didn't have anything at his home. I knew there was too much at stake, so I stayed by his side for weeks until I learned what I needed. I even opened my mind in the dream; sharing ideas and emotions with him, always trying to hide my true intent while gleaning any knowledge I could from his errant thoughts. It was agonizing. I hated it…and him."

Angst gnawed at Abbie's stomach at the thought of being with someone she didn't love…or worse, detested. Opening her mind and being vulnerable, while burying her true self. "How did you keep your emotions hidden from him in Consciousness? If he were as powerful then as he is now, he would have known how you felt."

"He knew. It seemed the more my disgust materialized, the more he wanted me. Whatever love he had soured to obsession. I was a treasure to be locked away; prey to be forever pursued. But he didn't realize what I was really after, or why I stayed. It was a difficult few months. Eventually his ego got the better of him. He shared what he was doing and took me to the penthouse where he kept his machines and trained his acolytes. He had rebuilt all of Khatri's designs."

"I thought you had destroyed all the research," Abbie said.

"But I hadn't destroyed Khatri," Alice admitted. "He and Alexander met up after he left the university. They recreated everything together. Wealthy patrons paid them millions to learn how to control the dream and remember everything when they woke up. I stuck around until I could steal the designs, and then I ran away. I wanted to destroy what they'd built, but I knew they would just put the devices back together again. Alexander hunted me in Consciousness and in the physical world, but I knew where to go and how to hide. I built my own computers and programs from Khatri's notes to combat him."

"So that's how you and he are so powerful," Abbie said. "You're using machines to keep your higher cognitive functions fully aware while in Consciousness. What about Khatri? I've never heard of him before."

An old yearbook opened across the black expanse. Blurry photos filled the page, until one snapshot came into focus. An attractive man with dark hair and mocha skin smiled brilliantly behind a thick beard. His large nose seemed perfectly balanced with a chin that jutted out a little too far. Under the photo read the words: *Dr. Jihan Khatri, Professor of Cognitive Psychology and Computer Engineering.*

"He taught Cognitive Psychology and Computer Engineering?" Abbie asked. "That's a weird combination."

Alice nodded. "Those two disciplines allowed him to forge some pretty interesting theories though. And build what would eventually take Alex and me into the dream. I don't know where he is now. He and Alexander parted ways probably ten years ago. He doesn't make waves in the dream, so I haven't had a need to track him down."

Everything began to make sense to Abbie. What started as a simple thought experiment had opened Consciousness to people more dangerous and powerful than evolution would naturally allow. Alice had sacrificed to try and stop them, going so far as to feign love for a man she had long since reviled just to gain an advantage. Hate ruled their relationship; one hiding while the other furiously hunted.

"Now you understand," Alice said. Visions of war, hunger, and despair flared on the empty black canvas like fires in a starless sky. Confusion followed, riding wings of corruption and greed. "Human civilization follows a pattern of destruction, death, rebirth, and enlightenment. For the past thousand years that pattern has constantly led to progress in all forms; technology, social interaction, philosophy, democracy, you name it. If things continue as they are, that pattern will cease. Things are only going to get worse. As Alexander grows stronger, and he trains more hunters, things will decay in the psychological world, and then spiral out of control in the physical. No one will be safe in their own minds. Even now he is on the cusp of gaining real control in Consciousness, beyond what anyone else has ever experienced. Imagine, true emotional control, where minds are open to him to steal thoughts, or manipulate emotions. Imagine an entire population sedated with depression so they never rise up and fight for anything more than what their oppressors are willing to throw to them."

After her recent fight with Vincent, Abbie had gained a new appreciation for the power of emotional manipulation. The grief and melancholy she had felt were almost too much for her, a highly trained Proctor. She had seen their impact on individual dreamers being hunted by Pursuants, but to think of such a phenomenon reaching thousands…millions all at the same time, seemed cataclysmic.

An image of a protestor being beaten by police morphed into

a dragonfly with bat wings. It flew over and landed on Alice's open palm before licking at her silver skin. She squashed it in her fist with a wet crunching sound.

"We're only now beginning to see the signs," she continued. "Powerful men holding sway over millions like despots always have, but now influencing them in Consciousness as well. Look at the upcoming presidential election this fall in the United States for example. The front-runners from both parties have each been trained by Alexander."

"Wait, what?" Abbie stammered. "Both the Democrat and the Republican? But I like Warren Newhouse!"

"We've come to a tipping point, Moon. Fear grows, and those who know how to use it thrive. That is power that cannot be broken. You fight to protect dreamers, which is admirable. I fight to protect everyone in and out of Consciousness from being manipulated and controlled. Your anger toward Auspice is palpable all around you. He's manipulating you. Imagine that experience spread exponentially through all human minds across the world. It would lead to an age of despair, slavery, and absolute power unlike anything else in history. That cannot be allowed to happen. That's what I'm fighting against. That's what my team is fighting against."

Indigo sky peaked through the darkness, turning the nothingness of the void back into a desert of rolling dunes. Warm air kissed Abbie's skin; a smell of water and dust permeating the area. Sand crunched against her bare feet. A pink bird laughed in the sky above.

"You have a team?" Abbie asked.

"Yes. One of them will be waiting for you and Auspice when you arrive at the airfield. He will agree to fly you out, and then kill both of you as soon as you land."

The matter-of-fact way Alice said, 'kill both of you as soon as you land,' caught Abbie off guard, as if she had been talking about picking up groceries or going to see a movie.

"You don't have to do that," Abbie said.

"Yes, I do," Alice replied in the same steady tone. "You won't remember any of this when you wake up. Auspice will continue to manipulate you. You're already too close. I never should have merged with you."

"I've been wishing you hadn't…for three days now. Why did you merge our minds? I thought it was to stop Catharsis, but you said you didn't even think the fight was worth participating in, so why try to link with me?"

Once again, the sand billowed on the air and formed the image of the dark man with his hands held behind his back. Again, Abbie felt his power.

"Alexander began focusing on you," Alice said. "I don't know why. This wasn't the first time either. I'd noticed it before when he and I were playing one of our regular games of trying to kill one another. We were both hiding in the fabric of Consciousness, but I could feel him drawn to you as we came upon your conclave in a fight with some Pursuants months ago. I didn't understand why he singled you out, and I still don't. I've been watching you closely ever since. His presence has come and gone several times since then, always moving closer to Moon."

"I would have known if he was around," Abbie contested. "I can feel the presence of others."

"Not someone like Alexander. Trust me. If he wants to remain hidden, he'll remain hidden. During Catharsis' attack, all Alexander's mental energy suddenly turned on you. I was afraid he would enter the fight, so I acted. Things went crazy from there. Catharsis wrapped one of his gross tentacles around your ankle, and I felt Alexander reaching toward you to make a connection. If I were in your mind when that happened, I could read his thoughts before he knew I was there. I could find out where he was and send someone to take care of him in the physical world. So, I connected you and I. Alexander pulled back though, and you used our combined power to smash Catharsis and send his crew running. When we separated, Alexander had already gone."

"And now I'm going to die for your choice, because you decided to use me as a pawn against your ex-boyfriend?" Abbie spat.

"You have to understand: if Alexander had connected with you, I could have learned so much. It was worth the risk for both of us."

Abbie spun around and wanted to punch Alice in the face. "Says the woman who is safe somewhere while letting me set myself up to die. Nothing I say will change your mind, will it?"

"Can you remember the dream in the real world?" Alice asked.

"No," Abbie said through grit teeth.

"Then, no, my mind will not be changed."

For a moment, the two women stood there in the sun without speaking. Abbie had no recourse. If she could remember in the waking world, maybe something could be done, but at this point, that option seemed too distant to grasp. Still, she couldn't abandon hope.

"What do I need to do to remember everything?" she asked. "You have to know some trick or something."

Alice reached over and touched Abbie's shoulder. Electricity seemed to jump from the chrome woman's palm, through Abbie's dark purple unitard, and directly to her heart. A shockwave rippled through the sand, singing on the air like a symphony of power, before echoing to nothing in the distance.

"What was that?" Abbie asked, still feeling the weakening

reverberations.

"We could be very powerful if we worked together," Alice said. Regret seemed to pull at her shiny lips, tightening the lines around her eyes. "But that can't be. I can't sacrifice everything we've accomplished, give the entire human race over to Alexander, for your life, little Abigail-Moon-Kinder. If you unified and remembered Consciousness, then we could make a different choice, but without that, Auspice will only be the first to try and extract the information from you, one way or another. Now that they know who you are in the dream and the real world, the hunters will never stop. Very soon they'll find my home in that case. We have too much built there to just abandon it and run. We would be conceding defeat and giving this world to Alexander. I will not let that happen. I am sorry."

"Then tell me how to remember; how to take control in Basic!"

"You're too divided," Alice said, sounding like Hanker…and Merquery…and Vincent. "Memory comes from unity, not control. You have to make the choice."

"Well, I'm choosing it then," Abbie shouted as she spun around in the sand. "I'm choosing to unify! I'm making the choice!"

Alice laughed, showing real emotion for the first time. "If only it were that simple. I can't tell you how to do it. All I can say is that you need to really *want* to unify; to give up control and be vulnerable with yourself. I'm not sure you're ready for that yet."

The sky suddenly darkened. Water seeped into the sand at Abbie's feet and made the ground squishy and sticky.

"What's going on?" Abbie asked. "Don't you have control over this section of the dream, or something?"

Alice looked up at the swirling clouds overhead. "I told you before. No one has control over Consciousness. Only influence. But this is your doing."

"I'm making the storm?"

A silver hand reached up and touched Abbie's chin with an unexpected warmth. "Auspice, and probably Catharsis too, will be here soon," Alice said. "When I touched you, your power amplified my own and rippled through the dream. They felt it."

"We can fight them off!" Abbie stated with confidence. Her armor formed without a premeditated thought. "They don't stand a chance against the two of us together."

"There will be no fight," Alice said. "Auspice can't know we interacted in Consciousness. If he thinks you've told me you are coming, he may call in reinforcements and try a different strategy. I need you both on that plane---"

"So, we can die?" Abbie interrupted.

Silver eyes faded toward black, as if Alice knew the pain her words would cause. "So, you can die," she confirmed.

For a brief moment, the chrome on Alice's face softened to pink skin. Frizzy brown hair fell over her shoulders. Freckles covered her nose and cheeks. The visage passed away quickly however, morphing into a completely different face with proud lips, dark hair, skin with a slight blue tint, and a white line down the left side of her cheek, ending in a dot.

Abbie looked over at herself, as if staring in a mirror. The woman before her didn't just look like Moon...she *was* Moon, down to the throbbing anger and layer of self-deception that seemed to smell of sawdust. Never before had Abbie seen herself from the outside in such a potent, naked way. The judgment and rage, focused equally outwardly and inwardly, gave her a powerful presence...but not as powerful as she would have expected.

"What are you..." Abbie stumbled.

"I'm sorry, Abigail-Moon-Kinder," Alice said, as purple armor materialized around her new form. "When my enemies arrive, I need them to think we never spoke. They must believe it with all their core understanding. You need to be on that plane with Auspice. You both need to die."

Wind blew like a hurricane, lifting Alice/Moon into the air. Abbie ran after her, arms waving frantically.

"We don't have to do this!" she cried. "There has to be another way!"

Alice looked down. "There isn't." Pity seemed to overwhelm her for a moment. She raised her hand, palm pointing toward Abbie. "I wish we could have met in the waking world, Abigail-Moon-Kinder. I truly wish that."

A blast of pure white sympathy exploded from Alice's outstretched hand. The emotion slammed against Abbie in a devastating blow that turned the sand to crystalized obsidian. Abbie fought against the crush, but she was no match for the power of Alice Ashling.

Consciousness tattered. Abbie crumbled. Blackness sucked her from the dream.

CHAPTER THIRTEEN

A metal woman. A river. Grief. Depression. A jumble of mixed images and feelings.

Abbie sat forward in the bed, trying to grip each thought and every memory. Sunlight peaked through the gaps in the thick curtains telling her it was still daytime. The digital clock on the nightstand read 2:05. Vincent continued sleeping. Occasionally he would twitch, face tightening as if stressed. For a moment Abbie wondered if she should wake him up but decided against it. She hadn't enjoyed a moment alone for two days and needed time to process. Besides, if everything Vincent had told her was true, he could handle himself in the dream.

Making her way to the small bathroom, Abbie turned on the faucet and examined her reflection. A feeling of nervousness, deep and unending, reverberated with each heartbeat and seemed to age her face. Cold water pooled in her hands, and she splashed her eyes. Fatigue retreated like a frightened kitten. Staring at herself in the mirror, Abbie tried to make sense of the muddled thoughts and impressions she retained from her experience in Consciousness.

Something had happened in the dream. Something with a silver woman. Something that made her afraid.

Something about Vincent.

She crept from the bathroom back over to the bed and sat down quietly. Vincent continued breathing steadily with an occasional tremor. Abbie closed her eyes and tried to piece everything together. She swam in a river. She had been in a fight. Vincent had been there. A hand reached up from the ground, coiled by a striking serpent. The woman. The woman dominated her thoughts. Was the woman Alice? Whoever she was, the thought of her filled Abbie with dread, as if someone had started digging her grave while she sat and watched. But she also felt admiration. Such a confusing mixture of emotion couldn't be reconciled until she had more information.

Vincent sat up suddenly, making Abbie jump in surprise. A bead of perspiration dripped down his nose. The blankets fell from his shirtless body, revealing the glistening skin of an athlete after a run. Veins rippled up his forearms as if he had been flexing in his sleep. He still seemed tired.

"It's alright," Abbie said, not moving from her spot on her own bed. "Just breathe." It felt good to be the one to help him come back to reality, as opposed to the other way around.

"We were…" Vincent gasped. "Attacked."

"I wondered," Abbie said. "All I feel is nervousness and dread right now."

"Do you remember anything?" Vincent asked, turning toward her. He blinked several times and wiped at his eyes with the back of his hand.

Abbie opened her mouth to tell him about the silver woman, but something screamed for her to leave out that detail. "I remember…" she began slowly, "Running. Searching. A river."

A smile warmed Vincent's face. "You fell into the River of Subconscious. We were separated for a while. I eventually found you, but things got crazy from there. We should draw the picture." He turned, ready to jump out of bed.

"It's a hand with a snake wrapped around it," Abbie said,

pinching the bridge of her nose.

Vincent sat forward, a concerned look on his face. "Yeah, that's it. You okay?"

"I'm ready for all of this to be over."

"We're close," Vincent said. He moved from his bed and sat next to Abbie. His hand covered hers in a comforting gesture that filled her with anxiety. "We are so close. Do you have any more details about Alice's location?"

The words 'Triple Z' came to Abbie's mind, along with the same distant landing strip. Mountain peaks she'd never seen before seemed suddenly familiar, as if she looked up at them from a meadow sometime in the past. In that moment Abbie knew the exact direction they needed to fly. Again, she felt hesitant to give Vincent all the details.

"Triple Z," she said. "I'll know it when I see it."

Vincent squeezed her hand and scooted closer. His face drew within inches of hers.

"You're an amazing woman," he whispered. "More so than any I think I've ever met. I feel…drawn to you, out here and in the dream. It's almost like I have no…"

He kissed her.

Unexpected emotions rocked Abbie's brain in that moment. Pleasure bubbled to the surface, but so did anger and fury. It seemed as if a voice from somewhere far away screamed at her to stop and then gouge Vincent's eyes out.

Abbie pulled away from the kiss this time, hands gripping the comforter beneath her.

"Sorry," she said. "You were right. We need to get all of this craziness taken care of before we figure out this thing between us."

"So, there is something between us?" Vincent said with a

playful nudge of his elbow.

"Maybe," Abbie admitted.

Despite the nervousness churning her stomach, she smiled. Abbie didn't know what was happening in the dream world, but Vincent had a way of making her feel better, no matter what the circumstances. They had run from kidnappers, hidden from the police, and avoided getting shot. Through it all, Vincent had reassured her and been a gentleman.

Even so, her instincts told her to be wary. Part of her didn't want to listen. She wanted to trust Vincent fully. She wanted it so badly.

"Let's get our shoes on and grab a quick bite before heading over to the airstrip," Vincent said as he jumped from the bed. He threw his white shirt on and grabbed his jacket from the nightstand. "Hopefully, a pilot will be available to take us where we need to go. The website for the lodge here said sometimes pilots would take people on paid rides. Maybe we'll get lucky."

At the mention of a pilot, Abbie again grew nervous.

They ate quickly at the hotel restaurant before waiting for a line of pick-up trucks to pass on the highway so they could jog across to the grass runway and its corrugated metal hangar. The afternoon sun shined behind them with just enough warmth to tease spring, but not enough to bring relief from the chill. A cold breeze blew into their faces from the east, bringing with it the promise of potential snow in the forecast. An ocean of green pasture waved in the wind all around them. Abbie rubbed her arms to keep the lingering claws of winter at bay. Three airplanes lined up next to the rounded hangar: all single engine Cessnas. Two of them looked fairly new, with blue and white paint stretching from front to back, while the third appeared more rugged and worn. Red wings cast a shadow on the grass, a compass logo with a lightning strike down the middle adorning the side door.

"How you folks doing?" a smiling man with a gray beard and red ball cap said. He stood just outside the hangar's entrance next to the orange windsock, wiping grease from his hands with a blue rag.

"We're looking to hire a pilot to fly us out to a backcountry airstrip north of here," Vincent said, shaking the man's smeared hand. "I can pay cash."

"Where you lookin' to go?" the man asked.

Vincent turned toward Abbie, then back at the man. "We'll know it when we see it. My girlfriend here used to fly out of this airfield as a teenager and she wants to go back to where her grandma would take her on their summer trips. She knows where she's going, but as the crow flies, if you know what I mean."

The man rubbed the back of his neck with the rag and looked over at the planes. "You'll have better luck tomorrow or Saturday, honestly," he said, pointing toward the planes. "Tomorrow night we'll have probably six more aircraft flying in, to camp across the street. More than likely, somebody would be happy to fly you out if you're willing to pay. Right now, it's just me and Carl. He flew in last night and has just been working on his plane all day. Carl might be willing to do it, but he mentioned earlier about needing to pick up a forest service ranger from one of the cabins where he's been on fire watch the last few weeks."

"You guys have forest fires this early in the year?" Vincent asked.

"Not normally," the man answered. "But sometimes the Forest Service does training stuff. I don't know. You can talk to Carl though. He'll have all the details. But like I said, tomorrow or Saturday you'll have a better chance."

Vincent and Abbie said goodbye to the old pilot and walked around the far side of the hangar. Beneath the wing of the older aircraft a man sat in a lawn chair with a cowboy hat pulled down over his eyes. His faded brown leather jacket contrasted against the pale skin of his neck. Tufts of red hair poked out over his collar. Abbie couldn't see his face under the hat but assumed she would see freckles across his cheeks. A logo of a lightning compass was sewn to the left breast of the jacket, matching the one on the older, red-winged aircraft.

"Excuse me, are you Carl?" Vincent asked.

A snore rumbled under the cowboy hat.

"Excuse me," Vincent repeated with greater volume. "Are you Carl?"

The man jumped and sat forward, pulling the cowboy hat from his face. As expected, Abbie saw a collection of orange freckles covering the man's nose and cheeks, matching his scruffy hair. He looked to be in his early thirties, handsome, with a pointed jaw that seemed somewhat familiar to Abbie, as if they'd met before somewhere. The feeling of nervousness she'd been feeling subsided slightly, but only slightly. Then she saw the holster on his belt, with a shiny revolver strapped inside like an Old West sheriff. Her nervousness reasserted itself.

"Sorry, what was that?" he asked in a surprising British accent.

"Are you Carl?" Abbie questioned.

"Oh, yeah, that's me. Carlton's my full name, which I prefer, honestly. Only Pete over there calls me Carl, 'cause he knows it'll get a rise out of me." Carlton stretched his arms over his head and rotated his neck. "What time is it?"

"Just before three," Vincent replied.

"Damn," Carlton said, standing up. "I gotta go. Got me a pick-up."

"Yeah, Pete told us you're flying out to grab a Forest Service

Ranger from a backcountry airstrip," Vincent said. "We wanted to see if we could hire you to fly us north to a strip as well."

"Which one?"

Vincent pointed his thumb at Abbie. "My girlfriend knows it by sight from when she was a teenager. We're willing to pay cash for the trip. $500 about do it?"

Carlton adjusted the cowboy hat on his head and squinted. "You want me to fly you out to a backcountry airfield, and you don't know where it is? How far away is it?"

"About an hour," Abbie answered. As she spoke, the words filled her with trepidation. Why was she so nervous? Everything in her mind told her to run away.

"Like I said," Vincent continued. "We'll pay whatever is necessary. This is important to her…to both of us."

Stretching his back, Carlton adjusted his belt and the revolver. "Alright. I'll do it for $500. And you'll have to let me pick up the ranger first, since he's got priority right now."

"That's great," Vincent said. He reached into his back pocket and pulled out a leather wallet. "Here's $500."

As Vincent placed five $100 bills in Carlton's hand, the Brit chuckled. "I should've asked for a thousand."

Carlton prepped the plane quickly, kicking the tires and spinning the propeller. Vincent ran back to the hotel gift shop to buy Abbie a coat. She stood there alone for a few minutes with her confusing thoughts. Chills continued to prick at Abbie's skin, but it wasn't the cold that made her hesitate. She did not want to get on that plane. It wasn't fear of flying either. Some dread hung over her that she couldn't explain.

"You okay?" Carlton asked after a few minutes. "You look nervous. Afraid of flying?"

"Not usually," Abbie replied, eyes glancing quickly down to the pistol on his belt.

"Me open-carrying make you queasy? You're in Idaho, love; everybody and their cousin's got a gun on their hip. You gotta get used to that."

"No, it's just…" Abbie wavered. She glanced over her shoulder as an 18-wheeler rumbled by on the highway. Vincent stepped out of the giftshop across the street holding a gray coat on his arm. He made eye contact with Abbie and waved with a smile. Even from a hundred yards away he could warm her spirits.

"You don't have to fly anywhere today," Carlton said, bringing Abbie's attention back to his freckled face. "If you're nervous…about anything, you can walk away. I'll give back the $500. No problem for me at all."

Abbie wanted to take the offer.

Why was she so nervous? What had happened in the dream? Did it have something to do with the silver woman?

"Have we…met before?" Abbie asked, pressing her lips together. "You seem familiar."

"You ever been to England?" Carlton questioned. "Specifically, the north, around Newcastle?"

"Nope."

"Then I doubt it. I've only been in the States for a couple years now, and most of it has been around these parts. Unless you come to Stanley Idaho on the regular, we wouldn't be likely to know one another. And I'd probably remember a pretty lady like you. I just have one of those faces, as they say."

"Makes sense," Abbie replied, though she couldn't shake the feeling she knew the pilot somehow.

"We ready to go?" Vincent asked as he ran up to them on the

grass. "Here's a coat, Abbie. That should warm you up a bit."

"Abbie?" Carlton said with a smile. "That's a right nice name. And yes, we are ready to go…except the lady here seems nervous to fly."

"I'm okay," Abbie assured. She threw on the coat, feeling its fur lining and smelling oiled leather.

"Let's get going," Vincent said to Carlton. He put his arm around Abbie and pulled her close. "Just give us a second, okay, Carlton?" They turned away from the pilot. Vincent rubbed her arms as if trying to cast out the cold. "Are you afraid of flying?"

"No," Abbie said. "I just feel nervous is all. Like something happened in the dream and now I'm scared to go further."

Vincent nodded as if he understood. "It makes sense. There is so much fear and confusion about all of this. The people we're facing in Consciousness have done a number on me too. They're scared, and they're trying to make us scared. That was the emotion they were throwing at us before we woke up. I feel it too, but we can't stop now. We're too close. Everything is going to be okay once we land wherever Alice is. Trust me. I'm going to be by your side the entire time. You don't need to be nervous. Within two hours we'll be with Alice. You'll be safe, I'll be safe, and we can plan our next move from there. Do you trust me?"

"I…" Her eyes dropped and focused on the grass at her feet. Abbie didn't know what to say. Right now, she felt nervous about Vincent *and* the pilot. None of it made sense. Why couldn't she remember the dream? All of this would be so much simpler.

"Abbie, look at me," Vincent said.

She looked up at his kind eyes. He seemed pained, as if her hesitation hurt him deeply. He had done nothing to make her doubt, only putting himself at risk since she met him. After their first shared sleep at the cabin, she had felt drawn to him. That desire remained, but now suspicion and hesitation controlled her; suspicion of a man who had only ever been kind to her, and toward a pilot she'd never even met.

"I'm sorry I'm having a hard time," Abbie said quietly.

A laugh sang from Vincent's mouth, and he beamed at her. "Abbie, you are the most amazing woman I've ever met, whether here or in the dream. You've been through so much and come so far in the past few days. I'm in awe of you. I just…I just…"

He leaned forward and kissed her on the cheek quickly. Warmth flowed through Abbie's face at the sweetness of the gesture.

"I'm sorry," Vincent stammered. He stepped back and nervously rubbed his hands together in the cold air. "I shouldn't have done that. I shouldn't have kissed you in the hotel either. It was out of turn."

Abbie reached up and touched her cheek. He could have kissed her on the lips, and she would have accepted it, but the cheek somehow seemed so intimate in that moment, so kind. "No, that was very gentlemanly and charming." Her nerves steadied. "I think I'm ready to get on the plane."

"Awesome," Vincent glowed, practically bouncing up on his toes.

"We good?" Carlton called as a stiff gust blew from the east.

Vincent led Abbie to the open plane door and nodded. "Yeah, we're good to go."

"You sure?" Carlton asked Abbie. His eyes seemed almost sad. "We can wait if you're not comfortable."

"I'll be alright," Abbie said.

Glancing down, Carlton nodded. "Whatever you want."

The plane rocked slightly as Vincent climbed into the back seat. Abbie took the chair next to the pilot and began strapping herself into the harness.

"Go ahead and put on your seatbelts and headsets before I start the engine," Carlton said. "It's going to get pretty loud in here, so we'll use the speaker system that runs through the cab."

Abbie put on a set of headphones that looked like something from 1985. The large ear cushions pressed against her head, a small microphone extending from the right unit toward her mouth.

"Alright, let's get this show on the road," Carlton's voice squawked in her ear.

The propeller spun, sending tremors through the plane and up Abbie's legs. The last time she had flown had been for a trip with college friends to Cancun. During that vacation they had soared with a tour company over the ocean in a small plane similar to Carlton's. Of course, it hadn't rattled and shook quite like this one, but Abbie kept her calm.

Sunlight shone through the windshield as they took off from the grass runway and turned northwest toward the mountains. Lakes and streams appeared below them, reflecting the afternoon rays. Pockets of snow remained in the shadows between trees or rocky overhangs. Abbie stared out the window in awe at the diverse terrain. A handful of deer ran through the trees. A bull moose stood in a pond. They flew over a large deep blue body of water that Abbie remembered seeing in her mind the day before.

"What lake is that down there?" she asked.

"That's Redfish Lake," Carlton said through the speaker system. "It's a nice spot. You two should check it out while you're in the area."

Mountains, meadows, pine trees, and stone ridges passed beneath them as they flew north. On Abbie's left she watched dark clouds gathering in the east. Constant vibrations from the plane's engines soothed Abbie's mind. She wanted to close her eyes and sleep but figured this wouldn't be a good time to doze. Occasionally a peak or shape on the horizon would flash with a memory that didn't belong to her. Vincent had been right: they were close.

After about a half hour of flying, Carlton pushed against the yoke, and they began to descend toward a brown strip of dirt in the middle of a dense pine forest that ran east to west.

"This is where we gotta pick up the ranger," the pilot said. "It'll only take a few minutes. We'll land, and then walk over to the cabin, which is just in the trees. You guys think you can help me grab his luggage? It'll make things quicker, and we can head off to that airstrip you want to hit."

"Sure," Abbie agreed. She looked back at Vincent, who quickly glanced up from his phone.

"Yeah, that's fine," he said, placing the cell next to him on the seat.

"You have signal up here?" Abbie asked.

"No," Vincent confirmed. "Just checking the time. It'll be getting dark in the next couple hours, so I wanted to see how much time we had."

Dust billowed around them as the plane touched down on the runway. The metal groaned and bounced, making Abbie's stomach twist like dropping on a rollercoaster. The aircraft quickly came to a stop and Carlton turned off the engines.

"The cabin is over there through those trees, just on the north side of the runway," Carlton said, pointing off to their right.

"I don't see anything," Vincent replied. "Is there a path or something?"

Carlton unlocked his seatbelt and opened the door. "You'll see it once we get closer. These cabins are used during the fire season and for training stuff. They're small, but they'll keep you alive."

The world seemed completely silent before Abbie removed her headset. Sounds rushed to her ears as she pulled the large cushions away from her skin. Birds chirped in the trees, along with the occasional cry of an eagle or other large avian predator. Vinyl squeaked as Vincent adjusted the pilot seat forward so he could reach the door to exit. Abbie pulled on her own handle and pushed the light fiberglass barrier open on the forest. She stepped down toward the dirt, smelling strong pine fragrance on the cold air. The gray coat Vincent had purchased retained enough warmth to keep her comfortable despite the chill. She stretched her legs and back, breathing in the pleasant scents of undisturbed wilderness.

"Follow me," Carlton said as he stepped past Abbie.

Feet crunched against dry pine needles. The trio crossed the airstrip and entered the trees, Carlton leading, Abbie just behind him, and Vincent taking up the rear. Deep shadows swallowed them in the closeness of the forest. Abbie glanced around for any sign of a cabin but saw only more trees.

"It's just up here," Carlton said.

After another thirty seconds, Abbie realized she no longer heard three sets of footprints on the arid ground: only two. She turned around and saw no one behind her.

"Vincent?" she asked, stopping. Trees dominated her view. She could barely see back to the clearing where they had landed. Vincent had disappeared. "Vincent?!" she called.

"Shit," Carlton breathed.

Abbie spun back toward her guide, catching the glint of metal in the dim forest. Carlton's revolver shifted back and forth in his left hand as the pilot looked around frantically. His feet shuffled, grinding dry grass, leaves, and pinecones beneath his boots.

"Carlton, why is your gun---" Abbie began.

Somewhere to their left, a twig snapped, followed by the pounding of heavy footsteps running toward them. Vincent burst out from behind a tree and slammed into Carlton. A cowboy hat flew into the air. The men tumbled to the ground, rolling on top of each other.

"Abbie!" Vincent yelled, trying to pull the gun from Carlton's hand. "Run back to the plane!"

Carlton punched Vincent in the face and kicked him off. For some reason Abbie tried to form a sword in her hand, but nothing materialized. Instead, she picked up a dried branch about the size of her arm and hit Carlton across the head. The stick broke, and the Englishman struggled to his feet unharmed. Vincent grabbed at his leg, but Carlton turned and kicked him in the jaw. Vincent slumped and didn't move.

"Help!" Abbie screamed, stepping away from the pilot as he wiped dirt from his chin. "Help us!"

"I'm sorry Moon," Carlton said. His voice sounded mournful, not angry, or antagonistic.

"What did you call me?"

"No one can hear you out here." Carlton walked toward her slowly, right hand forward as if trying to calm her, left pointing the gun at her chest. Leaves stuck to his face, along with slivers of brown pine needle. "I'm sorry. I didn't want to have to do this. I didn't want you to get on the plane."

Abbie continued stepping backward, feeling desiccated stalks and undergrowth crushed beneath her shoes. "Who are you?"

"I'm a friend," Carlton said. Tears came to his eyes. "I really am. I'm sorry."

Straightening his arm, Carlton pointed the revolver directly at Abbie's face.

Dirt rustled behind the gunman. Vincent bolted forward on his hands and knees, yanking Carlton to the ground.

"Run, Abbie!" he shouted.

An ear-splitting crack exploded in the quiet forest as the gun went off. A shockwave hit Abbie's ears and she turned, running without thought or direction. Like a deer fleeing from hunters, she charged into the forest, dodging trees and rocks as she dashed. Her hair blew in her face as she looked back, seeing nothing but trees. Another gunshot clapped like thunder and urged her onward. Her heart pounded in her ears, sweat beading on her brow. Cold air beat against her face, but she felt warm enough to cast off her coat. Glancing back quickly again, Abbie expected to see a gunman chasing her, firing indiscriminately in her direction, but only shadowed forest stared back.

While looking behind her, Abbie's foot hit a fallen log and she tumbled forward. The ground sloped down at an angle, and she found herself toppling end over end into a shallow ravine. Sticks scratched her face as she fell. Grasping for anything to stop her plunge, Abbie opened her eyes in time to see a tree rush up to her face.

The impact sent a dull thud from the side of her head, rebounding through her skull like fluttering waves on a pond. Her body came to a stop, face-first in a thick bramble of scrub oak. She smelled dirt and rotting wood. She was alive.

Tiny, thorned leaves bit into the palms of her hands as Abbie pushed against the bush. She struggled slowly to her feet, a wave of dizziness overcoming her. The pain in her head throbbed, spinning the earth like a marry-go-round. Fragments of foliage clung to her cheeks and tickled her skin. Her hands shook. Vertigo spun her around again. She tried to stay upright but found the world going dark. Reaching for the nearest tree, Abbie pitched forward.

Blackness devoured her.

CHAPTER FOURTEEN

Pain.

All her consciousness in that moment seemed molded from aching and suffering. Three-dimensional shapes convulsed before Abbie's eyes, as if they couldn't settle on a form. No trees or plants greeted her view, only the strange forms on a dark purple expanse that stretched like a barren world before her. She pushed onto her hands and knees, trying to gain perspective in a place where she swore the smell of oranges whispered in her ear. Darkness surrounded her, save for ghostly mists of color that shuddered back and forth as if trying to reach her and avoid her at the same time.

"Where…I can't…" she mumbled. Her head palpitated like a spastic snare drum. Colors flashed before her face in-time with the beat.

Finally, after what seemed like an hour, Abbie stood up and blinked at the odd world. Everything, from the reflective ground at her feet, to the formless shapes surrounding her, flickered like an old TV signal, slightly out of tune. Ripples spread from where her shoes touched the floor, like she stood on water. The world rattled and twitched. Abbie tried to gain her bearings but found only throbbing soreness.

"Where am I?" she asked with more strength.

"You're in pain," the planet seemed to echo back at her.

"Where am I?!" she screamed, instantly regretting the effort. She swooned and stumbled back. The ground seemed to be soft and squishy suddenly, where seconds before it had been firm and steadfast.

"You're in Consciousness…kind of," a woman's voice answered.

It was Abbie's voice.

"Who are you?" she asked. "Why do you sound like me?"

Indistinct shapes and colors coalesced in front of her, continuing to stutter and shift. A woman formed; long dark hair, shiny sapphire bodysuit, pale complexion, a line of glowing white paint running down her left forehead and cheek. Abbie squinted, trying to steady the seizing world and focus on the being.

She opened her mouth to ask the question again, but instinctively knew who the woman was.

"You're Moon," Abbie said.

"Yes." The woman's voice vibrated as if the air itself shuddered violently. Sections of translucent purple armor formed around the doppelganger's shoulders, arms, and legs. "I'm Moon."

Abbie stared at her twin's face, recognizing every line, mole, and imperfection. "We look almost exactly the same, except your skin is a bit smoother than normal. Wild. Vincent was right. And when you said, 'I'm Moon,' shouldn't you say, 'We're Moon?'"

The flickering woman stepped closer and shook her head. "You're not Moon. You're Abbie."

"We're the same person."

Again, Moon's neck swiveled her head back and forth as if to silently dispute the sentence. "We are not." She started walking around Abbie in a circle, slowly looking her up and down as if judging the price of something she wasn't sure she wanted to buy. "I know your life, but you don't know mine."

Abbie stood firm, pushing past the pain. "That isn't my fault. I had no idea this other world existed until two days ago. How do you expect me to figure any of this out when I'm completely in the dark about everything?"

"Hanker tried to reach you," Moon said. "You drew the pictures, and yet you still couldn't grasp anything outside your physical realm."

"Well, I'm here now, aren't I? How is it we can be here at the same time? And where is *here*?"

Moon looked around the shifting environment and shrugged. "I don't know. It's possible you've been getting closer to Consciousness over the past few days. Maybe it's because you just smashed our head against a tree. We're not fully in Consciousness though. It's like we're part way, but not in sync."

"Shouldn't we merge or something at this point?" Abbie asked. "That's what Vincent talked about."

"I don't want to merge with you," Moon scoffed. A cold wind seemed to blow from every direction at once.

"Why not?"

The strange mental biosphere groaned and billowed dark brown clouds in the distance. Moon looked Abbie in the eye as if the strange environment didn't bother her at all. "You have nothing to offer me. Merging with you would be a waste. I want to take over in Basic. That's the only way we're going to survive this."

"What does that even mean, 'take over?' We're the same person!"

Moon's armor flared purple as if glowing along with her emotional state. "No. We. Are. Not."

So that was it. Abbie's own subconscious didn't like her.

Instead of feeling inadequate, Abbie felt irritation. Who was this dream-person to judge *her*? A sanctimonious bitch with a superiority complex?

"So, are you just my subconscious then?" Abbie shot back. "Something that gets to watch and critique, but never help out?"

Moon seemed to bristle at the accusation. She stopped circling and stood directly in front of Abbie. "I tried to keep you from getting on that plane. I tried to warn you about Vincent."

"What do you mean?" Abbie asked. "Vincent has been helping me."

"Wake up!" Moon shouted. "Vincent has been manipulating you! He doesn't care about you. All he cares about is finding Alice so Alexander can track her down and kill her so she can't stand in his way anymore. His plans are too big to risk having a monkey wrench like her thrown in to gum everything up. Vincent doesn't care about you beyond getting him to Alice. Think about it! He's been playing you from the moment you met in the parking lot. It's obvious."

Tears filled Abbie's eyes. She bit her lip, not wanting to admit the truth. "No, he just tried to save me in the forest---"

"The only reason he did that was so that he wouldn't fail in his mission. He thought you were nervous to get on the plane because Hanker told me everything about him being nothing but a self-absorbed, vicious little bastard. Vincent and I even battled in Consciousness after that. But it was Alice that told me we would be killed if we got on the plane to come find her. That's why you were nervous to fly. I was screaming at you not to board the plane! Vincent thought it was my hate for him that was making you hesitate. If he'd had any inkling Alice had sent Pinely to kill us, he never would have gotten on that aircraft."

"It's not true! He's been nothing but kind and helpful."

"Think about it!" Moon screamed. "I don't care if you're falling in love with him. You need to wake the hell up. I know you've had suspicions. Don't throw them back on me because you don't want what I'm saying to be true. You think I'm going to lie to myself about something like this? Take your feelings out of it and really look!"

Moon's words cut deep. In truth, Abbie *didn't* want her counterpart to be telling the truth. Looking more closely at Vincent would be like looking in a mirror and seeing flaws you knew were there but chose not to see. There were plenty of things about Vincent that didn't add up, however. Abbie had to admit that. She didn't even fully understand Vincent's motivations to find Alice. He claimed to simply want to help, but if that were the case, why the rush? Why not find a safe place to hunker down until Abbie learned to remember the dream? And if he was so trustworthy, why not wait until Moon trusted him enough to simply tell him Alice's location while they trained in Consciousness?

She began playing all their encounters back through her mind; every detail that seemed off about the handsome and charming man. Vincent's inexhaustible supply of money. The fact that Mozzie found them at the store. How Vincent arrived in her apartment in time to save her. How he knew just how to comfort her at just the right moment to keep her from doing something he didn't want; holding her hand, speaking encouraging words, rubbing her scalp.

A kiss in a hotel room.

'If you can't trust me, you can't trust anybody.'

It all made sense.

No more covering up the truth. No more accepting his words because she wanted him to be something he wasn't.

Abbie sat down and cried. She knew in that moment, everything Moon said was true. Everything. Just as she'd known the dream world existed when Vincent described it to her in his Tesla. Knowledge weighed on her like a sack of rocks tied around her neck.

"Oh, stop crying," Moon hissed.

"Shut up!"

"Stop crying!"

Abbie bolted to her feet. The grays and browns wafting around them morphed into purples and reds. Moon's shifting body stabilized and held firm. "You don't get to judge!" Abbie screamed. "You get to know my life *and* yours, while I don't know anything about you at all? You get to judge my feelings for a guy I trusted? You get to create whatever you want from nothing without ever worrying about food or rent, or anything else. If I starved to death out there, you think you'd just be fine and dandy in here? You don't get to disrespect me and what I worry about. You don't have the right!"

"I don't?" Moon asked. "You're not the one who has to slog through hours of pointless TV shows every night without ever getting a hold of the steering wheel to actually make any decisions. I tried to wake you up a million times so I wouldn't have to watch you lumber through existence. You have no idea how long I've tried to get into the driver's seat so that we could avoid some stupid mistake or prevent you from making a fool out of yourself."

"Well, aren't you lucky you get to see all and hear all," Abbie spat. Now it was her turn to circle like a predator. The shapes around them became more definite, as dark clouds merged above them. The ground turned dry and brown, covered in pine needles and crunchy leaves. "I can smell your perceived superiority. But if I got to see your life and you couldn't see mine, that would switch things around a bit, wouldn't it? You wouldn't be so smug then."

"Of course," Moon replied. "And then you could run back to your protector Vincent. Even now I can feel your affection for him;

even after knowing he's been exploiting you this whole time."

"It's not something you can just shut off like a light switch! But that wouldn't matter to you because you've never cared about anyone."

A tremor ran through the area, again affecting the environment and sending shapes spasming like shock therapy patients.

"You know nothing," Moon countered. "I whispered to you that Vincent was a threat, but he would bat his eyes and flex his pecks, and suddenly you would go anywhere he wanted."

"Really?" Abbie shot back. "Because I remember sitting in the car after a man attacked me in my apartment, and Vincent comforted me. I was all alone. You weren't there for me! If you're so grand, why didn't you save us from this mess? And, what about after our first shared dream? I don't know what happened, but you do; you were there with Vincent. And somehow, I woke up with an even greater trust for him. Turns out, that wasn't my trust, it was yours."

Lips and eyebrows compressed toward Moon's nose. It was a look of anger Abbie recognized all too well.

"You're right. You weren't the only one manipulated by him," Moon admitted.

"Finally, a bit of humility," Abbie said, hands in the air. "So, I'm not the only one who can have someone they trust pull the rug out from under them."

"You're the only one who runs from a fight."

"I don't fight?! I hit Mozzie with a damn wine bottle! I tried to get that pilot Carlton off Vincent before the gun went off; and then yeah, I got scared and ran. You can't die in the dream, but I sure as hell can out there. I'd love to see how you dealt with having a real gun shoved in your face!"

"You wouldn't even draw a damn picture because you were afraid of not being as good as Emma," Moon countered.

"And I'm sure you've never felt self-doubt either. My whole life would be so easy for you, I'm sure."

"It would!" Moon seethed. "If you gave me control, I could get us out of this mess. I could breathe the memories of a pilot somewhere and then be able to fly us directly to Alice. I could punch Pinely in his freckled face and take the gun from him."

"Who's Pinely?" Abbie asked. "That's the second time you've mentioned that name."

"You see?" Moon said, turning around with arrogant swagger. "You can't even draw the connection between the physical and the mental. Pinely is a member of my conclave, who obviously secretly works as an agent for Alice. He's that pilot Carlton. They have the same stupid logo, both here in Consciousness and out there in Basic. They look and sound the same. Hell, they smell the same! I'm pretty sure even Hanker doesn't know about Pinely's deception…tricky little Brit."

"That's why Carlton called me 'Moon' when he had the gun pointed at me," Abbie said. "I thought he looked familiar when I saw him."

"Yeah, he's just as handsome in Basic as he is in the dream, which I'll admit, is even more of a surprise than him secretly working for Alice. He always seemed to try too hard."

"Can Alice help us?" Abbie questioned.

Moon snorted. "She just sent someone to kill us. If you just let me take control, then she'd probably lend a hand. Other than that? Not likely."

The two women stood silent for a moment. Sounds and smells converged in paradoxical shapes all around them. Abbie had so many questions but knew herself well enough to admit Moon wouldn't answer any of them without making her feel stupid.

"Why am I this way?" Abbie asked the empty universe around them. She rubbed her sore head and eyes.

"What do you mean?" Moon asked.

Abbie waved her hand between the two of them. "Why am I this way? Why do I hate myself so much that I can't even get a straight answer from my own subconscious? What the hell happened to me to make me this adversarial toward…myself?"

Moon nodded, opening her mouth to speak, but then closing it again.

"You see?" Abbie continued. "Not even super-awesome-wonderful Moon knows the answer to that one. Look at us. Our body is literally lying in a ditch a hundred miles from the nearest road in the middle of nowhere Idaho, while a friend of yours is about to shoot us in the head. But here we stand, in this weird psychedelic mind space, hating ourself so much that we can't even admit we're the same person."

"We're not!" Moon yelled.

Shockwaves blew from Abbie as she stomped closer to Moon. The warrior's purple armor faded somewhat for an instant before surging back. Similar defensive plates manifested around Abbie in a matching shade of violet. She looked down at the armor. It had appeared without a conscious thought. No wonder Moon was so arrogant; creating something from nothing felt incredibly empowering.

Looking back up, Abbie stared at her counterpart with more confidence than ever before. "You think you're so amazing, don't you? You think you're so much better than me. You can create anything you want because you live in a world that isn't real."

"Consciousness is real!" Moon defended with conviction, though her eyes focused on Abbie's armor with a hint of worry.

"No, it's not!"

The shout shattered the world around them like a glass sphere dropped on the sidewalk in a rainstorm. Wind screamed in a whirl of blue liquid and fear.

Abbie seemed to tower over Moon; an angry teacher frustrated with a mouthy student. An odor, like burning oil in a pan, puffed from Moon's hair. "What's that I smell, Moon?" Abbie asked. "Do you doubt your own words? No, you don't know uncertainty. Everything comes easy to you in your imaginary world. You don't know what it's like to put everything you have into something and still come up short; to be afraid of making the wrong choice and impacting the next ten years of your career. You've been watching my life like I watch one of those 'pointless TV shows' you seem to hate, but you're not really even experiencing it, are you?"

"I don't need to experience it," Moon said, turning away from her mirror image.

"Because you're afraid."

Lavender fire flared from Moon's eyes as she turned back. "I'm not afraid of you," her voice growled. "I have nothing to fear from you. I've heard your complaints, but you've never faced fear in its purest form, or felt the depression of someone you're trying to save from being tortured. You've never been swarmed by creatures intent on stealing your emotions, or to rape your thoughts. You're nothing but a weak, cowardly little thing that worries about your sister being a better artist and businesswoman, and whether Nana Gayle is proud of you or not."

"Yeah," Abbie hissed. "And you have your life in Consciousness all figured out."

"I do! You will never have anything to offer me. I have no need for you beyond you stuffing your face with ice cream so you don't starve to death, and maybe going to bed on time so I can do important work that you'll never understand."

Abbie had heard enough. Maybe it was her anger with Vincent's betrayal; maybe it was her realization that she truly was her own worst enemy. Whatever the case, she acted without thinking. Grabbing Moon's head with both hands, Abbie screamed and released all her pent-up frustration, fear, self-loathing, and doubt. The emotions rushed from her body and flooded Moon in a cascade of intertwining, muted color. The two women seemed to glow in a gray light that brightened nothing. Moon's eyes widened, threatening to burst from her face. Mouth open, muscles tense, the great warrior cracked like dry mud on a hot day, but somehow remained solid. As the emotions ebbed, the flow seemed to reverse, filling Abbie with the overwhelming responsibility of protecting the threatened, the fear of being too slow to save a tormented dreamer, and the terror of being hunted by beings who knew more about your doubts than you did.

The emotions swirled around Abbie and Moon like a figure-eight, passing from one woman to the other and back around again; an endless loop of light made up of misgivings, mistakes, and missed opportunities. Their armor shattered into tiny pieces and popped like puffs of smoke into the void. Memories that had been viewed from afar like a voyeur now seared themselves into place along with the corresponding crush of sentiment. As the flow slackened, light faded, leaving them limp and exhausted.

Moon collapsed to her knees and wept. Abbie toppled backwards and spun around onto her belly. Tears flowed freely from her eyes as well, dripping onto a starfield that reflected her bloodshot visage. No shame accompanied the sobs, only understanding, insight, and humility.

"I'm sorry," Abbie whispered. She rolled onto her back and sat up slowly, trying to wipe away the cascade of saline covering her face. "I'm so sorry I didn't understand."

Head down, Moon continued to cry. After a moment, she looked up and Abbie noticed the white line on her face had disappeared. Moon's features had softened, and she seemed even more like Abbie than she had before.

"I didn't know..." Moon gasped. "I didn't know what it's like. I didn't want to know."

"We couldn't have...either of us." Abbie sniffed and looked up at swirling galaxies and endless stars that took shape above them. A calm spread over the environment. Tortured shapes ceased convulsing.

Pity. It smelled like moist grass on a rainy day. Abbie had never sensed anything so painfully peaceful. It brought an ache that spread from her chest to her limbs; not a consuming pain, just a discomfort that brought empathy.

She understood Moon now. The burden she carried for everyone threatened by greedy Pursuants; the doubts that she wouldn't be fast enough or strong enough, and that one night she would choose to give up and waste away in a Thought Bubble like so many others.

They were the same person, the same frustrations, worries, and suspicions, simply different mountains to climb. Moon was indeed amazing. But so was Abbie.

"You're incredible," Abbie said after a fleeting silence. "Vincent may have lied about a lot of stuff, but he didn't lie about that. You're something special, Moon."

"No," Moon replied with a weak smile. Tears continued to trickle down her cheeks. "No, my name is Abbie. I've always been Abbie; I just couldn't accept it. Merquery was right. I'm not two, I'm one. I'm Abbie. And Abbie is pretty incredible too."

Whimpering, Abbie scooted forward and wrapped her arms around Moon as if hugging a beloved sister. Moon embraced her, and the two women cried in each other's warmth and acceptance. The emotion surrounded them like welcoming fire on a cold night. Eyes closed, they allowed themselves a moment to exist without expectation, uncertainty, or self-judgement. They were at peace, tranquil like a calm ocean under a slowly rising sun.

A deep breath filled Abbie's lungs and she opened her eyes, seeing she sat by herself in the endless space. Moon was nowhere to be seen. Abbie was alone.

No, alone wasn't the right word.

Whole. One. Unified.

Abbie stood, remembering how she felt when Hanker told her Vincent was playing her; how she felt when Nana Gayle told her how good her drawings were.

She remembered everything. The dream world and the physical world. The whole world.

What had Alice called her? Abbie-Moon-Kinder. That name felt right.

Standing, Abbie stretched her back and breathed deeply. She knew what she had to do.

"Looks like it's time to wake up," she said.

'But you can't wake yourself up from the dream,' a voice in her head seemed to say.

Abbie nodded as if recognizing the statement's logic. "I'm not going to let that stop me anymore." She closed her eyes and felt herself lift toward open space above. Nothing would hold her back.

Nothing would stop her from reaching her goals ever again.

She needed to see Alice. And she knew just how to make it happen.

CHAPTER FIFTEEN

Cold pebbles dug into Abbie's cheek as she awoke. Her head still pounded from hitting the tree, but her mind seemed crisp and focused. A squirrel pattered through the brush to her right, and she opened her eyes in time to see a bushy tailed rodent dart up a pine tree ten feet away. Leaves crumpled against her palms as she pushed herself up next to the scrub oak where she had fallen. Shadows deepened in the forest. The sun drew close to the mountains in the west. Orange clouds kissed a purple sky overhead. It seemed the most beautiful sunset Abbie had ever seen; more spectacular than five suns rotating in the sky over Consciousness. More beautiful than anything she could ever create in the dream.

She was whole for the first time in her life. Everything from the smells of the dirt between her fingers, to the creaking of pine branches, seemed elevated and amplified. Her understanding now encompassed the full range of the human experience, both physical and mental. She wanted to sing and dance, but knew threats still loomed that would snuff out her joy if given the chance. She needed all her wits and knowledge to find Alice.

Abbie sat behind the bush for a moment listening. No sounds beyond distant bird calls or wind in the treetops drew her attention in any given direction. She strained her ears for a plane engine roar anywhere nearby but heard nothing. Questions remained: who had fired the gun after the initial struggle? Vincent or Pinely? Had someone been shot, and if so, whom? Was the plane still on the runway, or was she stranded, unprepared for a very cold night in the wilderness?

A twig snapped somewhere to her left. Abbie shifted silently, remaining hidden behind the scrub oak. Nothing came into view around any of the trees. Pine needles crunched from the same direction as the broken twig. A footstep. Movement soon drew her eye to a tall man with red hair, wearing a brown leather jacket with a lightning compass logo on the breast.

Carlton/Pinely.

He crouched low to the ground, eyes searching in every direction. The silver revolver in his left hand reflected the dying light. Blood dripped from his forehead all the way down his chin.

Where was Vincent? Dead? Shot somewhere in the forest? If so, it would make her job so much easier. A morbid thought, but one that didn't bother Abbie. She didn't necessarily want Vincent dead, even after all the manipulation, but if Pinely had shot him, at least she could appreciate the simpler road that fact afforded.

Pinely drew closer to the scrub oak, but still didn't see Abbie through the brush. She held perfectly still, waiting for the right moment.

Just as the pilot stepped within a few feet, Abbie jumped up and punched him in the throat. Pinely stumbled back, eyes wide. Not waiting for a better moment, Abbie lunged for the gun, twisting Pinely's wrist while lodging her elbow under his chin. The revolver came loose in her hand. She jumped back out of arm's reach of the tall man and fingered the trigger.

"Bloody hell!" Pinely choked and coughed.

"Back off, Pinely Daymare," she said, voice calm. "I understand why you needed to shoot me before, but I'll do the same if you step any closer."

Arms raising, Pinely nodded his head. “Sorry about that,” he croaked, rubbing his throat with his left hand. “Got a job. You know how it is.”

“Where’s Vincent?” Abbie asked.

“Run off,” Pinely answered with a shrug. “I shot him in the leg, but he bashed my head with a rock, so I didn’t see where he went. I followed some spots of blood as best I could, along with some footprints, but I lost him pretty quick. He seemed to be running north, which would get him deeper into the forest, that’s for sure. Not the direction I would have picked. I came back this way to see if I could find you. Then I figured I’d fly off and leave the two of you to freeze overnight, or starve, or whatever. And here I found you.”

“I found *you*,” Abbie corrected. “What would Hanker think if he saw us here? I’m sure he’d be disappointed you’ve been lying to him this entire time.”

Pinely’s eyes blinked several times in rapid succession. “You remember,” he said finally. “You didn’t before though…when we were about to take off. I would have noticed. You were afraid. That wasn’t an act. You didn’t remember at that point, right?”

“I didn’t, but I do now. Aspira, Merquery, that stupid pointed green hat of yours and the British flag for a cape? I remember all of it. Why have you been lying to us?”

“I had to,” Pinely said, shifting weight from his left foot to his right as if trying to warm himself. “Alice recruited me three years ago when I still lived in Newcastle in the North of England. She needed eyes and ears, that’s all. I came out here to help. But I never lied directly, now did I, Moon? You never asked me if I worked for Alice.”

Abbie stepped closer, pointing the gun directly at Pinely’s chest. “You never offered the information though, did you? You pretended to not be able to remember Consciousness once you woke up, but that's obviously crap. Does Aspira work with you and Alice here in Idaho too?"

Wind blew from the east and Pinely shivered. "Can we discuss all of this someplace else? It's getting cold, and the sun is setting. Plus, your boyfriend is somewhere out here, and I'd hate to get hit in the head again with a rock, if you follow me."

"Take us back to the plane then," Abbie said. "You're flying me to Alice right now."

"Could you put the gun down at least?" Pinely asked. "Now that I know you remember the dream, I'm not going to try to hurt you."

"I'll hold onto it just the same," Abbie said, motioning for Pinely to start walking. "After the last few days, I have some trust issues. Get moving and I'll follow behind."

Pinely led the way through the trees, stepping loudly on the dry grass and underbrush with his hands still in the air. At first, Abbie couldn't tell which direction they walked, but soon saw the trees beginning to thin, opening on the backcountry runway. No sight or sound of Vincent revealed itself anywhere in the area.

"Could we take a minute and maybe find my hat?" Pinely asked. "That was a right nice western cap. I'd hate to lose it."

"Keep walking," Abbie answered. "It was at least better than that Robin Hood hat you wear in Consciousness."

"It's called a bycoket, if you must know," Pinely continued without looking back. "You really do remember everything. That's wild. It makes me happy though. I wasn't excited about this particular mission. Not a fan of killing people, especially ones I know and respect; meaning you, not that wanker Auspice. Anyway, to answer your earlier question: Aspira doesn't know about any of this."

"So, you've kept it all a secret from your little kitty girlfriend too?" Abbie asked.

"She's not my girlfriend. Aspira wants to be with me, and I let her play the role, but I don't share any of myself with her. I'm with…someone else."

"Well, isn't she lucky?"

They cleared the forest and walked back onto the dirt airstrip. The red-winged airplane sat exactly where they had landed. Rays of sunlight shot over the jagged peaks on the horizon, now less than ten minutes from sunset. Abbie focused on every sensory detail in her field of view. The birds had quieted down. The air grew cooler. Footprints in the dust to her right made their way from the forest toward the plane. A crosshatching pattern covered the prints, like deceptively expensive shoes worn by casual professionals. One glance at Pinely's worn cowboy boots told Abbie the prints didn't belong to him. Spots of red spattered the ground ahead: blood, possibly from a leg wound.

"Vincent came this way," Abbie said, eyes locked on the trail of blood. "How badly did you hurt him?"

"I shot him in the upper thigh, I think. Again, I was getting bashed in the skull with a rock, so the details are vague."

They drew closer to the aircraft. The footprints seemed to run around to the pilot's side of the Cessna. Abbie pointed the gun at the plane, half expecting Vincent's head to pop up in the cockpit and fly off without them. As she circled around the propeller, she noticed the prints running toward the passenger door, and then toward the opposite end of the runway, leaving the plane behind.

Abbie bit her lip, trying to make sense of the scene before her. "Did he run off into the---"

"Abbie!" Vincent shouted. Abbie turned to see the dark-haired man limping heavily from behind the trees on the south side of the runway, less than thirty yards away. Blood darkened his gray pants from the mid-thigh down past his knee. "Abbie! Are you alright? What happened? How'd you get the gun from him?"

"Stay back, Auspice!" Abbie shouted. She spun the revolver toward Vincent and cocked back the hammer. "Don't take another step."

"What are you talking about?" Vincent said. He stopped; a pained expression pulling his handsome face down like melting wax. "You've got the gun on this asshole. We should be safe now. Shoot him and we can keep going."

"I don't like this prick," Pinely breathed.

"I know who you are, Auspice," Abbie said. "I remember everything. You said I had no idea what was really going on. Well, I have a much better understanding now. Stay back, and I won't have to shoot you."

Vincent's head tilted to the left. He nodded slightly. "Whatever this guy told you, it's a lie, Abbie. I promise you. He tried to kill us. You can't trust him."

"He didn't tell me anything," Abbie said. "I remember it all myself. I know you're Auspice. I know you cast Fraelig from the dream that first time we met in Consciousness. I know you were Resin. I know you manipulated me every step of the way. You can't trick me anymore."

"Abbie," Vincent said, taking a step forward and then grimacing as he put weight on his right leg. "Are you sure you know what's true and what's not? Are you sure no one else has been manipulating you? I've only ever---"

A gunshot split the silence and cut off Vincent's gaslight maneuvering as Abbie fired over his head. Frightened birds flew from nearby trees in caws and cries. He stopped, holding his hands out toward Abbie as if asking for a parlay.

"Shut up, Vincent," Abbie ordered. She turned to Pinely and

motioned her head toward the aircraft. "Get the plane started, Pinely. And if I feel like you're planning on screwing me over at any point, I'll blow a hole in that pretty face of yours."

"You really think I'm handsome, Moon?" the Brit asked with a smile.

"Get in the damn plane!"

"Yes, my lady." Pinely opened the pilot door and stepped up to the cockpit.

"What about me?" Vincent asked, voice suddenly hard and tense. "Are you going to leave me out here to starve to death? Freeze in that storm coming in? We can still help each other Moon. Now that you know everything, you also have to see what I can do for you both here and in Consciousness. I can show you things you never realized; things you couldn't comprehend. Just take me to Alice, and everything can be yours. Everything you ever wanted."

The engine sputtered and the propeller started spinning. Abbie's hair blew into her face, and she brushed it aside with her left hand.

Abbie stepped over to the passenger-side door, gun still pointed at Vincent. "You know," she shouted over the roaring motor and turbine. "I don't doubt you're telling the truth about all of that. I'm sure you could show me everything you claim and more."

"I can."

"But it doesn't matter. You're a liar. You've done nothing but manipulate me since the moment we met in the hospital parking lot. You can rot in hell for all I care."

"I don't think you really mean that," Vincent called. "And you still don't know what's really going on. Either way, I promise you, I have some surprises left up my sleeve."

"I'm sure you do," she yelled as she pulled herself up toward the plane's cab. "But unless one of those surprises involves pulling a tent and a sleeping bag out of your ass, you're going to have a cold night ahead of you. Sleep well. I'll see you in the dream."

She slammed the door behind her and looked at Pinely. He smirked, putting his headset over his ears. Abbie followed his lead and watched through the window as Vincent took a few shaky steps toward the plane.

"You're as scary out here as you are in Consciousness, Moon," Pinely grinned. "I say that as a way to butter you up, so you don't shoot me, just so I'm being honest. It's true all the same, though."

"Take me to Alice," Abbie replied. She placed the gun on her lap, finger laying across the guard, ready to slip over the trigger at the slightest need.

Vincent grew smaller and smaller in the window as the plane raced down the runway and lifted into the darkening sky. They turned north, spinning one more time over the airstrip. Abbie looked down on the tiny figure lost in a sea of trees. Would Vincent survive the night? Would he be able to eventually make his way 100 miles back to civilization? She doubted it. Perhaps they could come back for him in the morning. Perhaps Alice would show Vincent some mercy. Maybe she'd send a rescue crew once Pinely brought Abbie to their hidden headquarters at the Triple Z cabin she had seen in Alice's mind.

Perhaps. But not likely.

Vincent was on his own. Whatever tricks he had up his sleeve, he better use them quick, otherwise he'd be too dead to surprise anyone.

They flew for another half hour as the sky transitioned from dark blue, to purple, and finally to formless gray.

"Do you prefer 'Pinely,' or 'Carlton?'" Abbie asked after an extended silence.

"Pinely is fine," he replied. "That's how you know me. One name I was given, the other I chose. Both are appropriate, in my opinion. You want me to call you 'Moon,' or 'Abbie?'"

She thought about it for a second. "I think we'll go with Abbie while we're out here in Basic. Before all of this I never would have accepted that name. I was Moon, or nothing. Now I think I understand myself better than I did before though. It's nice."

"Yeah, once you have both worlds reconciled, it certainly changes your perspective in each."

They sat silently again except for the rumble of the propeller. The trees beneath them turned into an unbroken mass of black. Lightening occasionally flashed to the east and bathed the forest in an instantaneous flicker of radiance. No other lights appeared on the horizon as far as the eye could see. Just as Abbie began to fear things would be too dark for them to land safely, a woman's voice squawked on the radio.

"Carlton, we've got you on infrared," she said. "You're one minute out."

"Lovely," Pinely answered. "I think I can see the runway, but if you wouldn't mind flashing the light at the tail end for shits and giggles, I'd appreciate it. Make sure the hatch is unlocked too, please. And tell her we've got an unexpected visitor, but that she'll be happy with who she meets."

"Will do," The woman responded.

A yellow flash blinked in the dark mass of trees just ahead of them. Abbie could make out a pale strip of gray in the blackness that appeared to be another backcountry airstrip. After three blinks, the light went out. No other points of illumination could be seen anywhere in the area. Night claimed the world and refused to relinquish its hold.

Tires touched down on the airstrip and bounced Abbie up and down. Something clattered to the floor in the back seat, but Abbie couldn't make anything out in the dark cabin, outside the few lights glowing on the control board next to the yoke. Pinely pushed forward on the stick, and they came to a stop next to pine trees huddled in shadow. The propeller slowed, lessening the vibrations running through the vessel. Silence once again engulfed them.

"Alright," the pilot said, removing his headset. "That was not the calmest landing I've ever had. Bit nerve-racking it was in the dark, but we made it, so all's good."

"Don't you have lights on the front you could have turned on, like a car's headlights?" Abbie asked.

"It's better not to use them at this point," Pinely said. He unbuckled his belt and opened the door. Cold air rushed in, reminding Abbie of Vincent, now stranded in the middle of nowhere. "We've come close enough to showing our enemies where we are," Pinely continued. "I think caution is our only ally tonight."

He stepped down and walked around the plane toward Abbie's door. She threw it open and jumped next to him. Moisture clung to the air, with a hint of gasoline from the aircraft engine. Spires of black pine stood against a dark gray sky. Stars began to peak out on the world like children poking their heads from under a blanket. No other details took shape in the night. Only the barest silhouette of Pinely's face could be seen in the murk.

"You can keep the gun for now," he said. "But Alice will make you give it back, just so you know."

"I'll keep it till then," Abbie informed. The revolver made her feel more secure. She couldn't conjure a blade in Basic after all. Alice had sent someone to kill her. Best to be prepared for anything.

"Stay close behind me," Pinely said. "There's a path up here that I know pretty well, even in the dark. We've got a little ways to walk, and I'm not going to use any flashlights till we're under the cover of the trees."

He led Abbie toward the forest. The ground seemed level enough, though occasionally Abbie's foot would step on a pinecone and send her slightly off balance. After a few minutes, a single red light came into view through the trees.

"What's that?" Abbie asked.

"A marker. We're close."

Metal clicked somewhere in front of Abbie, and suddenly Pinely's face lit up. He'd turned on a small pocket flashlight. The beam moved from his feet to the trees around them. He shined it on the closest pine, where Abbie saw a trail camera strapped to the trunk; it's red light indicating battery life. After waving his hand at the camera as if to say, 'good evening,' Pinely turned to their right and motioned for Abbie to follow. He shone the flashlight at their feet, allowing them to see any surprise roots or rocks that could impede their progress. No sound reached Abbie's ears beyond the crunching of their shoes on the forest floor, and the occasional rumble of thunder somewhere off to the east.

A deer sprinted across their path, eyes reflecting the glare from the flashlight. Abbie jumped at the surprise visitor but kept her nerves in check. She held the gun up, happy she didn't have her finger on the trigger.

"Here we are," Pinely said after another few minutes. "Home sweet home."

He shined the flashlight in front of them, illuminating the porch of a small red cabin, no bigger than twenty-feet-by-twenty-feet square. Dark windows reflected the flashlight glare and gave the entire structure the feel of a lifeless skull left to decay in the woods. Rotting boards made up the front steps, with nails poking out here and there. A railing ran along the porch with red and white accents.

Faded white shutters covered several of the windows. Above the door two small chains hung a carved wooden sign that read 'Triple Z Ranch' in yellow letters.

"This doesn't look much like a ranch," Abbie said.

"It's not much of a cabin either," Pinely replied. "But you'll see what we've really got going on in a second."

Cowboy boots thumped against squeaking boards as Pinely stepped onto the porch. Abbie followed, feeling the wood shift under her feet. The smell reminded her of the Woodland cabin porch where she had taken Vincent that first night, with its pile of musty dried logs next to the front door. Hinges squealed when Pinely opened the entrance and stepped inside. Dust and stuffy old furniture tickled Abbie's nostrils and threatened to send her into a sneezing fit. She plugged her nose and avoided making a scene.

"Step back for a second," Pinely said. He bent over and pulled at a rusted metal loop attached to the wooden floor. A trap door opened, revealing what looked like a metal submarine hatch beneath, complete with a circular locking mechanism. Pinely grabbed the latch wheel and spun it. A hiss of air escaped from the hatch as he pulled it open. Light shot from the hole in the floor, illuminating a steel ladder that descended underground at least twenty feet down a circular shaft.

"You guys have a subterranean lair, or something?" Abbie asked without hiding her sarcasm.

"Pretty much," Pinely said. "You want to go first?"

"Sure," Abbie said. She stepped over and handed Pinely back his revolver. "I'm sure at this point I won't be needing a gun anymore. If you guys wanted to take me down, you'd probably be able to do it whether I'm armed or not."

"Yeah, there's not really anywhere else to go from here anyway. It's either down, or back out to the forest."

Cold metal pressed against Abbie's palms as she lowered herself down the ladder. Rounded steel walls encircled her. She sank lower rung by rung. Warm air billowed up from below, sending goosebumps tingling along her arms. After about twenty feet, the shaft opened on a large concrete chamber filled with blue water barrels and wooden crates. Generators hummed somewhere in the space, along with what sounded like a laugh track from an old 1970's sitcom. Thick metal doors stood in alcoves on the walls to her left and right. In front of her, a long hallway arched to the left, with a similar corridor going in the opposite direction behind her. Thick, brass pipes ran along the ceilings to each door and down the halls, probably for water, Abbie figured. Footsteps echoed from somewhere, but the tall ceilings made discerning the exact direction difficult.

"Watch out," Pinely said as he slid down the ladder in a single motion.

"Well, who am I meeting here?" a woman said, drawing Abbie's attention to the hallway behind her. Out stepped the silver woman she'd met in Consciousness, only instead of chrome skin, pink flesh and freckles, framed by frizzy brown hair with streaks of gray, met her gaze. Lines on her forehead placed the woman in her mid-forties by Abbie's estimation, but her body looked tight and fit, ready to run or fight at a moment's notice. She wore a white tank top and baggy canvas pants, along with combat boots that gave her the air of a soldier about to go on leave. Two other women followed her, one with dark skin, short coarse hair, and striking eyes, the other with Hispanic features, large lips, and black ponytails falling all the way to the small of her back. Both wore similar clothing to their leader, with the long-haired woman sporting a camouflage jacket over her ensemble.

"Sorry about the surprise guest," Pinely said with a slight bow to the woman. "She got the drop on me, but I think you won't be too mad."

"You can make it up to me later," the woman said as she leaned in and kissed Pinely on the lips. "You've got some blood on your face, sweety. Are you okay?"

"I got hit in the head by a certain Proctor while I was trying to murder her and that prig Auspice," Pinely smiled. "But there's no hard feeling, at least for my part. I think the blood is from the rock Auspice hit me with anyway."

"As long as you're okay," Alice said, rubbing his chin. "You better get cleaned up real quick before we get everyone together." After the fleeting moment of affection, she turned to Abbie and looked at her from the toe of her shoes to the top of her tussled hair. "Abbie-Moon-Kinder, I presume."

"I'm going to guess you're Alice Ashling," Abbie stated with confidence. She held out her hand and Alice took it firmly.

"You would be correct."

"You look exactly like you did on the shores of the subconscious river, except less shiny," Abbie said.

A smile warmed Alice's face; her eyes dropping for a second as if conceding Abbie's appraisal. "So, I take it sometime in the last six hours you somehow figured everything out and now remember the psychological world alongside the physical one? I'm going to be honest, I'm pretty damn surprised. Not disappointed, mind you, just surprised."

Abbie shrugged. "Well, a knock on the head and a pointed argument with oneself opens up all kinds of doors, I guess. You were right; I wasn't ready. Not until I understood myself a bit better. This is your hidden lair, I take it?"

"It's our sanctuary," Alice said, looking up at the cement ceiling overhead. "It's not a penthouse overlooking Kowloon Bay like what Alexander would have, but it's been safe so far."

“And you and Pinely are…together?” Abbie motioned toward the couple as the pilot put his arm around Alice.

“We don’t like to label it,” she said with a smile.

“I would, if she’d let me,” Pinely added. “The age difference bothers her, I think,” he winked.

Alice elbowed him in the ribs and motioned for the group to follow her down the far corridor. “Abbie, there’s a lot you need to learn, and not a lot of time for me to teach it to you. Come with me. You’re about to get a crash course in what we’re up against.”

CHAPTER SIXTEEN

"Did you build this place?" Abbie asked as they stepped into a large conference-style room off the main corridor. A large man in army fatigues sat on a sofa across the chamber watching what looked like an episode of *Sanford and Sons* on an old square television. He jumped up as they entered and turned off the TV. The walls of the compound appeared to be solid concrete, with rounded corners and pipelines running along the ceiling, like in the adjacent hallways. All the doors were made of heavy cast-iron, with few accoutrements accenting the space beyond the occasional chair, table, or dusty couch. Everything felt dated, as if picked up from a thrift store specializing in furniture from the 1950's. A smell, like baked beans, seemed to waft from a room on their right.

"Have a seat," Alice said as they stepped over to a long yellow linoleum table surrounded by eight matching chairs with fraying plastic pads on the backrests. "I'll update you on everything once the entire night crew is here."

Abbie took a seat in one of the worn chairs, feeling torn plastic rubbing against her back. Alice sat across from her, next to Pinely, while the others either took flanking chairs or stood along the walls silently watching. Within a few minutes, seven more people entered the room and joined the six already present. All together Alice had five men and six women on her crew besides herself, all dressed in either simple military-type clothing, or wearing jeans and collared shirts as if it were Casual Friday at a local call center.

"Everyone," Alice began, "let me introduce you to Moon."

Several looks of surprise rippled from the gathered group. One of the men, sporting a thick beard and sunburnt cheeks, nodded his head in approval.

"You've all heard of her by reputation, if you haven't met her in Consciousness," Alice continued. "As you are all aware, our original plan was to terminate, if necessary, but as you can see, she's quite persistent. Moon has bridged the gap between the mental and physical and is here before us now as a whole individual. This means we have another ally in our fight against Alexander and the cat." Alice turned back to Abbie and focused on her. "I'm sure you have plenty of questions, but to answer your first one: no, we didn't build this place. It was constructed in the early 1950's by a man by the name of Roland Ingram. He was a multi-millionaire from Chicago who thought the world was going to end in nuclear war, so he had this compound built as far away from civilization as possible so he and his extended family could survive the apocalypse. Unfortunately, he died a few years later and the family held onto it for decades until I learned of its existence and bought it from them. I had it removed from all public records, including Google maps, through a bit of dream influencing, and it's been the perfect hideout ever since."

Abbie nodded in understanding. Hiding from someone as well-connected and powerful as Alexander, would be almost impossible. Alice had found a perfectly elegant solution.

"How do you make money?" Abbie asked. "I assume nobody here has a day job as a fry cook in Stanley Idaho."

"I have plenty of investments at this point, " Alice said. "Being able to navigate Consciousness as I do, allows me to glean all kinds of information and see lots of patterns. It's not exactly insider trading, but when you're at my level it's hard not to get a feel for where things are headed in the financial markets. You'll catch on too, I'm sure."

A woman to Abbie's left, the one with dark brown skin who had accompanied Alice in the hallway, stood up and pressed her hands against the table. "Not to speak out of turn," she said in an unfamiliar African accent, "but I think it's a mistake to bring her here. She was within a hundred miles of us with Auspice. He had to have passed-on what information he learned about our location. They'll be combing this area with everything they have; satellites, hunters, whatever. She puts us at risk, and it will be her fault if we have to abandon basecamp."

"No, Incandice," Alice said. "It was my fault."

Incandice? Abbie had heard that name many times before. They had actually fought together one time against a group of Pursuants trying to corner children to feed on their innocence. Incandice was a legend that rarely slept in a single sleep cycle and could carve a trained Pursuant from the dream with a thought. Now Abbie understood why she was so talented. Perhaps everyone in the room was a famous Proctor with an impressive history longer than Abbie's arm.

"With all due respect," Incandice continued. "I still---"

Alice put her hand up to silence her subordinate. "Let me stress to all of you right now again, it wasn't Moon's fault. It was my fault. Alexander acted as though he was going to make contact with Moon, and in my impatience in trying to learn his location, I reached out to her, and we merged for a moment. Alexander pulled back, but the damage had been done. Whether that was his plan all along, I can't be sure. That wasn't the first time he showed interest in Moon. In any case, the discovery of our location and the subsequent hunt is not Moon's fault. We acted in the best way to protect ourselves and all of humanity, but now we don't need to take those measures anymore. Moon lives and will be considered our ally. Understood?"

Heads nodded around the room. Incandice sat back down but continued to eye Abbie distrustfully.

"Good," Alice continued. "Now that we have that covered, Incandice is right about one thing: Auspice is sure to have been in contact with his superiors; possibly Alexander himself. We still don't know exactly who he was working for and what they want, so we need to be extra careful and begin planting misleading information in the dream so that he, and whoever's in charge, thinks Moon was working with us the entire time just to throw him off. We need to sow confusion and doubt. This will need to be like the Bezos operation we pulled last year. Chaos and skepticism; that's what we need to create. Now that Moon is fully conscious, she can help take part in our little deception. We got lucky. We should also do whatever we can to discredit Auspice. That shouldn't be terribly difficult since he's known for having screwed over a number of Proctors and Pursuants over the past decade."

"I can meet with some of my Brazilian Proctors in a few hours," a large muscular man sitting on the far side of the table said in a South American accent. Large biceps strained against his short-sleeve green shirt. "Once Kaberi wakes up I'll pass everything on to her team too."

"Thank you, Tiago," Alice said.

Abbie raised her hand, as more questions began to fill her mind. She realized these eleven people may be only the team members in the complex currently awake at that moment. Dozens more could potentially be sleeping in other rooms. "How many people do you have down here?" she asked.

"Currently we have 24 of us," Alice answered. "We sleep in shifts, while taking turns delving deeper using the machines."

"The machines?" Abbie questioned. "Like what you and Alexander used back in the day? You have them here?"

Alice rubbed her lips and glanced sideways to different members of her crew as if silently asking them their opinions. "Well, if you're here, then we might as well bring you all the way in." She stood and motioned toward the hallway to her left. "Follow me, Moon. Incandice and Pinely will come with us, the rest of you get back to what you were doing. And Francis…"

"Yes ma'am," a short young man in a pale-yellow golf shirt said as he leaned against the side wall.

"Finish cleaning the damn bathrooms on the west side of the complex. I'm tired of the smell in the hallway outside the doors every time I walk by."

"Yes ma'am," Francis said slowly, as several of his colleagues chuckled.

The farther Abbie traveled inside the compound, the more impressive it became. She followed Alice down another arching hallway past a kitchen area, workout room, and several more cast-iron doors. Each hallway ended in another metal flap that could be shut and sealed in case of nuclear contamination. The paranoid builder of this underground bunker certainly hadn't spared any expense in creating his doomsday contingency. Abbie assumed they were traveling west, as a smell of overflowing toilet filled the area. After one more turn Alice led her to a large double door made of dark polished wood instead of steel.

"This was going to be Mr. Ingram's master bedroom," Alice said as she pushed open the doors. "He died before he ever slept here, but this room ended up being the biggest and the best; perfect for our needs."

Varnished wood covered the walls instead of the concrete common throughout the rest of the base. Maroon shag carpet scrunched under Abbie's shoes. A series of four out-of-date hospital beds acted as the centerpiece to the room, along with several desks covered in top-of-the-line computers, monitors, and soldering equipment. Two of the beds were occupied by sleeping individuals; a man and a woman, both wearing helmets that covered most of their faces. They were hooked to cables similar to what Abbie had witnessed in Alice's memories of her first shared consciousness experience with Alexander. Two other helmets sat unused on the adjacent beds. A technician sat at one of the desks, typing at a keyboard with a half-eaten donut next to it. Dark black dreadlocks fell over the man's glasses. He yawned and scratched his chest over a t-shirt with a Green Lantern logo on the front.

"Welcome to the Incubus," Alice said, arms wide like a tour guide at the White House. "This is an update of Alexander and Professor Khatri's original design. We've had to cobble some things together, but Dr. Dlamini does a good job of keeping things up-to-date and competitive, don't you Hakim?"

"I do my best," the doctor said in a South African accent. He adjusted his glasses and looked at Abbie. "We got a new recruit?"

"This is Moon," Alice introduced. "We haven't had a chance to talk about the future just yet, but for now, she's here to learn."

Abbie shook the doctor's hand firmly. "Pleasure to meet you, Dr. Dlamini? Did I pronounce that right?"

"You did. Call me Hakim, please."

Picking one of the helmets off the closest bed, Pinely tightened several cables hooked to the back with his left hand. "How are Maggie and Vlad doing?" he asked.

"Vitals good," Hakim said, turning to his computer monitor. He took a quick bite from his colorfully sprinkled donut and pointed to the screen. "Their theta waves are strong; mental acuity at 68 percent. They have about another hour is all. Hopefully Vlad will come out with more information about that Bolivian guy, The Ascendent, that's blacked things out down there in South America. I'll let you know what he gets."

The two sleeping individuals lay completely at peace as far as Abbie could tell. The man wore a t-shirt and flannel pants, while the woman slept in shorts and a tank top. Other than the futuristic headgear, Abbie would have assumed they were taking a nap or just resting their eyes. Neither moved in the slightest beyond the rhythmic rising and falling of their chests.

"What do these helmets do, exactly?" she asked. "Do they just make your brain stronger, or something like that?

"They induce a powerful theta state," Alice replied. She leaned back against Hakim's desk and grabbed a file folder full of documents. Slipping several paperclips from the pages, she threw the file back where she found it. "Let me illustrate for a second," she continued, slipping the paperclips together and holding them tight. "Imagine your consciousness is like these paperclips, okay? Minds naturally link when in a subconscious state. You can connect to a certain number of minds at any given time. It depends on the person, but most can do a dozen or so before needing to drop one off in order to link with another. Six or seven is usually optimal, which is why most conclaves of both Proctors and Pursuants run at about that number.

"Those links, multiplied across billions of individuals and their links, produce the dream world and all the environments you encounter. It's how thoughts and memories get left behind in the subconscious of other people and stay in rivers of thought for centuries after individuals have died. Everything from cities of light to barren wastes are built from the collective minds of everyone in the psychological space. What the helmets do is allow users to enter that plane of existence and make those connections without falling fully asleep. More of their conscious mind is taken into the dream, giving them more power over the space and its inhabitants. So, imagine one of these paperclips suddenly growing four or five times in size and linking directly to thousands of minds instead of just a handful. That's what they do for us."

Pinely handed Abbie the helmet and she turned it over in her hands. Heavier than she expected, the unit featured padding on the inside, along with a visor that came down over the eyes, and a series of what looked like audio speakers along where your scalp would rest.

"Are those speakers in there, or something?" Abbie asked.

Papers shuffled on the desk as Hakim stood and took the helmet from her. "They work in a similar way, inducing the brain into a vibrational state that allows one to enter Consciousness. It's a little more complicated than that when you get down to it, but those are the basics."

"They can also be very dangerous," Incandice said, stepping forward.

"That's true," Alice confirmed. "It takes training. A lot of training. You can actually get lost between conscious and subconscious thought, touching minds that are awake, losing your sense of reality, frying your synapses. Alexander uses them too, but I've come across some of his trainees as they've pushed themselves too hard, and they're never the same after that; in the dream or out here in the physical world."

"Only a few of us are skilled enough to use them on a consistent basis," Incandice continued. "You think feeling other people's emotions is addictive? Try being so powerful you can merge with Consciousness. That right there can mess you up. It's like swimming deep into the River of Subconscious but without the ability to escape."

"Okay, but if Alexander is teaching people how to use them and building, like, an army to take over, shouldn't we make more than four?" Abbie asked.

"The Incubus Helmets aren't the answer," Alice said. "Even

Alexander seems to understand that. The more people who have access to tech like this, the more likely another version of Alexander will pop up and start it all over again. So far, our intel points to Alexander only having a few helmets as well. That's all he had when I was with him trying to steal the blueprints back in the day too. He doesn't want any challengers to his throne. Even so, he's probably trained over a thousand Pursuants, and has access to the most powerful people in the world. Think of Rasputin; the guy who ran the Russian court back in the early 20th century. He wasn't the tsar or a political figure, but he had all the power; more than even the king he served. That's Alexander. That's what we're dealing with."

Wheels on the bed legs squeaked as Abbie sat down on one of the unoccupied mattresses. Seeing all the technology, the compound, the trained fighters, and knowing that Alexander had even more resources than this, left her feeling small and insignificant. After a moment, Alice sat next to her and tapped Abbie on the knee.

"This is all a bit much for somebody who just a few hours ago couldn't remember both worlds," Alice said.

Looking over at the man in the helmet lying next to her, Abbie focused on his bare feet. She couldn't help but think about the power he currently enjoyed in Consciousness, while at the same time being completely helpless here in the physical world. The dichotomy struck her for the first time.

"What are they doing in there right now?" Abbie asked.

"Learning," Alice said. "Oftentimes we stay below the surface of the dream, trying to find out where Alexander is going to be next. He travels a lot. We don't fight Pursuants while hooked up to the Incubus. It's too easy to damage someone, or ourselves."

"You talked about Alexander basically taking over in the dream," Abbie continued, sitting forward on the bed. "How close do you think he is?"

"Pretty close," Pinely answered. "We're finding more and more sections of dream, particularly in Asia and Eastern Europe, where the emotional current is incredibly dark and depressing. Another area has been almost completely cut off in Bolivia. Just last week there was a military incursion into Kazakhstan from Russia. Normally the locals fight back tooth and nail, but this time they just sort of stepped aside. It matched what we were seeing in Consciousness."

"Soon there will be pockets like that all over the world, where a handful of trained Pursuants are manipulating enough people to take control of entire governments," Incandice added.

"Holy crap," Abbie breathed. Suddenly her problems seemed minimal in comparison to the full depiction of what they faced. "You said a couple times that Alexander had been paying attention to me before that night when Catharsis attacked. Why?"

Alice looked away and seemed to stare at the wood panels on the walls. "I don't know. He's very calculating. It may have been to get me to do exactly what I did when I linked our minds so he could discover my location, but that feels too much like a conspiracy theory to me. He couldn't have known exactly what information you would have gleaned. You learning my location would never have been guaranteed, though it is on my mind enough that it tends to linger near the surface of my thoughts. Even so, he wouldn't know that. No, there's something else there, I just haven't figured it out yet. What I do know, Abbie-Moon-Kinder, is that there is more going on than even I know."

Abbie took a deep breath, filling her lungs with the recirculated air of an underground bomb shelter in the Idaho wilderness. Thoughts of a man like Alexander pawing around her life made her feel dirty and exposed.

"What do I do now?" she asked. "I remember everything, but Catharsis knows who I am. He said my full name when we met at

Capacious' Thought Bubble. He's still going to hunt me if he can and try to extract what I know. You guys won't be safe if I'm still out there. Vincent may be out of the picture, but Mozzie knows who I am now too. I never really thought about anything beyond getting to you. Now that I'm here, I'm not sure what to do next. My life is over, possibly in both realms. I can't protect people every night if I'm always the target. I can't go to work during the day if somebody is going to try to kidnap me once a week. This whole thing has gotten out of control."

"It has," Alice agreed. She stood back up and pursed her lips as if coming to a decision. "And at this point I can only offer one solution."

"What's that?"

"We have to get you into the dream wearing one of the helmets so you can scare the shit out of anyone that would ever come after you."

Laughter bubbled up from Abbie's chest; real laughter like she hadn't felt in days. "Scare the shit out of them, huh?" she chuckled.

"Yep," Alice smiled. "It will take a bit of practice before you should confront anyone up there, but I'm willing to let you have a go with the Incubus tonight, if you're willing. After that, we figure out what to do here in the physical world. Now that you're united, you were bound to make some changes in your life anyway, right?"

Abbie rubbed her thumbs together and thought about Alice's words.

Changes.

Yeah, there would be changes. Abbie no longer feared pursuing her art. She no longer feared not having a job. The world would open to her in a way that she never imagined. But she still had people she cared about. She never wanted to be far from Nana

Gayle. Mom and Dad always brought her joy, even when they pushed for her to play it safe. She wanted to spend time with her sister again too.

"Aren't you afraid I'll hurt myself using one of those things?" Abbie questioned.

"Not really," Alice said. "You have enough control to keep yourself from going too far and damaging your mind. You'll feel Consciousness fighting against you if you push things. I'm actually interested in seeing what you could do in there if given a little boost. Pinely is set to go to sleep and hook up with your team here pretty soon. Meet up with Hanker and the rest and just allow yourself to experience things. Let's keep you here at the compound for a couple days, practice with the Incubus, and then kick Catharsis and anybody else right in the face once you're comfortable with the tech. Sound good?"

"Mistress," Incandice said slowly as if about to step on glass. "I don't think---"

Alice held up her index finger "It will be fine. I know what I'm doing. Either way, It's Moon's choice at this point."

After a moment of pondering, Abbie looked at Alice and nodded. "Alright, what do I need to do with these helmets?"

"How about we get you something to eat, and maybe a shower too first," Alice replied. "Then we'll wake up Vlad and Maggie here so we can monitor you solo. We'll pop you into Consciousness with a whole new bag of tricks, how does that sound?"

The helmet covered Abbie's eyes and nose, but light still poured in around the edges and over her mouth. The bed shook as she shifted her weight to make herself more comfortable. Even without seeing them, Abbie knew Alice, Incandice, and three other team members continued to stand over her while Hakim typed at his computer.

"I don't like this," Incandice said.

"I know you don't," Alice replied.

"You made me wait a month after I unified before letting me use the Incubus," Incandice continued. "Now she gets to use it a few hours after she remembers the dream?"

"Are you jealous?" Alice asked.

"Are you desperate?"

No one spoke for a moment and Abbie wondered if they were all still standing there.

"Yes, I am desperate," Alice answered finally. "Hakim, are we ready? Pinely should be asleep by now. A little TLC always calms his mind and helps him enter Consciousness more quickly. He'll be waiting for her already."

"Just give me a second," the tech responded. Keys clacked under his fingers. "I've been in here since 5 a.m. this morning and I'm a bit tired. I don't want to dop it up. I need to get everything synced with her natural wavelengths. Normally I'd want at least two days to get everything configured. This isn't as easy as I make it look. Now, Moon, keep your eyes closed, but the screen on the helmet will flash different colors and things that will help attune your brain. Don't pay attention to it, just let it happen. You'll begin to see things in your mind, kind of like if you were on a psychedelic."

"Well, that doesn't make me worry or anything," Abbie said. "I've heard LSD doesn't cause any problems at all."

"You won't be on drugs," Hakim assured. "The device tricks the brain into reaching those kinds of heights without the damage that accompanies narcotics. Plus, it's far more controllable here. I'll be monitoring the whole time. Give me one more minute and we should be good to go."

Shapes and colors appeared in Abbie's field of vision as she waited. With her eyes closed, her other senses heightened. She could hear shoes scraping against the carpet as people shifted around. The smell of Hakim's cologne began to bother her slightly. Air blew from the vents somewhere to Abbie's left, sending a cool ripple between her bare toes.

"Moon," Alice said, suddenly close to her ear.

Abbie jumped slightly at the surprise proximity of the sound. "Yes?"

"Find Pinely and talk to your team. Don't try to exert yourself. Things will feel different right away. Take it slow. Hanker will know what to do and how to help."

"Should I tell him Pinely has been spying on him for you?" Abbie asked. "I'm sure he'll be overjoyed to hear about it."

"Pinely wasn't spying on him," Alice said, voice drawing farther away, as if she stood back with the group like before. "Pinely was spying on you."

"On me?"

"I told you, Alexander showed interest in you for some reason. I needed to know how much interest. Hakim! Can we get this going now, please?"

"Yes, yes," Hakim said. "We're good to start. You ready, Moon?"

"Ready as I'll ever be," Abbie said.

"Alright, here we go."

Vibrations slowly built along Abbie's scalp. A deep tone resonated, though she couldn't tell whether it was an audible sound, or just a product of the frequency pumping through the helmet. Lights flashed on the other side of her eyelids in patterns Abbie couldn't comprehend. Slowly, despite her trepidation, the muscles along her back relaxed. For a moment she felt like her arms and legs floated alongside her. The colors morphed together and seemed to enter her entire body. Voices called from far away. Memories became more vivid than ever before. Dreams and nightmares took shape in a swirl of emotion.

Abbie opened her eyes and the world around her exploded in color and sound; a thousand hallelujahs in a chorus of joy and thanksgiving. Thoughts and sensations rushed to her, but she somehow felt above it all, as if the fabric of reality would bend to her every thought.

Consciousness was no longer something she moved through. Consciousness was hers to play with and mold.

Before she even fully arrived in the dream, Abbie knew she was more than she had ever been before.

She wasn't a dreamer. She wasn't a Proctor.

Abbie-Moon-Kinder was a god.

CHAPTER SEVENTEEN

Two red suns rose on Consciousness as Abbie took her first heightened steps into the realm while under the influence of the Incubus helmet. Everything seemed more vibrant, like a fly under a microscope where every individual lens along the surface of its eye can be seen in sharp relief. Fields of green stretched out before her with a grove of pink and purple marshmallow trees off to the left. Water flowed through the sky like liquid clouds, while butterflies fluttered in wandering tribes discussing the politics of resentment. Dreamers filled the area as they always did, popping up here and there for a few seconds before drifting away like mist on a lake.

From the detail on the bark of an aspen, to the flowers jumping up and down at Abbie's feet, it became clear this would be an elevated experience when compared to her nightly dream cycle. A multitude of smells mingled and blended on the wind, but Abbie could tell the difference between every one; lemon, nectarine, lime, peach, bacon, ham, a cake with raspberry filling. For the first time ever, Abbie looked down and focused on the grass between her toes. Each blade twisted and danced independent of the plants around it, as if every single individual stalk were a manifestation of a unique thought from a dreamer. Never before had Abbie felt psychologically connected to a lawn, but in that moment, she wanted to whisper to the shrubs and hear them respond with images and memory.

The emotions of a hundred thousand people flooded Abbie's brain through a direct connection, but instead of being overwhelmed, she processed each thought easily, with keen understanding. Her mind expanded and comprehended the underlying sentiment of this section of dream, and what brought people's subconscious to this particular sphere.

Frivolity, mixed heavily with childhood exuberance.

Abbie drew a pensive breath through her nose and wondered whether she could continue filling her lungs until all of Consciousness was inside her.

"Moon," Pinely said, somewhere to her right. "Moon, are you okay?"

Opening her eyes, Abbie looked at Pinely in his green pointed hat, British flag cape, and lightning compass symbol on his chest. Normally she would see him simply as he manifested, but under the influence of the Incubus, Abbie could feel his anxiety, smell his affection for Alice, and see the natural features of his physical face beneath the slightly more perfect dream version.

"Moon," Pinely repeated. Even the sound of his British accent seemed somehow crisper and more melodic. Each syllable…each change in tone between the individual letters carried his emotional meaning better than if he had tried to describe his feelings in an entire novel.

"I'm fine, Pinely," she answered.

"You're not wearing any clothes," Pinely said, looking Abbie over with a confused look on his face.

Peeking down, Abbie saw that she was indeed naked, but felt no shame. The fear of being exposed was a common one in Consciousness, hence the customary dream of arriving at a high school class in your underwear, but Abbie no longer felt fear, so covering up never even occurred to her.

"Sorry," she said, forming her purple body suit over her dream flesh. "Things just feel so different right now; so much more…pure, if that makes sense."

Pinely looked at her closely, lips tight together. "You feel different. I mean…I can feel the difference in you. It's not like when others have used the machine. It's really…unique."

Dreamers flocked toward Abbie suddenly as if drawn like insects to a bug zapper. A man sighed in Spanish about how he longed to hold her. A young girl with a Texan accent asked if she could fly. A woman wrapped in an ethereal Canadian flag spoke in French about how she wanted to learn how to overcome her fear of water. More and more voices chimed in. Abbie understood them all.

"What are they doing?" Pinely asked as a dreamer passed through his body and left him panting for air.

"They can feel me," Abbie answered. "And I can feel them. It's all loud emotion here; excitement and silliness."

"Well can you turn down the volume a bit?" Pinely asked. "It's overwhelming with so many coming at you. I can't keep my thoughts straight."

Abbie closed her eyes and pushed away the ideas and feelings of the enamored dreamers. They slowly wandered back toward the fields and colorful forests, confused and lost, as if they no longer knew why they had come over to her in the first place.

"This is amazing," Abbie gasped, looking at her hands. "Have you entered Consciousness before using the Incubus?"

"I have," Pinely admitted, while readjusting his hat. "A couple times. I always feel fuzzy for a few days afterward though, so I don't like the 'hangover,' as it were. But dreamers never swarmed around me as if I was some celebrity like they did with you just now. That was wild. I don't know if it's ever happened to Alice either."

"How did the dream feel to you when you used the

machine?"

Air blew between Pinely's flapping lips. "I felt more Like I was a part of Consciousness, for sure. I understood more languages, I could hide my presence more easily. Overall, it was like switching from an old black and white TV like my granddad used to have, to one of those big 4K flat screens."

"Yes, it's like that…" Abbie said, looking around at minute transitions between shades of indigo in the sky. "…but so much more."

The ground rippled and friendly voices blew on the breeze.

"Moon!" Merquery shouted. Her golden hair twirled around her face; white robes flowing like water in a stream. Behind her bounced squat Gaze in his glimmering orange armor, Tommy in his jeans and a black *Sound Garden* t-shirt, and Brainstorm with his gigantic video game character body, thumping his massive boots against the ground like a lumbering dinosaur. Aspira, with her cat-like features and jealous smell, leaped from a watery cloud just above Abbie's head and landed in between her and Pinely.

"What are you two talking about," Aspira hissed. She rubbed against Pinely and ran her pink whiskers across his neck. The Brit smiled dutifully and rolled his eyes in Abbie's direction.

"Moon!" Merquery yelled again as she rushed over. Statuesque arms threw themselves around Abbie. Her friend embraced her as if they hadn't seen each other in years. "You're okay! We've been so worried. Hanker told us that Auspice was manipulating you in Basic and making you sleep at different times so we couldn't contact you. Is that true? Are you alright?"

"I'm fine, Merquery," Abbie said, pulling herself from the hug. "I'm better than fine. All the work has finally paid off. I remember everything. I'm united now."

"You remember the dream in Basic?" Brainstorm asked as he

rubbed his ridiculously muscular neck.

"I do. I was just telling Pinely, wasn't I?"

"Yeah," Pinely answered with less than convincing speed. "She was telling me how she got away from Auspice and is heading home tomorrow."

Tommy ran his fingers through greasy hair and squinted. "You seem different Moon. You feel…different."

"Did you find Alice?" Gaze interrupted, his black and auburn armor glistening with enthusiasm.

"No," Pinely replied before Abbie could open her mouth. "Turns out there was nothing where Moon thought Alice would be. Must have been misdirection. I'm sure it pissed off Auspice to no end…before you escaped, of course."

"Yeah…" Abbie said. She tried to control her annoyance. Pinely had every reason to protect his girlfriend, but his lack of trust irritated her. She could speak for herself. "It's a long story," she continued, "but we're in good shape now, and I'm back. Where's Hanker?"

"He told us to gather and find Pinely, and that he would meet back up with us," Merquery said. "Since you got pulled from the dream a few days ago, things have been weird. We've had fewer individual Pursuants, but more news of concentrated emotional attacks in different parts of Consciousness. I heard from a lizard last night that the dream city Guāng in the Asian time zone was assaulted sometime before I fell asleep. Why would anyone do that? There are too many dreamers and Proctors there to make any Pursuant hunt worthwhile."

"They're not hunting," Abbie said. "Large-scale synchronized emotional attacks are going to become more frequent, trust me. I've met a lot of dreamers and different Proctors over the past few days. We're going to have our work cut out for us. When will Hanker be back to meet the group?"

Merquery looked out on the horizon. "He didn't say, but I figured he'd be back by now. We felt his emotional connection until just a little bit ago, so either he woke up, or he broke the link so he could concentrate on something else. He's been hunting for you in different sleep times, so that may have been his plan all along."

That sounded like Hanker: searching Consciousness at all times of day to find someone he cared about. To have a mentor as powerful and caring as Conrad Rossi was the dream of every Proctor. Abbie couldn't help but feel suddenly emotional at the thought of her friend and trainer sacrificing so much to try and help her. An overwhelming feeling of gratitude swelled in Abbie's chest, radiating like a tiny sun, and warming her flesh. The faces of her team brightened as the glow manifested and poured from her entire body.

"Whoa…" Gaze breathed. "You guys feel that?"

"Smells like…" Tommy said, a massive grin spreading across his scruffy face, "birthday cake and cinnamon rolls." He closed his eyes as if inhaling a memory from childhood.

Aspira swayed and leaned against Pinely. Fur twitched across her body and changed color from pink to blue. "Yeah…Wow…I just…"

"I love Hanker so much!" Brainstorm bawled. His oversized hands flew to his face as he cried like a spasming boulder on a hillside.

"He's amazing!" Merquery sobbed.

"Whoa, guys," Pinely said, stepping away from his crew. "Let's all just…pull it together. Right, Moon?"

"Uh…Yeah," Abbie agreed, dragging her emotions back inside her mind like a fishing net from the ocean. Her body stopped beaming light, and the team seemed to regain their composure.

Brainstorm wiped his tears and sniffed. “Hanker is just so awesome…”

“Yeah, we know, buddy,” Pinely said, patting the giant young man across the back awkwardly, as if he’d never consoled a crying teenager before in his life. “It’s alright. Deep breath.” He looked at Abbie, concern practically dripping from his face.

The power of the Incubus became even more apparent to Abbie in that moment. Her deep appreciation for Hanker had not only amplified in her mind, but it had infected those around her with no effort at all. Absolutely amazing. Pinely’s discomfort would be warranted, if not for Abbie’s emotional control. She had unified, after all. She was stronger than ever.

She could control it.

Her thoughts returned quickly to Hanker, and the fact that he had not yet returned. Abbie didn’t share Merquery’s opinion that he had cut off his emotional connection because he left the dream, or merely needed to concentrate on another group of Proctors. No, Hanker was in a scrape somewhere. She could feel it. Hanker could take care of himself in pretty much any situation, but even so, it wouldn’t hurt to take a deeper look. With her newly acquired powers, Abbie decided to reach out with her mind and see if she could verify if Hanker had indeed abandoned the dream for the night, or if he was in trouble.

“Give me a second, everyone,” Abbie said. “I’m going to see if I can reestablish a connection with Hanker, so we can see if he needs our help somewhere.”

“How?” Tommy asked. “He’s nowhere around here.”

Abbie didn’t answer, instead focusing her mind on her link with Hanker. He had been her rock in the dream world when she first started understanding her ability to feel the emotions of dreamers. Without him, she may have ended up on a completely different path.

Her consciousness reached out and touched others in the dream, searching for anyone who had come into contact with Hanker. A trail began to form, leading her deeper, down from the common manifestation points toward Thought Bubbles filled with decadence and corruption. The link grew stronger, and she could feel Hanker's anger like a pinpoint of light on a dark mountain. In her mind she saw her mentor's bald head shining in the light of a Thought Bubble she recognized by its gold inlay, oversized paintings, and naked Greek statues. Hanker stood before a group of Pursuants, blue armor glowing, weapons at the ready.

'Where is he?!' Hanker barked. The eagle emblem on his chest flared like a phoenix.

'You don't ask questions here,' a woman with a porcelain doll face said as drool dripped from her painted mouth. *"He knows you're here, Hanker, but he'll only come out to play when he wants to, not when you call."*

Who was Hanker searching for? Was it Alexander? If so, even with his impressive mental powers, he wouldn't stand a chance against the dream titan.

Opening her eyes, Abbie's purple armor formed around her body. "I found him."

Brainstorm looked around as if expecting Hanker to come walking out from behind one of the trees. "Where? I don't see him."

"He's in trouble," she said. "I'll take us there."

"Wait, what?" Merquery asked.

Pinely jumped forward. "I don't think that's a good idea, Moon. Maybe we could---"

The ground convulsed, air spinning like a cyclone. Emotions switched from happiness to despair like someone flicking off a light. The suns on the horizon vanished as if churning down a drain with a mixture of acrylic paints. Trees pulled from the ground and dropped with them into empty space. After a moment, Abbie held up her arms and everything stopped. Chunks of dirt tumbled in slow motion next to her face while leaves shuddered on air currents. Brainstorm wobbled as if he were about to fall over. Dropping her hands, Abbie pulled the team into an emotionally sterile spot where connections with dreamers frayed to nothing. Several trees that had followed them from the higher emotional sphere slammed against shadowed ground and began decaying instantly. A dark mist converged all around them like a ghostly predator. It smelled of onion and carbonized bread. Strange birds and feathered creatures screeched overhead and glowed in unnatural colors that seemed to absorb the light around them.

"How…did you do that?" Tommy asked with a queasy look on his face.

"I've never dropped from one mental state to another so fast," Brainstorm agreed. "We even yanked some of the trees with us. That's crazy!"

"Follow me," Abbie said as she walked into the fog. "I know where we're going."

"Where *are* we going?" Gaze called after her. "I don't think this is a good spot for somebody as inexperienced as Brainstorm."

"I'm fine!" Brainstorm argued. "I'm not a kid."

Abbie didn't look back. The team's confused emotional state would only interfere with finding Hanker. For a moment she thought about leaving them behind but realized they could still be of use in a battle.

Battle. She almost laughed out loud.

The word itself seemed silly in Abbie's mind. In that moment she felt like no one could ever pose a threat to her; not even a challenge. Consciousness belonged to her, and no one else.

Pinely ran up to her, waving away an orange bat holding

what looked like a miniature nuclear bomb. "This isn't a good idea," he warned. "Remember what Alice said: don't push yourself. It's all too new for you to run off and start a row."

"I'm not going to let Hanker fight alone. Not after everything he's done to try and help me over the past few days...and years. If not for him, I wouldn't have known Vincent was my enemy. Things could have turned out way worse. Vincent would have arrived on your doorstep if not for Hanker. Think about that."

"And I appreciate his efforts, truly," Pinely said, practically running to keep pace with Abbie. "But I think we should wrap this in a bow right now and have you wake up and report to Alice. I know you feel amazing, but there are dangers. Addiction is always a possibility, no matter how strong you think you are."

"I'm fine," Abbie assured. "If I feel out of control, I'll let you wake me up."

Pinely's eyes narrowed. "I'm sure you will."

A granite building with crystalline revolving doors took shape through the haze. Brainstorm looked up at the Greek statues of gods and goddesses in various stages of disrobe.

"I've never been here before," the young man said, eyes locked on a nude sculpture of Aphrodite.

"Eyes forward, kid," Gaze ordered. "I'm not letting Brainstorm go into that place."

"None of us should be here right now," Aspira replied. She grabbed Pinely's hand and glared at Abbie. "This is a dangerous spot for a fight. If Hanker is here, he should know better than to start a fuss. There are enough trained Pursuants in places like this that they won't even try to wake you up. They'll lick your brain and see what they can experience."

"We'll be fine, trust me," Abbie said.

Next to the entrance stood wrinkled, bulbous Capacious in his tight gray business suit. Fat ashen lips curled as Abbie approached.

"What do you want, Moon?" He growled in his gravely bass. "You and Auspice caused quite a bit of trouble the other day. Scared a lot of my clients."

"If I remember correctly," she said sweetly, "it was Catharsis that made a mess, not me. We're here for Hanker. I know he's inside."

Capacious looked past her to the other members of the crew. He seemed to linger on Aspira and Brainstorm before turning his attention back to Abbie. "I'm a forgiving man, especially if the price is high enough. Hanker's throwing his weight around inside…if I'm reading the emotions right. I was surprised to see him here when I woke up in Consciousness, but then again, rumor has it he's been tearing places up looking for you and Auspice. But it seems he wasn't the only high roller looking to shake things around tonight. Something good is going on in the Palace. People are cheerin'…and runnin'."

"Step aside," Abbie ordered.

Belly fat jiggled and sloshed as Capacious burst out laughing. "Step aside? You think I got here by being pushed over by little Proctors like you and your friends? No, no, no. I can handle you and your whole damn conclave without twitchin'. That's not how it goes. You pay. Like everybody else. Thoughts; memories. You pay, and you go inside. So, let's settle up, shall we? I want something secret from you, Moon, like a thought you hide from others; something adventurous from the guy with the stupid pointy hat…"

"It's called a bycoket, if you must know," Pinely said under his breath.

"…a nice sexy memory each from the cat lady and the

blonde…"

Aspira hissed.

"…and maybe a juicy little fear from the child who makes himself look like a muscular Overwatch character to hide his inferiority." Capacious licked his lips and winked at Brainstorm.

A compression wave blew from Abbie's chest, driving the fog away in all directions. Her disdain manifested in pulses of solid sound that beat like snare drums and smelled of ammonia. The rotating door on the building rattled, glass cracking. Capacious stepped back as if punched in the chest.

"You'll get nothing, you lecherous piece of crap," Abbie spat. She placed her right hand under Capacious' flabby chin and lifted him off the ground. All his worries and concerns lay bare to her eyes as if she stared directly into his soul. In the dream Capacious had power, but in the physical world he knew nothing but doubt, loneliness, and impotent hate. She could see it written into the lines on his face.

Capacious opened his mouth to call out, but before words could form, Abbie grabbed hold of his feelings of isolation like she would a rotten plum…and squeezed. Black bile spat from his mouth as boils formed beneath his suit and across his face. He coughed and shook, legs kicking at the air trying to find purchase.

"Moon, what are you doing?" Pinely asked. "Let him go!"

"Let her take the bastard out of the dream," Aspira argued.

"Yeah!" Brainstorm agreed. "He called me a child."

With a burst of pickle brine and chunky pie filling, Capacious exploded like a balloon full of shaving cream. Spectral entrails hit the air in front of Abbie's face and sizzled to nothing before they could touch her skin. Goo spattered the front of the building and slopped all over Pinely in thick globs.

"Gaaahhh!" the Brit groaned. "That's gross."

"That was awesome!" Brainstorm gushed as dark green slime dripped from his chin.

Aspira peeled a dollop of viscera from her shoulder and tossed it away in disgust.

Power flowed through Abbie's body in warm throbs of confidence and understanding. Capacious hadn't been lying when he boasted of his mental strength. After feeling his control first-hand, she had to admit Capacious would have beaten her in a fight with no trouble. He had stolen dark emotions and underhanded tricks to spare. Even so, under the influence of the Incubus, Abbie had cast him from Consciousness without even needing to conjure a weapon. Her mind raced with the possibilities now before her. Could she go head-to-head with Catharsis' entire army? Alexander himself? How could she go back to being a lowly Proctor after experiencing such raw dominance?

"Moon," Pinely whispered while wiping sticky lumps of Capacious from his cape. "We need to leave. Right now. I've never seen anyone---"

"Let's get inside," Abbie said as if Pinely hadn't spoken. She waved her hands, and the front of the building crumbled away like a sandcastle on a beach.

Unlike the last time Abbie had ventured to the Pleasure Palace with Vincent, tonight the entire emotional spectrum inside fluctuated from panic to surprise to excitement. The main gallery stood empty, save for a few dreamers huddled in the alcoves along the walls like frightened lemmings. Cries echoed down the hall and off the tall columns, along with angry shouts and the sound of exploding masonry. A pair of dancers manifesting as half-man, half-parrot, ran up the marble stairs towards the shattered front entrance and passed the group, leaving behind a trail of colorful feathers. Cracks ran along the walls, tables sat overturned, all highlighted in a red and orange glow, like dying embers.

"Where is everybody?" Merquery asked.

Lightning charged the air and lit up the main entryway, followed by booming thunder that shattered the tiles. Two Pursuants crashed against a pillar leading to the main hallway. The larger of the duo pulled himself up and howled as spikes extended across his entire body. The other, smaller and more waifish, with green skin and scraggly hair hanging from his back, locked eyes with Abbie and ran toward her in a frenzy.

"I'll take him," Pinely said. He formed a bow and arrow, aiming at the charging wretch's face. Before the psychic projectile twanged from the bowstring, the Pursuant doubled over in pain and screamed.

"I've got him," Abbie said as she stepped past Pinely. "He's weak. This will be easy."

The green Pursuant clawed at the ground and reached for Abbie, but she waved her hand and he turned inside out like a sweater tossed into the laundry. Abbie rounded the corner without slowing her step and entered the arched hallway. Half a dozen Pursuants threw themselves forward in an explosion of greedy anger and thrilling overconfidence. Color and imagination converged in a scene almost too chaotic to comprehend. The large, spiked hunter tossed a marble pillar at someone encased in a ball of light that smelled like cookies, while several others smashed themselves against the barrier trying to tear it open. Terrible shrieks and rumbles assaulted the senses and rattled the brain. In the center of the energy sphere stood Hanker in his pale cobalt armor and glowing eagle emblem. The powerful Proctor obliterated two advancing Pursuants with a swipe of a crackling razor whip.

"It's Hanker!" Abbie shouted.

Running forward, she cleared a path, pressing Pursuants

against the walls with a thought. A purple blade manifested in her hand, and she decapitated the spiked brute with a single stroke. A group of parasites scurried away in surprise at the powerful new addition to the fight. Through the ball of white energy, Hanker's face lit up at the sight of his student.

"Moon!" he cried. "You're okay!"

"It's Moon!" a wolf-like Pursuant squealed through serrated teeth. He pointed a boney finger while jumping up and down. "She's here! Tell him she's here!"

A flash of lightning cracked from Hanker's shield, hitting the beastly hunter, turning him to ash. He didn't even have time to scream. The remaining Pursuants chattered like insects and bounded back as if waiting for orders from some unseen general.

Abbie used the relative calm to run over to her mentor. "I knew you were in trouble," she said. "I could feel it a mile away."

"And I can feel you've gotten a boost," Hanker nodded. His protective bubble thinned. He reached for Abbie as if to give her a hug. "I assume that means you've---"

The oxygen itself screamed all around them, cutting off Hanker's words and blowing in a gale as if the air ran away from something horrifying. Humidity increased. Water seeped from the walls before spraying in tiny shoots like holes in a dam. The walls around Abbie and the team broke apart and exploded forward, propelled by a surging flood.

"The River of Subconscious!" Hanker cried. He stumbled back as if unable to form an effective mental defense against a force of nature. The worry on his face told Abbie everything she needed to know.

Things were about to go bad.

"Run!" she screamed.

CHAPTER EIGHTEEN

Whitecaps roared like a horizontal waterfall, obliterating columns, stone blocks, and dreamers in its wake. An uncontrollable collection of unconscious thought, billions upon billions of memories, beliefs, and forgotten moments, swept through Capacious' palace with indiscriminate fury. The entire citadel heaved and toppled as the River of Subconscious destroyed everything in sight.

"Get everyone---" Hanker shouted before disappearing in the rush, along with everyone else around Abbie.

A wave of subliminal thought thundered over her. She held firm, forcing the water around her body, even as thoughts and memory pummeled her mind with punishing ferocity. Pursuants and Proctors alike washed away in a tsunami of ideas. A woman with scorpion tails for arms slammed into a pillar and scratched at the stone for dear life before disappearing into a swirl of blackness and bubbles. Even with her new-found strength, the river began to push Abbie aside. Stone tiles around her feet cratered and broke free from their emotional foundations, spinning her about in vortices of memory that didn't belong to her.

'How did the river get here?' she thought. *'I've got to get out and find Hanker.'*

She swam toward the surface as if soaring through the sky. Breaking the water's churning face, Abbie flew into the air and watched as the river fell from above in a massive cataract right next to what had moments before been Capacious' Pleasure Palace. The waterfall seemed to originate in the emotional layers above. Someone had forced the river deeper into Consciousness. Abbie had never seen anything like it, nor remembered ever hearing of the waterway shifting course. Its power had cleansed everything in its path and left behind broken columns and collapsed walls in the darkness.

"Hanker!" Abbie shouted. She descended to the shoreline and looked around. A few Pursuants pulled themselves from the surprise deluge and limped along the banks like half-drowned rats. Pinely and Merquery did the same on the other side of the river, helping each other avoid getting stuck in a thick layer of mud now forming along the water's edge. No other movement stood out against the shadowy horizon. No sign of Tommy, Gaze, Brainstorm, or Aspira. No Hanker. He had to have escaped the flood. If Pinely and Merquery made it out, Hanker had to as well.

A geyser exploded along the river's surface a few yards to Abbie's right. A large blue gauntlet emerged, grabbing hold of the mud. Hanker pulled himself from the reek, gagging on forgotten recollections and unknown languages.

"Hanker!" Abbie called. She rushed over, feet squishing in the sludge, and helped her teacher stumble from the river. His bulk dwarfed hers, but Abbie lifted him effortlessly. "Are you okay?"

"I'm alright," he coughed. Dirt and grime stuck to his cheeks and scalp. Pale cracks ran along the surface of his armor. His right shoulder pauldron had broken off in the deluge, along with the bracer on his left forearm.

"Hey! You two okay?" Pinely shouted from the other side of the waterway. "Give us a second to clean off and we'll fly over to help."

"We're fine!" Hanker waved without looking at them. He

spat and hacked. "Where the hell…did the river come from?"

"I don't know," Abbie said. She pulled him farther from the shore, leaving the sticky mud behind. "I came to find you. I could feel you even from across the void without a mental link. I'm stronger now than ever before. I'm unified, just like you hoped. I'm with Alice."

"You made it to her?" he asked. Joy seemed to fill his face and light up his countenance. "Safe? You're safe?"

"Yes."

"What about Vincent?"

"Bleeding in a forest a hundred miles away. We're good. We've won."

Hanker looked at the river and shook his head. "No. Something else is going on. How did the subliminal stream get down here? No one can control the subconscious like that."

Warm, humid air billowed suddenly from the ground with the stench of rancid potatoes. A crow called from somewhere overhead before morphing into innocent laughter.

"Don't be so sure…" a voice echoed in a playful sing-song cadence.

"Catharsis!" Abbie yelled. She spun about but saw nothing beyond mist and gray shadows. "Where are you, stupid cat?"

Water sloshed loudly behind her. Abbie turned around to see the giant pink feline with its purple stripes step out of the river and shake like a housecat after a bath. He towered twenty feet tall; a colorful Sphynx of the dream world. Fur glistened and then seemed to stretch; a thousand hairy fingers clawing for the thoughts of innocent dreamers. Glowing orange eyes stared down at Hanker and Abbie with a lust that seemed unquenchable. The darkness dissipated all around them, replaced by a crimson sky with deep clouds, and a barren stone terrain, like the floor of a cave with jutting stalactites. Red shafts of light broke through the storm overhead with kisses of pride and determination.

A group of Pursuants scrambled around, cackling at their leader's feet. Over Catharsis' shoulder appeared the glowing female angel with long blond hair and impressive bird wings that Abbie had faced previously in the palace. The woman floated with a smirk, tickling Catharsis' ear and staring at Abbie. Though she looked every bit a Celestial being, nothing but malice flowed from her aura in droplets of stinky sulfur.

"You're half right about not being able to control the River of the Subconscious," Catharsis said, kicking mud from his paw. "It goes where it wants to go, but if you put something in its path, well…it has no choice but to destroy it."

"You can't move a Thought Bubble any more than you can shift the river," Hanker yelled. He stood tall. The cracks in his armor healed instantly. "You can't move an entire emotional plain."

"But you can bridge two points in Consciousness," Catharsis said. "Your friend Abbie certainly knows how to do it now, don't you sweetie? If you do it fast enough you can cause all kinds of problems and pull objects and dreamers with you. It just requires willpower and some help from friends. In fact, I've been practicing---"

"Shut you're damn mouth, you feline bitch!" Pinely screamed as he flew into the air and sliced at Catharsis with a double-bladed battle axe made of rage. The weapon buried itself in the cat's shoulder with a sickening 'thunk' sound. The Cheshire tiger shrieked and swiped at the British Proctor, missing by a wide margin. Catharsis' angelic companion flew toward Pinely, but he spun around in time to kick her in the face. "It doesn't matter how many bastards you have by your side, cat, I'm going to prune every one!"

Merquery followed behind her teammate, launching a volley of energy bursts that hit Catharsis in the eye. "I usually like cats," she said, "but I think at the moment I'm more of a dog person! Pain is in the mind, and I hope you're feeling it!"

Pursuants in the shape of rock monsters and shadowy cloud formations ran toward Hanker and Abbie, laughing as if they stood a chance. The angel flew after Pinely with a flaming sword in her hand.

Hanker took out three enemies with a swipe of his energy whip. Abbie blinked her eyes and exploded two more into puffs of green mist and flower pollen.

"Did you just do that?" Hanker asked as he punched the only remaining hunter hard enough to spin his head around and cast him from the dream.

"I've gained a few new skills since we met last," Abbie grinned.

Tentacles wiggled from Catharsis' left ear and groped for Merquery. Slobber flew from his mouth as he stomped and retreated from the golden-haired Proctor's continued assault.

"Prickly little insurgents," Catharsis' voice echoed through the barren realm as more blasts pummeled his fur. "A bit of pain is good for the soul. I'll give you more than you can manage!"

Pinely landed beside Abbie and winked. "He makes himself look big, but I think old Catharsis is really more of a fluffy little pussy, afraid of---"

A glowing yellow blade burst from Pinely's chest and cut downward toward his belly. The Brit gasped in shock and stumbled backward.

"Pinely!" Abbie screamed. She looked to see where the blade had originated, but it seemed to grow directly from her friend's sternum. No attacker stood behind him.

Merquery flew over with a cry. "Pinely! Somebody help---"

Golden hands grabbed her by the neck and yanked Merquery back into the sky. Catharsis' personal angel tore at the blonde Proctor's throat. Merquery reached back and scraped at her assailant's eyes. The two women tumbled behind a bluff while explosions of light burst into the air.

"I'll be…okay…" Pinely coughed as a hole opened in his chest. "Save Merquery…I'll wake up…and then…"

The sword retracted, replaced by a pair of hands grabbing from inside the wound. They stretched it opened as if something had been trapped and was escaping. Pinely tore apart with a rip and a shriek. Vincent stepped out of the Brit's open chest as if strolling into a party. He tossed what remained of Pinely aside like a damp towel. His creamy armor appeared as robust and impenetrable as always, but his skin seemed pale, dry, and cracked, like shriveled leaves after a summer drought.

"Stupid little Carlton!" Vincent spat, kicking Pinely's dissipating form in the face as it billowed to nothing. "Shoot me in the leg? Rot in hell!"

"Vincent!" Abbie seethed. She leaped from Hanker's side, prepared to cause her enemy enough pain to wake him up screaming.

A cat's paw slammed into the ground in front of her. Chunks of rock and broken spikes flew into the air on impact. Abbie paused. She looked up at Catharsis, ready to use her growing powers to decimate him as well. She would crush both men's minds and send them whimpering into the physical world.

"I'll destroy both of you!" she yelled. Blades appeared in her hand instinctively, though she wouldn't need them.

"Now just hold on for a second, little Moon," Catharsis said, smiling. "I didn't come here to fight. I felt your power the moment you entered Consciousness. I know you're with Alice, using one of her helmets. And may I say, you seem to rival Alexander with your natural ability."

"Moon, don't engage!" Hanker yelled. He stomped over and flanked his student. "Those helmets are dangerous. That's what I felt when you arrived at the Thought Bubble. Something else is going on if the two of them followed you down here."

Vincent stepped around Catharsis' paw and glared at Abbie. "Yeah, Moon. You should listen to your protector. He knows all. He understands all."

"Shut up, Vincent!" Abbie shouted. "After I'm done with you, you'll look even more cracked and weak than you do now. Let me guess; you're cold out there in the forest and your leg is bleeding out? I bet it's hard to hold any kind of form here in Consciousness when you're afraid you won't survive the night."

Pallid skin fractured and flaked as a scowl tore at Vincent's normally handsome face. "Shows how much you know, Abbie."

The angel woman flew up from behind the ridge with a slight sag to one of her wings. Scars stretched across her beautiful face but healed quickly. She soared over to Catharsis and resumed her place beside his left shoulder.

Merquery didn't emerge behind her. She had been torn from the dream too, just like Pinely. No matter, Abbie thought. Catharsis and Vincent were barely a threat at all anymore. They would know her power. They would feel it and beg for her to stop.

"We don't need pretenses anymore, Vincent," Abbie said. "I can cast you and Catharsis out of Consciousness with so little effort it'll be embarrassing. But Hanker here always taught me to take the higher ground, so I'll give you one chance. How about this? You turn on Catharsis right now and help us banish him from the dream, and maybe I'll send someone from Alice's team to pick you up in the morning, so you don't die. First and last offer."

Catharsis chuckled and licked at his wounded shoulder. "Moon, you are wonderful! Hanker was so right to take you under his wing all these years. But now you've surpassed your mentor, haven't you? You don't need him anymore." The cat turned to his Celestial servant, angel wings flapping just to his left. "Cherub, are you ready?"

"Yes sir," she answered, voice hauntingly beautiful.

Tilting his head toward Cherub, Catharsis reared back and opened his mouth. Octopus limbs slithered between his teeth and grabbed the angelic woman roughly by the head and feet.

"What are you doing, Catharsis?" Hanker asked.

The tentacles twisted around the angel and pulled, ripping the woman in half in a splash of golden light and silver liquid. Her body dropped to the ground and vaporized like rain evaporating off hot pavement.

Abbie stepped back, confused. Why would Catharsis wake up one of his faithful servants?

"So, you're attacking your own people now?" Abbie questioned. "Keep that up and you'll make all our jobs easier."

"Oh, silly Moon," Catharsis said, wiping his lips with cephalopod appendages. "You still think of things in such a straightforward way. As soon as you arrived here, I knew I wouldn't be able to defeat you. Your power in the dream is indescribable so long as you have access to Alice's technology. But you won't have access for long, trust me. And until then, I knew I'd need some insurance policies. You see, this is all a giant chess game; you have to be able to see your opponent's moves a mile away…or at least know their weaknesses. Cherub knows that. When I got her the fake documents claiming she was one Dr. Julie Lorien, she understood her part in all this. I'll tell you your part in it too soon enough. After a little…object lesson."

"Who's Dr. Julie Lorien?" Abbie asked. "You think I care about who your little angel is when she wakes up?"

Catharsis' eyes narrowed as he smiled. "You should. That's your problem: always so focused on what's in front of you as opposed to what's coming up from behind."

"That's it," Abbie spat, stepping forward. "I'm going to---"

An indigo armored hand raised in front of her, keeping her from jumping up to rip out Catharsis' throat. Hanker blinked quickly and looked down at the stone ground.

"Moon…" he whispered. Hanker looked at her with tears in his eyes. "Abbie…there is still so much I wanted to teach you. So many wonderful things you could pass on. Stay close to Alice. Don't give into the power. You can be just like me without any of it."

"What are you talking about?" Abbie asked. "Let's take down Ass Number One and Ass Number Two, and then you can teach me anything you want."

"She doesn't understand, does she Auspice?" Catharsis laughed. "Conrad's going to have to explain it to her."

Vincent shook his head and smiled. "I told you she wouldn't. As much pain as I'm in right now, I wouldn't trade being here for anything."

"Shut up!" Abbie said, pointing her sword at Vincent. He flipped her the bird and sneered.

"Abbie," Hanker said again. He put his large hands gently on her shoulders and stood directly in front of her. Sadness and gratitude leaked from his armor in wisps of ripe orange and candied banana, along with his natural fresh cookie dough scent . "You can't stop no matter what. You can't let them win."

Abbie pulled away in frustration and shook his hands from her shoulders. "What are you talking about?! I've already won!

They've lost!"

"No, they haven't." Hanker shook his head and again pulled her close to him. Consciousness suddenly shook, like a weak aftershock from a much larger earthquake. "You're united, but there are still two worlds we inhabit. Dr. Lorien…I know that name."

"So?" Abbie said, growing more anxious to pummel Catharsis and Vincent with each passing second.

"You don't understand…" Hanker's face grew pale, breathing shallow. "Dr. Lorien is one of the new interns who started working for Dr. Chabra yesterday to monitor me during the night shift. She works in the building where I live. She's there now. I can feel her. She's injected something into my arm."

Eyes blinked as the realization dawned on Abbie. "That Cherub angel lady…"

"Has just killed me," Hanker said.

The large, kind man in his blue armor and eagle symbol stumbled back and fell to the side. He braced himself on his hands and knees but seemed to shrink slightly before their eyes. His skin grew paler as his armor became translucent.

"Hanker!" Abbie screamed. She rushed to his side and tried to help him up, but her hands passed through his body as if he weren't even there.

"Cyanide," Catharsis said as he lowered his nose close to Hanker and sniffed. "It's cliched, I know. I would have used whatever poison worked fastest and was hoping for some really cool compound with an awesome name, but cyanide turned out to be best. I was disappointed, honestly, but I trust Cherub's methods. She's done this a couple times before. Direct shot to the vein with enough to kill a horse. Brain death occurs first, which is kind of poetic if you think about it. Old Conrad Rossi here will be mist in a few seconds, I'd assume."

"Abbie..." Hanker coughed. He slumped forward and rolled onto his back. Armor disappeared completely. The ground became visible behind his body as he grew less and less opaque.

"Sorry Uncle Conrad," Vincent waved. "It's nothing personal. Just business. You understand."

"Hanker! What do I do?" Abbie asked. Tears streamed down her face. Her mentor lay dying in his sleep in a hospital in Utah while she watched his mind fade right in front of her. Somewhere in that dark room across the mountains stood a woman with a hypodermic needle in her hand. Abbie imagined her smiling; proud of herself for extinguishing the flame of one of the greatest Proctors of his generation. She wanted to kill her...slowly.

"Abbie..." Hanker repeated weakly. His eyes bulged and twitched back and forth as if taking in all the details around him one last time.

"I can't do it without you!" she sobbed. In that moment Abbie wanted to hear him preach to her about being one person in the real world and in the dream; see him smile over the flavor of a fruit that tasted like contentment. She needed his insight and encouraging words. What would she do when he was gone?

And suddenly he *was* gone. No explosion of power, no grand farewell with key words of wisdom. Just a choking sound and hollow eyes that disappeared from Consciousness as if he'd never existed.

Gone. Never to dream again.

The smell of warm cookies lingered on the air for a moment before dispersing. Abbie continued crying. Loneliness poured from her with each tear, taking the shape of leeches that writhed on the ground before sizzling to pus in the dirt.

"Hanker has always been a pain in my ass," Catharsis said in a voice that seemed almost comforting in its soothing timbre. "I know it was a sacrifice for Auspice to tell me who his uncle was in the physical world. After all, he'd been manipulating Hanker effectively to get information about powerful proctors for years. It was good business, I assure you. But Auspice understands what's at stake, and why sacrifices need to be made."

"And what's…at stake?" Abbie gasped between sobs.

"All of creation," Vincent answered.

Sorrow sculpted like clay in Abbie's mind before twisting and contorting into something closer to fury. Wrath. Anger. Ire. Madness. Rage. Every word in the dictionary seemed insufficient to describe the depth of her emotion. All of Consciousness would rattle with the echoes of her power as she crashed against her enemies like a sentient hurricane.

Abbie stood, body glowing purple and black. Her eyes flared and spit flame like a demon about to drag a rapist down to purgatory for eternal damnation.

Instead of cowering or running away, Catharsis scratched his furry crotch and cracked his neck to the side.

"Oh Abbie-Moon, Abbie-Moon, Abbie-Moon," he sang. "I know you want to kill us both; scar our minds so we're vegetables once you're done, and you'd be right to hurt us however you like."

"I'm glad we're on the same page," Abbie said, walking slowly toward her targets.

"But there's a reason we are where we are, and you are where you are," Vincent replied.

"Yes, yes," Catharsis continued. "I wanted Hanker out of the way, and I wanted you to see it, because you need to know that you still have a part to play in all of this."

"You're right," she agreed. "My part is to destroy both of you so completely that even your unconscious thoughts will be too damaged to linger in the River of Subconscious over there."

Catharsis stooped low and brought his whiskered face down to Abbie's level. "Remember how I said this was all a chess match? Well, chess is a simple, uncomplicated game. I've just removed your bishop from the board. I'm not afraid to sacrifice a few pawns either. Especially when they belong to you and not me."

The air rippled to Abbie's left like someone had thrown a stone at the surface of reality. Vincent stepped over toward the rift and pulled out a dreamer, tied with ghostly bonds that wrapped around her fluctuating consciousness.

Abbie recognized the woman instantly. The smell of lavender filled the air.

"Nana Gayle…" she breathed, taking a step toward her grandmother. The flames in her eyes died to nothing, as did her glowing aura.

"I grabbed myself a stray dreamer a little bit ago," Vincent said. "I held onto her so you could say hi."

"…Abbie?" Nana Gayle questioned, as if lost in a dark room and needing help escaping. She looked around frantically, face changing color from light pink to sickly yellow. "I see mushrooms, but I know the airplane will take off before the dinner plates are finished."

"She's a bit confused," Vincent chuckled. "Doesn't have your mental strength here in Consciousness, poor old lady. Makes her easy prey to all sorts of nasties when she goes to sleep, I'm sure."

"Abbie…? I think I hear you in the washing machine…"

The ground rumbled, and Abbie prepared to rip Nana Gayle from Vincent's arms and then tear him to pieces so small it would take a month for him to form a coherent thought.

"Ah, ah, ah," Catharsis said, wagging his paw in front of Abbie's face. "Now, we don't want to fight in front of your sweet Grandma, who, if I may say, is surprisingly attractive. I see where you get your looks. But before you go off using those new mental abilities of yours, let me paint you a picture first, okay? Your granny's asleep all comfy and cozy in that sweet little condo she shares with Grandpa Carl. If we wanted, we could single her out every night and torment her in Consciousness until her entire psyche breaks down and she ends up in an institution. Not the first time that's been done, and it won't be the last."

"I'll stop you, you son of a bitch!" Abbie bellowed. The air shook with her words as the sky above them ruptured in spastic lightning as if about to break apart.

"Oh, I'm sure you will," Catharsis said. He glanced up at the atmosphere and nodded his head.

"Abbie," Nana Gayle repeated. "Why is the sky cracking an egg?"

"She's so sweet, isn't she?" Vincent smiled as he put his arm around Grandma.

Catharsis stepped closer to Abbie, seeming to have no fear of her impressive powers. "Yes, I have no doubt you have the capacity to cause us unlimited trouble. More than Alice ever dared. But you didn't let me finish my painting, did you? We could torment her here in the dream and have tons of fun. Or I could send out the call and wake up my operative currently sleeping in his car in front of your grandma's place on Davinci Drive, and have him break in, maybe kill Grandpa, and then take Granny away and do whatever he wants with her. He could hurt her, play with her, smash her fingers for all I care. Now isn't that a lovely picture I've painted for you? Here's another object lesson: make her afraid, will you, Auspice?"

Vincent reached over and touched Nana Gayle's cheek. The look on her face changed instantly from confusion to fear. Her eyes opened wider, mouth hanging slightly open. Wrinkles along her forehead and around her eyes deepened, skin draining of color.

"I don't want…please," Nana gasped.

"Stop it!" Abbie screamed. "I'll kill you!"

"No. You. Won't." Catharsis' voice grew menacingly deep, affecting the world with as much force as Abbie's. His entire body seemed to slither, as if made up of worms and snakes ready to feed on decaying flesh. "You see, little Abigail Kinder, unless you have power both here and out there, you have no power at all. I will kill this woman in the most cruel way imaginable, and you will be able to do nothing to me! I will flay her brain like a fish and lick up the juices while you hide in a bunker in stupid Idaho!"

Fear distorted Nana Gayle's lovely face. "Help…please…anyone!"

"Let her go!" Abbie yelled. Despite her anger, she stepped away from Catharsis as he advanced like an oversized beast about to pounce.

"I don't think so," he said, voice returning to normal. "But we can make a deal, you and me. You see, even though Vincent failed in the end to arrive with you to Alice's little hidden sanctuary…"

"I got shot," Vincent interrupted.

"…he was still able to track you by leaving his phone in the back seat of the plane. Always such a clever boy."

"You're welcome, by the way," Vincent said.

Catharsis rolled his eyes. "And *you're* welcome that Mozzie and the team took time to fly in and pick you up before you had to spend the night in the forest."

'Damn it,' Abbie thought. That stupid phone. Vincent had been looking at it the whole time they were flying to the airstrip.

She'd heard something drop to the floor in the backseat when she and Pinely had landed. It had to have been Vincent's cell. Mozzie and Vincent, and now Catharsis, knew exactly where Alice was at that moment. They had tracked the plane. Vincent wasn't freezing in the woods; he was with Mozzie. Everything she thought she had escaped came suddenly crashing through the front door.

She had failed. If only she had unified sooner, none of this would have happened. If only she had been faster, or smarter, or stronger.

"Ah, the sweet silence of a mind at work," Catharsis mused. "Your emotions are pretty loud though. I feel you're figuring everything out. Good."

Abbie looked from Nana Gayle, to Vincent, to Catharsis. She stepped back again, feeling powerless despite the strength offered by the Incubus helmet. "You're going to kill Alice now, aren't you?"

Catharsis laughed under his breath as if he'd just heard a mildly funny joke.

"She still doesn't get it," Vincent said, head shaking.

"Whether she does or not, she needs to know her role." Catharsis shrunk down to the size of a large tiger and began circling Abbie. "I don't care about Alice. She wasn't even powerful enough to be a Proctor before her little experiment all those years ago. I was there that first night. I felt Alexander enter the dream with all his natural talent. I played with Alice so I could draw closer to him. No, Alice is nothing without the helmet."

"Then what do you want?" Abbie asked like an exasperated third-grader unable to understand the quadratic equation.

"I want the helmet," Catharsis grinned.

"Two, actually," Vincent added. "We know she has at least two."

"Yes, two. Vincent's earned one. You see, Abigail, Alexander is the king here, but he's a king that is more than happy to let his knights run amok and do their own thing. He's comfortable both here and in the physical world and doesn't make a fuss unless you try to upset his apple cart too much. You don't challenge him; he leaves you alone. Of course, no one *can* challenge him anyway, unless they have comparable tech to what he uses, so what would the point be?"

Understanding streaked in Abbie's mind like a shooting star on a moonless night. All the manipulation, finding Alice, everything, was so Catharsis could depose a king and take his place. He needed Alice's Incubus so he could be powerful enough to rip Alexander from his throne. He never intended to kill Alice…unless he needed to.

"You're not working for Alexander at all, are you?" she asked.

Catharsis continued circling. "No. He and I have an alliance of sorts, but I'm not a threat to him in here. Out in the real world I can hold my own, but like I said, if you don't have power in both places, you're nothing. I need those helmets. And you're going to get them for me."

"Oh, I am?" Abbie questioned.

"You are," Vincent confirmed. "Originally, the plan was for you to lead me to Alice, and from there I would steal the helmets. I didn't think you'd ever unify, honestly, and you gave up the info easily enough. Everything was working out…until I got shot."

"But I'm an adaptable man," Catharsis continued. "I would have gotten to Alice however I could. Vincent likes complicated plans, but I'm simple. And patient. It tends to work out for me. Because of that, I now know where she is in the middle of that forest. I know where the tools I need are located. Now that you're inside her compound, and we know who you are, and who you love, you're going to open the door and hand the helmets over to my team. They'll be landing sometime in the next hour. You give them the helmets and Alice can do whatever she wants at that point. None of her trained little puppets will be able to compete with me after that. Even Alexander will bow to me. You do this and everything can go back to normal. I'll leave you alone. I'll leave Granny alone, and your sister, and Mom and Dad, and those idiots you work with. No one else has to end up like poor Conrad Rossi. Piss me off though, and all bets are off. Your grandma will only be the first of your loved ones to get the dream torture treatment right alongside some Basic beatings."

Nana Gayle continued to twitch and cry in fear while Vincent rubbed his nose against her cheek. His serene face seemed almost pleasured by her terror.

Arms slumped to her side as Abbie's strength seemed to drain from her like water from a broken vase. If she saved Nana Gayle and everyone else she loved by giving Catharsis the Incubus, what would she be condemning the realm of Consciousness to suffer? What kind of 'king' would Catharsis become? Not a benevolent monarch. And Vincent would never be satisfied letting the cat take all the power. Whether allies now or not, eventually they would destroy each other and everyone standing between them. The war Hanker had feared, but ten times worse. But if she turned her back on the people she cared about, her life, and all of theirs, would be over. Worse; ripped from them by merciless fingers intent on causing physical and psychological pain that would never heal.

No good options. The sound of the river filled her ears as the water soaked into the dry gray landscape of Catharsis' personal torture chamber.

"Tick tock, little Moon," Catharsis whispered, coming up behind her and licking her ear.

Abbie jumped in surprise and smacked the cat across the face without thinking. The thought occurred to her to grab him and explode his feline construct from the inside out, but that would solve nothing. He would just come back into the dream and start everything over again.

"What's it going to be Abbie?" Vincent asked. "I could drop her into a nightmare. Plenty of hunters would be waiting to help me open her up. Nana Gayle is about to have the worst dream she's ever experienced, and let me tell you, there's going to be some fun stuff in there for me too…"

"Stop it!" Abbie shouted. The River of Subconscious seemed to freeze in time for an instant in reply to her anger. "Just…stop it. Let her go."

"So, you'll do it?" Vincent asked.

"Of course, she'll do it," Catharsis confirmed. "Attachments are so dangerous, Auspice. Look how long it took you to get rid of Uncle Conrad, even though you knew he was causing all of us so many headaches. The deeper the bonds, the harder they are to dig up and strangle. Let her grandma go. If things don't work out our way, we can always play with Granny again tomorrow night."

"Fine," Vincent said. "Want to say goodbye before she wakes up, Moon?"

Abbie stepped over to Nana Gayle and touched her cheek. The pain and sorrow on the older woman's face ebbed, replaced by a faint smile. "Go pick some flowers, Nana," Abbie said. "Grandpa always loves to see them in the vase before we sit down for breakfast."

"Yes, Abbie," Nana Gayle replied, a look of peace coloring her eyes. "I'll go pick some flowers. Everything smells so good outside."

A tear trickled down Abbie's cheek. "I'll see you soon, Nana. Now go."

The bonds holding Grandma captive faded away, followed by Nana Gayle's dream form. Mist surrounded her until all that remained were hints of memory from a fine summer morning with the smells of bacon and pancakes.

"We have a deal?" Catharsis asked before Nana Gayle's presence had fully dissipated.

"I don't know how I'm going to get the helmets and computers out without any members of Alice's team stopping me," Abbie admitted. "They're like a paramilitary force down there."

Catharsis stepped in front of Abbie and brought his face close enough that his whiskers tickled her cheek. She smelled his anticipation like sweat on a dog.

"You're resourceful," he said. "You are the great Moon, after all. How many people does she have down there?"

"24."

"My team has more than enough bullets for that many," Catharsis mused.

"And for me too, I assume?" Abbie asked. They wouldn't leave her alive if they intended on killing the others.

A broad, toothless grin spread Catharsis' feline face. "Not necessarily. I'll only kill if necessary. You let us in quietly and we can avoid any…messiness. I'm a man of my word. And in truth, I don't want you dead, Abbie. I've seen the amount of attention Alexander pays to you. You may not have noticed, but I have. After seeing you tonight and what you can do under the influence of Alice's technology, I think I'm beginning to understand why he's enamored with you. You're special. No, hurting you, especially after everything that's happened over the past few days, wouldn't be in my best interests. It would come back to me, and I don't need that kind of attention until I'm ready for it. I'd actually invite you to come with us if I thought you'd take the offer."

"Pass," Abbie said.

"Just as I thought," Catharsis replied. "Anyway, all I need from you is to open the door. My team got word to me an hour ago that satellite images show some sort of underground base buried not far from the runway where your plane landed. I'm assuming there's a locked hatch of some sort. You open it quietly, a few of my men arrive by helicopter and come inside, and if we can get in and out quickly, there shouldn't be too many bodies left behind. They have orders to bomb the compound if the door doesn't open, or if the helmets never come out. Again, I'd just as soon leave everyone, including you, alive, but like I said, I'm adaptable. If I can't have the helmets, Alice won't be left with them either, and I'll go to Alexander and tell him I've solved his opposition problem. Not my preferred course of action, but a viable one. It all comes down to you, little Moon."

Thunder rumbled in the distance. Abbie looked out on the desolate landscape with its spiked rocks and fractured red sky. It seemed to resemble her own mental state. No matter what she did, people would suffer. The question would be: how many?

"I open the door…" she began, "and as long as no one fights back, you leave everyone alive."

"I'm a man of my word, right Vincent?"

"He only stabbed me in the back a couple times," Vincent smiled.

"And those were fairly literal." Catharsis licked his lips and shivered. "You have limited options, Abbie-Moon, Moon-Abbie. I ask again: do we have a deal?"

"…Yes," Abbie replied slowly. "We have a deal. I'll bring you the helmets. I'll open the door and try to make things as easy and bloodless as possible."

"Good," Catharsis breathed, hot air moistening Abbie's face.

"My men will contact me in Consciousness once they're done, so I'll know right away whether I'll need to take action against any of your family. Remember, I know what type of person you are, Abigail. You're going to think about screwing me over for the greater good. I'd advise against that. I know where you are. One way or another I'm getting those helmets, even if I have to kill everyone in that underground base, or whatever it is Alice has down there. I'll kill them, and you, and I'll still torment everyone in your family after you're dead. That's a promise."

"I know what type of man you are, Catharsis," Abbie replied. "I don't doubt a word you say. I've seen what you do to dreamers and Proctors."

"So, we're on the same page then. Wonderful. I'll awaken one of my lieutenants currently enjoying a drug-induced sleep on the helicopter, and they'll be arriving shortly. Now it's time for you to wake up, sweet Moon. Auspice, if you wouldn't mind doing the honors."

Vincent stepped forward and formed a yellow blade the size of his arm. He lifted it over his head and sneered. "I've been waiting all night to do this."

The sword came down on Abbie's head, cutting her from the dream in a flash of brain-splitting agony, defeat, and anguish.

CHAPTER NINETEEN

Abbie's eyes opened inside the helmet, met by strange convulsing lights glowing from the front display. She sat forward, hearing the hum of computer fans and the whispers of hushed voices.

"Levels have dropped," she heard Dr. Hakim say from his desk on the left.

"She's awake," Pinely said, somewhere to her right.

"Moon, is everything alright?" Alice asked, voice growing closer.

Pulling off the helmet, Abbie's eyes adjusted to the fluorescent lighting. She squinted and rubbed her cheeks, feeling a layer of sweat on her clean face. The glare lessened, shapes forming into people she recognized. Pinely and Alice stepped over to her with concerned looks. Hakim pushed his dreadlocks out of his face and sat back in his chair, yellow glow from the closest monitor reflecting in his glasses. Incandice munched on an apple while leaning against the far wall, seemingly unconcerned with anything Abbie could offer.

"Other than that decline over the last few minutes she was in there," Hakim continued, "her levels were the highest I've ever seen."

Abbie closed her eyes and tried to process the sudden…nothingness that surrounded her. Everything seemed barren and lifeless. She felt no emotions from anything; not the people beside her, nor the sheets on the bed beneath her. An unknown thirst, not for water, but for a connection to life itself, made her want to throw the helmet back on and delve deeper into Consciousness.

The physical world seemed so desolate when compared with the experience she had just escaped.

"Are you alright?" Alice asked again. She leaned forward and brushed a strand of hair out of Abbie's eyes.

"I'm…okay," she answered. In truth, her mind felt fuzzy, as if thoughts required more effort to form than normal. Breaths filled her chest and helped slow her heartbeat. Memories from the dream seemed more vibrant and real than reality itself. The color of the grass; the emotions from her teammates.

The death of Hanker.

Nana Gayle's tears.

Grief suddenly hit like a freight train. The heightened sensations afforded by the Incubus seemed to linger, tearing into Abbie's mind like claws from a rabid racoon. She pulled her legs up onto the small hospital bed and held them close against her chest, while silent sobs began racking her body. For a moment she felt like nothing existed beyond her pain.

"It's alright," Alice soothed. "The first time coming down from the Incubus is really hard. Incandice cried like a baby, wanting to go back inside and feel the emotions again."

Pinely put his hand on Abbie's shoulder. "What happened after Auspice split me in half?"

"Give her a minute before we ask her any questions," Alice said. "You know how hard this can be, babe. Just let her breathe. Moon, you'll be able to go back soon. Let yourself feel it for a second."

So that was it. They thought she was crying because she wanted to go back to the dream. They had no idea about Hanker, or Nana Gayle, or Abbie's mission to betray all of them. Here in the cold, conditioned air of Alice's underground fortress, only Abbie knew the coming danger. Soon Catharsis' team would arrive and do whatever they had to do to get what they wanted. People would die.

And what would Abbie do about it? Her grief subsided as she tried to focus on what Catharsis had said. *'I'll kill them, and you, and I'll still torment everyone in your family after you're dead. That's a promise.'*

All she had to do was open the door. Simple. Maybe she could lure everyone into one of the conference rooms she saw and lock them in. They'd never be able to break down those metal hatches. That way everyone would be safe.

No. Even without the deep sorrow and Incubus-induced hangover, Abbie knew she could never get everyone in the compound into one room. Several of them already didn't trust her. That distrust would be justified in less than an hour when Abbie helped Catharsis' team in order to save Nana Gayle and everyone else she loved. There would be no way to trick Alice. She knew the compound better than Abbie ever could after only spending a couple hours inside. Alice would find a way to escape with her crew from whatever deception Abbie could concoct. A battle would most certainly ensue. Alice and her squad would fight to the death. There was too much at stake for them to hold back. They would all die. After that, who would watch over Consciousness and bring down those attempting to influence and oppress the innocent? Catharsis could not be allowed to get his hands on those helmets.

That left Abbie only one option: telling Alice the truth.

On paper it seemed easy. In reality? Not so much.

Nana Gayle's terrorized face filled her mind. Never before had Abbie considered she'd find herself in a situation requiring a choice between the greater good and the people she loved. The mass of faceless dreamers seemed so much less important than the handful of people she cared about. Her mom and dad, Grandma and Grandpa, they would all suffer unspeakable torments because of her choice. Everyone in the dream would be oblivious to their agony.

Could she make that horrible decision for her family members? Could she condemn her parents and friends to pain and suffering without them ever knowing why they had to pay the price for strangers?

"How are you doing, Moon?" Alice asked, pulling her from her plague of choices. "You need another minute? Pinely told me Catharsis shifted the River of Consciousness. I need to know what happened and if that's true."

In that moment, Abbie made up her mind. She lifted her face from her knees, wiped her tears, and sniffed.

"They're coming," she whispered. "Catharsis knows where you are. Vincent left a tracker on the plane. He never wanted to kill you. They're not working with Alexander at all. They want the Incubus so they can have more power. Catharsis has satellites and helicopters and knows right where we are. If I don't open the top hatch, they'll bomb us and kill everyone."

Incandice dropped her apple and practically leaped toward Pinely. "You let them track you?!"

"I didn't know," Pinely said as he stumbled back and tripped on one of the beds. "I had a gun pointed at me at the time, okay?"

"I'll beat you both to death, you---" Incandace seethed in her African inflection.

"Shut up!" Alice screamed. The sound caught everyone by surprise and echoed off the wood-paneled walls. Hakim almost fell from his chair.

"Sorry, love," Pinely said quietly.

Alice stood and looked at the far wall. "We need everyone awake. Implement Defense Plan Epsilon, along with---"

"Stop," Abbie said. She reached up and grabbed Alice's wrist lightly. "Stop for a second. If we fight, we die. Simple as that."

"Well, I'm not giving up the Incubus," Alice said, staring down at Abbie with dead eyes. "If they want a fight, I'll give them---"

"Hanker is dead," Abbie stated flatly. "They killed him."

Silence filled the room like black smoke. Pinely's eyes stared unblinking. Alice's mouth opened and then closed again as if trying to vocalize something unspeakable. Incandice seemed unfazed, though a bead of sweat ran down the dark skin along her temple.

No one spoke. Hakim coughed quietly; sound bouncing off the walls as if he'd screamed.

For a moment Abbie felt anger at the emotional sterility coming from Alice and Pinely, before remembering she couldn't experience people's feelings in Basic. Right now, it was probably a blessing. She could see the pain on Pjnely's face, the heartache in Alice's eyes. Even so, Abbie longed to commune with another person; share her grief, even if it meant being amplified by someone else's. Sitting on the bed, only aware of her own emotions, Abbie felt suddenly very alone.

Bigger things were in motion beyond her sorrow, however. Mourning would have to wait.

Mattress springs squeaked as she stood. "They wanted to make sure I understood what they were willing to do, and how much power they have out here in the physical world. They had someone in Hanker's hospital, that angel woman Catharsis has with him sometimes. She injected Hanker with cyanide, and his mind died right there in front of me. Catharsis wants the helmets, and he'll do whatever he has to so he can take Alexander's place as the most powerful person in Consciousness. He'll kill all of you one way or another."

"We can't let him take the Incubus," Incandice said with a headshake. "I'll kill whoever tries to get in here."

Abbie rubbed the sides of her sore forehead. Despite the fog clinging to her brain, several ideas poked through the murk. The deeper she dug, the clearer images from Consciousness became, along with their connection to the creative centers of her cerebellum. If Alice was willing to take a chance, they all might be able to live and fight another day.

"I think we can avoid anyone having to die," Abbie said. "Give me a second to think. I'm coming down from the Incubus, and my brain is fuzzy, but I still feel a connection to my deeper consciousness. I know I can think of something. I can feel it. Let me play with a few details---"

"We cannot wait," Incandice interrupted. "I'll initiate Plan Epsilon."

"Will you just give me a second?!" Abbie shouted. "If you're so keen to get everybody killed, go ahead and run off like an idiot. But I think I have an idea…if you'll let me grab a hold of it and look at different angles for a moment. It's about to slip through my fingers, so just shut up and stand over there."

Alice held up her hand toward Incandice. "Give Moon a minute before we sound any alarms."

A grunt rumbled in the angry woman's throat, but she nodded and stepped back.

Eyes closed, Abbie tried to picture every word Catharsis said before Vincent chopped her head open and woke her up. *'My team got word to me an hour ago;' 'they have orders to bomb the compound;' 'I'd just as soon leave everyone, including you, alive;' 'I'm a man of my word.'*

She could feel the cat's sticky-sweet emotions, along with Vincent's pent-up frustration. They both feared and admired Alexander. Catharsis wanted power…but not Vincent. What did Vincent want? She couldn't tell without going back into Consciousness.

Catharsis wanted glory and control. He was willing to leave Abbie alive. That hadn't been a lie. She could use it. Give the cat what he wanted, come along for the ride, and then boom, fire and darkness. Could she protect her family too along the way? They would still have one helmet if everything worked out the way she planned. A longshot, but one worth taking.

It could work.

"I have a way that will get everyone out of here alive," Abbie said finally. "And screw Catharsis at the same time. I told him I'd help get the Incubus. He had my grandmother; I didn't know what else to say to him. Vincent was manipulating her fears. He threatened my family."

"Too bad for them," Incandice said with a wave of her hand. "I won't sacrifice all of Consciousness for a handful of people, just because you know them."

"I'm not asking you to," Abbie assured, lip curling in an expression that would have killed someone in the dream world. "I know what's at stake here. But if all of us die, who's going to stand in the way of Alexander, and the people he's trained. Who's going to stop Catharsis? If he wants to take down Alexander, he'll find a way to do it, and everyone else will pay the price. It's idiotic to die for a cause that no one else can fight once we're dead."

Alice stepped between the two women and began pacing back and forth. "You said you had an idea about how to stop them without anyone getting killed, Moon. What is it?"

Mouth dry, tongue heavy, Abbie swallowed and nodded her

head. “I lock all of you in one of the side rooms. You bang on the doors as if you’re trying to escape. Pinely, or somebody else can be hiding somewhere to help you escape after we’ve left. Before Catharsis’ team arrives, we hide one of the Incubus helmets and one of the computers and then let them take the other three. Then---”

“No way,” Incandice interrupted. “We let them take three units, and trust that you’ll---”

“Let her finish!” Alice bellowed. Incandice stepped back half a step and pressed her lips together tightly. A small smirk fleeted across Pinely’s face.

“Thank you,” Abbie said to Alice. “Like I was saying, we let them take the other three units. They know you have two. If we have three waiting, they likely won’t go searching for more. Then I go with them into the helicopter.”

“Why?” Pinely asked. “Why would you do that? You don’t know what they’ll do to you if you go with them.”

Abbie smiled. “It’s not what they’ll do to me, but what I’ll do to them. Plus, it’s the only thing I can think of to make sure they don’t drop whatever bombs they have and destroy the base anyway. Catharsis claimed to want me alive, and I think he was telling the truth, but I wouldn’t put it past him to still try and kill the rest of you.”

“What did you mean, ‘what *you’ll* do to them?’” Alice questioned.

A tingle ran up Abbie’s spin as she thought about the answer to that question. “I assume you have some explosives around here somewhere?”

“You want to blow them up?” Pinely asked.

“Yes,” Abbie answered. “And then come back in here to use the Incubus and scare the living crap out of Catharsis so he’ll never threaten my family again.”

"That last part won't be an option," Hakim said, adjusting his glasses.

"Why not?" Abbie questioned. "I just used the helmet and felt more powerful than ever. I'll be able to tear Catharsis to shreds."

"If we unplug the units," Hakim began, "it will take several days to recalibrate them again. It's not like turning off a microwave. Everything in here is synced together. They feed off one another. I can't just flick a switch and have things work properly. That's why I stay in here when the Incubus is in use. This isn't an autopilot situation."

Abbie stood and rubbed her fingers along her scalp, half in annoyance, half in desperation. "It will take days to make them work again?! My family doesn't have days! Catharsis will torture them somewhere in Consciousness during that time. He might even have them killed. I need to get at him in the dream before he knows what's happened! I need the power of the Incubus to stop him."

"Moon," Alice said, touching her arm. "It's not that simple…"

"I don't know what to tell you," Hakim continued. He tapped the desk with his index finger and bit his lip. "I never turn them off for that reason. As long as they're on and ready to go they can flow with the changes in Consciousness. Once that connection is broken, it takes a while to reestablish, and a lot of calculation and subject testing. Two days, minimum."

A frustrated growl tightened Abbie's throat. She needed to protect Nana Gayle and everyone else. Catharsis would be waiting in Consciousness. She could find him and end this. Without the Incubus she wouldn't be strong enough to go toe-to-toe with him.

'I think I'm beginning to understand why he's enamored with you. You're special.' Catharsis' words pushed through the fog hanging over her brain. Maybe she *was* strong enough and just didn't

know it. Alexander had been paying attention to her for some reason. Could it have been because of her natural ability?

The thought reminded Abbie of one of Hanker's last statements. *'Don't give into the power. You can be just like me without any of it.'* Did she trust her mentor enough to let go of her fear and doubt?

Whether she could or not, Abbie had to try. She wouldn't be able to fall asleep fast enough to catch Vincent and the feline by surprise though. Too much adrenaline would be pumping through her veins for her mind to quiet itself and enter Consciousness.

Think, think, think!

'I'll awaken one of my lieutenants currently enjoying a drug-induced sleep on the helicopter.'

Drugs. What drugs had Catharsis been talking about? Could the drugs get her to sleep?

Too many variables. Too many chances to fail. Doubt, doubt, doubt.

But Abbie had to try. She wouldn't abandon anyone tonight, even if it cost her everything. Doubt would not rule her ever again.

"It's okay," she said, nodding toward Hakim. "I'll find another way. I can't let Catharsis win. Not today…not ever."

Alice sat back on the closest bed and blew out a heavy breath. "That's a risky plan, pretty much all around, Moon. Especially for you."

"I know it's a risk, but it's better than the alternative. Yes, you'll lose three helmets when I bring the helicopter down, but you'll still have one fully functional unit here, and you can build more. Yes, you'll have to abandon your base, but that's unavoidable at this point. And yes, I may get killed in the process, but that's not Plan A, or Plan B, or Plan C at this point." Abbie took a breath and stared Alice in the eyes. "And you don't need to call me 'Moon' anymore. My name is Abbie Kinder. Everybody knows who I am now anyway, so there's no sense in protecting an identity that's already lost. This is the only option that doesn't result in all your deaths and Catharsis overrunning Consciousness. Do you have any explosives or not?"

For the first time since she arrived inside Alice's compound, Abbie saw Incandice smile.

Rain pattered against the roof and dripped down the windowpane in front of Abbie. Dark trees dominated the view, illuminated by an occasional burst of lightning. The musty cabin offered little protection from the cold. She shivered in the coat Vincent had bought her from the lodge gift shop. It smelled of fake leather and imitation animal fur; a perfect representation of the counterfeit man who had given it to her.

Darkness consumed the old one-room cottage, except for a shaft of light shooting from the open hatch behind her. Misty breath caught the glow and reminded Abbie how thankful she was the temperature hadn't dropped enough for the rain to turn to snow. The helicopter might have a hard time landing in a snowstorm, and she'd hate for something to happen to any of Catharsis' men.

Before she got to them, of course.

A calm breath filled her lungs as a few raindrops hit the glass. This time yesterday her heart would have been pounding out of her chest at the thought of leading a bunch of mercenaries into a trap. Today though, she felt calm and in control. In her mind, there was no real difference between combat in the dream and combat in Basic. Yes, she could die in one of them, but that fact didn't bother her. What was death really, other than just another realm to wake up in? What was life, but a physical dream from which to be roused?

The thought eased her worries as she waited for the sound of propeller blades to cut through the tattling rain.

After another ten minutes the drizzle lessened to barely a sprinkle. Rotors thumping in the distance met Abbie's ears. The helicopter had arrived.

She stepped outside the cabin and down the crooked wooden steps. A small break in the clouds overhead revealed a black sky full of stars. It had to be after three in the morning at this point. Soon the horizon would brighten into dim shades of pink and blue.

The chopper burst suddenly from above the forest and blocked out the stars in a spinning mess of wind and pummeling water droplets. Abbie held her hand in front of her eyes to keep the rain from spraying her irises, while her hair twisted around and smacked her face in soggy strands. A floodlight suddenly flicked on from the helicopter and bathed Abbie in its cold rays. She tried to stare up but found the brightness too much after the darkness of the cabin. The chopper lowered to about twenty feet above; blade pounding with enough volume to rattle her teeth.

A line of rope hit the ground a few feet to her left, followed by a second, and then a third. Several men wearing full military tactical gear descended and splashed in puddles next to the cabin's front porch. Each one wore a full flack vest with pouches, military fatigues, and a combat helmet straight out of an army base in the Afghan desert. Abbie couldn't make out many other details in the shifting light, but the M-16 rifles on their backs couldn't be missed. The closest soldier unhooked himself from his repel line and raised his weapon in Abbie's direction. A flashlight turned on and shined in her face, followed by at least one more to her right.

"Abbie Kinder?" a man's voice asked over the helicopter roar.

"Yeah, that's me," Abbie shouted back. She raised her hands as a courtesy, but something told her the soldier wouldn't be shooting her…at this point at least.

"Are you alone?" he questioned.

"They're all locked in a room downstairs," she said. "You won't have any problem. Follow me inside."

The soldier lowered the rifle slightly and raised his right hand to his left shoulder, clicking a radio sewn into his flack vest. "Confirmed, she is alone on the ground. Any more heat signatures registering on the surface besides us?"

"Negative sir," a voice squawked from the radio. "Recording seven warm bodies, including the girl."

"Go ahead and land on the airstrip as planned," the soldier ordered. "Maintain radio contact for as long as possible. If anything goes south, we'll let you know, unless we lose signal underground. We don't know exactly what to expect. You see anything moving, take it out with the Fitty."

"Yes sir."

The helicopter pulled up and disappeared back over the treetops. The sound faded slightly but continued to dominate the area.

"You say everybody inside is locked in a room?" the soldier asked, returning his attention to Abbie.

"Yeah. I tricked them inside and then jammed a wrench into the round locking-thingy. You'll see for yourself in a minute."

The soldier stepped closer to her, never dropping the rifle's barrel from Abbie's face. Her eyes adjusted to the glaring flashlight and she made out more details about the lead soldier. His broad frame dwarfed Abbie, appearing to be of Pacific Island descent by his facial features.

"You say we're not going to meet any resistance in there?" he asked. "Is that what you're telling me?"

"Yes," Abbie answered, lowering her hands. "That's what I'm saying."

Footsteps splashed behind her and one of the other troopers shoved Abbie slightly with his shoulder as he walked by. "I wouldn't trust her too much, Manu," an Australian said with a bit of mirth. Mozzie's scruffy face caught the beam from the soldier's flashlight. A line of scabs still marked his cheek and forehead where Abbie had clawed at him when he'd attacked in her apartment. He probably still had a goose egg on his head from the wine bottle too. "This is a tricky bitch right here, I tell you," Mozzie scoffed. "We get in and out, and if anything she says proves false, I'm going to put a bullet in her."

"You don't do shit without my say so, got it?" the lead soldier said. "Let us do our jobs, and you can do yours. Sound good?"

"I'm all warm and fuzzy." Mozzie turned to Abbie and licked his teeth. "Where we goin', Moon?"

"Inside the old cabin and down the ladder. Like I said: follow me."

"Search her first," Mozzie demanded. "I don't want to have a gun put to my head at any point during this mission. I already have some wounds to tend to because of this Sheila."

"I'm a sergeant major; I don't take orders from you, Mosquito," the soldier snapped.

Mozzie growled. "You want more surprises on this shit-show, do you, Manu?"

"Fine," the sergeant breathed. "Search her."

One of the other mercenaries stepped forward and slung his rifle across his back before patting Abbie down thoroughly from top to bottom.

"She's good, sir," the man informed. "No weapons. No communication devices I could find."

"Excellent. Now let's move."

Abbie led a total of six soldiers into the cabin and toward the shaft of light beaming from the open hatch. Their boots stomped against the creaking wood floor. They circled the trap door and pointed their guns down the shaft as if expecting imminent attack from all angles.

"You go down first," the sergeant-major ordered with a nudge of his M-16.

Her shoes, now slick from the wet ground outside, slipped several times on the metal rungs as she descended. A short corporal jumped down next, instantly ready to fire the moment he hit the ground. The rest followed, and Abbie led them down the corridor toward the Incubus room. The sergeant-major walked at Abbie's side, eyes focusing on every door they passed. His camouflage military gear reflected in a series of pipes to their left. He smelled of sweat and dirt, but his square jaw and light brown skin hinted at an attractive man underneath all the grime. He reminded her of Vincent: handsome, well spoken, strong, and completely corrupted.

As they entered the main hallway, the sound of banging filled the room from one of the side doors, along with people shouting in muffled cries. A wrench had been lodged in the locking mechanism.

"That's where I trapped everybody," Abbie pointed as they walked past.

The sergeant stopped and pointed at the hatch. "Anders: stand guard here. Make sure nobody gets out and surprises us. Shoot any hostiles."

"Yes sir."

"You just got them in there all together, huh?" Mozzie asked, sarcasm seeping from the words.

Abbie tapped the wrench. "I told them I had found out where Alexander was and that we needed to hit him now before he had a chance to move. Everybody rushed in excited, and once they were all seated inside, I closed the door and shoved the wrench in there. What, did Catharsis think I would have a hard time?"

Several of the soldiers chuckled.

Concrete walls refracted the sound of each footstep as they neared the Incubus chamber. So far things had gone according to plan. Abbie hoped that would continue, otherwise a lot of people would likely die. Including her.

"Where's Vincent?" Abbie asked as they turned a corner. "I thought I heard Catharsis say you picked him up or something. I expected to see him here with you."

"Naw," Mozzie answered. "He was still bleeding pretty good from the leg wound. We had to get him to a doc right quick. He'll be okay though. They got him sedated. I'll tell him you were asking about him. Might perk him up."

"You can tell Vincent the next time I see him I'm going to flay him alive."

Mozzie snorted. "I can do that."

"This is where they keep it," Abbie said as they approached the Incubus room at the end of the hall.

The doors swung open onto wooden veneer and the smell of stale donuts. Three helmets, three beds, and three computers sat in the center of the space. The corresponding Incubus unit had been moved to an adjacent closet. Hakim had taken great care to make sure the carpet, even the dust on the desks, wouldn't leave evidence behind that any objects had been moved. The doctor paid attention to detail, that was for sure.

"Here they are," Abbie said, arms wide. She picked up a large terabyte external disk drive from the closest table and held it under her arm. "They have three units, not two like Catharsis thought. I didn't get a chance to learn a ton about them, since I arrived less than eight hours ago, but I know you'll want the helmets and all the computers. Don't forget the hard drives like this one either. There's a platform dolly over there behind the sink area we can use to take everything out."

"*We*?" Mozzie mocked. "There's no '*we*' here, Moon."

The sergeant pointed to the computers and snapped his fingers. "Get the dolly and start loading up, men. Take everything, even the monitors. I don't want anything left behind."

"Yes sir."

As the soldiers started unplugging cords and tossing screens onto the dolly, Abbie stepped over to Mozzie and looked at his military gear and green fatigues. "There's a '*we*' now, Mosquito-Man. What do you think Alice is going to do to me if I stay behind? She'll have me killed for sure. She was going to do it before I unified and remembered the dream. Alice isn't one to forgive being betrayed. I'm a dead woman. Catharsis offered me a chance to go with you. I may hate your guts…and his…but I'd rather be alive and hate you both as opposed to dead. Besides, he said Alexander wanted me alive, and I'd like to find out why that is."

"You think I'm going to let you go with us after everything you've done to me?" Mozzie asked through grit teeth. He rubbed the scratches on his face and glared.

"What?" Abbie smiled. "Like that time I broke into your apartment and assaulted you? Or when I threatened you in a grocery store? Oh wait, that was *you* doing it to *me*. Or are you talking about when I chopped your arms off at Capacious' palace? Because, that I *did* do to you."

The sergeant laughed and wiped sweat from his brow. "She can come with us."

"Bull shit!" Mozzie yelled.

"I have orders," the sergeant continued, raising his rifle calmly as if to let Mozzie know he was serious. "The General said she might change her mind if she was successful in getting us inside without a fight. Alice can be an angry lady, from what he said. Moon can come if she wants, so long as there are no problems."

Mozzie turned and kicked one of the beds.

"Thank you, Sergeant Major," Abbie said. She turned as if to look around the room and slipped the hard drive she held inside her coat. "Any of us ever met in the dream before? I'm starting to realize that I may have killed some of you in Consciousness."

The sergeant laughed and scratched his wide nose. "Yeah, you and I have met before."

"And here I thought we didn't know each other," Abbie said, leaning against one of the desks like a harmless co-ed at a frat party. "You one of those Pursuants who makes themselves look like a werewolf or something to scare kids?"

"Lava rock monster, most of the time," he grinned. "I'm Koa. It means 'warrior' in Hawaiian."

"I chopped off your arms and legs and then crushed your head between my fists a couple days ago," Abbie nodded, smacking her knuckles together to accent her words. "That was a good fight. No hard feelings?"

He tilted his head to the left and stuck his tongue between his teeth. "You get us out of here nice and easy with the gear, and we'll call it even."

"Deal. What were you doing that night, anyway? You wouldn't let those Pursusants you were with hunt."

Koa bit his lip. A flash of red colored his tan cheeks as if the temperature had risen. "I was trying to freak out some corporate guy from New York for Catharsis. I don't usually work with him, but things kind of…aligned. Normally I don't---"

"It's fine," Abbie cut him off. She had no desire to hear Koa's excuses.

The last of the computers piled onto the dolly, helmets resting on top. Soldiers stood at attention, awaiting further command.

"Move out, men," the sergeant ordered.

The group made their way back down the hall, passed the captives still banging against the metal door, and eventually to the ladder. Each soldier took turns carrying computers and monitors up to the cabin, and after ten minutes Abbie stood again in the cold forest air. Rain had stopped falling, though she could see no stars through the mists overhead. The sky in the east seemed to glow slightly with the promise of dawn.

"Load up the gear," the commander said, reaching toward his wireless receiver. "We carry everything from here. Skycap? You read?"

"Loud and clear, sir," the radio crackled.

"Report we have acquired objective. No rounds fired. Any movement in the forest on infrared?"

"Negative sir. Nothing but a couple deer that came by a few minutes ago. We see you clearly about one klick to our north."

The sergeant pointed toward the computers as if reminding his officers to start picking up the equipment. "Excellent, Skycap.

Start prep for takeoff. We're headed your way now."

Each soldier grabbed computers and helmets, until all the gear was accounted for in their strong arms. The group started walking south into the grove, leaving behind the cabin and hidden underground compound. Flashlights shone on trees and scurrying squirrels as boots crunched against wet pine needles. Mozzie walked in front of Abbie, angry breathing competing with the din of the distant engine rumbling to life. The other soldiers surrounded her, hunched over with screens and large hard drives. Each step brought Abbie closer to her goal. She still needed more information though, before she could see any potential victory. Her rapport with the Sergeant Major couldn't be pushed too far, but she felt safe in asking a few more questions.

"Hey, I have a question, if that's okay, Sergeant Major/Rock Monster Koa," Abbie said.

Mozzie turned his head, lip curled down. "Shut up, Moon."

"Ask whatever you want," the commander said from immediately behind her. "Mosquito is just pissed he's not as strong as you are in the dream. Makes him feel inadequate."

"Screw you, Manu," Mozzie seethed.

"Right back at you, prick. Go ahead, Moon."

"Thanks. First off, should I call you 'Koa,' or 'Manu?'"

"Manu is fine out here in Basic."

"Got it," Abbie said. "Question number two: in the dream, Catharsis mentioned one of you guys was drugged before, and he would wake you up once he knew if I was going to help. How does that work? Drugs usually make your connection weaker in Consciousness, not stronger. Even a psychedelic like PCP will make things more confusing even if it elevates your mind. Plus, wouldn't the drug make it so you couldn't wake up on your own? You'd have to wait for it to wear off, right?"

“We have a cocktail that we use,” one of the soldiers to Abbie’s left answered. “Inject it in your arm, and it works great. Gets you to sleep within seconds but doesn’t stop you from waking up. Doesn’t mess with your higher brain functions either, so no effect on your abilities in the dream. It’s good stuff. Sarge calls it the Drop Shot, since it will drop you damn fast.”

Abbie nodded her head. “You got any on you? I’d like to try it sometime. Alice is going to come after me in Consciousness, I’m sure. It would be nice to be able to control my REM cycle a little bit better so I can drop in and out if she tries to hunt me down; break up when I sleep, that sort of thing.”

The soldier patted a pocket on his vest. “Stick with us and I can hook you up.”

“I’ll keep that in mind.”

“So, you think Alice will make you a target after this?” Manu asked.

Abbie snorted, as if trying to hold back a laugh. “What would you do if you were in her position?”

“Hunt you down,” Manu smiled.

“Thus, having a drug that can put me to sleep when she’s awake, might come in handy.”

Manu walked a little closer. “You’re pretty impressive Moon, if you don’t mind me saying. You would have made a good soldier; if you’d chosen that route.”

“Thank you, sergeant major,” Abbie said. “The thought of working for Catharsis makes my skin crawl, but at least you don’t seem so bad. You’re not Mozzie, so you’ve got that going for you.”

A chuckle snorted from Manu’s nose. They continued walking in silence.

The helicopter engine vibrations intensified until the group stepped into the clearing for the backcountry landing strip. Abbie could make out the contours of Pinely's aircraft on the far side of the runway against the trees. She also got a better view of the helicopter than she had before. Not knowing anything about military aircraft, Abbie couldn't tell what type of machine it was exactly, only that it was large, with tires, a long fuel funnel on the front, and a sliding door on the side. Was it a Blackhawk? Darren at the Sign Hub would know that sort of thing; he always did. The thought of her boss reminded Abbie of the innocent minds currently in Catharsis' crosshairs. She stared forward, tapping the hard drive under her arm.

The soldiers loaded up the computer gear and Incubus headsets quickly. Light continued to slowly build in the eastern sky.

"Let's climb on the bird and get out of here," Sergeant Major Manu said, removing his protective helmet. Wind blew his thick black hair as he climbed into the helicopter and offered his hand to Abbie.

"Thanks," she said, taking the closest seat to the open door. The other troopers slumped into adjacent chairs or stood with their hands grasping loops hanging from the ceiling. Mozzie sat with his arms folded, grimacing in Abbie's direction from across the helicopter interior.

Despite her earlier calm, the danger of the situation finally started to eat away at Abbie's resolve. Now would be the moment of truth. She pulled the hard drive out from under her arm and placed it on her lap.

"You should get buckled in," Manu said. "I'll close the door once you're locked."

Abbie turned to the soldier who had mentioned the drug as they'd walked through the forest. "Can I get a Drop Shot now? I don't like flying without a few doses of Dramamine in me."

The guardsman laughed and pulled out a small rapid-shot

syringe from his chest pocket. "I only got two left on me, but if you want one, I'm cool with it. You okay with her having one, Sarge?"

"Yeah, but give me the other so I can tell Catharsis: mission accomplished as planned," Manu said. "You want to come with me, Moon? You won't smash my head or anything, will you?"

"I'll try and refrain," Abbie smiled.

The soldier tossed over an automatic injecting needle like what Abbie's uncle used for his insulin. She held the plastic syringe tightly as the helicopter shifted to the right and started to lift from the airstrip.

Only one thing left to do.

Abbie quickly reached down and pulled the cover off the hard drive, revealing a lump of plastic explosive and a flick-switch. Alice's team had worked fast and efficiently. The Brazilian guy, Tiago, had assured Abbie the bomb would cause the desired damage. She took a deep breath. *'Death was just another realm to wake up in,'* she reminder herself.

"Hey Mozzie," Abbie yelled.

"What do you want, Moon?" he scoffed.

She flicked the switch and tossed the hard drive. "Catch!"

As the explosive charge left her hand and flew toward Mozzie, Abbie jumped to the right toward the open door.

Three seconds. That's all she had until…boom.

The helicopter had already lifted ten feet off the ground, but she didn't hesitate. Knocking over a confused Sergeant Major Manu, Abbie leaped into the air and plummeted toward the moist ground. Manu lost his footing and tumbled out next to her, arms flailing. Wind blew through Abbie's hair, reminding her of the jump she had taken with Fraelig toward the River of Subconscious. That fall felt like a lifetime ago.

Her right ankle shrieked in pain as she hit wet earth and fell forward onto her face. Manu landed on his side a few feet to her left with a painful thump and didn't move. The needle remained tight in Abbie's hand. Before she had a chance to push herself up and assess the damage to her leg, heat from an explosion above smash into her back, followed instantly by a roar so loud she thought it might burst her ear drums.

The airstrip lit up like the Fourth of July. Fire blew in all directions. The helicopter spun around, teetering and tipping. Abbie jumped to her feet, feeling her right ankle protest at supporting the weight of her body. She ran toward the trees as fast as she could, looking back as the chopper leaned backward and slammed into the ground. Debris shot in all directions as a second explosion decimated the helicopter in a thunderous howl. A chunk of propeller whistled through the air and slammed into a tree twenty feet away. The smell of gasoline and burning plastic assaulted her senses. Heat seemed to overtake Abbie no matter how hard she sprinted. Trees flew by in her periphery. After a moment, the intense warmth subsided enough that she stopped just beyond the edge of the forest and turned around.

The entire clearing danced in the light of the bonfire, casting shadows that seemed to jitter and grasp like terrifying demons. Nothing moved; no soldiers rushed from the flames or chased Abbie into the woods. Whether the helicopter had landed on Manu or scorched him during the explosion Abbie couldn't guess. Her ears rang like after a heavy metal concert, ankle screaming at her to sit down, but other than that, she was fine.

Physically, at any rate.

She leaned forward, hands on her knees, and tried to catch her breath. Blood surged through her veins like a marathon runner. Abbie had just blown up a helicopter with plastic explosives. Men were dead because of that choice. They had been her enemies, but still, the realization hit her harder than expected. She had cut hundreds, maybe thousands of Pursuants from the dream world over the better part of a decade, but none of them had suffered permanent damage because of the act. Today she had taken a life.

'Lives,' plural.

Air blew from her lungs in a focused burst, expelling any doubts that would make her question her actions. Self-reflection had to wait, she told herself. Breaths calmed and she stood up straight.

Opening her left hand, Abbie looked down at the hypodermic full of customized sedatives. Manu had been ready to inject himself and report to Catharsis in Consciousness. The helicopter pilot had probably already radioed someone in their organization telling them they had acquired the Incubus Helmets. Soon their colleagues, wherever they were, would know something was wrong.

Abbie had no time. By now, Pinely would have left his hiding place in the air vents and extricated Alice's crew from the conference room. Catharsis would be waiting in Consciousness for news of his team's success. She could find the cat and catch him by surprise. Vincent too. Maybe she would be strong enough to take them both on even without the Incubus.

Maybe not.

Even if she wasn't, Abbie had to try. There could be no doubts in her mind today.

The syringe felt cold against her palm. She squeezed it and jabbed the plastic applicator into her right forearm, just below the bicep. A warm feeling instantly emanated from the vein and filled her chest.

Sitting back against a tree, Abbie watched the helicopter burning. She thought of Nana Gayle and Grandpa Carl's pancakes; of Mom and Dad gardening; her sister Emma painting in the backyard when they were teenagers. Images of Hanker came to mind as he trained her how to form a psychic weapon for the first time so long ago.

She thought of Catharsis and Vincent laughing smugly on the shores of the subconscious river.

They would pay for what they had done to Hanker and all the other dreamers they manipulated. They would fear Abbie-Moon-Kinder like they had never feared anyone, even Alexander. Amplified by the Incubus helmet or not, Abbie would rend the dream world under her own mental power if she had to.

Catharsis and Vincent would be so afraid of her that they wouldn't dare touch anyone she had ever met.

Her eyes closed and she rushed toward darkness with revenge as her primary weapon.

CHAPTER TWENTY

Chaotic feelings of overstimulation and stress interlaced Abbie's fingers like an oppressive lover. Automobile honks and rattling jackhammers competed for auditory dominance. She opened her eyes on the outskirts of the Asian dream city of Guāng, feeling the anxiety of dreamers addicted to high pressure jobs and too little sleep. Guāng meant 'light' in Chinese, but Abbie always felt that was a misleading name for a place that seemed to suck the light right out of you. Even so, every color in the rainbow illuminated the area from buildings and floating signs, twinkling all around like stars in the heavens. Winged serpents flew alongside robotic birds and floating heads chattering about buying and selling. Skyscrapers reached toward a dark green and purple sky, shuddering and twisting slightly as if stretching cramped muscles.

Everything about this area of dream space seemed repressive and restrained. Urban smells of car exhaust and stagnant water made Abbie long to return to training sessions with Hanker in the forest or mornings planting tomatoes with Nana Gayle. The funk of unreal sewers and self-abandonment from millions of dreamers couldn't compare with blossoms of faith from a newly manifested sapling. A pair of Proctors stood across the street talking with a group of ethereal women in tight dresses, while several giant panda bears bounced down the highway. Red advertisements flashed in Chinese characters before morphing into images of a rabid Hello Kitty or men getting hit in the crotch by golf clubs.

The city of Guāng only came online in the dream just as Abbie normally was waking up, so she rarely came anywhere near it. The place always reeked of desperation and unfulfilled ambition; too many businessmen droning out their lives drowning in monochromatic paperwork; too many dreamers trapped behind concrete and glass with no horizon to inspire them. It reminded her of a collection of towers populated by dreaming stockbrokers she encountered sometimes; full of thirst that can never be quenched. More reasons to avoid metropolitan constructs.

Tonight though, she felt the persistent wisps of Vincent's mind in the streets, so she would endure the stench.

While no longer augmented by the Incubus, Abbie's senses still seemed heightened. The crush of emotion from so many people in one place no longer affected her as it had the first time she had dreamed with Vincent in this time zone. Ideas and desires rolled off her back, unable to get a foothold in her psyche.

Her connection with Vincent lingered as well. Vanilla seemed to throb along the thoroughfare like melting ice cream in a gutter. Catharsis was close by somewhere too. She looked up at the towering buildings illuminated against a murky lavender sky. A smell of calamari and lilac settled on the street, as if pouring from a high-rise vent. The cat always smelled like confidence and tenacity.

He was up there, in one of the skyscrapers. Both of them were.

Abbie flew into the air, passing a bathtub full of sardines singing in some neglected language. Several dreamers soared alongside her, laughing, and pointing as if the woman in the purple bodysuit somehow amused them. The higher Abbie flew, the stronger the scent of Vincent's sweet vanilla became. One building in particular, a dark green structure with warping and spinning bricks, pulsed with bright multicolored lights. It grabbed Abbie's attention, overflowing with the sensations of powerful dreamers. She felt Catharsis laughing; Vincent brooding.

Opening her perception, she reached out mentally to try and form a psychological picture of the top few floors of the building. A posh penthouse took shape in her imagination, with hardwood floors, finely decorated carpets, leather furniture, and a fountain spraying envy into the air. Catharsis and Vincent, along with four other Pursuants dressed in suits and capes, talked and shared stolen thoughts. At least six dreamers flittered through the space like ghosts, going where they were ordered and doing whatever they were asked. Abbie tried to exert control over the emotions underpinning the area, just as she had done with the Incubus, but thoughts became slippery, and she found it difficult to connect with all the ideas present in such a psychologically overpowering location. The background emotions of the entire city cluttered her brain and she pulled back. She had hoped to manipulate the building itself, taking Catharsis and Vincent by surprise with an instant death blow, but now knew it was beyond her current ability.

Her doubts suddenly tried to manifest and push her away from such an impossible task.

"No," she whispered. "No doubts. You are Abbie-Moon-Kinder. They're already afraid of your potential. It's time to bring it to the surface."

Destroying the entire building may be out of the question, but she could still make one hell of an entrance.

The skyscraper drew closer as Abbie picked up speed. Windows enlarged, and she could see a lion-sized purple and pink cat giggling with men holding drinks like at an upscale cocktail party in Manhattan. They wouldn't be laughing for long.

Mind clear, emotions focused, Abbie extended her awareness until she felt each singular brick forming the walls around the penthouse. She smiled, crushing the individual thoughts holding the imaginative mortar together. Cinder Blocks and windows detonated like a nuclear bomb as Abbie tore the side of the penthouse to shreds. Wreckage flew into the room and hit two of the Pursuants in the face with crushing force. They fell back and rolled into furniture that broke apart in the intensity of their collision. Catharsis and Vincent jumped in shock while their servile dreamers screamed and disappeared. One Pursuant tripped into the fountain of envy and crawled out weeping about how everyone had more expensive suits than he did.

"Catharsis!" Abbie screamed. Her voice seemed to deepen and rumble through the air in vibrating surges.

Fur bristled along the cat's back. Vincent formed his yellow armor and jumped beside his ally along with the four Pursuants. Two of the hunters' skin turned deep black like shadows at midnight. The other two took forms of hideous, snarling beasts, with spiked pelts, bulging eyes, and slobbery snouts.

"Moon!" Catharsis bellowed. "How dare you?! How dare you?!"

"Abbie?" Vincent said. His skin remained dry and cracked, but it seemed to soften when he saw her.

"You've looked better, Vincent," she said. "Whatever party you're throwing hasn't helped clear up your complexion."

His eyes and lips narrowed in unison. "Getting shot in the leg and pumped full of drugs will do that to you. If you coming here means you've screwed over Catharsis, I'm sure you'll look as pretty as me soon enough."

"What have you done, Moon?" Catharsis fumed.

Abbie floated into the room, rippling the fabric of a Persian rug as she entered. "I've brought a message from your team. They wanted me to tell you that they got three Incubus helmets with my help, but that they encountered some problems when they tried to take off in the helicopter. There was a…fire. You won't be seeing any of them in the dream again."

Claws dug into the hardwood floor and spit splinters into the air as Catharsis' muscles tensed like writhing maggots. "Where is Koa?! Where is my Team?"

"Burning somewhere in the Idaho wilderness," Abbie answered.

A shockwave of rage blasted from Catharsis and pushed Abbie back toward the edge of the building. As if commanded, the four Pursuants charged toward her, manifesting talons, cannons, and in one case, a jagged mace. Abbie pivoted and dodged the first assault from an attacker with black skin that twinkled with a field of stars. Purple armor formed around her body; sword materializing in her hand. She countered by cutting off the first Pursuant's right arm. He screamed and ducked away from her just as a beast with eagle claws lunged forward. A streak of violet light cut him in two. He fell to the side and wheezed like air spitting from a balloon.

Orange blasts lit up the penthouse as one of the well-dressed leeches fired from a cannon growing where his arm should have been. The emotional projectiles hit Abbie in the chest with enough force to shatter bone. Her armor held up against the assault; cracking in places but protecting her from harm. He fired more blasts, each one smelling more and more like desperation. Abbie walked toward him unfazed.

"It's not working!" The man cried.

"She's mine!" another of the monsters yelled. His hairy body grew larger, as if size would intimidate Abbie.

Diving forward, she slammed her blade into the creature's throat, and twisted. His severed head bounced at Catharsis' feet. Saliva and mucus smeared across the cat's fur as the head slowly dematerialized.

The remaining hunters attempted to run behind their leader

for safety, but Abbie tossed her sword. It spun around the room like a boomerang. The razor edge caught both men by surprise and banished the emotional leeches from the dream with painful slices of anger. Mist wafted where the Pursuants fell; the only reminder they had even been in the room.

"Efficient," Catharsis said. Octopus arms covered in round suckers slithered from his mouth and nose. "You're more powerful than you've ever been, little Moon. You here to intimidate us, hmmm? I promised to hurt people if you didn't play along, and now you think you can come here and scare me? Make me afraid to hurt your friends and family because you stabbed us in the back?" He slinked toward her like a predator about to play with a meal. "Good luck!"

Catharsis lunged forward in a slimy mass of contorting tongues. They groped for Abbie, spitting slobber wherever they touched. Taking flight, Abbie soared over his head, only to have a tentacle grab her by the ankle and slam her back down to the floor. Wooden boards cracked and spun on the air as she left a crater behind on impact.

Vincent stood to Abbie's left and watched as Catharsis picked her up and slammed her down again. He seemed uninterested in engaging in the fight; instead pouring himself a drink and leaning against the damaged bar.

Before Abbie could cut herself loose, Catharsis threw her against the fountain. Demolished masonry ruptured in chunks and dust. Liquid envy spilled through the breach like syrup and poured over Abbie's head into a pool on the floor. For a second, resentment overcame her with thoughts of how much she wished she had tentacle arms as well. Sloughing off the counterfeit emotion, Abbie stood back up and reformed her blades while envy dripped from her armor and hair.

Massive paws smashed the floor each time the cat swiped at

her. Changing perspective, Abbie appeared behind Catharsis and sliced off a section of his tail before he had a chance to react.

"Do you have any idea what I'm going to do to you?" Catharsis roared. "I can tell you're not hooked up to one of Alice's helmets. I can feel your weakness; your doubt!"

Abbie swung her sword and severed three of his tangled worms, saying nothing in response to his taunts. In no way did she want to give him emotional fuel to use against her. Sweat dripped from her forehead, but she stood her ground.

"You don't have the strength to take me down, stupid Moon," he continued, throwing a chair at Abbie. "Vincent can sit over there drinking for all I care. I don't even need his help. I'll swallow you whole and let my leeches suck you dry from the inside. I'm going to enjoy destroying the minds of your grandma and parents. It'll be slow. I'll savor every time they beg me to stop; every time they call out for you to save them!"

A scream ruptured from Abbie's throat despite her attempts to remain silent. She rushed forward, carving with her blade. Catharsis raised his front paw to scratch at her, but Abbie slid underneath his leg and cut off the cat's foot. The feline reared back and howled. More slimy appendages wiggled from the wound and twisted toward their enemy. Madness poured from his eyes in riotous bursts of violet flame.

Clambering to the side on her hands and knees, Abbie prepared to throw her sword again so she could catch Catharsis behind the shoulders. Before the blade left her hand, a wet ganglia slithered around her neck and yanked her back to the floor. Another moist octopus' arm grabbed her by the right wrist, while others crushed her waist and ankles. Abbie choked and gasped, kicking against the restraints as she dropped her weapon. The appendages pulled her toward Catharsis' enraged face.

"This was fun to watch," Vincent said as he sipped liquid that smelled like gin blossoms and distraction. "It's been a while since I've caught a show as surprising as this one."

Gulps coughed from Abbie's mouth as she tried to breathe. Catharsis tightened his grip and forced her face even with his own. Hot breath burned her cheeks, smelling like rotten fish.

"You didn't think you actually stood a chance, did you, Moon?" he asked. "I wish I had a dime for every ridiculous Proctor who decided to try and make a name for themselves by challenging me. You have skill, to be sure, but in the end you're like all the rest: weak; stupid," the tentacles pulled her toward his mouth. "Tasty."

Sharp teeth drew close to her neck. Saliva dripped onto Abbie's bare toes. She remembered fighting Catharsis' army at Capacious' Pleasure Palace. A single memory had allowed her to break free of their constraints.

She could do it again. She knew it.

Abbie possessed more power than she realized. The time had come for her to accept that truth; to run toward it instead of away.

She smelled bacon. *Leader of the Band* played on the radio. Nana Gayle picked her up. *'There's my little Abbie, all awake and ready for breakfast!'* Nana smiled. More memories of playing with friends at the local swimming pool augmented the first. Impressions flooded her mind, all happy, all strengthening. Abbie sat at a school desk drawing. Her art teacher, Mrs. Payne, walked up behind her and told her what an impressive sketch she had done. Laughter with Emma. A walk through the mountains with dad. Crying on Mom's shoulder after a high school break-up.

Light poured from Abbie's body as if filled with enough positive energy to power a city. The tentacles holding her wrists sizzled as if in a frying pan. She pulled against them and felt her hands release from their grasp. Grabbing at the appendages holding her throat, she pulled them away from her neck and tasted air again.

Her left hand clasped one of the cat's fangs and pushed against his tug.

"I'm not…stupid," she choked. "I'm…not weak."

"Oh really?" Catharsis asked, pulling her closer to his mouth with the tentacle still attached to her waist. "You will be once I'm done with you. You'll pray for death, and it will never come. I'll make sure of it. I control everything."

Control. That's what life amounted to for Catharsis. The end result of all effort. He wanted to control the real world and the dream world and everyone in it. Control, control, control.

Abbie smiled. "Well, you know…the thing about control, don't you?"

"And what is that, pathetic Moon?"

"The more you want control, the more afraid you are."

A laugh rumbled in Catharsis' throat. His mouth widened. His incisor cut into Abbie's hand. "And what am I afraid of, Abbie?"

Using all her emotional resolve, she pushed against her restraints and tore through tendons and thick muscle. Catharsis' tooth ripped from his gums and bled in Abbie's firm grasp. Blobs of black slime shot from the severed tentacles as Catharsis shook his head violently as if trying to scare away a wasp.

Abbie grabbed his large, tiger-like face, and squeezed. "Let's find out what you're afraid of!"

The building, broken furniture, fractured walls, Vincent, and every emotion linked to the city of Guāng vanished instantly as Abbie pulled herself and Catharsis deeper into Consciousness. Colors blended into blackness, exploding in bright blues and yellows. Before the cat could retaliate, the two combatants dropped into a realm of azure sky and vast sand dunes. They fell to earth directly over the River of Subconsciousness. Tumbling, grasping at each other, the enemies clawed and held tight as air blew through hair and fur. Water rushed up to meet them. The surface of the river burst open as they impacted. Cold liquid splashed around them and filled their minds with thoughts and memories buried so deep they were impossible to find except by accident.

Tentacles once again twisted tight around Abbie's throat, but the pressure no longer bothered her. His claws dug into her armor trying to reach flesh. She pushed Catharsis deeper into the dim, pressing his mind with a force she didn't know she possessed.

"What are you afraid of cat?" she cried. "What forms your nightmares when you're all alone?"

Catharsis writhed, trying to pull himself free of Abbie's grasp, but no matter how hard he tugged, she held on like a vice.

"Kill you!" Bubbles flew from his mouth as he bellowed.

"Not today!"

Thoughts from the river battered them both, trying to pry back their mental defenses and fill in the cracks with long ignored emotions and desires. Catharsis' control began to waver first, and Abbie used that opening to her advantage. She connected with his mind, digging deep with her fingers like dredging up mud from a garden. Dark, childhood anxieties of insignificance and powerlessness simmered in Catharsis' mind. Abbie grabbed hold, feeling his weakness and insecurity. She saw a woman turning her back; a man with a belt reaching down. Limp skin clung to bone. Hunger gnawed. A military uniform hung in a closet, never ironed perfectly enough to impress himself. Depressing smells, like boiling onion soup with way too much salt, barfed from Catharsis' subconscious and twirled on whirlpools in the river. His fears, lust for power, and regret took form in the gloom and threatened to overcome them both.

Abbie suddenly stood in front of a mirror, staring back at a thin old man, seemingly in his late seventies, as he tightened a dark green tie that matched his crisp uniform. Metals and little colored rectangles covered his chest, along with four silver stars running across each shoulder. A name plate on his right pocket read 'Marshal' in bright white letters.

The man seemed frail and physically weak but hiding a mental fortitude that was almost unmatched. She felt his frustrated emotions, along with snippets of memory. His brown eyes, while not feline in nature, housed a malice and enmity Abbie recognized immediately.

Catharsis.

Another name came to her mind as the man in the mirror positioned his military dress cap on his head: 63-year-old Four-star General Ethan Marshal of the United States Army. He looked far older than 63.

Everything made sense in that moment. Catharsis enjoyed power both in the waking world and in the dream…but he didn't run the show in either. That's what he wanted. No more orders; no more kneeling to a superior of any type. His desire for the helmets, and the power they would afford, seemed to trickle from the general's pores as he looked his reflection up and down. In ten months, he would be forced to retire after turning 64. He had no choice. That fact infuriated him. No one would dictate to Catharsis what he did or did not do. No one. Not now, not ever.

All his thoughts lingered on the Incubus. There was no manipulation. He wanted those helmets, and he would do anything to get them.

Anything.

This pathetic man, so powerful and yet so stunted, would bend his will toward dominating others just so he wouldn't have to follow his last set of orders…so he would never have to take an order again, period.

Pitiful.

Dark emotions of wretchedness and defeat raged through Abbie's mind and slammed into Catharsis like a meteor in a barren desert. They cycled back and forth in a loop, filling the cat with his own pent-up inadequacies.

"Get…out of my…head!" he screamed.

Abbie held tighter. "Feel it, General!"

Orange cat eyes with their vertical black slit, spasmed and turned an all-too-human brown with flecks of green. Catharsis' strong body and octopus tentacles wasted into emaciated, wretched limbs with no muscle to speak of. The grip around Abbie's neck lessened to nothing. Catharsis' pink tongue sloughed from his mouth and flapped to the side as they moved through the water.

Swimming upward against the current, Abbie pulled Catharsis back toward the surface. They exploded into the air, sending a fountain bursting onto the dry sand on the river's bank. Abbie tossed Catharsis away roughly. He thumped like a drowned kitten into the sand and rolled to his side. Tears trickled down his fur and mingled with the left-over thoughts from the subconscious stream.

"Get up," Abbie ordered.

"Please…" Catharsis wept. He raised an emaciated paw and dropped it weakly to the sand in a puff of dust.

Abbie stomped over and grabbed him by the scruff around his neck. "This happens every night from now on, you understand? This happens every night if even one of your Pursuants so much as touches a hair on the head of anyone I've ever met. You have power in Basic? Good for you. I don't need power out there. I have enough in here to torment you until you're nothing but a pelt spread across my floor. Promise me, 'man-of-your-word;' promise me you'll call off any attacks in here or out there."

"I…" Catharisis gasped. "I…"

"Promise me!"

A shockwave rippled the sand a half mile in every direction. Power emanated from Abbie, turning her skin golden and shiny. Light reflected off her body in shafts of pure power. Several eagles swooped down and circled as if bowing to a superior being. Catharsis cowered and shook.

"I promise!" he shrieked. "I promise! Please, let me go…please…"

In that moment Abbie saw the terrifying cat for what he really was: a ridiculous brute unable to accept his own limitations.

"One more thing," Abbie said, grabbing Catharsis by the scruff of his neck and pulling his face close to hers. "I know who you are now, Four-star General Ethan Marshal. That means Alice will know who you are now too as soon as I wake up. That means all your enemies will know who you are if you try to cross me. Understood?"

The cat nodded and dropped his eyes. "Yes. Understood."

She released him. Catharsis slumped back against the dune and panted.

Abbie stepped aside and breathed. She had defeated the undefeatable. Now only Vincent remained.

"This isn't…over," Catharsis said weakly. Claws extended from his scrawny paw as he reached toward Abbie. Before he could swipe at her, thin rods of gold shot from the sand, encircling the cat and forming around him in the shape of a birdcage, complete with a tiny swing overhead like in an old Bugs Bunny cartoon. He growled and pushed against the bars; gnawing them with his teeth, but unable to break free.

"Yes, it is, kitty. It's over" Abbie replied, turning back toward the river. The gold layer covering her body soaked into her skin like lotion and disappeared. She felt stronger than ever. "Why don't you take a nap in your cage? You'll wake up feeling much better, I'm sure."

"There's more than…just me out there," he continued, still scratching at his prison. "Alexander is watching after all. And I'm not…going to just roll over for you."

"You better," Abbie waved. "Unless you want to get drowned again."

With that, Abbie focused her energies and reconnected with the city of Guāng. A broken skyscraper appeared in her mind. She called out to it, establishing a link that pulled like a magnet. The dunes swirled around her, leaving behind the pleasant smells of desert flowers and moist sand. She dropped herself back into the loud world of pressure and worry. Her feet touched the scratched hardwood floor of the penthouse once again. Liquid envy squished between her toes from the broken fountain. The urban world echoed with shouts and sirens while a dragon flew by and glanced at the fractured suite wall.

Abbie smelled vanilla.

Vincent remained sitting at the bar where she had left him. His yellow armor glowed lightly, ebbing and flowing like a plasma ball come to life. He drank from a green bottle and wiped his mouth.

"Where's Catharsis?" he asked with the calm of a person wondering where the dog had run off to.

"Licking his wounds," Abbie answered.

Eyebrows arched over Vincent's eyes as a look of surprise and admiration colored his face. "Wow. Look at you. Three days ago, you were screaming in your apartment, and now you're making the great Catharsis lick shit from your bare feet. No wonder

Alexander wants to get to know you better."

"And what do you want, Vincent?" Abbie asked. "When I was hooked up to the Incubus, I could feel Catharsis' lust for power and control, but I couldn't feel what you wanted. What are you after?"

Standing, Vincent nodded his head and stepped closer to Abbie. He tossed the green bottle aside and it shattered against what remained of the central fountain. "Isn't that obvious." His eyes seemed sad and sincere as they pleaded with her.

"What, you want me, is that it?"

"Maybe." Vincent reached for her, armor melting from his shoulders and arms. His dry, cracked skin smoothed out and glowed slightly. A breeze picked up his long hair and wafted it off his shoulders. His cape billowed like a dramatic hero arriving to save the day. "I lied to you; I know that. I admit it. I had a job to do, and I was going to do it. I never wanted to hurt Uncle Hanker. I never wanted to hurt you. There's more going on here than you know, Abbie. Believe me. But even with all that, I never lied to you about who you were. I never lied about how impressed I was with you. I never lied about my admiration…my affection."

A warm, pleasant feeling filled Abbie's chest, not unlike what she felt when sharing thoughts with Vincent. His words oozed truth. He seemed suddenly so kind and loving…so misunderstood and vulnerable. She could fix him. All he needed was love and affection, and he would become the perfect partner.

"Stop it," she said, pushing the emotions aside. "You can't manipulate me anymore."

"I'm not manipulating you. I know what you feel for me because I feel the same way for you. That's not a manipulation. That's truth."

"You don't know what truth is!"

"You want truth!?"

Vincent stepped toward her and opened his mind, just as he had in the quiet of the Atlantic Ocean two days before. Similar images of a young, lonely boy coalesced around her as they had then, but this time Vincent didn't pick and choose what she glimpsed. Abbie looked deep into his mind and saw how he would transform into different people like the blob Resin, believing himself to be different and thus becoming someone different. All his doubts and regrets would wash away, leaving behind someone new; someone fresh and clean.

That's what Vincent wanted: to be clean and new; to be redeemed.

He wanted to become someone else, a person who hadn't betrayed the people around him, who hadn't done terrible, selfish things. He wanted to be someone better…someone worthy.

Worthy of Hanker's pride.

Worthy of Abbie's love.

Maybe with the Incubus helmet he could truly become a new man…literally…without the baggage of a life spent stabbing people in the back. Vincent could use the power of the amplified mind to create a new personality and delete the old, or simply modify it so he could become a true hero in his own story. He could be who he always wanted to be and live up to the legacy of his selfless uncle.

"You see the truth?" Vincent asked. "There's no need for either of us to be trapped by the past. We can create something new for both of us. Become something different; something perfect."

Abbie wanted to believe it possible. She couldn't deny their attraction or the connection that pulled them toward one another. She couldn't control how she felt about him, no matter how dangerous those emotions proved to be.

Even so, Abbie would not be ensnared in a trap that would

eventually hold her hostage. Vincent had shown his true self, and the desire to change wouldn't be enough.

As his hand reached up to touch her cheek, Abbie grabbed his wrist and squeezed. "Nice try, Vincent. You want redemption but you don't want to work for it. You want the easy way out, just like you always have."

"Abbie, listen," Vincent urged, voice sounding so sweet and reasonable, filled with citrus and sandalwood.

She released his wrist and pushed it away. "You're really good, Vincent, but once someone's seen through the magician's trick, he'll never fool them again. You're a liar and a murderer. You deserve to rot right alongside Catharsis."

Vincent sneered. The skin on his face grew pale as fractures again spread across the surface. Pain held in his eyes, as if her words stung far more deeply than he would ever admit. "This could have gone so much easier, Abbie."

The air grew heavy and uncomfortably hot. An oppressive gust blew up from the floor like a belch of hate from a drunk man. Depression and doubt filled Abbie's chest in roaring waves of sewage. Suddenly she couldn't breathe again, but this time instead of tentacles wrapped around her neck, it was misery. Her legs grew weak.

"We could have been so good together, Abbie," Vincent continued. "We still can be. Don't make me do this."

Despite the force pushing against her, Abbie took a step toward Vincent. "I'll tell…you the…same thing I…told Catharsis."

"Let me guess: don't hurt my family and friends or I'll destroy you? Come on, Abbie! I know you. I know your pain and hesitation. I know your desires. I don't want to hurt your family. I don't want to hurt you. But I will."

Hopelessness and despondency bore fissures inside Abbie's

mind with the force of a power drill. It took all her strength to keep from falling over and kneeling before Vincent like a supplicant. She tried to form her swords but found them breaking to pieces before they'd fully manifested.

Vincent stepped closer and breathed in through his nose. "You're strong, but there's only one way this ends, Abbie."

The depression deepened, triggering memories of weakness and pain.

'Fight it,' Abbie said to herself. *'You're strong. You're strong. You're strong.'*

Even so, her doubts took shape once again. '*You're not good enough. You're the worst. You can't draw. You can't fight. Hanker is dead because of you. Most of Alice's helmets are destroyed because of you. Just give up. You can't win. There's only one way this ends.'*

There's only one way this ends.

"You're damn right," she said.

Feet planted, Abbie grabbed hold of her rotten emotions and doubt, shifting them like a river back toward Vincent. The flood hit him and knocked the man back. His eyebrows pressed against the ridge over his nose, teeth grinding. Black hair blew over his shoulder as if caught in a hurricane. Abbie's doubts mixed with his own, highlighting every mistake, every betrayal, every time he had acted egotistically. He shook as his emotions spilled out and filled the room in effervescent whisps.

"You think I doubt myself?" Abbie asked, stepping forward. "Of course, I do. We all do. The difference is I'm no longer a slave to my doubts. I'm not a slave to my regret. What about you, Vincent?"

Wind blew in a gale, billowing Vincent's yellow cape back toward the fountain. Abbie's melancholy flitted away like a butterfly and slammed into Vincent with freight train force. He leaned forward against the rush; a man trying to withstand a tornado. Chairs and chunks of debris lifted in the cyclone and began smashing into the walls. Vincent bellowed in protest but couldn't move his feet.

Abbie grabbed him by the neck and lifted Vincent off the ground. He weighed nothing to her; like a plastic bag, or an annoying cobweb stuck to your hand. He clawed weakly at her wrists to dislodge her grip but lacked the strength to remove even a finger from his throat. The wind stopped. A coffee table dropped to the floor with a crash along with several bottles of distilled emotion. She turned and walked toward the broken wall that opened on the city below.

"You're so good at reading everybody else's emotions, you never stop to acknowledge your own, do you, Vincent?" she asked, extending her arm past the edge of the floor. Vincent hung precariously over open air.

Feet dangling a hundred stories from the ground, he reached with his toes to find purchase. "Please, Abbie…"

"Now you sound like Catharsis."

"Please," he begged. "I know things. Life isn't…going to get…easier for you. Things are coming that will wash you away like a diaper on the ocean. Listen to me…Abbie. You need me."

"I don't," she said. Her fingers loosened.

"We're the same."

"We're not."

Vincent let go of Abbie's wrists and looked at her calmly. "I can fly, Abbie. We can all fly here. This isn't a very effective threat."

A smile beamed from Abbie's cheeks, full of joy and harmony. "You sure about that? Your doubts not getting the better of you?"

Vincent glanced down at the buildings and streets below him. His eyes blinked rapidly. Fear seeped from his flesh in spurts of burned caramel fumes.

"That's what I thought, Vincent. You have more than enough doubt clouding your mind to make you drop like a stone. I hope the fear takes you the entire way down. I never want to see you again."

Abbie opened her hand and Vincent plummeted with a terrified scream. His yellow cape flapped around him as he fell, disappearing against the lights and darkness of the city. The realm rumbled as he hit the street; exiled from the dream for another night.

Peace overcame Abbie and she started to cry. Tears of relief and joy flowed from her eyes. As impossible as it seemed, she had beaten both Catharsis and Vincent without the help of the Incubus. Flowers bloomed at her feet. Trees began to grow from the penthouse floor. Crisp smells of nature overpowered the choking vapors of Guāng City. Birds too colorful to be real flew into the building and nestled in fresh branches next to fruit that tasted like optimism.

The night air pulled at her. Abbie stepped out into nothingness and flew toward the stars. Butterflies swarmed, dragons watched in awe, and sardines in bathtubs stopped singing to watch a Dream Master soar. Nothing could hold her back. No barriers could stop her.

Abbie-Moon-Kinder looked down on Consciousness and laughed.

"I guess this is what it feels like to come to the end of a beginning."

CHAPTER TWENTY-ONE

Ripe peach juice dribbled from the edge of Abbie's mouth as she bit into the sweet fruit. The flavor assaulted her senses and threatened to send her into Consciousness with the overwhelming power of its tang. Never before had she enjoyed a peach straight from the tree and knew in that moment, going back to store-bought produce would be impossible.

"Good, right?" Incandice asked as she picked another fruit from a branch and placed it in a basket next to a dozen others. "Who'd have thought Alabama would have such amazing peaches. I always hear about Georgia peaches, but they can't be better than these."

Abbie took another bite and looked around the quiet orchard. Weeds sprouted high next to overgrown trees; pollen tickled the nose. Bees buzzed on the humid air as dark clouds gathered to the north.

"Looks like it's going to storm again this afternoon," she said.

"Let's get back inside," Incandice nodded. "I have more than enough fruit for Reilly to make his cobblers. And don't you need to get the canvas wrapped up and mailed today?"

"I do. Francis said he would box it up for me once I made any necessary changes along with my signature. He still has to falsify the documents and shipping labels so it can't be tracked back here. I'll finish up and pass it along to him to do his thing."

The two women walked along the lines of trees until they came to the edge of the grove. Tall grass rubbed against Abbie's bare legs just below her jean shorts. Sweat stuck to her white t-shirt as she swatted away a wasp searching for nectar. The Alabama humidity had taken getting used to, but now her perspiration didn't bother her as much as it had when they arrived at their temporary sanctuary. At least now she didn't feel the need to take a shower every time she walked outside.

Just beyond the orchard stood a large produce processing factory with a faded logo painted on the side reading: Avery Bros. Peaches; Since 1936. Rust streaked from the roof down the building's corrugated metal walls. Lines of iron carts sat empty in the sun, stained with juice from decades of peaches, and covered in a layer of dirt as if unused in many years.

Home-sweet-home. Or more appropriately, Abbie thought, hideout-sweet-hideout.

Hinges squeaked and sent a shiver through Abbie's body as she opened the door and let Incandice step inside with her basket of fruit. After two months, she thought she would be used to the screeching side entrance but admitted that it still rattled her jaw every time she opened it. Her eyes adjusted to the interior light, boots thumping against the concrete floor. A Row of twelve beds lined the far wall below the windows where a series of conveyor belts had originally been. Four people currently slept comfortably in the quiet factory; sleep masks covering their eyes so the sunlight wouldn't interfere with their theta cycle. Soft spa music played from an iPad plugged into one of the few outlets along the north side of the workshop. Several tables filled the center of the warehouse where Pinely chopped carrots next to Tiago, who peeled potatoes into a metal trash can.

"We got Reilly his peaches," Incandice whispered as she

placed the basket next to Pinely. "Where do you need us?"

"Could you go fill those pots with water, Incancice?" Pinely asked. "I need to start boiling the potatoes for dinner."

"What about me?" Abbie questioned quietly. One of the sleeping men grumbled something from his bed and rolled over.

"Alice wants to see you if you have a minute," Pinely answered. "She's up in the office. And be careful going up the stairs. Remember, that one step has rusted out. We don't need anyone else cutting themselves like Frances did, and then waking everybody up with their screams. Nobody wants to be pulled form Consciousness like that."

"I'll watch my step, thanks. Let me take one last look at the painting real quick so Francis can get it mailed, and I'll head up to talk to her."

Abbie made her way past an old orange pick-up truck that still smelled of peaches and waved at Francis as the short young man waddled over carrying a bucket full of onions.

"Is Pinely still making fun of me from when I cut my ankle on the stairs?" Francis asked.

"Does he ever stop making fun of anybody?" Abbie rubbed his shaggy brown hair. "Don't worry. As long as you don't spill the onions, you won't add anything to your clumsiness tally."

He smiled and nodded. "I finished the crate for your canvas. If you're ready, I can box it up and take it to town after dinner on my supply run. I have the fake shipping barcodes printed too."

"Let me add one finishing touch," Abbie said, "and you should be good to do your thing."

In the far southeastern corner of the factory directly under Alice's second-floor office, stood a small area with a painting easel, chair, and selection of high-quality acrylics on a small table. Abbie smelled the light scent of ammonia from the preservatives in the paint as she stepped toward her work of art. The last two weeks had been a creative flurry for her, as she let her mind create an image that could hang proudly next to her sister's paintings in New York. Never had a piece come so effortlessly to Abbie as this one, nor the ease of using a mixture of paint and pencil in an experimental style. Perhaps her united mind found more freedom in creation than it had when divided between two plains of consciousness.

The 20-by-24-inch canvas, now covered in pale yet vibrant strokes that seemed to almost move and come alive depending on the angle, featured an impressionistic painting of a bald man in azure armor standing in a world of mixing color. In places he seemed to blend into the background, while still standing distinctly apart from the rest of the painting. Over his shoulder floated a half photo-realistic, half cartoonish butterfly. The remainder of the piece seemed to manifest directly from consciousness and pull the mind toward a place of peace and comfort.

Abbie beamed, looking into the caring eyes of her mentor, happy he would be remembered after his death in more than just memory. She had worried earlier that morning that more work would need to be done on the painting before mailing it off. After a few hours away from the piece however, Abbie now realized any additional brush strokes would do nothing more than detract from the purity of the image.

She reached over and picked up a tube of blue paint and a small clean brush. Dipping the soft bristles into the acrylic, Abbie reached toward the lower left-hand corner of the canvas and signed her initials in a quick but fluid motion.

"You look good, Hanker," she whispered. "You're all done. Even Emma will be impressed, I think."

Metal steps groaned under her feet as she bounded up the stairs toward Alice's office, careful to skip the corroded section. As she reached the landing, Abbie looked down on the factory floor. Pinely continued chopping his vegetables. Francis placed several onions on the table next to him. Tiago hummed a Brazilian tune that could barely be heard against the music playing on the far end of the warehouse.

"Come in," Alice waved as Abbie opened the door. The woman sat at a wooden desk covered in papers and a laptop, with a window to her left looking out on the orchards. She wore a brown t-shirt and jeans; a pair of reading glasses hanging on the bridge of her nose. Hair pulled back into a tight ponytail, Alice looked like a cross between a librarian and a general preparing troops for battle.

"What's up?" Abbie asked as she sat across from her. The plastic chair creaked as if about to break away from the bolts holding it to the aluminum legs.

"I got a message from Hakim about twenty minutes ago," Alice said.

"How's he doing in Nevada?"

"Sweating. At least that's what he complains about most. I think out of everybody, no one misses Idaho as much as he does. Luckily his team seems to be adjusting well, until we can all get back together again in one place. Hakim will be flying in next week to recalibrate the Incubus again. Without him around it gets out of tune so fast we can hardly use it. It's hard being separated, but there's nothing we can do for the time being. Hopefully in a couple more months we'll be safe to move again. I'm working on getting some better accommodations that won't draw attention, but it will still be a little while."

"Living in the factory hasn't bothered me too much," Abbie admitted. "It's not every day you can say you sleep with twelve different people every night, so there's that…"

"I'm glad you like it," Alice chuckled. She looked up at the metal beams running along the ceiling overhead. "It just gets so damn loud in here when it rains."

"Drowns out the moans from when you and Pinely are fooling around."

A deep belly laugh burst from Alice's mouth. She rested her head against her knuckles while getting herself back under control. "Well, I'm glad the noise of rain on corrugated metal has served some good during our exile in Alabama. This whole thing is a pain in the ass, I know, but it's temporary. Pinely always said I was paranoid for having contingency bases across the country, but he's not complaining now, is he? I just wish I'd put more thought into them instead of simply buying foreclosed properties. Next time I'll try and acquire a Hilton," she joked. "Anyway, Hakim found some interesting information that could point us toward where Alexander is. I thought you'd like to know."

Alice turned the computer around so Abbie could see the screen. A document with two mugshot photos drew her attention. Written in French, the booking report featured the standard front and side view of a man holding a series of numbers just below his chin. The man appeared to be in his 50's, attractive, dark hair, bushy beard, and sad eyes. Abbie recognized him from somewhere but couldn't put her finger on exactly where she had seen him before. Then she read the name, and everything made sense.

"Jihan Khatri," she said. "The guy who helped Alexander build the first machine you guys used back in college."

"The same," Alice confirmed. "He was just arrested in France yesterday trying to smuggle in drugs from Russia; the same drugs Catharsis uses in his Drop Shots. I was never sure if he still worked with Alexander or not, but this certainly points in that direction. He was always one of the few people Alex trusted. This could be a huge break for us. It may be worth spending some of our savings for a trip to France. I'll talk to the group and see what everyone thinks, but are you up for taking a trip to Europe if I decide to send a couple operatives?"

"...Yeah, I'll do it," Abbie said after a pause.

Papers crinkled under Alice's elbows as she leaned forward. "How long has it been since you've been able to talk to your grandma?"

The chair grumbled under Abbie's weight as she shifted against the backrest. "A couple weeks is all. She and my mom are still freaking out that I haven't come back home since everything happened. I've told them I'm taking time and drawing with friends; just trying to figure out my next move after quitting my job. That's true enough. I have been drawing a lot, so I'm not lying to them, and the painting for Emma's gallery opening is finished finally. They're proud I decided to do a piece. It's just hard not seeing them, and not being able to tell them everything. I miss them. They're afraid I've joined a cult."

"It won't be like this forever, Abbie," Alice said. "Things have stabilized in Consciousness, but that won't last. Catharsis is still building his forces. Even though we know who he is, General Marshal is not an easy man to undermine. He sits next to the President of the United States at official functions for God's sake. Vincent still slinks around too. And after Incandice ran into Koa last week in Consciousness we know he survived the fall from the helicopter when you knocked him out. It was probably him who lead the team that torched the Idaho base after we escaped. You wouldn't be safe if you went back. You're like me now; you need to keep your eyes focused both ahead and behind."

"I know. We have a job to do. I'm fully onboard."

Alice smiled. "I know you are. Your Dream Team is amazing everyone with their progress since you took over training from Hanker. Pinely can't stop talking about it, and Catharsis seems to be giving you a wide berth, which is good. Hanker would be proud."

An image of her mentor in his blue and yellow armor laughing and conjuring images to draw flickered in Abbie's mind like an old film reel. She remembered his kind words and tough criticisms, always pushing her, and the entire team, to be better. After Hanker's death, that responsibility had fallen to her.

"They're a good group," Abbie replied. "I've added a few new people to my core crew, and the one I'm building in Asia when I sleep midday is really starting to come together. One of them in particular, a young Proctor named Sapana, shows a lot of promise. He and I started out on the wrong foot when I first met him, but he's eager to learn and has a lot of energy, as does Fraelig, whom I've mentioned to you before."

Alice stood and nodded. "Well, I'm excited to take a look in the next couple days. I'm pretty busy with the whole Bolivia dream blackout thing that keeps getting worse, but I'll make time. We'll get everyone together and awake tomorrow morning to discuss our next move."

"If you want…" Abbie began, choosing her words carefully, "I could use the Incubus again to find Khatri in Consciousness. We could get information from him in the dream. It would be easy. You said so yourself that I'm the most gifted user you've ever known."

The muscles on Alice's neck twitched. "Abbie…you know what I'm going to say. I don't think it's a good idea for you to use it for now, especially since we only have one helmet left and I couldn't go in with you to help train. Yes, you're talented, but from what Pinely told me about your experience, it poses too great a danger right now."

"I got carried away is all."

"It's about more than getting carried away." Alice leaned forward over the desk; hands planted firmly. "You exploded Capacious, an incredibly powerful Pursuant, with a thought. You pulled your team into hazardous conditions without reflecting on whether or not their abilities matched the challenge. You attracted dreamers like a beacon without even trying. I'm not going to risk you falling into an addictive hole unless I'm there to guide you. For right now it's off the table."

Nodding, Abbie conceded. "Okay. It was just an idea."

"You'll use the Incubus again, I promise. Hakim will be here next week, like I said, to recalibrate it, and he's currently working on building another one. When that happens, believe me, we'll go in together. Besides, you've proven you don't need it, and from what I can see, you're a better leader without it. Trust that."

Abbie looked at the collection of papers strewn around Alice's laptop. A question had been eating at her ever since she first used the Incubus. Part of her feared the answer, or potential lack thereof, so she hesitated to ask.

"What makes me so special in Consciousness?" Abbie questioned. "Why did I have so much power when I used the helmet? I'm not a genius or anything like that. I'm not even as creative or talented as my sister. I'm a normal person. Why can I do what I do in the dream?"

"I honestly can't answer that, Abbie, because I don't know," Alice said.

"That's what I was afraid of."

Alice nodded her head. "If I knew what type of person would make a powerful Proctor, I would find those people and train them before they even understood their own potential in Consciousness. But unfortunately, it doesn't come down to any one thing. It's a combination that we don't understand at all; creativity, intelligence, spatial awareness, good brain chemistry, extra folds in the cerebellum, whatever. Why did Alexander have so much power the first time we used the helmets, while I wasn't even strong enough to be a Proctor before that? I don't know. I'm sure he doesn't know.

It's like asking why one person is a master architect while the next has an aptitude for languages. Some things we just have to accept. You're you. You're a powerful dreamer. That's going to have to be enough for now."

And there it was: no answer to the most important question Abbie had ever asked. Another mystery that might never be solved.

Chair legs scraped against the metal floor, and she stood. "Thanks, Alice. I'll go down and help finish dinner before I go back into Consciousness."

"Abbie," Alice said as she reached the door. "I just…want to say 'thank you' again for everything you did. We all owe you more than I think we realize. Without you, I'm not sure where this operation would be…where I would be. Thanks, again."

Embarrassment warmed Abbie's cheeks. She appreciated the sentiment, but they were all in this together now. No one stood higher than anyone else. No one's individual sacrifice eclipsed anyone else's.

"I appreciate that," she replied. "I better get back down and help, otherwise Pinely won't have dinner ready, and my team will be waiting for me in Consciousness wondering why I never go to bed on-time."

"What image moves from mind to hand today?" Alice asked with a chuckle.

Abbie grinned and scratched the back of her neck. "A pink cat trapped in a birdcage."

“A pink cat trapped in a birdcage?” Brainstorm asked, looking up at the glowing image of a kitten trying to escape gilded bars. “That’s more complicated than yesterday. I don’t know if my Basic-self will get all the details right.”

Abbie walked past an upside-down tree and plucked an apple from its roots. The fruit tasted almost as good as the peach from earlier in the afternoon, except with a bit more annoyance as an aftertaste. Each member of her team stared at the construct of the cat in the cage and breathed deeply. Pinely, Merquery, Aspira, Brainstorm, Tommy, and Gaze, along with several new recruits, waited for their leader to impart wisdom before embracing the image. The forest blossomed around them, dreamers popping in and out with their customary babbling and playful laughter. Abbie turned attention back to her troops and put her hands on her hips.

“That’s where you’re making your first mistake, Brainstorm,” she replied, taking another bite of her apple.

“It’s not Brainstorm anymore Moon,” the young man said. “I’m going by Hanker 2.0 now.”

“Hanker 2.0?”

He dropped his eyes as if embarrassed. “I just thought…you know…I would honor him…or something. If you don’t like it---”

“We all get to choose who we are in Consciousness,” Abbie said. “It’s one of the perks of being a Proctor. If you want to be like Hanker, then more power to you. He is worthy of emulation. Just remember, that name will put a target on your back, so you need to be ready for that. Maybe we can call you ‘Duce’ for now, or something, until you’re ready.”

“’Duce’ sounds like somebody taking a crap,” Pinely said with a giggle. “I think that works perfectly for Brainy over there.”

“Shut up, Pinely,” Hanker 2.0 whined.

“Be nice,” Merquery said, swatting Pinely on the arm. Aspira hissed as if threatened by the woman

Abbie blinked her eyes slowly and smiled. “Hanker 2.0 will be fine, I guess. Kind of a mouthful though. Anyway, like I was beginning to say when you mentioned your ‘Basic-self,’ you’re perpetuating one major misconception that will keep you from uniting as a single mind.”

“What’s that?” he asked in his overly deep voice.

“That you are two different people in the dream and in Basic,” Abbie answered. She started pacing back and forth, feeling the grass between her bare toes. “All of you listen to me right now. Some of you have already had this drilled into your head, but even so, you need to embrace the fact that you are one person in here and out there. You are not merely remembering things someone else did; *you* did them. You’re not a voyeur in your own life, watching someone else go through the tedium of the day. The tedium belongs to you, not just the power of the dream. Accept that and you’ll bridge the gap between memory and experience. That is the key to unifying. Don’t fight it. Embrace it and move on.”

“Yes ma’am,” Pinely winked.

“Now, back to our drawings,” Abbie said, tossing the apple core away. It hit a tree and puffed into smoke before morphing into a hummingbird with enlarged cartoon wings. Raising her hands back toward the image of the cat in the birdcage, Abbie breathed and closed her eyes. “This is the image that moves from mind to hand today.”

“This is the image that moves from mind to hand today.” They all repeated.

“Memorize it,” Abbie continued. “Feel the emotion behind it. After you draw it, I want you to remember my words. Remember how you feel right now. And know that you are all one person, just waiting to be united. Don’t judge your actions in Basic. Don’t judge yourself. Understand why you act in that way, why you fear the things you fear. Get to know yourself better. Love yourself. All of this will bring unification."

Thunder rumbled in the distance, followed by a slight wind, bringing with it the smell of caramel and onion. Dreamers paused in their dancing, staring toward the north and the uncertain emotions wafting through the grass.

"Alright people," Abbie said. "The time for learning has to be paused for now. Action is required. You know the drill. Cut down whatever Pursuants you find, but focus on feeling, hearing, and seeing. We fight, yes, but we are more than just a revolving door knocking hunters out of the dream. We're here to end this onslaught once and for all. Alice is watching. I'm watching. This is only the beginning, understand?"

"Yes, Moon!" they all shouted.

"Alright, you see that storm coming? We hold the line and keep people safe. Today may be rough, but tomorrow doesn't have to be. It's time to start forging something better! Let's go out there and do some good."

With that, the group bounded toward the horizon, weapons in hand.

Abbie smiled, wind in her hair and emotions coursing through her body.

'Who's to say that dreams and nightmares aren't as real as the here and now?' she thought to herself. *'I can certainly say they are. I'm lucky that way.'*

Maybe John Lennon knew what he was talking about after all.

THE END

COMING SOON:

Dreamforgers Book 2:

DREAM ADDICTS

If you enjoyed Dreamforgers,

please leave an Amazon review.

Join Steve's Sci-fi Thriller team at

Stevenheumann.com

Other novels by Steven Heumann

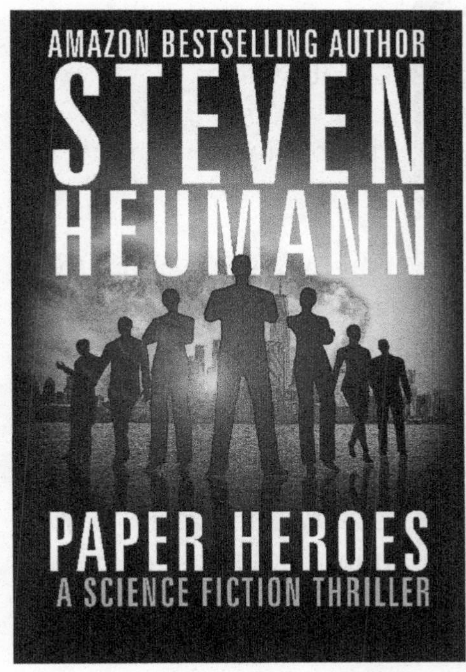

PAPER HEROES: Would you choose to become a hero - even if you knew it was all a lie?

After witnessing a terrorist attack involving advanced weaponry in the heart of New York City, corporate middle manager Stewart Mitchell is offered the chance to inspire the world as a real-life superhero. The only catch is that it would all be a lie; the good-guys and bad-guys are all in it together.

With seemingly limitless resources suddenly at his disposal, Stewart brings his friends into the conspiracy and soon they discover how deep the deception goes on all sides. Who can they trust? Can they even count on each other? Are they heroes or villains?

Can Stewart salvage his life, or will his deceit bring ruin down on everyone he cares about? The road to hell is paved with good intentions, and Stewart has his foot on the gas.

BUY PAPER HEROES NOW!

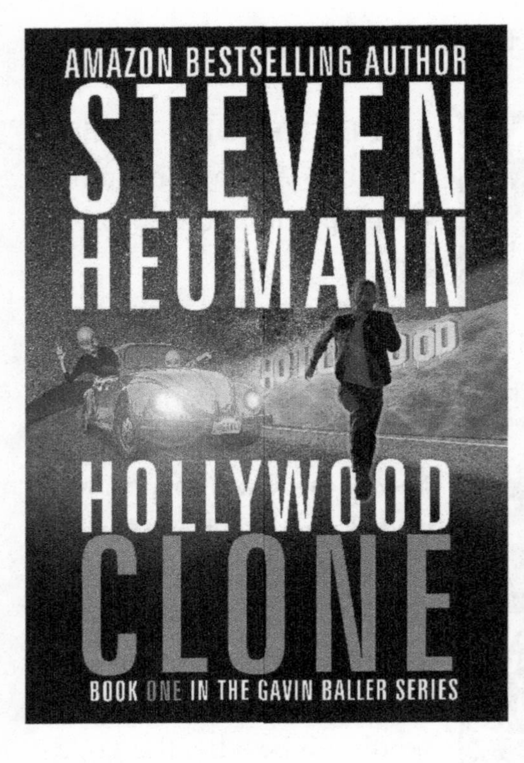

THE GAVIN BALLER SERIES:

Greatest actor in Hollywood...Biggest disappointment in the universe!

Gavin Baller is about to learn that both of those statements are 100% true. His Walk of Fame star can't help him now!

Aliens are on is trail across Los Angeles, and Gavin might not survive long enough to sell the movie rights.

Now with his estranged best friend and a beautiful protector by his side, Gavin is about to learn he's a key part of a bigger universe but hasn't quite lived up to intergalactic expectations.

Can he become the hero he's always pretended to be?

What will happen when Gavin is forced to go toe-to-toe with a galactic tyrant willing to rain down death and destruction merely to avoid his own boredom?

A self-absorbed celebrity verses the biggest threat in the universe? Yeah…this isn't going to end well!

PICK UP THE ENTIRE SERIES TODAY!

RETOOLED: SCI-FI TALES OF FAIRIES & FOLK

You only thought you knew the stories!

Jack and the Beanstalk. Bluebeard. The Pied Piper.

Experience them now like never before as you delve into worlds of arcane science, post-war depression, and killer cyborgs!

This collection includes brand new sci-fi retellings and twists, along with several of author Steven Heumann's previously published works that will keep you guessing despite what you think you know about the originals.

It isn't every day you get to experience something again for the first time, but now you can with RETOOLED: Sci-fi Tales of Fairies and Folk!

ENTER THE FANTASY NOW!

All of Steven Heumann's novels and short stories are currently available at

www.stevenheumann.com

Audiobooks available through Audible

Made in the USA
Monee, IL
03 March 2022